PENGUIN BOOKS

THE SECOND PENGUIN BOOK
OF SEA STORIES

Alun Richards has lived for most of his life in Wales, apart from service in the Royal Navy and a brief period as a probation officer in London. He is the author of several novels, including the much praised *Home to an Empty House* and *Ennal's Point*. *The Former Miss Merthyr Tydfil and Other Stories* is a selection from two volumes of short stories: *Dai Country*, which received the Welsh Arts Council literary prize for 1974, and *The Former Miss Merthyr Tydfil*, which was equally well received.

He is the editor of *The Penguin Book of Welsh Short Stories* (1976), and the first volume of *The Penguin Book of Sea Stories* (1977). He has also written a number of plays for the theatre, including *The Snowdropper*, which has been performed in the United Kingdom and abroad. His collected stage plays, *Plays for Players*, were published in 1975. He is perhaps best known for his many television plays and adaptations on the national networks, and he has also made frequent contributions to such popular series as *The Onedin Line* and *Warship*. His most recent work is *Barque Whisper* (1979), an historical novel dealing with the nightmares of a Cape Horn passage in 1858.

Alun Richards is married with four children and lives in Mumbles, near Swansea.

THE SECOND PENGUIN BOOK OF SEA STORIES

EDITED BY
ALUN RICHARDS

PENGUIN BOOKS

Penguin Books Ltd, Harmondsworth, Middlesex, England
Penguin Books, 625 Madison Avenue, New York, New York 10022, U.S.A.
Penguin Books, Australia Ltd, Ringwood, Victoria, Australia
Penguin Books Canada Ltd, 2801 John Street, Markham, Ontario, Canada L3R 1B4
Penguin Books, (N.Z.) Ltd, 182–190 Wairau Road, Auckland 10, New Zealand

—

First published as *Against the Waves* by Michael Joseph 1978
Published in Penguin Books 1980

—

—

Set, printed and bound in Great Britain by
Cox & Wyman Ltd, Reading
Set in Intertype Baskerville

CONTENTS

Part Two: Fact

INTRODUCTION

'A gone shipmate like any other man, is gone for ever.' Conrad's reflection as he watched the newly paid-off crew of the *Narcissus* drift towards a dockside tavern is one which might well be applied to the ships of yesterday as well as the seamen. The sea story, too, is very much a part of the past, and, with one or two exceptions, there are few contemporary writers whose names spring automatically to mind in connection with the sea. It might be that this is connected with our decline as a maritime power but I am rather more inclined to believe that the end of the sailing ship is in some way connected with a lack of interest in the sea on the part of writers, just as, in a contrary way, man's extraordinary achievements in space travel have been accompanied by an increase in science fiction.

But for me, nothing has ever quite taken the place of the sailing ship, certainly not in looks, nor the men who sailed them, and the stories of seamen and others with tales to tell continue to hold a fascination for those who like their tales full-blooded. There is also the matter of language. What terse technical instruction can compare with the telling maritime colloquialisms of the past? What handbook for the emergency medical treatment of astronauts would describe the appendix as being placed in the SSW corner of the abdomen? 'A-okay' is a poor substitute for 'sitting royal', and for this reason, the very flavour of the work-language of the sea is also a part of its fascination. There is a further difference and this is a matter of connection. I do not know how many science fiction writers have actually been personally acquainted with the technology of their trade, but I doubt whether any of the stories which follow could have been written without at least a nodding acquaintance with the essential character in every sea story, the sea itself.

7

The wise traveller, it has been said, travels only in the imagination, but this volume which is culled from famous and lesser known accounts of actual happenings at sea, with an equal salting of sea yarns and episodes whose authors range from Herman Melville to Nicholas Monsarrat, could not have been compiled if its creators had not, at the very least, placed themselves within earshot of the sea and seamen. The factual account, however, is inevitably much closer, usually an eye-witness report, often of a calamity or a disaster and the teller is a survivor. 'I was there', is the simple sentence which stops us in our tracks, while to the yarn spinner, tales of hearsay are fabric enough upon which to construct our entertainment.

Throughout I have had a guiding principle and have chosen what follows with Ernest Hemingway's cryptic phrase in mind, aiming to show the reader the true essence of 'the way it was', a statement closely paralleled by Conrad's equally well known declaration of his intention, 'to make you hear, to make you feel, above all, to make you see'. In particular, all the wartime stories, from Monsarrat's fiction to Peter Scott's factual memoir, fit this description. A further consideration has been to present as varied a picture as possible of all the multifarious happenings upon the sea, of the conflict between man and man, and between men and the sea, so that I have felt it necessary to select certain episodes from longer works to show aspects of sea life needed to complete the sea pie as it were. This was a rough weather dish which could be laid layer upon layer between crusts, the number of which denominated it a two- or three-decker, according to Admiral Smyth's *Sailor's Word Book* whose predilection for sea idiom would have the sailor with the aching tooth describe it as the 'aftermost grinder aloft, on the starboard quarter'!

My two-decker volume, then, divides itself into fact and fiction, but if you find yourself reading Melville's account of a fever epidemic amongst steerage passengers on a Liverpool packet ship, this is still a story of men pitted against the sea since, even though there was a physician aboard, only the captain would attend them. In the same way, Captain Bligh's dour account of his voyage in the ship's cutter after the mutiny on the *Bounty*, like Captain Slocum's battle with savages off Cape Froward, is an adventure in which the isolation provided by the sea is an essential element. In some stories there is only the sea and the narrator, but of course, most of the epic adventures, whether in fact or fiction, have in common the courage and will to survive of the central character. '*Hombre valiente?*' says Black Pedro with a sneer to Captain Slocum, finding him single-handed aboard the *Spray*, and this Black Pedro, 'the hardest specimen of humanity I had ever seen in all my travels', might well have stepped straight from the pages of Jack London.

Fact, of course, does not compete with fiction, and there are no meaningful generalizations to be made about either, except to say that stories, no matter what their origin, are concerned firstly with people. Even Noel Mostert's account of life aboard a fully automated supertanker with an engine room that can be left unmanned, with self-driving devices and all-seeing electric eyes, has plenty to say of her engineers' reservations. His own feelings, recorded here, describe the ship's gloomy metal acreage 'spreading all around' and he has a sense of a mechanical desert of indefinable purpose imposed upon the sea's own emptiness, a far cry this from the affectionate descriptions of sailing ship men of their favourite ships. The *Ardshiel*, nearly a quarter of a mile long and wider than a football field, is no 'regular roll along, blow along, old girl', nor 'one to be driven hard and never humoured'. Reading of her and other VLCCs (Very Large Crude Carriers) of over 200,000 tons, it is hard not to share his view that the old idea of a ship as a 'she' with all the marriage to the sea and its moods that this implies, is all but gone. No wonder that it is the adventures of the post-war yachtsmen which have captured our imagination, and although I have included a single chilling record of capsize from David Lewis's account of his lone voyage to Antarctica in *Ice Bird*, the voyages of the yachtsmen and women alone provide material enough to fill a separate volume. (You cannot, I have found, complete one anthology of sea stories without wanting to begin another!)

The yachtsmen are also well represented, however, in the fiction section, while the straightforward accounts to Quartermaster John

Hooper and Able Seaman Stanley Sutherland D.S.M., although separated by many years, are representative enough of the men of the sea whom Conrad described for all time: 'Men hard to manage, but very easy to inspire: voiceless men – but men enough to scorn in their hearts the sentimental voices that bewailed the hardness of their fate. It was a fate unique and their own; the capacity to bear it appeared to them to be the privilege of the chosen.'

Two other passages have remained with me from the reading undertaken in the preparation of this volume, one is the picture of the nameless seaman whose demise was described in the record of Anson's squadron rounding Cape Horn. Another is the plea of young Peter Heywood, Midshipman of the *Bounty* who, having remained on board with Fletcher Christian when the Captain was put over the side, was later brought to trial. He describes his situation at the precise moment of the mutiny.

To be starved to death or drowned appeared to be inevitable if I went in the boat and surely it is not to be wondered if at the age of sixteen years, with no one to advise with and so ignorant of the discipline of the Service (having never been to sea before) ... that I suffered the preservation of my life to be the first, and to supersede every other consideration?

This was one life placed in jeopardy at sea. His plea was happily listened to and he lived to make a distinguished career, but Anson's unknown seaman was not so lucky.

As our ship kept the wind better than any of the rest we were obliged, in the afternoon, to wear ship, in order to join the squadron to leeward which otherwise we should have been in danger of losing in the night, as we dared not venture any sail abroad, we were obliged to make use of an expedient which answered our purpose, this was putting the helm a-weather, and manning the fore-shrouds, yet in the execution of it one of our ablest seamen was canted overboard; we perceived that, notwithstanding the prodigious agitation of the waves, he swam very strong and it was with the utmost concern that we found ourselves incapable of assisting him; indeed we were the more grieved at his unhappy fate, as we lost sight of him struggling with the waves, and conceived from the manner in which he swam that he might continue sensible for a considerable time longer, of the horror of his irretrievable situation.

This account, written by Anson's chaplain, Richard Walter, relates that of six ships' companies which were with him on his voyage to the Pacific to harry Spanish possessions, only four men died from enemy action, but over 1,300 from disease, mainly scurvy. The crew of one ship alone, the *Gloucester,* had only 82 men left from 374 aboard at the commencement of the voyage. 'The prodigious agitation of the waves' was not the only enemy, and in the pages which follow, although the gone ships and the gone seamen predominate, something of their indomitable will is evident in the contemporary accounts and it is our good fortune that we can, without even suffering so much as the discomfort of a wet boot, garner something of that glorious and obscure toil upon the sea which was the privilege of the chosen.

ALUN RICHARDS

ACKNOWLEDGEMENTS

The Editor would like to express his thanks to Douglas Matthews B.A., F.L.A., Deputy Librarian of The London Library, Dr F. G. Cowley of the University College Library, Swansea, and their staffs, and to Macdonald Hastings, for their help in the compilation of this volume.

Thanks are due to the following authors, copyright holders and publishers for permission to reprint copyright material in this book:

A. D. Peters & Co. Ltd for 'H.M.S. *Sutherland*' from *A Ship of the Line* (published by Michael Joseph Ltd).

The Executors of the Ernest Hemingway Estate and Charles Scribner's Sons for 'After the Storm', which appears in *The First Forty-Nine Stories* (published by Jonathan Cape Ltd, London) and *Winner Take Nothing* (published by Charles Scribner's Sons, New York). Story Copyright © 1932 by Ernest Hemingway.

Tom Hopkinson and Richard Scott Simon Ltd for 'I Have Been Drowned' from *English Stories from New Writing* (1951) (published by John Lehmann).

The Estate of Weston Martyr and *Blackwood's Magazine* for 'Smith Versus Lichtensteiger'.

The Society of Authors as the literary representative of the Estate of John Masefield and Macmillan Publishing Co. Inc. for 'The Derelict' from *The Bird of Dawning* (published in the British Commonwealth except Canada by William Heinemann Ltd). Story Copyright © 1933 by John Masefield, renewed 1961.

Nicholas Monsarrat for 'Flying Dutchman Country' from *The*

Cruel Sea (published in the British Commonwealth by Cassell & Co. Ltd, and Penguin Books). Story Copyright © 1951 by Nicholas Monsarrat.

Miss Berta Ruck for 'Phantas' from *Widdershins* by Oliver Onions.

Alun Richards and Curtis Brown Ltd for 'The Search' from *Ennal's Point* (published by Michael Joseph Ltd).

The Estate of Capt. F. C. Hendry and *Blackwood's Magazine* for 'Easting Down' by Shalimar.

7C's Press Inc., PO Box 57, Riverside, Connecticut 06878, USA, for 'The Sinking of the *Titanic*' from *The Loss of the S.S. Titanic* by Lawrence Beesley.

Angus and Robertson Pty for 'H.M. Midget Submarine XE.3' from *Frogman V.C.* by Lt-Cdr Ian Fraser V.C., R.N.R.

Geoffrey Bles Ltd for 'The End of the Cable Ship *La Plata*' by John Hooper.

William Collins Sons & Co Ltd for 'Struggle Without Hope', from *Ice Bird* by David Lewis.

Macmillan London and Basingstoke for 'The Tanker Men', an abridgement by Noel Mostert from his book *Supership*.

Hodder and Stoughton Ltd for 'Fire at Sea' from *The Eye of the Wind* by Peter Scott.

King George's Fund for Sailors and George Harrap Ltd for 'Blockade Runner' by Stanley Sutherland D.S.M. from *Touching the Adventures*.

*

'On a Voyage Round Cape Horn' is from *Two Years Before the Mast* by Richard Dana.

'Emigrants' is from *Redburn* by Herman Melville.

'Savages' is from *Sailing Alone Around the World* by Captain Joshua Slocum.

PART ONE: FICTION

Joseph Conrad

YOUTH

THIS could have occurred nowhere but in England, where men and sea interpenetrate, so to speak – the sea entering into the life of most men, and the men knowing something or everything about the sea, in the way of amusement, of travel or of bread-winning.

We were sitting round a mahogany table that reflected the bottle, the claret-glasses, and our faces as we leaned on our elbows. There was a director of companies, an accountant, a lawyer, Marlow, and myself. The director had been a *Conway* boy, the accountant had served four years at sea, the lawyer – a fine crusted Tory, High Churchman, the best of old fellows, the soul of honour – had been chief officer in the P. & O. service in the good old days when mail-boats were square-rigged at least on two masts, and used to come down the China Sea before a fair monsoon with stun'-sails set alow and aloft. We all began life in the merchant service. Between the five of us there was the strong bond of the sea, and also the fellowship of the craft, which no amount of enthusiasm for yachting, cruising, and so on can give, since one is only the amusement of life and the other is life itself.

Marlow (at least, I think that is how he spelt his name) told the story, or rather the chronicle, of a voyage:

'Yes, I have seen a little of the Eastern seas; but what I remember best is my first voyage there. You fellows know there are those voyages that seem ordered for the illustration of life, that might stand for a symbol of existence. You fight, work, sweat, nearly kill yourself, sometimes do kill yourself, trying to accomplish something – and you can't. Not from any fault of yours. You simply can do nothing, neither great nor little – not a thing in the world – not even marry an old maid, or get a wretched 600-ton cargo of coal to its port of destination.

'It was altogether a memorable affair. It was my first voyage to the East, and my first voyage as second mate; it was also my skipper's first command. You'll admit it was time. He was sixty if a day; a little man, with a broad, not very straight back, with bowed shoulders and one leg more bandy than the other, he had that queer twisted-about appearance you see so often in men who work in the fields. He had a nut-cracker face, chin and nose trying to come together over a sunken mouth – and it was framed in iron-grey fluffy hair, that looked like a chin-strap of cotton-wool sprinkled with coal dust. And he had blue eyes in that old face of his, which were amazingly like a boy's, with that candid expression some quite common men preserve to the end of their days by a rare internal gift of simplicity of heart and rectitude of soul. What induced him to accept me was a wonder. I had come out of a crack Australian clipper, when I had been third officer, and he seemed to have a prejudice against crack clippers as aristocratic and high-toned. He said to me, "You know, in this ship you will have to work." I said I had to work in every ship I had ever been in. "Ah, but this is different, and you gentlemen out of them big ships; . . . but there! I dare say you will do. Join tomorrow."

'I joined tomorrow. It was twenty-two years ago; and I was just twenty. How time passes! It was one of the happiest days of my life. Fancy! Second mate for the first time – a really responsible officer! I wouldn't have thrown up my new billet for a fortune. The mate looked me over carefully. He was also an old chap, but of another stamp. He had a Roman nose, a snow-white, long beard, and his name was Mahon, but he insisted that it should be pronounced Mann. He was well connected; yet there was something wrong with his luck, and he had never got on.

'As to the captain, he had been for years in coasters, then in the Mediterranean, and last in the West Indian trade. He had never been round the Capes. He could just write a kind of sketchy hand, and didn't care for writing at all. Both were thorough good seamen of course, and between those two old chaps I felt like a small boy between two grandfathers.

'The ship also was old. Her name was the *Judea*. Queer name, isn't it? She belonged to a man Wilmer, Willcox – some name like that; but he has been bankrupt and dead these twenty years or more, and his name don't matter. She had been laid up in Shadwell basin for ever so long. You may imagine her state. She was all rust, dust, grime – soot aloft, dirt on deck. To me it was like coming out of a palace into a ruined cottage. She was about 400 tons, had a primitive windlass, wooden latches to the doors, not a bit of brass about her, and a big square stern. There was on it, below her name in big letters, a lot of scroll-work, with the gilt off, and some sort of a coat of arms, with the motto 'Do or Die' underneath. I remember it took my fancy immensely. There was a touch of romance in it, something that made me love the old thing – something that appealed to my youth!

'We left London in ballast – sand ballast – to load a cargo of coal in a northern port for Bangkok. Bangkok! I thrilled. I had been six years at sea, but had only seen Melbourne and Sydney, very good places, charming places in their way – but Bangkok!

'We worked out of the Thames under canvas, with a North Sea pilot on board. His name was Jermyn, and he dodged all day long about the galley drying his handkerchief before the stove. Apparently he never slept. He was a dismal man, with a perpetual tear sparkling at the end of his nose, who either had been in trouble, or was in trouble, or expected to be in trouble – couldn't be happy unless something went wrong. He mistrusted my youth, my common sense, and my seamanship, and made a point of showing it in a hundred little ways. I dare say he was right. It seems to me I knew very little then, and I know not much more now; but I cherish a hate for that Jermyn to this day.

'We were a week working up as far as Yarmouth Roads, and then we got into a gale – the famous October gale of twenty-two years ago. It was wind, lightning, sleet, snow, and a terrific sea. We were flying light, and you may imagine how bad it was when I tell you we had smashed bulwarks and a flooded deck. On the second night she shifted her ballast into the lee bow, and by that time we had been blown off somewhere on the Dogger Bank. There was nothing for it but go below with shovels and try to right her, and there we were in that vast hold, gloomy like a cavern, the tallow dips stuck and flickering on the beams, the gale howling above, the ship tossing about like mad on her side; there we all were, Jermyn the captain, every one, hardly able to keep our feet, engaged on that grave-digger's work, and trying to toss shovelsful of wet sand up to windward. At every tumble of the ship you could see vaguely in the dim light men falling down with a great flourish of shovels. One of the ship's boys (we had two), impressed by the weirdness of the scene, wept as if his heart would break. We could hear him blubbering somewhere in the shadows.

'On the third day the gale died out, and by-and-by a north country tug picked us up. We took sixteen days in all to get from London to the Tyne! When we got into dock we had lost our turn for loading, and they hauled us off to a tier where we remained for a month. Mrs Beard (the captain's name was Beard) came from Colchester to see the old man. She lived on board. The crew of runners had left, and there remained only the officers, one boy and the steward, a mulatto who answered to the name of Abraham. Mrs Beard was an old woman, with a face all wrinkled and ruddy like a winter apple, and the figure of a young girl. She caught sight of me once, sewing on a button, and insisted on having my shirts to repair. This was something different from the captains' wives I had known on board crack clippers. When I brought her the shirts she said: "And the socks? They want mending I am sure, and John's – Captain Beard's – things are all in order now. I would be glad of something to do." Bless the old woman. She overhauled my outfit for me, and meantime I read for the first time *Sartor Resartus* and Burnaby's *Ride to Khiva*. I didn't understand much of the first then but I remember I preferred the soldier to the philosopher at the time; a preference which life has only confirmed. One was a man and the other was either more – or less. However, they are both dead and Mrs Beard is dead, and youth, strength, genius, thoughts, achievements, simple hearts – all die . . . No matter.

'They loaded us at last. We shipped a crew. Eight able seamen and two boys. We hauled off one evening to the buoys at the dock gates, ready to go out, and with a fair prospect of beginning the voyage next day. Mrs Beard was to start for home by a late train. When the ship was fast we went to tea. We sat rather silent through the meal – Mahon, the old couple, and I. I finished first, and slipped away for a smoke, my cabin being in a deck-house just against the poop. It was high water, blowing fresh with a drizzle; the double dock-gates were opened, and the steam-colliers were going in and out in the darkness with their lights burning bright, a great plashing of propellers, rattling of winches, and a lot of hailing on the pier-heads. I watched the procession of head-lights gliding high and of green lights gliding low in the night, when suddenly a red gleam flashed at me, vanished, came into view again, and remained. The fore-end of a steamer loomed up close. I shouted down the cabin, "Come up, quick!" and then heard a startled voice saying afar in the dark, "Stop her, sir." A bell jingled. Another voice cried warningly, "We are going right into that barque, sir." The answer to this was a gruff "All right", and the next thing was a heavy crash as the steamer struck a glancing blow with the bluff of her bow about our fore-rigging. There was a moment of confusion, yelling, and running about. Steam roared. Then somebody was heard saying, "All clear, sir" . . . "Are you all right?" asked the gruff voice. I had jumped forward to see the damage, and hailed back, "I don't think so." "Easy astern," said the gruff voice. A bell jingled. "What steamer is that?" screamed Mahon. By that time she was no more to us than a bulky shadow manoeuvring a little way off. They shouted at us some name – a woman's name, Miranda or Melissa – or some such thing. "This means another month in this beastly hole," said Mahon to me, as we peered with lamps about the splintered bulwarks and broken braces. "But where's the captain?"

'We had not seen anything of him all that time. We went aft to look. A doleful voice arose hailing somewhere in the middle of the dock, *"Judea* ahoy!" How the devil did he get there? "Hallo!" we shouted. "I am adrift in our boat without oars," he cried. A belated water-man offered his services, and Mahon struck a bargain with him for half-a-crown to tow our skipper alongside; but it was Mrs Beard that came up the ladder first. They had been floating about the dock in that mizzly cold rain for nearly an hour. I was never so surprised in my life.

'It appears that when he heard my shout "Come up" he understood at once what was the matter, caught up his wife, ran on deck, and across, and down into our boat, which was fast to the ladder. Not bad for a sixty-year-old. Just imagine that old fellow saving heroically in his arms that old woman – the woman of his life. He set her down on a thwart, and was ready to climb back on board when the painter came adrift somehow, and away they went together. Of course in the confusion we did not hear him shouting. He looked abashed. She said cheerfully, "I suppose it does not matter my losing the train now?" – "No, Jenny – you go below and get warm," he growled. Then to us: "A sailor has no business with a wife – I say. There I was, out of the ship. Well, no harm done this time. Let's go and look at what that fool of a steamer smashed."

'It wasn't much, but it delayed us three weeks. At the end of that time, the captain being engaged with his agents, I carried Mrs Beard's bag to the railway station and put her all comfy into a third-class carriage. She lowered the window to say, "You are a good young man. If you see John – Captain Beard – without his muffler at night, just remind him from me to keep his throat well wrapped up." "Certainly, Mrs Beard," I said. "You are a good young man; I noticed how attentive you are to John – to Captain – " The train pulled out suddenly; I took my cap off to the old woman: I never saw her again . . . Pass the bottle.

'We went to sea next day. When we made that start for Bangkok we had been already three months out of London. We had expected to be a fortnight or so – at the outside.

'It was January, and the weather was beautiful – the beautiful sunny winter weather that has more charm than in the summertime, because it is unexpected, and crisp, and you know it won't, it can't, last long. It's like a windfall, like a godsend, like an unexpected piece of luck.

'It lasted all down the North Sea, all down Channel; and it lasted till we were three hundred miles or so to the westward of the Lizards: then the wind went round to the sou'-west and began to pipe up. In two days it blew a gale. The *Judea* hove to, wallowed on the Atlantic like an old candle-box. It blew day after day: it blew with spite, without interval, without mercy, without rest. The world was nothing but an immensity of great foaming waves rushing at us, under a sky low enough to touch with the hand and dirty like a moked ceiling. In the stormy space surrounding us there was as much flying spray as air. Day after day and night after night there was nothing round the ship but the howl of the wind, the tumult of the sea, the noise of water pouring over her deck. There was no est for her and no rest for us. She tossed, she pitched, she stood on her head, she sat on her tail, she rolled, she groaned, and we had to hold on while on deck and cling to our bunks when below, in a constant effort of body and worry of mind.

'One night Mahon spoke through the small window of my berth. It opened right into my very bed, and I was lying there sleepless, in my boots, feeling as though I had not slept for years, and could not if I tried. He said excitedly:

' "You got the sounding-rod in here, Marlow? I can't get the pumps to suck. By God! it's no child's play."

'I gave him the sounding-rod and lay down again, trying to think of various things – but I thought only of the pumps. When I came on deck they were still at it, and my watch relieved at the pumps. By the light of the lantern brought on deck to examine the sounding-rod I caught a glimpse of their weary, serious faces. We pumped all the four hours. We pumped all night, all day, all the week – watch and watch. She was working herself loose, and leaked badly – not enough to drown us at once, but enough to kill us with the work at the pumps. And while we pumped the ship was going from us piecemeal: the bulwarks went, the stanchions were torn out, the ventilators smashed, the cabin-door burst in. There was not a dry spot in the ship. She was being gutted bit by bit. The long-boat changed, as if by magic, into matchwood where she stood in her gripes. I had lashed her myself, and was rather proud of my handiwork, which had withstood so long the malice of the sea. And we pumped. And there was no break in the weather. The sea was white like a sheet of foam, like a caldron of boiling milk; there was not a break in the clouds, no – not the size of a man's hand – no, not for so much as ten seconds. There was for us no sky, there were for us no stars, no sun, no universe – nothing but angry clouds and an infuriated sea. We pumped watch and watch, for dear life; and it seemed to last for months, for years, for all eternity, as though we had been dead and gone to a hell for sailors. We forgot the day of the week, the name of the month, what year it was, and whether we had ever been ashore. The sails blew away, she lay broadside on under a weather-cloth, the ocean poured over her, and we did not care. We turned those handles and had the eyes of idiots. As soon as we had crawled on deck I used to take a round turn with a rope about the men, the pumps, and the mainmast, and we turned, we turned incessantly, with the water to our waists, to our necks, over our heads. It was all one. We had forgotten how it felt to be dry.

'And there was somewhere in me the thought: By Jove! this is the deuce of an adventure – something you read about; and it is my first voyage as second mate – and I am only twenty – and here I am lasting it out as well as any of these men, and keeping my chaps up to the mark. I was pleased. I would not have given up the experience for worlds. I had moments of exultation. Whenever the old dismantled craft pitched heavily with her counter high in the air, she seemed to me to throw up, like an appeal, like a defiance, like a cry to the clouds without mercy, the words written on her stern: *Judea*, London. Do or Die.

'O youth! The strength of it, the faith of it, the imagination of it! To me she was not an old rattle-trap carting about the world a lot of coal for a freight – to me she was the endeavour, the test, the trial of life. I think of her with pleasure, with affection, with regret – as you would think of someone dead you have loved. I shall never forget her . . . Pass the bottle.

'One night when tied to the mast, as I explained, we were pumping on, deafened with the wind, and without spirit enough in us to wish ourselves dead, a heavy sea crashed aboard and swept clear over us. As soon as I got my breath I shouted, as in duty bound, "Keep on, boys!" when suddenly I felt something hard floating on deck strike the calf of my leg. I made a grab at it and missed. It was so dark we could not see one another's faces within a foot – you understand.

'After that thump the ship kept quiet for a while, and the thing whatever it was, struck my leg again. This time I caught it – and it was a saucepan. At first being stupid with fatigue and thinking of nothing but the pumps, I did not understand what I had in my hand. Suddenly it dawned upon me, and I shouted, "Boys, the house on deck is gone. Leave this, and let's look for the cook."

'There was a deck-house forward, which contained the galley, the cook's berth, and the quarters of the crew. As we had expected for days to see it swept away, the hands had been ordered to sleep in the cabin – the only safe place in the ship. The steward, Abraham, however, persisted in clinging to his berth, stupidly, like a mule – from sheer fright, I believe, like an animal that won't leave a stable falling in an earthquake. So we went to look for him. It was chancing death, since once out of our lashings we were as exposed as if on a raft. But we went. The house was shattered as if a shell had exploded inside. Most of it had gone overboard – stove, men's quarters, and their property, all was gone; but two posts, holding a portion of the bulkhead to which Abraham's bunk was attached, remained as if by a miracle. We groped in the ruins and came upon this, and there he was, sitting in his bunk, surrounded by foam and wreckage, jabbering cheerfully to himself. He was out of his mind; completely and for ever mad, with this sudden shock coming upon the fag-end of his endurance. We snatched him up, lugged him aft, and pitched him head-first down the cabin companion. You understand there was no time to carry him down with infinite precautions and wait to see how he got on. Those below would pick him up at the bottom of the stairs all right. We were in a hurry to go back to the pumps. That business could not wait. A bad leak is an inhuman thing.

'One would think that the sole purpose of that fiendish gale had been to make a lunatic of that poor devil of a mulatto. It eased before morning, and the next day the sky cleared, and as the sea went down the leak took up. When it came to bending a fresh set of sails the crew demanded to put back – and really there was nothing else to do. Boats gone, decks swept clean, cabin gutted, men without a stitch but what they stood in, stores spoiled, ship strained. We put her head for home, and – would you believe it? The wind came east right in our teeth. It blew fresh, it blew continuously. We had to beat up every inch of the way, but she did not leak so badly, the water keeping comparatively smooth. Two hours' pumping in every four is no joke – but it kept her afloat as far as Falmouth.

'The good people there live on casualties of the sea, and no doubt were glad to see us. A hungry crowd of shipwrights sharpened their chisels at the sight of that carcass of a ship. And, by Jove! they had pretty pickings off us before they were done. I fancy the owner was already in a tight place. There were delays. Then it was decided to take part of the cargo out and caulk her topsides. This was done, the repairs finished, cargo reshipped; a new crew came on board, and we went out – for Bangkok. At the end of a week we were back again. The crew said they weren't going to Bangkok – a hundred and fifty days' passage – in a something hooker that wanted pumping eight hours out of the twenty-four; and the nautical papers inserted again the little paragraph: *"Judea. Barque, Tyne to Bangkok; coals; put back to Falmouth leaky and with crew refusing duty."*

'There were more delays – more tinkering. The owner came down for a day, and said she was as right as a little fiddle. Poor old Captain Beard looked like the ghost of a Geordie skipper – through the worry and humiliation of it. Remember he was sixty and it was his first command. Mahon said it was a foolish business, and would end badly. I loved the ship more than ever, and wanted awfully to get to Bangkok. To Bangkok! Magic name, blessed name. Mesopotamia wasn't a patch on it. Remember I was twenty, and it was my first second-mate's billet, and the East was waiting for me.

'We went out and anchored in the outer roads with a fresh crew – the third. She leaked worse than ever. It was as if those confounded shipwrights had actually made a hole in her. This time we did not even go outside. The crew simply refused to man the windlass.

'They towed us back to the inner harbour, and we became a fixture, a feature, an institution of the place. People pointed us out to visitors as "That 'ere barque that's going to Bangkok – has been here six months – put back three times." On holidays the small boys pulling about in boats would hail, *"Judea,* ahoy!" and if a head showed above the rail shouted, "Where are you bound to? – Bangkok?" and jeered. We were only three on board. The poor old skipper mooned in the cabin. Mahon undertook the cooking, and unexpectedly developed all a Frenchman's genius for preparing nice little messes. I looked languidly after the rigging. We became

itizens of Falmouth. Every shopkeeper knew us. At the barber's or
obacconist's they asked familiarly, "Do you think you will ever get
■ Bangkok?" Meantime the owner, the underwriters, and the char-
rers squabbled amongst themselves in London, and our pay went
n . . . Pass the bottle.

'It was horrid. Morally it was worse than pumping for life. It
emed as though we had been forgotten by the world, belonged to
obody, would get nowhere; it seemed that, as if bewitched, we
ould have to live for ever and ever in that inner harbour, a der-
ion and a byword to generations of longshore loafers and dis-
onest boatmen. I obtained three months' pay and a five days'
ave and made a rush for London. It took me a day to get there
nd pretty well another to come back – but three months' pay went
ll the same. I don't know what I did with it. I went to a music-
all, I believe, lunched, dined, and supped in a swell place in
.egent Street, and was back to time, with nothing but a complete
:t of Byron's works. The boatman who pulled me off to the ship
.id: "Hallo! I thought you had left the old thing. *She* will never
et to Bangkok." – "That's all *you* know about it," I said scornfully
but I didn't like that prophecy at all.

'Suddenly a man, some kind of agent to somebody, appeared
ith full powers. He had grog-blossoms all over his face, an in-
omitable energy , and was a jolly soul. We leaped into life again.
. hulk came alongside, took our cargo, and then we went into dry
ock to get our copper stripped. No wonder she leaked. The poor
ning, strained beyond endurance by the gale, had, as if in disgust,
oat out all the oakum of her lower seams. She was recaulked, new
oppered, and made as tight as a bottle. We went back to the hulk
nd reshipped our cargo.

'Then on a fine moonlight night, all the rats left the ship.

'We had been infested with them. They had destroyed our sails,
onsumed more stores than the crew, affably shared our beds and
ur dangers, and now, when the ship was made seaworthy, con-
luded to clear out. I called Mahon to enjoy the spectacle. Rat
ter rat appeared on our rail, took a last look over his shoulder,
nd leaped with a hollow thud into the empty hulk. We tried to
ount them, but soon lost the tale. Mahon said: "Well, well! don't

27

talk to me about the intelligence of rats. They ought to have le
before, when we had that narrow squeak from foundering. The
you have the proof how silly is the superstition about them. Th
leave a good ship for an old rotten hulk, where there is nothing
eat, too, the fools! . . . I don't believe they know what is safe
what is good for them, any more than you or I."

'And after some more talk we agreed that the wisdom of rats ha
been grossly overrated, being in fact no greater than that of men.

'The story of the ship was known, by this, all up the Chann
from Land's End to the Forelands, and we could get no crew on t
south coast. They sent us one all complete from Liverpool, and v
left once more – for Bangkok.

'We had fair breezes, smooth water right into the tropics, and t
old *Judea* lumbered along in the sunshine. When she went eig
knots everything cracked aloft, and we tied our caps to our head
but mostly she strolled on at the rate of three miles an hour. Wh
could you expect? She was tired – that old ship. Her youth w
where mine is – where yours is – you fellows who listen to this yar
and what friend would throw your years and your weariness
your face? We didn't grumble at her. To us aft, at least, it seem
as though we had been born in her, reared in her, and lived in h
for ages, had never known any other ship. I would just as soon ha
abused the old village church at home for not being a cathedral.

'And for me there was also my youth to make me patient. The
was all the East before me, and all life, and the thought that I ha
been tried in that ship and had come out pretty well. And
thought of men of old who, centuries ago, went that road in shi
that sailed no better, to the land of palms, and spices, and yello
sands, and of brown nations ruled by kings more cruel tha
Nero the Roman, and more splendid than Solomon the Jew. Th
old bark lumbered on, heavy with her age and the burden of h
cargo, while I lived the life of youth in ignorance and hope. S
lumbered on through an interminable procession of days; and t
fresh gilding flashed back at the setting sun, seemed to cry out ov
the darkening sea the words painted on her stern, "*Judea*. Londo
Do or Die."

'Then we entered the Indian Ocean and steered northerly f

Java Head. The winds were light. Weeks slipped by. She crawled on, do or die, and people at home began to think of posting us as overdue.

'One Saturday evening, I being off duty, the men asked me to give them an extra bucket of water or so – for washing clothes. As I did not wish to screw on the fresh-water pump so late, I went forward whistling, and with a key in my hand to unlock the forepeak scuttle, intending to serve the water out of a spare tank we kept there.

'The smell down below was as unexpected as it was frightful. One would have thought hundreds of paraffin lamps had been flaring and smoking in that hole for days. I was glad to get out. The man with me coughed and said, "Funny smell, sir." I answered negligently, "It's good for the health they say," and walked aft.

'The first thing I did was to put my head down the square of the midship ventilator. As I lifted the lid a visible breath, something like a thin fog, a puff of faint haze, rose from the opening. The ascending air was hot, and had a heavy sooty, paraffiny smell. I gave one sniff, and put down the lid gently. It was no use choking myself. The cargo was on fire.

'Next day she began to smoke in earnest. You see it was to be expected, for though the coal was of a safe kind, that cargo had been so handled, so broken up with handling, that it looked more like smithy coal than anything else. Then it had been wetted – more than once. It rained all the time we were taking it back from the hulk, and now with this long passage it got heated, and there was another case of spontaneous combustion.

'The captain called us into the cabin. He had a chart spread on the table, and looked unhappy. He said, "The coast of West Australia is near, but I mean to proceed to our destination. It is the hurricane month, too; but we will just keep her head for Bangkok, and fight the fire. No more putting back anywhere, if we all get roasted. We will try first to stifle this 'ere damned combustion by want of air."

'We tried. We battened down everything, and still she smoked. The smoke kept coming out through imperceptible crevices; it forced itself through bulkheads and covers; it oozed here and there and everywhere in slender threads, in an invisible film, in an incomprehensible manner. It made its way into the cabin, into the forecastle; it poisoned the sheltered places on the deck, it could be sniffed as high as the mainyard. It was clear that if the smoke came out the air came in. This was disheartening. This combustion refused to be stifled.

'We resolved to try water, and took the hatches off. Enormous volumes of smoke, whitish, yellowish, thick, greasy, misty, choking, ascended as high as the trucks. All hands cleared out aft. Then the poisonous cloud blew away, and we went back to work in a smoke that was no thicker now than that of an ordinary factory chimney.

'We rigged the force-pump, got the hose along, and by-and-by it burst. Well, it was as old as the ship – a prehistoric hose, and past repair. Then we pumped with the feeble head-pump, drew water with buckets, and in this way managed in time to pour lots of Indian Ocean into the main hatch. The bright stream flashed in sunshine, fell into a layer of white crawling smoke, and vanished on the black surface of coal. Steam ascended mingling with the smoke. We poured salt water as into a barrel without a bottom. It was our fate to pump in that ship, to pump out of her, to pump into her; and after keeping water out of her to save ourselves from being drowned, we frantically poured water into her to save ourselves from being burnt.

'And she crawled on, do or die, in the serene weather. The sky was a miracle of purity, a miracle of azure. The sea was polished, was blue, was pellucid, was sparkling like a precious stone, extending on all sides, all round to the horizon – as if the whole terrestrial globe had been one jewel, one colossal sapphire, a single gem fashioned into a planet. And on the lustre of the great calm waters the *Judea* glided imperceptibly, enveloped in languid and unclean vapours, in a lazy cloud that drifted to leeward, light and slow; a pestiferous cloud defiling the splendour of sea and sky.

'All this time of course we saw no fire. The cargo smouldered at the bottom somewhere. Once Mahon, as we were working side by side, said to me with a queer smile: "Now, if she only would spring a tidy leak – like that time when we first left the Channel – it would put a stopper on this fire. Wouldn't it?" I remarked irrelevantly, "Do you remember the rats?"

'We fought the fire, and sailed the ship as carefully as though nothing had been the matter. The steward cooked and attended on us. Of the other twelve men, eight worked while four rested. Everyone took his turn, captain included. There was equality, and if not exactly fraternity, then a deal of good feeling. Sometimes a man, as he dashed a bucketful of water down the hatchway, would yell out, "Hurrah for Bangkok"! and the rest laughed. But generally we were taciturn and serious – and thirsty. Oh! how thirsty! And we had to be careful with the water. Strict allowance. The ship smoked, the sun blazed . . . Pass the bottle.

'We tried everything. We even made an attempt to dig down to the fire. No good, of course. No man could remain more than a minute below. Mahon, who went first, fainted there, and the man who went to fetch him out did likewise. We lugged them out on deck. Then I leaped down to show how easily it could be done. They had learned wisdom by that time, and contented themselves by fishing for me with a chain-hook tied to a broom-handle, I believe. I did not offer to go and fetch up my shovel, which was left down below.

'Things began to look bad. We put the long-boat into the water. The second boat was ready to swing out. We had also another, a 14-foot thing, on davits aft, where it was quite safe.

'Then, behold, the smoke suddenly decreased. We redoubled our efforts to flood the bottom of the ship. In two days there was no smoke at all. Everybody was on the broad grin. This was on a Friday. On Saturday no work, but sailing the ship of course, was done. The men washed their clothes and their faces for the first time in a fortnight, and had a special dinner given them. They spoke of spontaneous combustion with contempt, and implied *they* were the boys to put out combustions. Somehow we all felt as though we each had inherited a large fortune. But a beastly smell of burning hung about the ship. Captain Beard had hollow eyes and sunken cheeks. I had never noticed so much before how twisted and bowed he was. He and Mahon prowled soberly about hatches and ventilators, sniffing. It struck me suddenly poor Mahon was a very, very

old chap. As to me, I was as pleased and proud as though I ha
helped to win a great naval battle. O! Youth!

'The night was fine. In the morning a homeward-bound shi
passed us hull down – the first we had seen for months; but we we
nearing the land at last, Java Head being about 190 miles off, an
nearly due north.

'Next day it was my watch on deck from eight to twelve. A
breakfast the captain observed, "It's wonderful how that sme
hangs about the cabin." About ten, the mate being on the poop,
stepped down on the main-deck for a moment. The carpenter
bench stood abaft the mainmast: I leaned against it sucking at m
pipe, and the carpenter, a young chap, came to talk to me. H
remarked, "I think we have done very well haven't we?" and then
perceived with annoyance the fool was trying to tilt the bench.
said curtly, "'Don't Chips," and immediately became aware of
queer sensation of an absurd delusion – I seemed somehow to be i
the air. I heard all round me like a pent-up breath released – as if
thousand giants simultaneously had said Phoo! – and felt a du
concussion which made my ribs ache suddenly. No doubt about it
I was in the air, and my body was describing a short parabola. B
short as it was, I had the time to think several thoughts in, as far a
I can remember, the following order: "This can't be the carpente
– What is it? – Some accident – Submarine volcano? – Coals, ga
– By Jove! we are being blown up – Everybody's dead – I ar
falling into the afterhatch – I see fire in it."

'The coal-dust suspended in the air of the hold had glowed dull
red at the moment of the explosion. In the twinkling of an eye, i
an infinitesimal fraction of a second since the first tilt of the bench
I was sprawling full length on the cargo. I picked myself up an
scrambled out. It was quick like a rebound. The deck was a wilder
ness of smashed timber, lying crosswise like trees in a wood after
hurricane; an immense curtain of solid rags waved gently befor
me – it was the mainsail blown to strips. I thought: The masts wil
be toppling over directly; and to get out of the way bolted on all
fours towards the poop-ladder. The first person I saw was Mahor
with eyes like saucers, his mouth open, and the long white hai
standing straight on end round his head like a silver halo. He wa

just about to go down when the sight of the main-deck stirring, heaving up, and changing into splinters before his eyes, petrified him on the top step. I stared at him in unbelief, and he stared at me with a queer kind of shocked curiosity. I did not know that I had no hair, no eyebrows, no eyelashes, that my young moustache was burnt off, that my face was black, one cheek laid open, my nose cut, and my chin bleeding. I had lost my cap, one of my slippers, and my shirt was torn to rags. Of all this I was not aware. I was amazed to see the ship still afloat, the poop-deck whole – and, most of all, to see anybody alive. Also the peace of the sky and the serenity of the sea were distinctly surprising. I suppose I expected to see them convulsed with horror . . . Pass the bottle.

'There was a voice hailing the ship from somewhere – in the air, in the sky – I couldn't tell. Presently I saw the captain – and he was mad. He asked me eagerly, "Where's the cabin-table?" and to hear such a question was a frightful shock. I had just been blown up, you understand, and vibrated with that experience – I wasn't quite sure whether I was alive. Mahon began to stamp with both feet and yelled at him, "Good God! don't you see the deck's blown out of her?" I found my voice, and stammered out as if conscious of some gross neglect of duty, "I don't know where the cabin-table is." It was like an absurd dream.

'Do you know what he wanted next? Well, he wanted to trim the yards. Very placidly, and as if lost in thought, he insisted on having the foreyard squared. "I don't know if there's anybody alive," said Mahon, almost tearfully. "Surely," he said, gently, "there will be enough left to square the foreyard."

'The old chap, it seems, was in his own berth winding up the chronometers, when the shock sent him spinning. Immediately it occurred to him – as he said afterwards – that the ship had struck something, and ran out into the cabin. There, he saw, the cabin-table had vanished somewhere. The deck being blown up, it had fallen into the lazarette of course. Where we had our breakfast that morning he saw only a great hole in the floor. This appeared to him so awfully mysterious, and impressed him so immensely, that what he saw and heard after he got on deck were mere trifles in comparison. And, mark, he noticed directly the wheel deserted and his barque off her course – and his only thought was to get that miserable, stripped, undecked, smouldering shell of a ship back again with her head pointing at her port of destination. Bangkok! That's what he was after. I tell you this quiet, bowed, bandy-legged, almost deformed little man was immense in the singleness of his idea and in his placid ignorance of our agitation. He motioned us forward with a commanding gesture, and went to take the wheel himself.

'Yes; that was the first thing we did – trim the yards of that wreck! No one was killed, or even disabled, but everyone was more or less hurt. You should have seen them! Some were in rags; with black faces, like coal-heavers, like sweeps, and had bullet heads that seemed closely cropped, but were in fact singed to the skin. Others, of the watch below, awakened by being shot out from their collapsing bunks, shivered incessantly, and kept on groaning even as we went about our work. But they all worked. That crew of Liverpool hard cases had in them the right stuff. It's my experience they always have. It is the sea that gives it – the vastness, the loneliness surrounding their dark stolid souls. Ah! Well! we stumbled, we crept, we fell, we barked our shins on the wreckage, we hauled. The masts stood, but we did not know how much they might be charred down below. It was nearly calm, but a long swell ran from the west and made her roll. They might go at any moment. We looked at them with apprehension. One could not foresee which way they would fall.

'Then we retreated aft and looked about us. The deck was a tangle of planks on edge, of planks on end, of splinters, of ruined woodwork. The masts rose from that chaos like big trees above a matted undergrowth. The interstices of that mass of wreckage were full of something whitish, sluggish, stirring – of something that was like a greasy fog. The smoke of the invisible fire was coming up again, was trailing, like a poisonous thick mist in some valley choked with dead wood. Already lazy wisps were beginning to curl upwards amongst the mass of splinters. Here and there a piece of timber, struck upright, resembled a post. Half of a fife-rail had been shot through the foresail, and the sky made a patch of glorious blue in the ignobly soiled canvas. A portion of several boards hold-

ing together had fallen across the rail, and one end protruded overboard, like a gangway leading over the deep sea, leading to death –
as if inviting us to walk the plank at once and be done with our
ridiculous troubles. And still the air, the sky – a ghost, something
invisible was hailing the ship.

'Someone had the sense to look over, and there was the helmsman, who had impulsively jumped overboard, anxious to come
back. He yelled and swam lustily like a merman, keeping up with
the ship. We threw him a rope, and presently he stood amongst us
streaming with water and very crestfallen. The captain had sur-
rendered the wheel, and apart, elbow on rail and chin in hand,
gazed at the sea wistfully. We asked ourselves, What next? I
thought, Now, this is something like. This is great. I wonder what
will happen. O youth!

'Suddenly Mahon sighted a steamer far astern. Captain Beard
said, "We may do something with her yet." We hoisted two flags,
which said in the international language of the sea, "On fire. Want
immediate assistance." The steamer grew bigger rapidly, and by-
and-by spoke with two flags on her foremast, "I am coming to your
assistance."

'In half an hour she was abreast, to windward, within hail, and
rolling slightly with her engines stopped. We lost our composure,
and yelled all together with excitement, "We've been blown up." A
man in a white helmet, on the bridge, cried, "Yes! All right! all
right!" and he nodded his head, and smiled, and made soothing
motions with his hands as though at a lot of frightened children.
One of the boats dropped in the water, and walked towards us
upon the sea with her long oars. Four Calashes pulled a swinging
stroke. This was my first sight of Malay seamen. I've known them
since, but what struck me then was their unconcern: they came
alongside, and even the bowman standing up and holding to our
main-chains with the boathook did not deign to lift his head for a
glance. I thought people who had been blown up deserved more
attention.

'A little man, dry like a chip and agile like a monkey, clambered
up. It was the mate of the steamer. He gave one look, and cried,
"O boys – you had better quit."

'We were silent. He talked apart with the captain for a time — seemed to argue with him. Then they went away together to the steamer.

'When our skipper came back we learned that the steamer was the *Somerville*, Captain Nash, from West Australia to Singapore *via* Batavia with mails, and that the agreement was she should tow us to Anjer or Batavia, if possible, where we could extinguish the fire by scuttling, and then proceed on our voyage — to Bangkok! The old man seemed excited. "We will do it yet," he said to Mahon, fiercely. He shook his fist at the sky. Nobody else said a word.

'At noon the steamer began to tow. She went ahead slim and high, and what was left of the *Judea* followed at the end of seventy fathom of tow-rope — followed her swiftly like a cloud of smoke with mast-heads protruding above. We went aloft to furl the sails. We coughed on the yards, and were careful about the bunts. Do you see the lot of us there, putting a neat furl on the sails of that ship doomed to arrive nowhere? There was not a man who didn't think that at any moment the masts would topple over. From aloft we could not see the ship for smoke, and they worked carefully, passing the gaskets with even turns. "Harbour furl — aloft there!" cried Mahon from below.

'You understand this? I don't think one of those chaps expected to get down in the usual way. When we did I heard them saying to each other, "Well, I thought we would come down overboard, in a lump — sticks and all — blame me if I didn't." "That's what I was thinking to myself," would answer wearily another battered and bandaged scarecrow. And, mind, these were men without the drilled-in habit of obedience. To an onlooker they would be a lot of profane scallywags without a redeeming point. What made them do it — what made them obey me when I, thinking consciously how fine it was, made them drop the bunt of the foresail twice to try and do it better? What? They had no professional reputation — no examples, no praise. It wasn't a sense of duty; they all knew well enough how to shirk, and laze, and dodge — when they had a mind to it — and mostly they had. Was it the two pounds ten a-month that sent them there? They didn't think their pay half good enough. No; it was something in them, something inborn and subtle and everlasting. I don't say positively that the crew of a French or German merchantman wouldn't have done it, but I doubt whether it would have been done in the same way. There was a completeness in it, something solid like a principle, and masterful like an instinct – a disclosure of something secret – of that hidden something, that gift of good or evil that makes racial difference, that shapes the fate of nations.

'It was that night at ten that, for the first time since we had been fighting it, we saw the fire. The speed of the towing had fanned the smouldering destruction. A blue gleam appeared forward, shining below the wreck of the deck. It wavered in patches, it seemed to stir and creep like the light of a glow-worm. I saw it first, and told Mahon. "Then the game's up," he said. "We had better stop this towing, or she will burst out suddenly fore and aft before we can clear out." We set up a yell; rang bells to attract their attention; they towed on. At last Mahon and I had to crawl forward and cut the rope with an axe. There was no time to cast off the lashings. Red tongues could be seen licking the wilderness of splinters under our feet as we made our way back to the poop.

'Of course they very soon found out in the steamer that the rope was gone. She gave a loud blast of her whistle, her lights were seen sweeping in a wide circle, she came up ranging close alongside, and stopped. We were all in a tight group on the poop looking at her. Every man had saved a little bundle or bag. Suddenly a conical flame with a twisted top shot up forward and threw upon the black sea a circle of light, with the two vessels side by side and heaving gently in its centre. Captain Beard had been sitting on the grating still and mute for hours, but now he rose slowly and advanced in front of us, to the mizzen-shrouds. Captain Nash hailed: "Come along! Look sharp. I have mail-bags on board, I will take you and your boats to Singapore."

' "Thank you! No!" said our skipper. "We must see the last of the ship."

' "I can't stand by any longer," shouted the other. "Mails – you know."

' "Ay! ay! We are all right."

' "Very well! I'll report you in Singapore . . . Good-bye!"

'He waved his hand. Our men dropped their bundles quietly. The steamer moved ahead, and passing out of the circle of light, vanished at once from our sight, dazzled by the fire which burned freely. And then I knew that I would see the East first as commander of a small boat. I thought it fine; and the fidelity to the old ship was fine. We should see the last of her. Oh, the glamour of youth! Oh, the fire of it, more dazzling than the flames of the burning ship, throwing a magic light on the wide earth, leaping audaciously to the sky, presently to be quenched by time, more cruel, more pitiless, more bitter than the sea – and like the flames of the burning ship surrounded by an impenetrable night.

'The old man warned us in his gentle and inflexible way that it was part of our duty to save for the underwriters as much as we could of the ship's gear. Accordingly we went to work aft, while she blazed forward to give us plenty of light. We lugged out a lot of rubbish. What didn't we save? An old barometer fixed with an absurd quantity of screws nearly cost me my life: a sudden rush of smoke came upon me, and I just got away in time. There were various stores, bolts of canvas, coils of rope; the poop looked like a maritime bazaar, and the boats were lumbered to the gunwales. One would have thought the old man wanted to take as much as he could of his first command with him. He was very very quiet, but off his balance evidently. Would you believe it? He wanted to take a length of old stream-cable and a kedge-anchor with him in the long-boat. We said "Ay, ay, sir," deferentially, and on the quiet let the things slip overboard. The heavy machine-chest went that way, two bags of green coffee, tins of paint – fancy, paint! – a whole lot of things. Then I was ordered with two hands into the boats to make a stowage and get them ready against the time it would be proper for us to leave the ship.

'We put everything straight, stepped the long-boat's mast for our skipper, who was to take charge of her, and I was not sorry to sit down for a moment. My face felt raw, every limb ached as if broken, I was aware of all my ribs, and would have sworn to a twist in the backbone. The boats, fast astern, lay in a deep shadow, and all around I could see the circle of the sea lighted by the fire. A gigantic flame arose forward straight and clear. It flared fierce, with noises like the whirr of wings, with rumbles as of thunder. There were cracks, detonations, and from the cone of flame the sparks flew upwards, as man is born to trouble, to leaky ships, and to ships that burn.

'What bothered me was that the ship, lying broadside to the swell and to such wind as there was – a mere breath – the boats would not keep astern where they were safe, but persisted, in a pig-headed way boats have, in getting under the counter and then swinging alongside. They were knocking about dangerously and coming near the flame, while the ship rolled on them, and, of course, there was always the danger of the masts going over the side at any moment. I and my two boatkeepers kept them off as best we could, with oars and boathooks; but to be constantly at it became exasperating, since there was no reason why we should not leave at once. We could not see those on board, nor could we imagine what caused the delay. The boatkeepers were swearing feebly, and I had not only my share of the work but also had to keep at it two men who showed a constant inclination to lay themselves down and let things slide.

'At last I hailed "On deck there," and someone looked over. "We're ready here," I said. The head disappeared, and very soon popped up again. "The captain says, All right, sir, and to keep the boats well clear of the ship."

'Half an hour passed. Suddenly there was a frightful racket, rattle, clanking of chain, hiss of water, and millions of sparks flew up into the shivering column of smoke that stood leaning slightly over the ship. The cat-heads had burned away, and the two red-hot anchors had gone to the bottom, tearing out after them two hundred fathom of red-hot chain. The ship trembled, the mass of flame swayed as if ready to collapse, and the fore top-gallant-mast fell. It darted down like an arrow of fire, shot under, and instantly leaping up within an oar's length of the boats, floated quietly, very black on the luminous sea. I hailed the deck again. After some time a man in an unexpectedly cheerful but also muffled tone, as though he had been trying to speak with his mouth shut, informed me, "Coming directly, sir," and vanished. For a long time I heard nothing but the whirr and roar of the fire. There were also whistling sounds. The boats jumped, tugged at the painters, ran at each other playfully, knocked their sides together, or, do what we would, swung in a bunch against the ship's side. I couldn't stand it any longer, and swarming up a rope, clambered aboard over the stern.

'It was as bright as day. Coming up like this, the sheet of fire facing me was a terrifying sight, and the heat seemed hardly bearable at first. On a settee cushion dragged out of the cabin Captain Beard, his legs drawn up and one arm under his head, slept with the light playing on him. Do you know what the rest were busy about? They were sitting on deck right aft, round an open case eating bread and cheese and drinking bottled stout.

'On the background of flames twisting in fierce tongues above their heads they seemed at home like salamanders, and looked like a band of desperate pirates. The fire sparkled in the whites of their eyes, gleamed on patches of white skin seen through the torn shirts. Each had the marks as of a battle about him – bandaged heads, tied-up arms, a strip of dirty rag round a knee – and each man had a bottle between his legs and a chunk of cheese in his hand. Mahon got up. With his handsome and disreputable head, his hooked profile, his long white beard, and with an uncorked bottle in his hand, he resembled one of those reckless sea-robbers of old making merry amidst violence and disaster. "The last meal on board," he explained solemnly. "We had nothing to eat all day, and it was no use leaving all this." He flourished the bottle and indicated the sleeping skipper. "He said he couldn't swallow anything, so I got him to lie down," he went on; and as I stared, "I don't know whether you are aware young fellow, the man had no sleep to speak of for days – and there will be dam' little sleep in the boats." "There will be no boats by-and-by if you fool about much longer," I said, indignantly. I walked up to the skipper and shook him by the shoulder. At last he opened his eyes, but did not move. "Time to leave her, sir," I said quietly.

'He got up painfully, looked at the flames, at the sea sparkling round the ship, and black, black as ink farther away; he looked at the stars shining dim through a thin veil of smoke in a sky black, black as Erebus.

"Youngest first," he said.

'And the ordinary seaman, wiping his mouth with the back of his hand, got up, clambered over the taffrail, and vanished. Others followed. One, on the point of going over, stopped short to drain his bottle, and with a great swing of his arm flung it at the fire. "Take this!" he cried.

'The skipper lingered disconsolately, and we left him to commune alone for a while with his first command. Then I went up again and brought him away at last. It was time. The ironwork on the poop was hot to the touch.

'Then the painter of the long-boat was cut, and the three boats, tied together, drifted clear of the ship. It was just sixteen hours after the explosion when we abandoned her. Mahon had charge of the second boat, and I had the smallest – the 14-foot thing. The long-boat would have taken the lot of us; but the skipper said we must save as much property as we could – for the underwriters – and so I got my first command. I had two men with me, a bag of biscuits, a few tins of meat, and a breaker of water. I was ordered to keep close to the long-boat, that in bad weather we might be taken into her.

'And do you know what I thought? I thought I would part company as soon as I could. I wanted to have my first command all to myself. I wasn't going to sail in a squadron if there were a chance for independent cruising. I would make land by myself. I would beat the other boats. Youth! All youth! The silly, charming, beautiful youth.

'But we did not make a start at once. We must see the last of the ship. And so the boats drifted about that night, heaving and setting on the swell. The men dozed, waked, sighed, groaned. I looked at the burning ship.

'Between the darkness of earth and heaven she was burning fiercely upon a disc of purple sea shot by the blood-red play of gleams; upon a disc of water glittering and sinister. A high, clear flame, an immense and lonely flame, ascended from the ocean, and from its summit the black smoke poured continuously at the sky. She burned furiously; mournful and imposing like a funeral pile kindled in the night, surrounded by the sea, watched over by the stars. A magnificent death had come like a grace, like a gift, like a

41

reward to that old ship at the end of her laborious days. The surrender of her weary ghost to the keeping of stars and sea was stirring like the sight of a glorious triumph. The masts fell just before daybreak, and for a moment there was a burst and turmoil of sparks that seemed to fill with flying fire the night patient and watchful, the vast night lying silent upon the sea. At daylight she was only a charred shell, floating still under a cloud of smoke and bearing a glowing mass of coal within.

'Then the oars were got out, and the boats forming in a line moved round her remains as if in procession – the long-boat leading. As we pulled across her stern a slim dart of fire shot out viciously at us, and suddenly she went down, head first, in a great hiss of steam. The unconsumed stern was the last to sink; but the paint had gone, had cracked, had peeled off, and there were no letters, there was no word, no stubborn device that was like her soul, to flash at the rising sun her creed and her name.

'We made our way north. A breeze sprang up, and about noon all the boats came together for the last time. I had no mast or sail in mine, but I made a mast out of a spare oar and hoisted a boat-awning for a sail, with a boat-hook for a yard. She was certainly over-masted, but I had the satisfaction of knowing that with the wind aft I could beat the other two. I had to wait for them. Then we all had a look at the captain's chart, and, after a sociable meal of hard bread and water, got our last instructions. These were simple; steer north, and keep together as much as possible. "Be careful with that jury-rig, Marlow," said the captain; and Mahon, as I sailed proudly past his boat, wrinkled his curved nose and hailed, "You will sail that ship of yours under water, if you don't look out, young fellow." He was a malicious old man – and may the deep sea where he sleeps now rock him gently, rock him tenderly to the end of time!

'Before sunset a thick rain-squall passed over the two boats, which were far astern, and that was the last I saw of them for a time. Next day I sat steering my cockle-shell – my first command – with nothing but water and sky around me. I did sight in the afternoon the upper sails of a ship far away, but said nothing, and my men didn't notice her. You see I was afraid she might be homeward bound, and I had no mind to turn back from the portals of the East. I was steering for Java – another blessed name – like Bangkok, you know. I steered many days.

'I need not tell you what it is to be knocking about in an open boat. I remember nights and days of calm, when we pulled, we pulled, and the boat seemed to stand still, as if bewitched within the circle of the sea horizon. I remember the heat, the deluge of rain-squalls that kept us baling for dear life (but filled our water-cask), and I remember sixteen hours on end with a mouth dry as a cinder and a steering-oar over the stern to keep my first command head on to a breaking sea. I did not know how good a man I was till then. I remember the drawn faces, the dejected figures of my two men, and I remember my youth and the feeling that will never come back any more – the feeling that I could last for ever, outlast the sea, the earth, and all men; the deceitful feeling that lures us on to joys, to perils, to love, to vain effort – to death; the triumphant conviction of strength, the heat of life in the handful of dust, the glow in the heart that with every year grows dim, grows cold, grows small, and expires – and expires, too soon, too soon – before life itself.

'And this is how I see the East. I have seen its secret places and have looked into its very soul; but now I see it always from a small boat, a high outline of mountains, blue and afar in the morning; like faint mist at noon; a jagged wall of purple at sunset. I have the feel of the oar in my hand, the vision of a scorching blue sea in my eyes. And I see a bay, a wide bay, smooth as glass and polished like ice, shimmering in the dark. A red light burns far off upon the gloom of the land, and the night is soft and warm. We drag at the oars with aching arms, and suddenly a puff of wind, a puff faint and te-pid and laden with strange odours of blossoms, of aromatic wood, comes out of the still night – the first sigh of the East on my face. That I can never forget. It was impalpable and enslaving, like a charm, like a whispered promise of mysterious delight.

'We had been pulling this finishing spell for eleven hours. Two pulled, and he whose turn it was to rest sat at the tiller. We had made out the red light in that bay and steered for it, guessing it must mark some small coasting port. We passed two vessels, outlandish and high-sterned, sleeping at anchor, and, approaching the light, now very dim, ran the boat's nose against the end of a jutting wharf. We were blind with fatigue. My men dropped the oars and fell off the thwarts as if dead. I made fast to a pile. A current rippled softly. The scented obscurity of the shore was grouped into vast masses, a density of colossal clumps of vegetation, probably – mute and fantastic shapes. And at their foot the semi-circle of a beach gleamed faintly, like an illusion. There was not a light, not a stir, not a sound. The mysterious East faced me, per-fumed like a flower, silent like death, dark like a grave.

'And I sat weary beyond expression, exulting like a conqueror, sleepless and entranced as if before a profound, a fateful enigma.

'A splashing of oars, a measured dip reverberating on the level of water, intensified by the silence of a shore into loud claps, made me jump up. A boat, a European boat, was coming in. I invoked the name of the dead; I hailed: *Judea* ahoy! A thin shout answered.

'It was the captain. I had beaten the flagship by three hours, and I was glad to hear the old man's voice again, tremulous and tired. "Is it you, Marlow?" – "Mind the end of that jetty, sir," I cried.

'He approached cautiously, and brought up with the deep-sea lead-line which we saved – for the underwriters. I eased my painter and fell alongside. He sat, a broken figure at the stern, wet with dew, his hands clasped in his lap. His men were asleep already. "I had a terrible time of it," he murmured. "Mahon is behind – not very far." We conversed in whispers, in loud whispers, as if afraid to wake up the land. Guns, thunder, earthquakes would not have awakened the men just then.

'Looking around as we talked, I saw away at sea a bright light travelling in the night. "There's a steamer passing the bay," I said. She was not passing, she was entering, and she even came close and anchored. "I wish," said the old man, "you would find out whether she is English. Perhaps they could give us a passage somewhere." He seemed nervously anxious. So by dint of punching and kicking I started one of my men into a state of somnambulism, and giving him an oar, took another and pulled towards the lights of the steamer.

'There was a murmur of voices in her, metallic hollow clangs of the engine-room, footsteps on the deck. Her ports shone, round with dilated eyes. Shapes moved about, and there was a shadowy man high up on the bridge. He heard my oars.

'And then, before I could open my lips, the East spoke to me, but it was in a Western voice. A torrent of words was poured into the enigmatical, the fateful silence; outlandish, angry words, mixed with words and even whole sentences of good English, less strange but even more surprising. The voice swore and cursed violently; it riddled the solemn peace of the bay by a volley of abuse. It began by calling me Pig, and from that went crescendo into unmentionable adjectives – in English. The man up there raged aloud in two languages, and with a sincerity in his fury that almost convinced me I had, in some way, sinned against the harmony of the universe. I could hardly see him, but began to think he would work himself into a fit.

'Suddenly he ceased, and I could hear him snorting and blowing like a porpoise. I said:

' "What steamer is this pray?"

' "Eh? What's this? And who are you?"

' "Castaway crew of an English barque burnt at sea. We came here to-night. I am the second mate. The captain is in the long-boat and wishes to know if you would give us a passage somewhere."

' "Oh, my goodness! I say ... This is the *Celestial* from Singapore on her return trip. I'll arrange with your captain in the morning, ... and, ... I say, ... did you hear me just now?"

' "I should think the whole bay heard you."

' "I thought you were a shore-boat. Now, look here – this infernal lazy scoundrel of a caretaker has gone to sleep again – curse him. The light is out, and I nearly ran foul of the end of this damned jetty. This is the third time he plays me this trick. Now, I ask you, can anybody stand this kind of thing? It's enough to drive a man out of his mind. I'll report him ... I'll get the Assistant Resident to give him the sack, by ...! See – there's no light. It's out isn't it? I take you to witness the light's out. There should be a light, you know. A red light on the – "

' "There was a light," I said, mildly.

' "But it's out, man! What's the use of talking like this? You can see for yourself it's out – can't you? If you had to take a valuable steamer along this God-forsaken coast you would want a light too. I'll kick him from end to end of his miserable wharf. You'll see if I don't. I will – "

' "So I may tell my captain you'll take us?" I broke in.

' "Yes, I'll take you. Good night," he said, brusquely.

'I pulled back, made fast again to the jetty, and then went to sleep at last. I had faced the silence of the East. I had heard some of its language. But when I opened my eyes again the silence was as complete as though it had never been broken. I was lying in a flood of light, and the sky had never looked so far, so high, before I opened my eyes and lay without moving.

'And then I saw the men of the East – they were looking at me. The whole length of the jetty was full of people. I saw brown, bronze, yellow faces, the black eyes, the glitter, the colour of an Eastern crowd. And all these beings stared without a murmur, without a sigh, without a movement. They stared down at the boats, at the sleeping men who at night had come to them from the sea. Nothing moved. The fronds of palms stood still against the sky. Not a branch stirred along the shore, and the brown roofs of hidden houses peeped through the green foliage, through the big leaves that hung shining and still like leaves forged of heavy metal. This was the East of the ancient navigators, so old, so mysterious, re-splendent and sombre, living and unchanged, full of danger and promise. And these were the men. I sat up suddenly. A wave of movement passed through the crowd from end to end, passed along the heads, swayed the bodies, ran along the jetty like a ripple on the water, like a breath of wind on a field – and all was still again. I see it now – the wide sweep of the bay, the glittering sands, the wealth of green infinite and varied, the sea blue like the sea of a dream, the crowd of attentive faces, the blaze of vivid colour – the water reflecting it all, the curve of the shore, the jetty, the high-sterned outlandish craft floating still, and the three boats with the tired men from the West sleeping, unconscious of the land and the people and of the violence of sunshine. They slept thrown across the thwarts, curled on bottom-boards, in the careless attitudes of death. The head of the old skipper, leaning back in the stern of the long-boat, had fallen on his breast, and he looked as though he would never wake. Farther out old Mahon's face was upturned to the sky, with the long white beard spread out on his breast, as though he had been shot where he sat at the tiller; and a man, all in a heap in the bows of the boat, slept with both arms embracing the stem-head and with his cheek laid on the gunwale. The East looked at them without a sound.

'I have known its fascination since; I have seen the mysterious shores, the still water, the lands of brown nations, where a stealthy Nemesis lies in wait, pursues, overtakes so many of the conquering race, who are proud of their wisdom, of their knowledge, of their strength. But for me all the East is contained in that vision of my youth. It is all in that moment when I opened my young eyes on it. I came upon it from a tussle with the sea – and I was young – I saw it looking at me. And this is all that is left of it! And this is all that is left of it! Only a moment; a moment of strength, of romance, of glamour – of youth! . . . A flick of sunshine upon a strange shore, the time to remember, the time for a sigh, and – good-bye! – Night – Good-bye . . .!'

He drank.

'Ah! The good old time – the good old time. Youth and the sea. Glamour and the sea! The good, strong sea, the salt, bitter sea, that could whisper to you and roar at you and knock your breath out of you.'

He drank again.

'By all that's wonderful, it is the sea, I believe, the sea itself – or is it youth alone? Who can tell? But you here – you all had something out of life: money, love – whatever one gets on shore – and, tell me, wasn't that the best time, that time when we were young at sea; young and had nothing, on the sea that gives nothing, except hard knocks – and sometimes a chance to feel your strength – that only – what you all regret?'

And we all nodded at him: the man of finance, the man of accounts, the man of law, we all nodded at him over the polished table that like a still sheet of brown water reflected our faces lined, wrinkled; our faces marked by toil, by deceptions, by success, by

47

love; our weary eyes looking still, looking always, looking anxiously for something out of life, that while it is expected is already gone – has passed unseen, in a sigh, in a flash – together with the youth, with the strength, with the romance of illusions.

C. S. Forester

H.M.S. 'SUTHERLAND'

(from *A Ship of the Line*)

C. S. Forester confessed to having a special affection for H.M.S. Sutherland, whose round bow and ungainly lines caused him to think of her as an ugly duckling. Aboard her, Captain Horatio Hornblower is about to begin a new commission, and although Forester wrote a number of complete short stories, this excerpt is preferred since it perfectly expresses his ability to set a scene, as well as giving us an insight into one of the most renowned sailors in fiction. No one who has served in the Royal Navy can fail to respond to the Master at Arms' terse, ' 'Alt! Orf 'ats!'

CAPTAIN Horatio Hornblower was reading a smudgy proof which the printers had just sent round to his lodgings.

'To all Young men of *Spirit*', he read. 'Seamen, Landsmen, and Boys, who wish to strike a Blow for Freedom and to cause the Corsican Tyrant to wish that he had never dared the Wrath of these British Isles. His Majesty's Ship *Sutherland* of two decks and seventy-four guns is at present commissioning at Plymouth, and a few *Vacancies* still exist to complete her Crew. Captain *Horatio Hornblower* in command has lately returned from a Cruize in the *South Sea* during which in command of the Frigate *Lydia* of thirty-six guns, he engaged and *sank* the Spanish vessel *Natividad* of two decks and more than *twice the force*. The Officers, Petty Officers, and men of the *Lydia* have all joined him in the *Sutherland*. What Heart of Oak can resist this Appeal to Join this Band of Heroes and Share with them the new Glories which await them? Who will teach Monsieur *Jean Crapaud* that the Seas are *Britannia's* where no Frog-eating *Frenchman* can show his Face? Who wishes for a Hatful of Golden Louis d'or for *Prize Money*? There will be *Fiddlers* and *Dancing* every evening, and Provisions at *six-*

teen ounces to the Pound, the Best of Beef, and Best of Bread, and *Grog* at midday every Day of the Week and *Sundays*, all in addition to the *Pay* under the *Warrant* of His Most Gracious Majesty King *George!* In the *Place* where this notice is read can be found an Officer of His Majesty's Ship *Sutherland* who will enlist any *Willing Hearts* who Thirst for Glory.'

Captain Hornblower struggled against hopelessness as he read the proof. Appeals of this sort were to be read in dozens in every market town. It hardly seemed likely that he could attract recruits to a humdrum ship of the line when dashing frigate captains of twice his reputation were scouring the country and able to produce figures of prize money actually won in previous voyages. To send four lieutenants, each with half a dozen men, round the southern counties to gather recruits in accordance with this poster was going to cost him practically all the pay he had accumulated last commission, and he feared lest it should be money thrown away.

Yet something had to be done. The *Lydia* had supplied him with two hundred able bodied seamen (his placard said nothing of the fact that they had been compulsorily transferred without a chance of setting foot on English soil after a commission of two years' duration) but to complete his crew he needed another fifty seamen and two hundred landsmen and boys. The guardship had found him none at all. Failure to complete his crew might mean the loss of his command, and from that would result unemployment and half pay – eight shillings a day – for the rest of his life. He could form no estimate at all of with how much favour he was regarded at the Admiralty, and in the absence of data it was natural to him to believe that his employment hung precariously in the balance.

Anxiety and strain brought oaths to his lips as he tapped on the proof with his pencil – silly blasphemies of whose senselessness he was quite well aware even as he mouthed them. But he was careful to speak softly; Maria was resting in the bedroom through the double doors behind him, and he did not want to rouse her. Maria (although it was too early to be certain) believed herself to be pregnant, and Hornblower was sated with her cloy tenderness. His irritation increased at the thought of it; he hated the land, the necessity of recruiting, the stuffy sitting-room, the loss of the indeendence he had enjoyed during the months of his last commission. Irritably he took his hat and stole quietly out. The printer's messenger was waiting, hat in hand, in the hall. To him Hornblower abruptly handed back the proof with a curt order for one gross of placards to be struck off, and then he made his way into the noisy streets.

The tollkeeper at the Halfpenny Gate Bridge at sight of his uniform let him through without payment; a dozen watermen at the ferry knew him as the captain of the *Sutherland* and competed to catch his eye – they could expect an ample fee for rowing a Captain to his ship up the long length of the Hamoaze. Hornblower took his seat in a pair-oared wherry; it gave him some satisfaction to say no word at all as they shoved off and began the long pull through the tangle of shipping. Stroke oar shifted his quid and was about to utter some commonplace or other to his passenger, but at sight of his black brow and ill-tempered frown he thought better of it and changed his opening word to a self-conscious cough – Hornblower, acutely aware of the by-play although he had spared the man no open glance, lost some of his ill-temper as a result. He noticed the play of muscles in the brown forearms as the man strained at his oar; there was a tattooing on the wrist, and a thin gold ring gleamed in the man's left ear. He must have been a seaman before he became a waterman. Hornblower longed inexpressibly to have him haled on board when they should reach the *Sutherland*; if he could only lay his hands on a few dozen prime seamen his anxiety would be at an end. But the fellow of course would have a certificate of exemption, else he would never be able to ply his trade here in a part where a quarter of the British Navy came seeking for men.

The victualling yard and the dockyard as they rowed past were swarming with men, too, all of them able bodied, and half of them seamen – shipwrights and riggers – at whom Hornblower stared as longingly and as helplessly as a cat at goldfish in a bowl. The rope walk and the mast house, the sheer hulk and the smoking chimneys of the biscuit bakery went slowly by. There was the *Sutherland*, riding to her moorings off Bull Point; Hornblower, as he gazed at her across the choppy water, was conscious of a queer admixture of conservative dislike in the natural pride which he felt in his new command. Her round bow looked odd at a time when every British-built ship of the line had the beakhead to which his eye had long grown accustomed; her lines were ungainly and told their tale (as Hornblower noticed every time he looked at her) of more desirable qualities sacrificed for shallow draught. Everything about her – save the lower masts which were of English origin – proved that she was Dutch built, planned to negotiate the mudbanks and shallow estuaries of the Dutch coast. The *Sutherland*, in fact, had once been in the Dutch 74 *Eendracht*, captured off the Texel and now rearmed, the ugliest and least desirable two-decker in the Navy List.

God help him, thought Hornblower, eyeing her with a distaste accentuated by his lack of men to man her, if ever he should find himself trying to claw off a lee shore in her. She would drift off to leeward like a cocked-hat paper boat. And at the subsequent court martial nobody would believe a word of the evidence regarding her unweatherly qualities.

'Easy!' he snapped at the wherrymen, and the oars ceased to grind in the rowlocks as the men rested; the sound of the wave slapping the side of the boat became suddenly more apparent.

As they drifted over the dancing water Hornblower continued his discontented examination. She was newly painted, but in as niggardly a fashion as the dockyard authorities could manage – the dull yellow and black was unrelieved by any white or red. A wealthy captain and first lieutenant would have supplied the deficiency out of their own pockets, and would have shown a lick of gold leaf here and there, but Hornblower had no money to spare for gold leaf, and he knew that Bush, who kept four sisters and a mother on his pay, had none either – not even though his professional future depended in some part on the appearance of the *Sutherland*. Some captains would by hook or by crook have cozened more paint – gold leaf, too, for that matter – out of the dockyard, as Hornblower ruefully told himself. But he was no good at cozening; not the prospect of all the gold leaf in the world could lead him to slap a dockyard clerk on the back and win his favour with flattery and false bonhomie; not that his conscience would stop him, but his self-consciousness would.

Someone on deck spied him now. He could hear the pipes twittering as preparations were made to receive him. Let 'em wait a bit longer; he was not going to be hurried today. The *Sutherland*, riding high without her stores in her, was showing a wide streak of her copper. That copper was new, thank God. Before the wind the ugly old ship might show a pretty turn of speed. As the wind swung her across the tide she revealed her run to him. Looking over her lines, Hornblower occupied his mind with estimates of how to get the best performance out of her. Twenty-two years of sea-going experience helped him. Before his mind's eye he called up a composite diagram of all the forces that would be at work on her at sea - the pressure of the wind on her sails, the rudder balancing the headsails, the lateral resistance of the keel, the friction of the skin, the impact of waves against her bows. Hornblower sketched out a preliminary trial arrangement, deciding just how (until practical tests gave him more data) he would have the masts raked and the ship trimmed. But next moment he remembered bitterly that at present he had no crew to man her, and that unless he could find one all these plans would be useless.

'Give way,' he growled to the wherrymen, and they threw their weight on the oars again.

'Easy, Jake,' said bow oar to stroke, looking over his shoulder.

The wherry swung round under the *Sutherland*'s stern - trust those men to know how a boat should be laid alongside a ship of war - giving Hornblower a sight of the stern gallery which constituted to Hornblower one of the most attractive points about the ship. He was glad that the dockyard had not done away with it, as they had done in so many ships of the line. Up in that gallery he would be able to enjoy wind and sea and sun, in a privacy unattainable on deck. He would have a hammock chair made for use here. He could even take his exercise there, with no man's eye upon him - the gallery was eighteen feet long, and he would only have to stoop a little under the overhanging cove. Hornblower yearned inexpressibly for the time when he would be out at sea, away from all the harassing troubles of the land, walking his stern gallery in the solitude in which alone he could relax nowadays. Yet without a crew all this blissful prospect was withheld from him indefinitely. He must find men somewhere.

He felt in his pockets for silver to pay the boatmen, and although silver was woefully short his self-consciousness drove him into overpaying the men in the fashion he attributed to his fellow captains of ships of the line.

'Thank 'ee, sir. Thank 'ee,' said the stroke oar, knuckling his forehead.

Hornblower went up the ladder and came in through the entry port with its drab paint where in the Dutchmen's time gilding had blazed bravely. The pipes of the boatswain's mates twittered wildly, the marine guard presented arms, the sideboys stood rigidly at attention. Gray, master's mate – lieutenants kept no watch in harbour – was officer of the watch and saluted as Hornblower touched his hat to the quarterdeck. Hornblower did not condescend to speak to him, although Gray was a favourite of his; the rigid guard he kept on himself for fear of unnecessary loquacity forbade. Instead he looked round him silently.

The decks were tangled with gear as the work of rigging the ship proceeded, but the tangle, as Hornblower was careful to note, carried under its surface the framework of orderliness. The coils of rope, the groups at work on the deck, the sailmaker's party sewing at a topsail on the forecastle, gave an impression of confusion, but it was disciplined confusion. The severe orders which he had issued to his officers had borne fruit. The crew of the *Lydia* when they had heard that they were to be transferred bodily to the *Sutherland* without even a day on shore, had nearly mutinied. They were in hand again now.

'Master-at-arms wishes to report, sir,' said Gray.

'Send for him, then,' answered Hornblower.

The master-at-arms was the warrant officer responsible for enforcing discipline, and was a man new to Hornblower, named Price. Hornblower concluded that he had allegations of indiscipline to lodge, and he sighed even while he set his face in an expression of merciless rigidity. Probably it would be a matter of flogging, and he hated the thought of the blood and the agony. But, at the beginning of a commission like this, with a restive crew under his orders, he must not hesitate to flog if necessary – to have the skin and flesh stripped from the offenders' backbones.

Price was coming along the gangway now at the head of the strangest procession. Two by two behind him came a column of thirty men, each one handcuffed to his neighbour, save for the last two who clanked drearily along with leg irons at their ankles. Nearly all of them were in rags, and the rags had no sort of nautical flavour about them at all. The rags of a great many of them were sacking, some had corduroy, and Hornblower, peering closer, saw that one wore the wrecks of a pair of moleskin breeches. Yet another wore the remains of what had once been a respectable black broadcloth suit – white skin showed through a rent in the shoulder. All of them had stubbly beards, black, brown, golden, and grey, and those who were not bald had great mops of tangled hair. The two ship's corporals brought up the rear.

"Alt,' ordered Price. 'Orf 'ats.'

The procession shuffled to a halt, and the men stood sullenly on the quarterdeck. Some of them kept their eyes on the deck, while the others gaped sheepishly around them.

'What the devil's all this?' demanded Hornblower sharply.

'New 'ands, sir,' said Price. 'I signed a receipt to the sodgers what brought 'em, sir.'

'Where did they bring them from?' rasped Hornblower.

'Exeter Assizes, sir,' said Price, producing a list. 'Poachers, four of 'em. Waites, that's 'im in the moleskin breeches, sir, 'e was found guilty of sheepstealing. That 'un in black, 'is crime's bigamy, sir – 'e was a brewer's manager before this 'appened to 'im. The others is larceny mostly, sir, 'cept for them two in front what's in for rick burning and t'other two in irons. Robbery with violence is what they done.'

'Ha – h'm,' said Hornblower, wordless for the moment. The new hands blinked at him, some with hope in their eyes, some with hatred, some with indifference. They had chosen service at sea rather than the gallows, or transportation, or the gaol. Months in prison awaiting trial accounted for their dilapidated appearance. Here was a fine addition to the ship's company, thought Hornblower, bitterly – budding mutineers, sullen sulkers, half-witted yokels. But hands they were and he must make the most of them. They were frightened, sullen, resentful. It would be worth trying to

55

win their affection. His naturally humanitarian instincts dictate
the course he decided to pursue after a moment's quick thinking.

'Why are they still handcuffed?' he demanded, loud enough fo
them all to hear. 'Release them at once.'

'Begging your pardon, sir,' apologized Price. 'I didn't want t
without orders, sir, seeing what they are and 'ow they come 'ere.'

'That's nothing to do with it,' snapped Hornblower. 'They'r
enlisted in the King's service now. And I'll have no man in irons i
my ship unless he's given *me* cause to order it.'

Hornblower kept his gaze from wavering towards the new hand
and steadily addressed his declamation to Price – it was mor
effective delivered that way, he knew, even while he despised him
self for using rhetorical tricks.

'I never want to see new hands in charge of the master-at-arm
again,' he continued, hotly. 'They are recruits in an honourabl
service, with an honourable future before them. I'll thank you t
see to it another time. Now find one of the purser's mates and se
that each of these men is properly dressed in accordance with m
orders.'

Normally it might be harmful to discipline to rate a subordinat
officer in front of the men, but in the case of the master-at-arm
Hornblower knew that little damage was being done. The me
would come to hate the master-at-arms anyway sooner or later
his privileges of rank and pay were given him so that he might be
whipping boy for the crew's discontent. Hornblower could drop th
rasp in his voice and address the hands directly, now.

'A man who does his duty as best he can,' he said, kindly, 'ha
nothing to fear in this ship, and everything to hope for. Now I war
to see how smart you can look in your new clothes, and with th
dirt of the place you have come from washed off you. Dismiss.'

He had won over some of the poor fools, at least, he told himsel
Some of the faces which had been sullen with despair were shinin
with hope now, after this experience of being treated as men an
not as brutes – for the first time in months, if not the first time i
their lives. He watched them off the gangway. Poor devils; i
Hornblower's opinion they had made a bad bargain in exchangin
the gaol for the navy. But at least they represented thirty out c

he two hundred and fifty additional human bodies which he
needed to drag at ropes and to heave at capstan bars so as to take
his old *Sutherland* out to sea.

Lieutenant Bush came hastening on to the quarterdeck, and
touched his hat to his captain. The stern swarthy face with its
incongruous blue eyes broke into a smile just as incongruous. It
gave Hornblower a queer twinge, almost of conscience, to see the
evident pleasure which Bush experienced at sight of him. It was
odd to know that he was admired – it might even be said that he
was loved – by this very capable sailor, this splendid disciplinarian
and fearless fighter who boasted so many of the good qualities in
which Hornblower felt himself to be lacking.

'Good morning, Bush,' he said. 'Have you seen the new draft?'

'No, sir. I was rowing guard for the middle watch and I've only
just turned out. Where do they hail from, sir?'

Hornblower told him, and Bush rubbed his hands with pleasure.

'Thirty!' he said. 'That's rare. I never hoped for more than a
dozen from Exeter assizes. And Bodmin assizes open today. Please
God we get another thirty there.'

'We won't get topmen from Bodmin assizes,' said Hornblower,
comforted beyond measure at the equanimity with which Bush regarded the introduction of gaolbirds into the *Sutherland*'s crew.

'No, sir. But the West India convoy's due this week. The guards
ought to nab two hundred there. We'll get twenty if we get our
rights.'

'M'm,' said Hornblower, and turned away uneasily. He was not
the sort of captain – neither the distinguished kind nor the wheed-
ling kind – who could be sure of favours from the Port Admiral. 'I
must look round below.'

That changed the subject effectively enough.

'The women are restless,' said Bush. 'I'd better come, too, sir, if
you don't object.'

The lower gun deck offered a strange spectacle, lit vaguely by
the light which came through half a dozen open gun ports. There
were fifty women there. Three or four were still in their hammocks,
lying on their sides looking out on the others. Some were sitting in
groups on the deck, chattering loud-voiced. One or two were

chaffering for food through the gun ports with the occupants o
shore boats floating just outside; the netting which impeded deser
tion had a broad enough mesh to allow a hand to pass through. Tw
more, each backed by a supporting group, were quarrelling vic
lently. They were in odd contrast – one was tall and dark, so tall a
to have to crouch round-shouldered under the five-foot deck beam
while the other, short, broad, and fair, was standing up boldl
before her menacing advance.

'That's what I said,' she maintained stoutly. 'And I'll say
again. I ain't afeared o' *you*, Mrs Dawson, as you call yourself.'

'A-ah,' screamed the dark one at this crowning insult. Sh
swooped forward, and with greedy hands she seized the other b
the hair, shaking her head from side to side as if she would soo
shake it off. In return her face was scratched and her shins wer
kicked by her stout-hearted opponent. They whirled round in
flurry of petticoats, when one of the women in the hammock
screamed a warning to them.

'Stop it, you mad bitches! 'Ere's the cap'n.'

They fell apart, panting and tousled. Every eye was turne
towards Hornblower as he walked forward in the patchy light, h
head bowed under the deck above.

'The next woman fighting will be put ashore instantly,' growle
Hornblower.

The dark woman swept her hair from her eyes and sniffed wit
disdain.

'You needn't put *me* ashore, Cap'n,' she said. 'I'm goin'. Ther
ain't a farden to be had out o' this starvation ship.'

She was apparently expressing a sentiment which was shared k
a good many of the women, for the speech was followed by a litt
buzz of approval.

'Ain't the men *never* goin' to get their pay notes?' piped up th
woman in the hammock.

'Enough o' that,' roared Bush, suddenly. He pushed forwar
anxious to save his captain from the insults to which he was e
posed, thanks to a government which left its men still unpaid aft
a month in port. 'You there, what are you doing in your hammo
after eight bells?'

But this attempt to assume a counter offensive met with disaster.

'I'll come out if you like, Mr Lieutenant,' she said, flicking off er blanket and sliding to the deck. 'I parted with my gown to buy ıy Tom a sausage, and my petticoat's bought him a soop o' West 'ountry ale. Would you have me on deck in my shift, Mr Lieuten-ıt?'

A titter went round the deck.

'Get back and be decent,' spluttered Bush, on fire with em-ırrassment.

Hornblower was laughing too – perhaps it was because he was .arried that the sight of a half-naked woman alarmed him not :arly as much as it did his first lieutenant.

'Never will I be decent now,' said the woman, swinging her legs ɔ into the hammock and composedly draping the blanket over :r, 'until my Tom gets his pay warrant.'

'An' when he gets it,' sneered the fair woman. 'What can he do ith it without shore leave? Sell it to a bumboat shark for a quar-r!'

'Fi' pound for twenty-three months' pay!' added another. 'An' ɛ a month gone a'ready.'

'Avast there,' said Bush.

Hornblower beat a retreat, abandoning – forgetting, rather – the ɔject of his visit of inspection below. He could not face those omen when the question of pay came up again. The men had ɛen scandalously badly treated, imprisoned in the ship within ;ht of land, and their wives (some of them certainly were wives, though by Admiralty regulations a simple verbal declaration of ɛ existence of a marriage was sufficient to allow them on board) id just cause for complaint. No one, not even Bush, knew that ɛ few guineas which had been doled out among the crew rep-sented a large part of Hornblower's accumulated pay – all he ɔuld spare, in fact, except for the necessary money to pay his ficers' expenses when they should start on their recruiting ɔurneys.

His vivid imagination and absurd sensitiveness between them ɛrhaps exaggerated part of the men's hardships. The thought of ɛ promiscuity of life below decks, where a man was allotted

eighteen inches' width in which to swing his hammock, while h
wife was allowed eighteen inches next to him, all in a long ro
husbands, wives, and single men, appalled him. So did the thoug
of women having to live on the revolting lower deck food. Possib
he made insufficient allowance for the hardening effect of lor
habit.

He emerged through the fore hatchway on to the maindeck
little unexpectedly. Thompson, one of the captains of the for
castle, was dealing with the new hands.

'P'raps we'll make sailors of you,' he was saying, 'and p'raps v
won't. Overside with a shot at your feet, more likely, before v
sight Ushant. And a waste o' good shot, too. Come on wi' th
pump, there. Let's see the colour o' your hides, gaolbirds. When t
cat gets at you we'll see the colour o' your backbones, too, you – '

'Enough of that, Thompson,' roared Hornblower, furious.

In accordance with his standing orders the new hands we
being treated to rid them of vermin. Naked and shivering, th
were grouped about the deck. Two of them were having the
heads shorn down to the bare skin; a dozen of them, who h
already submitted to this treatment (and looking strangely sick
and out of place with the prison pallor still on them) were bei
herded by Thompson towards the washdeck pump which a coup
of grinning hands were working. Fright was making them shiver
much as cold – not one of them, probably, had ever had a ba
before, and what with the prospect, and Thompson's bloodcurdli
remarks and the strange surroundings, they were pitiful to see.

It enraged Hornblower, who somehow or other had never fc
gotten the misery of his early days at sea. Bullying was abhorrent
him like any other sort of wanton cruelty, and he had no sympat
whatever with the aim of so many of his brother officers, to bre
the spirit of the men under him. One of these days his professio
reputation and his future might depend on these very men riski
their lives cheerfully and willingly – sacrificing them, if need be
and he could not imagine cowed and broken-spirited men doi
that. The shearing and the bath were necessary, if the ship was to
kept clear of the fleas and bugs and lice which could make life
misery on board, but he was not going to have his precious m

cowed more than was unavoidable. It was curious that Hornblower, who never could believe himself to be a leader of men, would always lead rather than drive.

'Under the pump with you, men,' he said kindly, and when they still hesitated – 'When we get to sea you'll see *me* under that pump, every morning at seven bells. Isn't that so, there?'

'Aye, aye, sir,' chorused the hands at the pump – their captain's strange habit of having a cold seawater pump over him every morning had been a source of much discussion on board the *Lydia*.

'So under with you, and perhaps you'll all be captains one of these days. You, there, Waites, show these others you're not afraid.'

It was blessed good fortune that Hornblower was able not only to remember the name, but to recognize in his new guise Waites, the sheepstealer with the moleskin breeches. They blinked at this resplendent captain in his gold lace, whose tone was cheerful and whose dignity still admitted taking a daily bath. Waites steeled himself to dive under the spouting hose, and, gasping, rotated heroically under the cold water. Someone threw him a lump of holystone with which to scrub himself, while the others jostled for their turn – the poor fools were like sheep; it was only necessary to set one moving to make all the rest eager to follow.

Hornblower caught sight of a red angry welt across one white shoulder. He beckoned Thompson out of earshot.

'You've been free with that starter of yours, Thompson,' he said.

Thompson grinned uneasily, fingering the two-foot length of rope knotted at each end, with which petty officers were universally accustomed to stimulate the activity of the men under them.

'I won't have a petty officer in my ship,' said Hornblower, 'who doesn't know when to use a starter and when not to. These men haven't got their wits about 'em yet, and hitting 'em won't remedy it. Make another mistake like that, Thompson, and I'll disrate you. And then you'll clean out the heads of this ship every day of this commission. That'll do.'

Thompson shrank away, abashed by the genuine anger which Hornblower displayed.

'Keep your eye on him, Mr Bush, if you please,' added Hornblower. 'Sometimes a reprimand makes a petty officer take it out of the men more than ever to pay himself back. And I won't have it.'

'Aye, aye, sir,' said Bush, philosophically.

Hornblower was the only captain he had ever heard of who bothered his head about the use of starters. Starters were as much part of Navy life as bad food and eighteen inches per hammock and peril at sea. Bush could never understand Hornblower's disciplinary methods. He had been positively horrified when he had heard his captain's public admission that he, too, had baths under the washdeck pump – it seemed madness for a captain to allow his men to guess that they were the same flesh as his. But two years under Hornblower's command had taught him that Hornblower's strange ways sometimes attained surprising results. He was ready to obey him, loyally though blindly, resigned and yet admiring.

Ernest Hemingway

AFTER THE STORM

IT wasn't about anything, something about making punch, and then we started fighting and I slipped and he had me down kneeling on my chest and choking me with both hands like he was trying to kill me and all the time I was trying to get my knife out of my pocket to cut him loose. Everybody was too drunk to pull him off me. He was choking me and hammering my head on the floor and I got the knife out and opened it up; and I cut the muscle right across his arm and he let go of me. He couldn't have held on if he wanted to. Then he rolled and hung on to that arm and started to cry and I said:

'What the hell you want to choke me for?'

I'd have killed him. I couldn't swallow for a week. He hurt my throat bad.

Well, I went out of there and there were plenty of them with him and some came out after me and I made a turn and was down by the docks and I met a fellow and he said somebody killed a man up the street. I said, 'Who killed him?' and he said, 'I don't know who killed him but he's dead all right,' and it was dark and there was water standing in the street and no lights and windows broke and boats all up in the town and trees blown down and everything all blown and I got a skiff and went out and found my boat where I had her inside of Mango Key and she was all right only she was full of water. So I bailed her out and pumped her out and there was a moon but plenty of clouds and still plenty rough and I took it down along; and when it was daylight I was off Eastern Harbour.

Brother, that was some storm. I was first boat out and you never saw water like that was. It was just as white as a lye barrel and coming from Eastern Harbour to Sou'west Key you couldn't recognize the shore. There was a big channel blown right out through

63

the middle of the beach. Trees and all blown out and a channel cut through and all the water white as chalk and everything on it branches and whole trees and dead birds, and all floating. Inside the keys were all the pelicans in the world and all kinds of birds flying. They must have gone inside there when they knew it was coming.

I lay at Sou'west Key a day and nobody came after me. I was the first boat out and I seen a spar floating and I knew there must be a wreck and I started out to look for her. I found her. She was a three-masted schooner and I could just see the stumps of her spars out of water. She was in too deep water and I didn't get anything off of her. So I went on looking for something else. I had the start on all of them and I knew I ought to get whatever there was. I went on down over the sand-bar from where I left that three-masted schooner and I didn't find anything and I went on a long way. was way out toward the quicksands and I didn't find anything so I went on. Then when I was in sight of the Rebecca Light I saw all kinds of birds making over something and I headed over for there to see what it was and there was a cloud of birds all right.

I could see something looked like a spar up out of the water and when I got over close the birds all went up in the air and stayed all around me. The water was clear out there and there was a spar of some kind sticking out just above the water and when I come up close to it I saw it was all dark under water like a long shadow and I came right over it and there under water was a liner; just lying there all under water as big as the whole world. I drifted over her in the boat. She lay on her side and the stern was deep down. The port holes were all shut tight and I could see the glass shine in the water and the whole of her; the biggest boat I ever saw in my life laying there and I went along the whole length of her and then went over and anchored and I had the skiff on the deck forward and I shoved it down into the water and sculled over with the birds all around me.

I had a water glass like we use sponging and my hand shook so could hardly hold it. All the port holes were shut that you could see along over her but way down below near the bottom something must have been open because there were pieces of things floating out all the time. You couldn't tell what they were. Just pieces. That's what the birds were after. You never saw so many birds. They were all around me; crazy yelling.

I could see everything sharp and clear. I could see her rounded over and she looked a mile long under the water. She was lying on a clear white bank of sand and the spar was a sort of foremast or some sort of tackle that slanted out of the water the way she was laying on her side. Her bow wasn't very far under. I could stand on the letters of her name on her bow and my head was just out of water. But the nearest port hole was twelve feet down. I could just reach it with the grains pole and I tried to break it with that but I couldn't. The glass was too stout. So I sculled back to the boat, and got a wrench and lashed it to the end of the grains pole and I couldn't break it. There I was looking down through the glass at that liner with everything in her and I was the first one to her and I couldn't get into her. She must have had five million dollars' worth in her.

It made me shake to think how much she must have in her. Inside the port hole that was closest I could see something but I couldn't make it out through the water glass. I couldn't do any good with the grains pole and I took off my clothes and stood and took a couple of deep breaths and dove over off the stern with the wrench in my hand and swam down. I could hold on for a second to the edge of the port hole, and I could see in and there was a woman inside with her hair floating all out. I could see her floating plain and I hit the glass twice with the wrench hard and I heard the noise clink in my ears but it wouldn't break and I had to come up.

I hung on to the dinghy and got my breath and then I climbed in and took a couple of breaths and dove again. I swam down and took hold of the edge of the port hole with my fingers and held it and hit the glass as hard as I could with the wrench. I could see the woman floating in the water through the glass. Her hair was tied once close to her head and it floated all out in the water. I could see the rings on one of her hands. She was right up close to the port hole and I hit the glass twice and I didn't even crack it. When I came up I thought I wouldn't make it to the top before I'd have to breathe.

65

I went down once more and I cracked the glass, only cracked it, and when I came up my nose was bleeding and I stood on the bow of the liner with my bare feet on the letters of her name and my head just out and rested there and then I swam over to the skiff and pulled up into it and sat there waiting for my head to stop aching and looking down into the water glass, but I bled so I had to wash out the water glass. Then I lay back in the skiff and held my hand under my nose to stop it and I lay there with my head back looking up and there was a million birds above and all around.

When I quit bleeding I took another look through the glass and then I sculled over to the boat to try and find something heavier than the wrench but I couldn't find a thing; not even a sponge hook. I went back and the water was clearer all the time and you could see everything that floated out over that white bank of sand. I looked for sharks but there weren't any. You could have seen a shark a long way away. The water was so clear and the sand white. There was a grapple for an anchor on the skiff and I cut it off and went overboard and down with it. It carried me right down and past the port hole and I grabbed and couldn't hold anything and went on down and down, sliding along the curved side of her. I had to let go of the grapple. I heard it bump once and it seemed like a year before I came up through the top of the water. The skiff was floated away with the tide and I swam over to her with my nose bleeding in the water while I swam and I was plenty glad there weren't sharks; but I was tired.

My head felt cracked open and I lay in the skiff and rested and then sculled back. It was getting along in the afternoon. I went down once more with the wrench and it didn't do any good. That wrench was too light. It wasn't any good diving unless you had a big hammer or something heavy enough to do good. Then I lashed the wrench to the grains pole again and I watched through the water glass and pounded on the glass and hammered until the wrench came off and I saw it in the glass, clear and sharp, go sliding down along her and then off and down to the quicksand and go in. Then I couldn't do a thing. The wrench was gone and I'd lost the grapple so I sculled back to the boat. I was too tired to get the skiff aboard and the sun was pretty low. The birds were pulling out and leaving her and I headed for Sou'west Key towing the skiff and the birds going on ahead of me and behind me. I was plenty tired.

That night it came on to blow and it blew for a week. You couldn't get out to her. They come out from town and told me the fellow I'd had to cut was all right except for his arm and I went back to town and they put me under five hundred dollar bond. It came out all right because some of them, friends of mine, swore he was after me with an axe, but by the time we got back out to her the Greeks had blown her open and cleaned her out. They got the safe out with dynamite. Nobody ever knows how much they got. She carried gold and they got it all. They stripped her clean. I found her and I never got a nickel out of her.

It was a hell of a thing all right. They say she was just outside of Havana harbour when the hurricane hit and she couldn't get in or the owners wouldn't let the captain chance coming in; they say he wanted to try; so she had to go with it and in the dark they were running with it trying to go through the gulf between Rebecca and Tortugas when she struck on the quicksands. Maybe her rudder was carried away. Maybe they weren't even steering. But anyway they couldn't have known they were quicksands and when she struck the captain must have ordered them to open up the ballast tanks so she'd lay solid. But it was quicksand she'd hit and when they opened the tanks she went in stern first and then over on her beam ends. There were four hundred and fifty passengers and the crew on board of her and they must all have been aboard of her when I found her. They must have opened the tanks as soon as she struck and the minute she settled on it the quicksands took her down. Then her boilers must have burst and that must have been what made those pieces that came out. It was funny there weren't any sharks though. There wasn't a fish. I could have seen them on that clear white sand.

Plenty of fish now though; jewfish, the biggest kind. The biggest part of her's under the sand now but they live inside of her; the biggest kind of jewfish. Some weigh three to four hundred pounds. Sometime we'll go out and get some. You can see the Rebecca Light from where she is. They've got a buoy on her now. She's right at the end of the quicksand right at the edge of the gulf. She only

missed going through by about a hundred yards. In the dark in the
storm they just missed it; raining the way it was they couldn't have
seen the Rebecca. Then they're not used to that sort of thing. The
captain of a liner isn't used to scudding that way. They have a
course and they tell me they set some sort of a compass and it steer
itself. They probably didn't know where they were when they ran
with that blow but they came close to making it. Maybe they'd los
the rudder though. Anyway there wasn't another thing for them to
hit till they'd get to Mexico once they were in that gulf. Must have
been something though when they struck in that rain and wind and
he told them to open her tanks. Nobody could have been on deck in
that blow and rain. Everybody must have been below. They
couldn't have lived on deck. There must have been some scene
inside all right because you know she settled fast. I saw that wrench
go into the sand. The captain couldn't have known it was quick
sand when she struck unless he knew these waters. He just knew it
wasn't rock. He must have seen it all up in the bridge. He must have
known what it was about when she settled. I wonder how fast sh
made it. I wonder if the mate was there with him. Do you thinl
they stayed inside the bridge or do you think they took it outside
They never found any bodies. Not a one. Nobody floating. They
float a long way with lifebelts too. They must have took it inside
Well, the Greeks got it all. Everything. They must have come fas
all right. They picked her clean. First there was the birds, then me
then the Greeks, and even the birds got more out of her than I did.

Tom Hopkinson

I HAVE BEEN DROWNED

(TO ANTONIA WHITE)

WHEN I was a boy my mother took me to a gipsy. She was a dirty old woman in a tent. My mother hoped, I suppose, that she would foretell me fame and fortune. I was hoping she would foretell me a pony for my birthday.

The gipsy looked for a long time into a crystal. Then she spoke, and in a clear voice quite unlike the gruff dialect in which she bargained, lied and quarrelled, the gipsy said, 'The boy will meet death by drowning.' Then she added, rather oddly, 'I see him drown; at least I think I do.'

Even at my age I realized that her hesitation set the stamp of truth on what she said. If she had wanted to invent a tale she would have made up a high-sounding one, full of the good fortune and grand events for which my mother longed.

Though I accepted death by drowning as my fate from that day on, I was never in the least haunted by the thought of it. I have always felt in my heart I should prefer to die that way, and now it is clear to me I never shall, I feel almost as though I had been cheated of a promised honour, degraded from my own peculiar destiny to be as other men.

Anyone who remembers being a child will recall the overwhelming desires which seized one for an object, not beautiful nor useful, which could only be a nuisance to one when one had it. I have been kept awake at night by a craving for a white mouse belonging to a friend. I stole the mouse, and was awake next night with the excitement of the theft and the mad joy of possession.

Something of the sort must have happened to me, I suppose, on the hot June afternoon when I saw *Stella*.

Stella, I could see straight away, was almost everything a boat ought not to be. She was too fine forward, so that she would thrust her nose into the waves instead of lifting to them. She was too square aft, so that a following sea would smash her from side to side with constant danger of a jibe. She had a long deep keel, making it impossible to run for shelter into the small muddy inlets of the coast where I should sail her.

I went into the builder's yard above which I had seen her much too tall mast tower, and looked her over inch by inch. When I had done I hated the very sight of her, hated her with the hatred one can only feel for something to which one is inextricably married, married not by force of circumstances which may change or weaken, but by an unchanging thing implanted in the substance of one's self.

There were some few points in *Stella*'s favour. I had hoped as I looked at her to find her rotten, and so to be given excuse for never seeing her again. She was as dry as a barrel and tough as a concrete pavement, built of teak.

'She don't make a cupful of water in two years,' said the builder, kicking angrily at her side – I could see he hated the boat as much as I did, and would gladly have scored off her by leaving her in his yard to rot unsold – adding in explanation, 'She've got two skins.'

Her enormous keel was of lead – worth money in itself – and she had a prodigious variety of sails, ranging from a tiny trysail and storm-jib to a towering mainsail and pot-bellied spinnaker. At the worst, I thought, I could ride out bad weather with two of the smallest pocket-handkerchiefs. Then I looked at the steepling mast and loaded keel and saw that without a stitch of sail the thresh and strain in any wind and sea would be terrific.

I bought *Stella*, as I had known all along I should. I paid £120 for her. It was nothing for a boat of her size and condition. From the point of view of anyone wanting a pleasant sail, it was money thrown down the drain. Sailing her could only be a nightmare.

As I went out of the yard I looked at the builder. 'She's a maniac's boat,' I said. 'Built by a lunatic, to be sailed by idiots. She ought to be broken up now, before someone injures themselves in her. If I had any sense, I'd pay you twice the money not to let me have her.'

The dealer looked at me under his wedged-down bowler hat. The deal was finished. I should not back out. 'She's a drowning boat,' he said.

I took *Stella* away from the yard a fortnight later. She scarcely needed touching. I had her painted black with varnished decks. She was copper-fastened all through and her fittings were brass.

I sailed her down the Medway and across to the Essex coast – where I lived aboard, and got to know her. But 'got to know' are not the words to use of *Stella*. I had known everything about her long before. She played no trick which I had not foreseen and dreaded. Her good qualities I had counted on without even proving they were there.

She buried her bows instead of lifting them, as I had known she would. When running before a wind, I had to be 'steering' all the time, spinning the wheel as a following wave crashed against her counter, spinning it back before the boom could fly over and snap the mast off like a hemlock stalk. A good boat steers herself. A good helmsman scarcely uses the wheel; he thinks instead. It was no good thinking at *Stella*. You had to take two hands to her and use all the strength of arms and planted legs and lever body.

As against that, she would sail almost into the wind's eye in defiance of all nature, and with her monstrous spread of canvas would go driving on, as if towed by an unseen army of porpoises, when other boats were tossing helplessly up and down, their crews playing nap for occupation.

At first I sailed *Stella* with a paid hand. That was all right for a week or two. But before long I began to find fault with everything he did. He could never set a sail just right. He left specks on the brass-work. At the wheel he let her fall away, shipped more seas than he needed. I sacked him. When he went off he looked not at all angrily at me, but sympathetically, as a man might look at another he must leave for the winter in the frozen North.

From that time I ministered to all *Stella*'s wants myself. I would let no one so much as splice a rope for her. By the end of the summer I would not even let other people come aboard. If in an access of friendship or desire I asked someone to stay on her for the weekend, I would be certain the day before to send a wire and put them off. My friends all gave me up.

I did not mind. During August and September I won seven firsts and two second prizes with *Stella* in ten races, sailing her with a young fisherman whom I paid for every race and packed off as soon as it was over. He hated the sea, and said so, and he hated me and my boat more than ever he could find words to say.

The day on which I was to drown was the day of the Yantlet Regatta. It was a dirty day, and a falling glass showed worse to follow. There was talk of calling the regatta off. All the competitors in my class – we had to sail an eighteen-mile course out of the estuary and back – agreed that if our race were to be held they would refuse to sail it.

I found a note in the rules of the Club saying that if one member of a class wished to sail the course he could do so and claim the race. I declared that I would sail and claim. The others held together and refused. 'It's a game for lunatics,' they said.

I found my fisherman and offered him double money for the race. 'You know what you can do with that,' he said. I offered him £20 – double the prize money – for himself. He looked down at his boots, round at the sky, and went to get his oilskins.

There was nobody except the officials of the Club to see us start. The race had been banned by the members. They were watching the dinghies race behind a breakwater.

We tacked out to the buoy, six miles in all, with four of open sea, *Stella* sailing as she had never sailed before. If the other boats had come out they would have looked like cart-horses. After that we had to beat windward – five further miles of open water, as 'open' as any water I ever sailed above and through – then we rounded a lightship and set off for home, doing ten knots and the boat half lost in spray.

We had covered perhaps a quarter of the way on this last leg when mist came down, not a nice gentle mist, but a foul blinding mist; not a mist that is laid round you like a blanket, but a mist that is flung at you like rough-cast. At the same time the tide turned.

The sea was now running out and the wind blowing in. The

waves got bigger every minute. *Stella* began to plunge her nose. Great slews of water flushed along the deck. I had been soaked for two hours before. Now the water was battering me solid. It was as much as I could do to stand. 'Better take in sail,' said the fisherman; they called him Jack.

'You'll take in nothing,' I shouted at him through the wind. Jack did not answer. He went forward and began to reef the foresail.

'Blast him,' I thought. 'I'll show him.'

We were running then over a sand-bar, a spit that would be dried out at low water. Now there was two or three fathoms over it. The waves were pounding and threshing, half breaking, instead of lifting and then sliding away beneath her keel. There was a big one just ahead and and as we came to it, instead of turning *Stella*'s bows away so that she met it slightly on her quarter, I drove them in. She took it solid. A great belch of water burst along the deck, splitting over every obstacle, re-uniting again the second it was past.

It took Jack waist-high, knocked him off his feet. I thought for a second he was gone. But it takes more than a wave to drown a fisherman, and as he swept down the scuppers he grabbed hold of one of the stays and clung till the burst of water had gone by. That happened in one second.

In the next there was a crack, a painful crack like the sound of a living body broken, then an outbreak of smaller cracks, wires and ropes whipped through the air or sank coiling by my feet, all of the decks forward and yards of sea on either side were suddenly over-spread with canvas, through which the water welled and over which it spread.

The weight and shock of that sea smashing her nose down, while a gust was bursting and lifting into her sails behind, had snapped the mainmast short.

I had thought very often of what I should do if *Stella* went down at sea, and she was going to go down now. Without way on her she would not steer. The next two or three waves would hammer her counter round and broach her to. Once broadside on, a couple of waves would fill her, and the tons of valuable lead on her bottom would do the rest.

I slithered and bolted forward to where a lifebelt was fixed on top of a skylight, tore it off, thrust head and arms inside, and went overboard in a patch of sea clear of sail and cordage. Two minutes later she was gone.

As soon as I found myself in the sea I knew what I must do. I never wore sea-boots on *Stella*. I did not trust her well enough. I could keep afloat with my lifebelt for several hours if I did not exhaust myself in swimming. A fool would have tried to make the coast against the tide. But to make those four or five miles – an hour's quick walking – I would have needed to swim twenty. I could not even hold my place and hope to be washed back when the tide turned in six hours' time. All I could do was to keep afloat and save my strength.

Having a lifebelt, I knew, is not everything. Plenty of drowned bodies are washed up with lifebelts underneath their arms. You have got to keep your face out of the water, not easy when the waves are running high, and you have got to keep yourself from dying of exhaustion, though normally you feel cold after a five-minutes bathe.

I reckoned I had two chances of life. One was to drift down to the lightship we had rounded, and hope to grab one of her chains or rouse her men by shouting. The other was that some of the men at the Yacht Club would set out to look for me.

They would not do that for several hours, because we had been making much faster time than ever they'd expect, and when we did not turn up they'd only think we had run into a creek for shelter, and would telephone round for a while to see if there was news of us. There was a chance of a stray steamer catching sight of me, but it was just as likely in the mist she would cut me down.

I decided to swim gently to keep the blood flowing, first on my breast, then on my back, shifting the lifebelt slightly as I turned from one position to the other. Once as I was swimming forward it slipped back and caught for a moment on my hips, lifting my body and pressing my face into the water. I rolled over on my back and worked it free. Once as I changed position my arm got pinned inside the belt. With muscles weakening, I had a horror that I could not get it back. I got it back quite easily and went on swimming.

I swam as I had been taught to swim, in long slow sweeping strokes, driving with my legs, which are strong and slow to tire, using my arms for direction and support, drawing great breaths of air upon the upward stroke, blowing it out from my mouth before me through the water as my arms came in and forward. I took as much care with my style as though I had been in for a competition, and there were judges pacing beside me in a bath, for in the swim I had embarked on, just one more stroke, or ten or twenty might serve, I knew, to keep me in the world.

At first, while I was over the bar where the waves were breaking, I thought I should be choked. Water beat up my nose, into my mouth. My throat was full of water and I thought my lungs must be filling too. A man must breathe to live, and every time I took in air I took in sea. Then I drifted into deep water where there was swell instead of breakers, and breath came more easily. I felt for a moment as glad as if I had been rescued. I looked round, and swam on almost gaily through the mist and swell.

I had been in the water for perhaps half an hour when I happened to catch sight of my fingers. Two of the fingers of my left hand and the little finger of my right hand were pale green. I have never been much at home in water, and after a short bathe it takes me half an hour to get my blood flowing properly through my limbs. There was no chance to get it flowing again now.

It was not long before my other fingers had gone dead. I imagined the paralysis moving up like the mercury in a thermometer, from wrist to elbow, elbow to shoulder, and then running on down inside my body. It became necessary for me to know if my toes were dead as well, to see if the paralysis were coming from both ends, or only one. I did actually raise my feet in the water and tried to take one of my shoes off to find out, but my dead fingers would no longer work.

I cannot say how long I had been in the sea before I saw the lightship. I was conscious one moment of something dark seen out of the corner of my eye. The next instant there she was, not as I had pictured her, a comfortable and friendly presence with men waiting ready to haul me out and take me in, but a great heaving mass rolling her iron belly up with every surge, then crashing back with showers of spray into the swell, a dreadful heap of metal uncontrolled, terrifying to a thing of flesh.

Her cables, which I had pictured as so firm and steady, almost like life-chains in a swimming-bath, whipped through the waves as though themselves alive, the links grinding and crashing like goods-trucks in a siding – but goods-trucks crashing and grinding of their own volition and capriciously, escaped from reason and control. I kicked away from her with all the strength I had, and as I kicked I shouted.

I shouted once, a high-pitched shriek. There came no sign or answer. I thought the thin sound might seem too like a seagull's cry. I gathered up air into my lungs, and burst it all out again in roars. In the wild clatter and grind of everything on board, in the explosions all round me of the bursting seas, I could scarcely hear the sound myself.

As the lightship passed away out of sight I began to expect death. It would not be possible for me much longer to keep my face out of the waves. It was already impossible to keep it from the crests, and I drew breath in deep gulps in the quiet troughs. Soon whether crests or troughs would be alike to me, my face would lie helplessly forward on the surge and water would make its way into my lungs, driving the last air out in bubbles from my nose.

My weary arms were becoming with every stroke more difficult to lift. I had to force them to serve my purpose, almost shouting my orders to them with my mouth, as they began to disregard the messages sent along sinews from my brain.

I was becoming a prey to bodily fancies that would have stopped me swimming altogether had I heeded them. It was not my arms that weighed so much and were so difficult to move, it was the burden of the clothing on my arms which had now grown weightier than I could lift. It was the thickness of the clothing on my body which prevented me dividing the waters like a fish.

So conscious was I of my painful arms that I forgot the existence of my legs, and when for some reason they came into my mind, I could not feel their presence for the cold. I imagined I had swum away from them entirely or else that they had kicked loose from their joints, and was urgent in myself to get them back, feeling I could never make land without their help.

Inside my body I endured a feeling of extreme and painful cold, as though my entrails had been taken out and ice sewn in. The sole remaining patch of warmth, it seemed to me, was around my heart, and in the upper part of my chest, between my ribs and shoulder-blades.

As I swam on, these various pains lifted and moved away from my outlying parts, becoming centred on my controlling, guiding head. The driving rain, the flung spume lashing from the waves against my face, the constant muscular effort to peer my eyes out of their sockets and lose no chance of sighting ship or boat, combined with the opposite effort to draw them right in beneath their brows for shelter, had caused inside my head a deadly pain, as though the metal of my forehead was on fire.

At the time these things were happening to me in the body, quite other things were happening in my mind.

I had no experience at all of that delightful coloured-cinema phenomenon in which the whole of one's past life is said to unroll progressively before one's eyes, and at the same time to be presented to one in a flash. Yet certain moments in my life, or as it were, pictures from my story, resurged before me with a more than natural vividness, rising and falling, growing sharper in image or receding, in time to the rising and falling of the waves.

I had, first, a picture of myself as infant, bundled together within my mother's womb, drawing life in through a tube as a diver draws air down from the surface.

I watched myself grow from a small swimming fish into a dwarf, enormous-headed, sightless-eyed, his useless limbs tucked round him for convenience, the whole creature shaken and quivering from the pulsing of his own determined heart.

This, the first vision that I saw, was curiously without colour. It had rather the grey appearance of a photograph, the nebulous vagueness of an X-ray picture.

Then, with no intervening stages, I was become a small boy of seven or eight, constructing for myself a house of packing-cases in the garden. No house, it seemed to me, is complete without store of food, and I was scratching with a trowel a hole in the turf floor, in order to let in a biscuit-tin larder for odd crusts and cakes, a green apple and a bottle which had once held lemonade.

And now, a few years older, I was making of my bicycle a sort of moving home, covering the handle-bars and frame with fittings, lashing a tiny tent against the saddle, delighting to show myself independent of the world on those two travelling wheels.

At seventeen, a senior boy at school, I owned a study. It had no door, consisted of no more than a slab of wood for desk, a seat close up against the slab, a bookshelf running round the sides. No bride ever lavished more care on her first home of love than I on that small wooden stall. Its sides I draped with flowered cloth, hung or pinned pictures over that, bargained with other boys for ornaments that caught my fancy.

My study and my youth washed by me on a wave.

Now, a young man, I walked through a town where I once lived. It was a seaport, whose tall, gabled warehouses darkened the street through which I passed.

Suddenly from a doorway ran a cat, a small and common tabby. At the sight I was filled with such a passion of tenderness I stopped still where I was, to follow with clenched hands its progress up the street. The cat turned off the road, crept low with flattened paunch beneath a warehouse door. My breath ran slowly out in a long sigh. The cat was safe. No wheel would break its back, no boot its belly.

I stopped there in the street to marvel at myself. What was the cat to me – that I should be its loving lord and father? And even as I stopped and asked, I saw the answer. The cat was pregnant. Two days before my love had told me there was a child of mine inside her body.

Over all these pictures as they dawned and faded, I experienced no emotion of regret. There was nothing I wished to bring back of what was gone, no untried course I wished that I had rather followed. I did not even wish or unwish the experience of seeing what I saw. The visions simply came before my eyes and glowed and died.

In between the vanishing of one and the appearance of the next were some few moments of absolute torment when I thought, not that my soul was being withdrawn from my body, but that my body was being wrenched by violence from my living soul.

Illusions of size and shape obsessed me. Now I traced all my suffering to the batterings of the waves which had compressed my frame to the substance of a tiny pellet, so that all I was bearing had been concentrated and rendered more intense by the small space in me available for suffering.

Now, now, it was the dreadful opposite. My racked and elongated body sprawled over so vast an acreage of water, that not one only, but a thousand waves attacked it from all sides. The tides both ebbed and flowed along its length. A million screaming gulls let fall their fishy droppings on my freezing back.

Again I was suffering, not from my size but from my shape. I had become a sponge. A hundred broad and narrow inlets carried the coldness of the sea into the very centre of my being.

'If only,' I shouted, 'I were smooth. If I were smooth and solid, then I should keep out the water as a house keeps out the rain. My skin would defend the secrets of my body. But now I am all spread out upon the sea. Salt water runs in all my vitals. It crystallizes in my heart and veins.' And I seemed in the darkness of the water under me to discern the flowing away from me of all my precious blood.

Throughout this time, as a man may feel in a limb which he has lost, so I swam on with strength that was long since spent. I had not died, and till I died my legs and arms, however in revolt, could not refuse their work. But what an hour ago was a smooth sweeping stroke had become the convulsive kick of a frog touched by a forceps on its nerve. I had no plan, no hope. I did not know if I was moving towards, or from, the shore, or whether perhaps there was no shore at all.

When I first entered the sea the world had withdrawn into two elements. There was the water upon which I rose and fell, and there was the mist that drove above me and from which I sucked in the dry air needed by my human lungs. But now the distinction between these elements was vanishing away. It seemed to me that the world as I swam had somehow been turned over. The water was now on the top, the needed air beneath. The breaths I was drawing from above had become too thick and watery to feed my lungs. I should do better, I saw, to draw breath from below.

79

With this discovery, that I could draw breath from the sea, there succeeded a strangely happy mood. I had done the most that could be expected of me. I had swum quite truly all I could. Exhausted but not terrified, I should swim now straight on from this life to the next. The dead would see me swimming as I entered upon the tideways of their world. I should come upon my new life, not drifting like a coward or amoeba, but swimming like a man. The thought gave comfort to me.

In life I had always loved and admired sailors above other men. Many sailors, I thought, must have passed from one life to the other in this way, upon cold bellies and with working arms and legs. I was proud and glad of the company I kept. I took a deep breath of water to sustain me, and swam on.

Of my sad, slow return to life one thing alone remains – a feeling of pain, compared to which all that I had gone through till now was only prelude.

The reason for this pain was clear. I had become caught between the elements. The sky, that had supported itself above the world for centuries, was fallen. I lay heavy upon the tossing waters of the sea. I alone among men had been trapped between the two.

Each cloud, collapsed upon the water, trailed its full weight across my chest, for I was held lying on my back. The surge and heaving of each wave forced my crushed body up, up, against the broken sky.

Clenching my teeth until they cracked, I lay waiting for the pain-storm to pass over, thinking in torment, but quite lucidly, 'This is the worst. This is the most. There can come no further pain than this.'

There could. One scorch of fire flared through me, and I sat up, shaking, crying, coughing, chattering. There were no angels by my side, but ordinary men. Their voices come to me from far away like the voices of men calling across an estuary at evening for a ferry.

'You have been drowned,' they said.

Jack London

'YAH! YAH! YAH!'

HE was a whisky-guzzling Scotsman, and he downed his whisky neat, beginning with his first tot punctually at six in the morning, and thereafter repeating it at regular intervals throughout the day till bed-time, which was usually midnight. He slept but five hours out of twenty-four, and for the remaining nineteen hours he was quietly and decently drunk. During the eight weeks I spent with him on Oolong Atoll, I never saw him draw a sober breath. In fact, his sleep was so short that he never had time to sober up. It was the most beautiful and orderly perennial drunk I had ever observed.

McAllister was his name. He was an old man, and very shaky on his pins. His hands trembled as with a palsy, especially noticeable when he poured his whisky, though I never knew him to spill a drop. He had been twenty-eight years in Melanesia, ranging from German New Guinea to the German Solomons, and so thoroughly had he become identified with that portion of the world, that he habitually spoke in that bastard lingo called 'bêche-de-mer'. Thus, in conversation with me, *sun he come up* meant sunrise; *kai-kai he stop* meant that dinner was served; and *belly belong me walk about* meant that he was sick at his stomach. He was a small man, and a withered one, burned inside and outside by ardent spirits and ardent sun. He was a cinder, a bit of a clinker of a man, a little animated clinker, and not yet quite cold, that moved stiffly and by starts and jerks like an automaton. A gust of wind would have blown him away. He weighed ninety pounds.

But the immense thing about him was the power with which he ruled. Oolong Atoll was one hundred and forty miles in circumference. One steered by compass course in its lagoon. It was populated by five thousand Polynesians, all strapping men and women, many of them standing six feet in height and weighing a couple of hundred pounds. Oolong was two hundred and fifty miles from the nearest land. Twice a year a little schooner called to collect copra. The one white man on Oolong was McAllister, petty trader and unintermittent guzzler; and he ruled Oolong and its six thousand savages with an iron hand. He said, come and they came, go, and they went. They never questioned his will nor judgement. He was cantankerous as only an aged Scotsman can be, and interfered continually in their personal affairs. When Nugu, the king's daughter, wanted to marry Haunau from the other end of the atoll, her father said yes; but McAllister said no, and the marriage never came off. When the king wanted to buy a certain islet in the lagoon from the chief priest, McAllister said no. The king was in debt to the Company to the tune of 180,000 cocoanuts, and until that was paid he was not to spend a single cocoanut on anything else.

And yet the king and his people did not love McAllister. In truth, they hated him horribly, and, to my knowledge, the whole population, with the priests at the head, tried vainly for three months to pray him to death. The devil-devils they sent after him were awe-inspiring, but since McAllister did not believe in devil-devils, they were without power over him. With drunken Scotsmen all signs fail. They gathered up scraps of food which had touched his lips, an empty whisky bottle, a cocoanut from which he had drunk, and even his spittle, and performed all kinds of deviltries over them. But McAllister lived on. His health was superb. He never caught fever; nor coughs nor colds; dysentery passed him by; and the malignant ulcers and vile skin diseases that attack blacks and whites alike in that climate never fastened upon him. He must have been so saturated with alcohol as to defy the lodgement of germs. I used to imagine them falling to the ground in showers of microscopic cinders as fast as they entered his whisky-sodden aura. No one loved him, not even germs, while he loved only whisky, and still he lived.

I was puzzled. I could not understand six thousand natives putting up with that withered shrimp of a tyrant. It was a miracle that he had not died suddenly long since. Unlike the cowardly Melanesians, the people were highstomached and warlike. In the big graveyard, at head and feet of the graves, were relics of past sanguinary history – blubber-spades, rusty old bayonets and cut-lasses, copper bolts, rudder-irons, harpoons, bomb guns, bricks that could have come from nowhere but a whaler's trying-out furnace, and old brass pieces of the sixteenth century that verified the tradi-tions of the early Spanish navigators. Ship after ship had come to grief on Oolong. Not thirty years before, the whaler *Blennerdale*, running into the lagoon for repairs, had been cut off with all hands. In similar fashion had the crew of the *Gasket*, a sandalwood trader, perished. There was a big French bark, the *Toulon*, becalmed off the atoll, which the islanders boarded after a sharp tussle and wrecked in the Lipau Passage, the captain and a handful of sailors escaping in the long-boat. Then there were the Spanish pieces, which told of the loss of one of the early explorers. All this, of the vessels named, is a matter of history, and is to be found in the *South Pacific Sailing Directory*. But that there was other history, unwritten, I was yet to learn. In the meantime I puzzled why six thousand primitive savages let one degenerate Scotch despot live.

One hot afternoon McAllister and I sat on the verandah looking out over the lagoon, with all its wonders of jewelled colours. At our backs, across the hundred yards of palm-studded sand, the outer surf roared on the reef. It was dreadfully warm. We were in 4° south latitude and the sun was directly overhead, having crossed the Line a few days before on its journey south. There was no wind – not even a catspaw. The season of the south-east trade was draw-ing to an early close, and the north-west monsoon had not yet begun to blow.

'They can't dance worth a damn,' said McAllister.

I had happened to mention that the Polynesian dances were superior to the Papuan, and this McAllister had denied, for no other reason than his cantankerousness. But it was too hot to argue, and I said nothing. Besides I had never seen the Oolong people dance.

'I'll prove it to you,' he announced, beckoning to the black Han-over boy, a labour recruit, who served as cook and general house servant. 'Hey, you, boy, you tell 'm one fella king come along me.'

The boy departed and back came the prime minister, perturbed, ill at ease, and garrulous with apologetic explanation. In short, the king slept, and was not to be disturbed.

'King he plenty strong fella sleep,' was his final sentence.

McAllister was in such a rage that the prime minister incontinently fled, to return with the king himself. They were a magnificent pair, the king especially, who must have been all of six feet three inches in height. His features had the eagle-like quality that is so frequently found in those of the North American Indian. He had been both moulded and born to rule. His eyes flashed as he listened, but right meekly he obeyed McAllister's command to fetch a couple of hundred of the best dancers, male and female, in the village. And dance they did, for two mortal hours, under that broiling sun. They did not love him for it, and little he cared, in the end dismissing them with abuse and sneers.

The abject servility of those magnificent savages was terrifying. How could it be? What was the secret of his rule? More and more I puzzled as the days went by, and though I observed perpetual examples of his undisputed sovereignty, never a clue was there as to how it was.

One day I happened to speak of my disappointment in failing to trade for a beautiful pair of orange cowries. The pair was worth five pounds in Sydney if it was worth a cent. I had offered two hundred sticks of tobacco to the owner, who had held out for three hundred. When I casually mentioned the situation, McAllister immediately sent for the man, took the shells from him and turned them over to me. Fifty sticks were all he permitted me to pay for them. The man accepted the tobacco and seemed overjoyed at getting off so easily. As for me, I resolved to keep a bridle on my tongue in the future. And still I mulled over the secret of McAllister's power. I even went to the extent of asking him directly, but all he did was to cock one eye, look wise, and take another drink.

One night I was out fishing in the lagoon with Oti, the man who had been mulcted of the cowries. Privily, I had made up to him an additional hundred and fifty sticks, and he had come to regard me with respect that was almost veneration, which was curious, seeing that he was an old man, twice my age at least.

'What name you fella kanaka all the same pickanniny?' I began on him. 'This fella trader he one fella. You fella kanaka plenty fella too much. You fella kanaka just like 'm dog – plenty fright along that fella trader. He no eat you fella. He no get 'm teeth along him. What name you too much fright?'

'S'pose plenty fella kanaka kill 'm?' he asked.

'He die,' I retorted. 'You fella kanaka kill 'm plenty fella white man long time before. What name you fright this fella white man?'

'Yes, we kill 'm plenty,' was his answer. 'My word! Any amount! Long time before. One time, me young fella too much, one big fella ship he stop outside. Wind he no blow. Plenty fella kanaka we get 'm canoe, plenty fella canoe, we go catch 'm that fella ship. My word – we catch 'm big fella fight. Two, three white men shoot like hell. We no fright. We come alongside, we go up side, plenty fella, maybe I think fifty-ten (five hundred). One fella white Mary (woman) belong that fella ship. Never before I see 'm white Mary. Bime by plenty, white man finish. One fella skipper he no die. Five fella, six fella white man no die. Skipper he sing out. Some fella white man he fight. Some fella white man he lower away boat. After that, all together over the side they go. Skipper he sling white Mary down. After that they washee (row) strong fella plenty too much. Father belong me, that time he strong fella. He throw 'm one fella spear. That fella spear he go in one side that white Mary. He no stop. My word, he go out other side that fella Mary. She finish. Me no fright. Plenty kanaka too much no fright.'

Old Oti's pride had been touched, for he suddenly stripped down his lava-lava and showed me the unmistakable scar of a bullet. Before I could speak, his line ran out suddenly. He checked it and attempted to haul in, but found that the fish had run around a coral branch. Casting a look of reproach at me for having beguiled him from his watchfulness, he went over the side, feet first, turning over after he got under and following his line down to the bottom. The water was ten fathoms. I leaned over and watched the play of his feet, growing dim and dimmer, as they stirred the wan phosphoresence into ghostly fires. Ten fathoms – sixty feet – it was nothing to him, an old man, compared with the value of a hook and line. After what seemed five minutes, though it could not have been more than a minute, I saw him flaming whitely upward. He broke the surface and dropped a tenpound rock cod into the canoe, the line and hook intact, the latter still fast in the fish's mouth.

'It may be,' I said remorselessly. 'You no fright long ago. You plenty fright now along that fella trader.'

'Yes, plenty fright,' he confessed, with an air of dismissing the subject. For half an hour we pulled up our lines and flung them out in silence. Then small fish-sharks began to bite and after losing a hook apiece, we hauled in and waited for the sharks to go their way.

'I speak you true,' Oti broke into speech, 'then you savve we fright now.'

I lighted my pipe and waited, and the story that Oti told me in atrocious bêche-de-mer I here turn into proper English. Otherwise, in spirit and order of narrative, the tale is as it fell from Oti's lips.

'It was after that that we were very proud. We had fought many times with the strange white men who live upon the sea, and always we had beaten them. A few of us were killed, but what was that compared with the stores of wealth of a thousand thousand kinds that we found on the ships? And then one day, maybe twenty years ago, or twenty-five, there came a schooner right through the passage and into the lagoon. It was a large schooner with three masts. She had five white men and maybe forty boat's crew, black fellows from New Guinea and New Britain; and she had come to fish bêche-de-mer. She lay at anchor across the lagoon from here, at Pauloo, and her boats scattered out everywhere, making camps on the beaches where they cured the bêche-de-mer. This made them weak by dividing them, for those who fished here and those on the schooner at Pauloo were fifty miles apart, and there were others farther away still.

'Our king and headman held council, and I was one in the canoe that paddled all afternoon and all night across the lagoon, bringing word to the people of Pauloo that in the morning we would attack the fishing camps at the one time and that it was for them to take the schooner. We who brought the word were tired with the paddling, but we took part in the attack. On the schooner were two white men, the skipper and the second mate, with half a dozen black boys. The skipper with three boys we caught on shore and killed, but first eight of us the skipper killed with his two revolvers. We fought close together, you see, at handgrapples.

'The noise of our fighting told the mate what was happening, and he put food and water and a sail in the small dinghy, which was so small that it was no more than twelve feet long. We came down upon the schooner, a thousand men, covering the lagoon with our canoes. Also, we were blowing conch-shells, singing war-songs, and striking the sides of the canoes with our paddles. What chance had one white man and three black boys against us? No chance at all, and the mate knew it.

'White men are hell. I have watched them much, and I am an old man now, and I understand at last why the white men have taken to themselves all the islands in the sea. It is because they are hell. Here are you in the canoe with me. You are hardly more than a boy. You are not wise, for each day I tell you many things you do not know. When I was a little pickaninny, I knew more about fish and the ways of fish than you know now. I am an old man, but I swim down to the bottom of the lagoon, and you cannot follow me. What are you good for, anyway? I do not know, except to fight. I have never seen you fight, yet I know that you are like your brothers and that you will fight like hell. Also, you are a fool, like your brothers. You do not know when you are beaten. You will fight until you die, and then it will be too late to know that you are beaten.

'Now behold what this mate did. As we came down upon him, covering the sea and blowing our conches, he put off from the schooner in the small boat, along with the three black boys, and rowed for the passage. There again he was a fool, for no wise man would put out to sea in so small a boat. The sides of it were not four inches above the water. Twenty canoes went after him, filled with two hundred young men. We paddled five fathoms while his black boys were rowing one fathom. He had no chance, but he was a fool. He stood up in the boat with a rifle and he shot many times. He was not a good shot, but as we drew close many of us were wounded and killed. But still he had no chance.

'I remember that all the time he was smoking a cigar. When we were forty feet away and coming fast, he dropped the rifle, lighted

a stick of dynamite with the cigar and threw it at us. He lighte
another and another, and threw them at us very rapidly, many o
them. I know now that he must have split the ends of the fuses an
stuck in match-heads, because they lighted so quickly. Also, th
fuses were very short. Sometimes the dynamite sticks went off in th
air, but most of them went off in the canoes. And each time the
went off in a canoe, that canoe was finished. Of the twenty canoes
the half were smashed to pieces. The canoe I was in was so smashed
and likewise the two men who sat next to me. The dynamite fel
between them. The other canoes turned and ran away. Then tha
mate yelled, "Yah! Yah! Yah!" at us. Also he went at us again witl
his rifle, so that many were killed through the back as they fle
away. And all the time the black boys in the boat went on rowing
You see I told you true, that mate was hell.

'Nor was that all. Before he left the schooner, he set her on fire
and fixed up all the powder and dynamite so that it would go off a
one time. There were hundreds of us on board, trying to put ou
the fire, heaving up water from overside, when the schooner blew
up. So that all we had fought for was lost to us, besides many mor
of us being killed. Sometimes, even now, in my old age, I have ba
dreams in which I hear that mate yell, "Yah! Yah! Yah!" In
voice of thunder he yells "Yah! Yah! Yah!" But all those in th
fishing camps were killed.

'The mate went out of the passage in his little boat, and that wa
the end of him we made sure, for how could so small a boat, wit
four men in it, live on the ocean? A month went by, and then, on
morning, between two rain squalls, a schooner sailed in through ou
passage and dropped anchor before the village. The king and th
headmen made big talk, and it was agreed that we would take th
schooner in two or three days. In the meantime, as it was ou
custom always to appear friendly, we went off to her in canoe
bringing strings of cocoanuts, fowls, and pigs, to trade. But whe
we were alongside, many canoes of us, the men on board began t
shoot us with rifles, and as we paddled away I saw the mate wh
had gone to sea in the little boat spring upon the rail and danc
and yell, "Yah! Yah! Yah!"

'That afternoon they landed from the schooner in three sma

boats filled with white men. They went right through the village, shooting every man they saw. Also they shot the fowls and pigs. We who were not killed got away in canoes and paddled out into the lagoon. Looking back, we could see all the houses on fire. Late in the afternoon we saw many canoes coming from Nihi, which is the village near the Nihi Passage in the north-east. They were all that were left, and like us their village had been burned by a second schooner that had come through Nihi Passage.

'We stood on in the darkness to the westward for Pauloo, but in the middle of the night we heard women wailing and then we ran into a big fleet of canoes. They were all that were left of Pauloo, which likewise was in ashes, for a third schooner had come in through the Pauloo Passage. You see, that mate, with his black boys, had not been drowned. He had made the Solomon Islands, and there told his brothers of what we had done in Oolong. And all his brothers had said they would come and punish us, and there they were in the three schooners, and our three villages were wiped out.

'And what was there for us to do? In the morning the two schooners from windward sailed down upon us in the middle of the lagoon. The trade-wind was blowing fresh and by scores of canoes they ran us down. And the rifles never ceased talking. We scattered like flying-fish before the bonita, and there were so many of us that we escaped by thousands, this way and that, to the islands on the rim of the atoll.

'And thereafter the schooners hunted us up and down the lagoon. In the night-time we slipped past them. But the next day, or in two days or three days, the schooners would be coming back, hunting us towards the other end of the lagoon. And so it went. We no longer counted nor remembered our dead. True, we were many and they were few. But what could we do? I was in one of the twenty canoes filled with men who were not afraid to die. We attacked the smallest schooner. They shot us down in heaps. They threw dynamite into the canoes, and when the dynamite gave out, they threw hot water down upon us. And the rifles never ceased talking. And those whose canoes were smashed were shot as they swam away. And the mate danced up and down upon the cabin-top and yelled, "Yah! Yah! Yah!"

'Every house on every smallest island was burned. Not a pig n
a fowl was left alive. Our wells were defiled with the bodies of tl
slain, or else heaped high with coral rock. We were twenty-fi
thousand on Oolong before the three schooners came. Today v
are five thousand. After the schooners left, we were but three tho
sand, as you shall see.

'At last the three schooners grew tired of chasing us back an
forth. So they went, the three of them, to Nihi, in the north-eas
And they drove us steadily to the west. Their nine boats were in tl
water as well. They beat up every island as they moved along. The
drove us, drove us, drove us day by day. And every night the thr
schooners and the nine boats made a chain of watchfulness th
stretched across the lagoon from rim to rim, so that we could n
escape back.

'They could not drive us for ever that way, for the lagoon w
only so large, and at last all of us that lived yet were driven up
the last sand-bank to the west. Beyond lay the open sea. There we
ten thousand of us, and we covered the sand-bank from the lagoo
edge to the pounding surf on the other side. No one could lie dow
There was no room. We stood hip to hip and shoulder to shoulde
Two days they kept us there, and the mate would climb up in tl
rigging to mock us and yell, "Yah! Yah! Yah!" till we were we
sorry that we had ever harmed him or his schooner a month befor
We had no food, and we stood on our feet two days and nights. Tl
little babies died, and the old and weak died, and the wounde
died. And worst of all, we had no water to quench our thirst, ar
for two days the sun beat down on us, and there was no shad
Many men and women waded out into the ocean, and we
drowned, the surf casting their bodies back on the beach. And the
came a pest of flies. Some men swam to the sides of the schoone
but they were shot to the last one. And we that lived were very sor
that in our pride we tried to take the schooner with the three mas
that came to fish for bêche-de-mer.

'On the morning of the third day came the skippers of the thr
schooners and that mate in a small boat. They carried rifles, all
them, and revolvers, and they made talk. It was only that the
were weary of killing us that they had stopped, they told us. Ar

e told them that we were sorry, that never again would we harm
white man, and in token of our submission we poured sand upon
ur heads. And all the women and children set up a great wailing
r water, so that for some time no man could make himself heard.
hen we were told our punishment. We must fill the three schoo-
rs with copra and bêche-de-mer. And we agreed, for we wanted
ater, and our hearts were broken, and we knew that we were chil-
en at fighting when we fought with white men who fight like hell.
nd when all the talk was finished, the mate stood up and mocked
, and yelled, "Yah! Yah! Yah!" After that we paddled away in
ur canoes and sought water.

'And for weeks we toiled at catching bêche-de-mer and curing
in gathering the cocoanuts and turning them into copra. By day
d night the smoke rose in clouds from all the beaches of all the
ands of Oolong as we paid the penalty of our wrong-doing. For
those days of death it was burned clearly on all our brains that it
as very wrong to harm a white man.

'By and by, the schooners full of copra and bêche-de-mer and
ur trees empty of cocoanuts, the three skippers and that mate
lled us all together for a big talk. And they said they were very
ad that we had learned our lesson, and we said for the ten thou-
ndth time that we were sorry and that we would not do it again.
lso, we poured sand upon our heads. Then the skippers said that it
as all very well, but just to show us that they did not forget us,
ey would send a devil-devil that we would never forget and that
e would always remember any time we might feel like harming a
hite man. After that the mate mocked us one more time and
lled, "Yah! Yah! Yah!" Then six of our men, whom we thought
ng dead, were put ashore from one of the schooners, and the
hooners hoisted their sails and ran out through the passage for
e Solomons.

'The six men who were put ashore were the first to catch the
evil-devil the skippers sent back after us.'

'A great sickness came,' I interrupted, for I recognized the trick.
he schooner had had measles on board, and the six prisoners had
een deliberately exposed to it.

'Yes, a great sickness,' Oti went on. 'It was a powerful devil-

devil. The oldest man had never heard of the like. Those of ou
priests that yet lived we killed because they could not overcome th
devil-devil. The sickness spread. I have said that there were te
thousand of us that stood hip to hip and shoulder to shoulder o
the sand-bank. When the sickness left us, there were three thousan
yet alive. Also, having made all our cocoanuts into copra, there wa
a famine.

'That fella trader,' Oti concluded, 'he like 'm that much dirt. H
like 'm clam he die *kai-kai* (meat) he stop, stink 'm any amoun
He like 'm one fella dog, one sick fella dog plenty fleas stop alon
him. We no fright along that fella trader. We fright because h
white man. We savve plenty too much no good kill white man. Tha
one fella sick dog trader he plenty brother stop along him, whit
men like 'm you fight like hell. We no fright that damn trader. Som
time he made kanaka plenty cross along him and kanaka want '
kill 'm, kanaka he think devil-devil and kanaka he hear that fell
mate sing out, "Yah! Yah! Yah!" and kanaka no kill 'm.'

Oti baited his hook with a piece of squid, which he tore with h
teeth from the live and squirming monster, and hook and bait san
in white flames to the bottom.

'Shark walk about he finish,' he said.

'I think we catch 'm plenty fella fish.'

His line jerked savagely. He pulled it in rapidly, hand unde
hand, and landed a big gasping rock cod in the bottom of th
canoe.

'Sun he come up, I make 'm that dam fella trader one presen
big fella fish,' said Oti.

Weston Martyr

SMITH VERSUS LICHTENSTEIGER

SMITH stood five feet five inches in his boots, weighed nearly ten stone in his winter clothes and an overcoat, and he had a flat chest and a round stomach. Smith was a clerk in a small branch bank in East Anglia; he was not an athlete or a fighting man, although he followed the fortunes of a professional football team in the newspapers with great interest, and he had fought for a year in France without ever seeing his enemy or achieving a closer proximity to him than one hundred and twenty yards. When a piece of shrapnel reduced his fighting efficiency by abolishing the biceps of one arm, Smith departed from the field of battle and (as he himself would certainly have put it) 'in due course' returned to his branch bank.

For forty-nine weeks each year Smith laboured faithfully at his desk. In his free hours during the winter he read Joseph Conrad, Stevenson and E.F. Knight, and he did hardly anything else. But every year in early April, Smith suddenly came to life. For he was a yachtsman, and he owned a tiny yacht which he called the *Kate* and loved with a great love. The spring evenings he spent fitting out, painting and fussing over his boat. Thereafter, as early as possible every Saturday afternoon, he set sail and cruised alone amongst the tides and sandbanks of the Thames Estuary, returning again as late as possible on Sunday night. And every summer, when his three weeks' holiday came round, Smith and his *Kate* would sail away from East Anglia together and voyage afar. One year Smith cruised to Falmouth in the West Country, and he likes to boast about that cruise still. Once he set out for Cherbourg, which is a port in foreign parts; but that time, thanks to a westerly gale, he got no farther than Dover. The year Smith encountered Lichtensteiger he had sailed as far east as Flushing, and he was on his

93

way back when a spell of bad weather and head winds drove him into Ostend and detained him there three days.

Lichtensteiger was also detained at Ostend; but not by the weather. Lichtensteiger had come from Alexandria, with a rubber tube stuffed full of morphine wound round his waist next to his skin, and he was anxious to get to London as quickly as he could. He had already been as far as Dover, but there a Customs official (who had suspicions but no proof) whispered to a friend in the Immigration Department, and Lichtensteiger found himself debarred as an 'undesirable alien' from entering the United Kingdom. He had therefore returned to Ostend in the steamer in which he had left that place.

Lichtensteiger stood six feet one inch in his socks, weighed fourteen stone stripped, and he had a round chest and a flat stomach. He was as strong as a gorilla, as quick in action as a mongoose, and he had never done an honest day's work in his life. There is reason to believe that Lichtensteiger was a Swiss, as he spoke Switzer Deutsch, which is something only a German-Swiss can do. His nationality, however, is by no means certain, because he looked like a Lombard, carried Rumanian and Austrian passports, and in addition to the various dialects used in those two countries, he spoke French like a Marseillais, German like a Würtemberger, and English like a native of the lower Westside of New York.

When Smith and Lichtensteiger first set eyes on each other Smith was sitting in the *Kate*'s tiny cockpit, smoking his pipe and worrying about the weather. For Smith's holiday was nearly over; he was due at his bank again in three days, and he knew he could not hope to sail back while the strong north-westerly wind continued to blow straight from East Anglia towards Belgium. Said Smith to himself, 'Hang it! I've got to sail tomorrow or get into a nasty fix. And if only I had two sound arms I *would* sail tomorrow and chance it; but a hundred-mile beat to wind'ard all by myself is going to be no joke. What I need is another man to help me; but there isn't an earthly hope of getting hold of any one in this filthy hole.'

Lichtensteiger was walking along the quay. He glanced at the *Kate* and her owner with a disdainful eye and passed on, because neither the boat nor the man held any interest for him. But in

Lichtensteiger's card-index-like mind, in which he filed without conscious effort most of the things he heard and saw, there were registered three impressions and one deduction:

'A yacht. The British flag. An Englishman. A fool.' Having filed these particulars, Lichtensteiger's mind was about to pass on to the problem of how to get Lichtensteiger to London, when an idea flashed like a blaze of light into his consciousness. To translate Lichtensteiger's multi-lingual thoughts is difficult; a free rendering of them must suffice. Said Lichtensteiger to himself, 'Thunder and lightning. Species of a goose. You poor fish. Of course. It is *that*! If *you* had a yacht – if *you* were a sailor – *there* is the obvious solution. Then there no more need would be to risk placing oneself in the talons of the sacred bureaucrats of Customs or within the despicable jurisdiction of blood-sucking immigration officials. Why, say! If I had a little boat I guess I wouldn't worry myself about smuggling my dope through no Dovers and suchlike places. With a boat of my own then veritably would I be a smuggler classical and complete. But what's the use! I ain't got no boat and I ain't no sailor. But hold! Attention! The English yacht. That fool Englishman. There are possibilities in that direction there. Yes. I guess I go back and take another look at that guy.'

Lichtensteiger's second survey of Smith was detailed and thorough, and it confirmed his previous judgement. 'Easy meat,' said Lichtensteiger to himself, and then aloud, 'Evening, stranger. Pardon me, but I see you're British, and I guess it'll sound good to me to hear someone talk like a Christian for a change. I'm from Noo York, and Otis T. Merritt's my name. I'm over this side on vacation; but I'll tell you the truth, I don't cotton to these darned Dagoes and Squareheads here, not at all. So I reckon to catch the next boat across to your good country, mister, and spend the balance of my trip there with white men. That's a peach of a little yacht you got. I'll say she certainly is. She's a pippin, and I guess you have a number one first-class time sailing around in her. It's just the kind of game I've always had in mind to try for myself. It 'ud suit me down to the ground, I reckon. If you've no objections, I'll step aboard. I'd sure like to look her over. Where are you sailing to next after here?'

'Harwich,' answered Smith. 'Come aboard and look round if you like, by all means; but I'm afraid you won't find very much to see here.'

'Why, she's the finest little ship I ever set eyes on,' cried Lichtensteiger a few minutes later, settling himself on the cabin settee 'And to think you run her all alone. My gracious! Have a cigar?'

'Thanks,' said Smith. 'I do sail her by myself usually, but this time I'm afraid I've bitten off more than I can chew. You see, I've got to get back to Harwich within three days. If I had another man to help me I'd do it easily, but with this wind blowing it's a bit more than I care to tackle alone.'

After that, of course, it was easy for Lichtensteiger. He did not ask Smith if he could sail with him, he led Smith on to make that suggestion himself. Then he hesitated awhile at the unexpectedness of the proposal, and when he finally yielded to persuasion, he left Smith with the impression that he was doing him a favour. It was very beautifully done.

That night Lichtensteiger transferred himself and two suitcases from his hotel and slept aboard the *Kate*. At daybreak next morning they sailed. Once outside the harbour entrance Smith found the wind had fallen to a moderate breeze, but it still blew out of the north-west, making the shaping of a direct course to Harwich impossible. Smith, therefore, did the best he could. He put the *Kate* on the starboard tack and sailed her to the westward along the Belgian coast.

It did not take Smith long to discover that Lichtensteiger was no sailor. He could not steer or even make fast a rope securely. In half an hour it became clear to Smith that Lichtensteiger literally did not know one end of the boat from the other, and within an hour he realized that his passenger, instead of helping him, was going to be a hindrance and an infernal nuisance as well. Lichtensteiger did all those things which must on no account be done if life is to be made livable in the confined space aboard a small boat. In addition to other crimes, Lichtensteiger grumbled at the motion, the hardness of the bunks and the lack of head-room in the cabin. He left his clothes scattered all over the yacht, he used the deck as a spittoon and he sprawled at ease in the cockpit, so that every time Smith had to move in a hurry he tripped over Lichtensteiger's legs. B midday Smith had had as much of Lichtensteiger's company as he felt he could stand. Now that the weather was fine and looked like remaining so, he knew he could easily sail the *Kate* home by himself. He said, 'Look here, Merritt; I'm afraid you don't find yachting in such a small boat is as much fun as you thought it was going to be. See those buildings sticking up on the shore there? Well, that's Dunkerque, and I'll sail in and land you, and then you can catch the night boat over to Tilbury nice and comfortably. I'll run you in there in half an hour.'

Smith's suggestion astounded Lichtensteiger, and produced in him so profound an alarm that he forgot for a moment that he was Merritt. His eyes blazed, the colour vanished from his face, and tiny beads of sweat hopped out upon it. Then Lichtensteiger emitted some most extraordinary sounds which, had Smith but known it, were Switzer-Deutsch curses of a horrid and disgusting kind, coupled with an emphatic and blasphemous assertion that nothing, not even ten thousand flaming blue devils, could force him to set foot upon the suppurating soil of France. In fairness to Lichtensteiger it must be stated that he very rarely forgot himself, or any part he might happen to be playing, and it was also always difficult to frighten him. But the toughest ruffian may be, perhaps, excused if he shrinks from venturing into a country which he has betrayed in time of war. And this is what Lichtensteiger had done to France, or, more precisely, he had twice double-crossed the French Army Intelligence Department, Section Counter-Espionage, Sub-section N.C.D. And the penalty for doing this, as Lichtensteiger well knew, is death. Since 1916, when Lichtensteiger succeeded in escaping from that country by the skin of his teeth, France was a place which he had taken the most sedulous pains to avoid, and at the sudden prospect of being landed there he lost his grip of himself for fifteen seconds. Then he pulled himself together and grinned at Smith and said, 'Dunkerque nix! Nothing doing. I guess not. And don't you make any mistake, brother; I think this yachting stuff's just great. I'm getting a whale of a kick out of it. So we'll keep on a-going for Harwich. Sure, we will. You bet. And no Dunkerque. No, sir. No Dunkerque for mine. Forget it.'

Smith said, 'Oh, all right,' and that was all he said. But he was thinking hard. He thought, 'By God! That was queer. That – was – *damned* queer. The fellow was scared to death. Yes – to *death*! For I'll swear nothing else could make a man look like that so suddenly. He turned absolutely green. And he sweated. And his eyes – He was terrified. And he yammered, panicked, babbled – in German, too, by the sound of it. By gosh! I wonder who he is? *And what it is he's been up to*? Something damnable, by the look of it. And whatever it was, he did it in Dunkerque – or in France, anyway. That's plain. To look like that at the mere thought of landing in France! My God, he might be a murderer, or anything. Cleared out into Belgium and hanging about, waiting his chance to get away probably. And here I am, helping him to escape. Oh Lord, what a fool I was to let him come. I actually *asked* him to come. Or did I? Yes, I did; but it seems to me now, with *this* to open my eyes, that he meant to come all the time. He did! He led me on to ask him. I can see it all now. He's a clever crafty devil – and he's twice my size! Oh, hang it all. This is *nasty*.'

Smith was so absorbed by his thoughts that he did not notice the change of wind coming. The *Kate* heeled suddenly to the puff, her sheets strained and creaked, and she began to string a wake of bubbles and foam behind her. 'Hallo,' said Smith, 'wind's shifted and come more out of the north. We'll be able to lay our course a little better now; she's heading up as high as nor'-west. I'll just see where that course takes us to if you'll bring up the chart.'

Lichtensteiger brought the chart from the cabin table, and Smith spread it out upon the deck. 'Not so good,' said he, after gazing at it for a while. 'We can't fetch within forty miles of Harwich on this tack. A nor'-west course only just clears the Goodwins and the North Foreland. Look.'

'Then why don't you point the boat straight for Harwich,' said Lichtensteiger, 'instead of going 'way off to the left like that?'

'Because this isn't a steamer, and we can't sail against the wind. But we'll get to Harwich all right, although if this wind holds we won't be there before tomorrow night.'

'Tomorrow night,' said Lichtensteiger. 'Well, that suits me. What sort of a kind of place is this Harwich anyway? Walk ashore there, I suppose, as soon as we get in, without any messing about?'

'Oh, yes. But we'll have to wait till the morning probably, for the Customs to come off and pass us.'

'Customs!' said Lichtensteiger. 'Customs! I thought – you'd think, in a one-hole dorp like Harwich, there wouldn't be no Customs and all that stuff. And anyway, you don't mean to tell me the Customs'll worry about a little bit of a boat like this?'

'Oh, yes, they will,' Smith answered. 'Harwich isn't the hole you seem to think it is. It's a big port. We're arriving from foreign, and if we went ashore before the Customs and harbour-master and so on passed us there'd be the very devil of a row.'

'Well, crying out loud!' said Lichtensteiger. 'What a hell of a country. Not that the blamed Customs worry me any; but – well, what about all this Free Trade racket you Britishers blow about? Seems to me, with your damned Customs and immigration sharps and passports an' God knows what all, you've got Great Britain tied up a blame sight tighter than the United States.' Saying which, Lichtensteiger spat viciously upon the deck and went below to think things over.

Before Lichtensteiger finished his thinking the sun had set, and when he came on deck again, with his plan of action decided upon, it was night. Said he, 'Gee! It's black. Say, how d'you know where you're going to when you can't see? And where the hell are we now, anyway?'

'A mile or so nor'west of the Sandettie Bank.'

'That don't mean nothing to me. Where is this Sandettie place?'

'It's about twenty miles from Ramsgate one way and eighteen from Calais the other.'

'Twenty miles from Ramsgate?' said Lichtensteiger. 'Well listen here, brother. I guess I've kind of weakened on this Harwich idea. It's too far, and it's going to take too long getting there. And I find this yachting game ain't all it's cracked up to be by a long sight. To tell you the truth, without any more flim-flam, I'm fed right up to the gills with this, and the sooner you get me ashore and out of it the better. See? Twenty miles ain't far, and I reckon Ramsgate, or anywhere around that way, will do me fine. Get me? Now you point her for Ramsgate right away and let's get a move on.'

'But, I say – look here!' protested Smith. 'I don't want to go to

Ramsgate. I mean, I've got to get back to Harwich by tomorrow night, and if we put into Ramsgate I'll lose hours and hours. We can't get there till after midnight, and you won't be able to land before daylight at the very earliest, because the Customs won't pass us till then. And – '

'Oh, hell!' broke in Lichtensteiger. 'Customs at Ramsgate, too, are there? Well, say, that's all right. I'll tell you what we'll do. We won't trouble no flaming Customs – and save time that way. You land me on the beach, somewheres outside the town, where it's quiet and there's no one likely to be around. I'll be all right then. I'll hump my suitcases into this Ramsgate place and catch the first train to London in the morning. That'll suit me down to the ground.'

'But, look here! I can't do that,' said Smith.

'What d'you mean, you can't? You can. What's stopping you?'

'Well, if you will have it, Merritt,' answered Smith, 'I'll tell you straight, I don't like being a party to landing a man – any man – in the way you want me to. It's illegal. I might get into trouble over it, and I can't afford to get into trouble. If they heard in the bank I'd lose my job. I'd be ruined. I'm sorry, but I can't risk it. Why, if we got caught they might put us in prison!'

'Caught! You poor fish,' said Lichtensteiger. 'How can you get caught! All you've got to do is to put me ashore in the dark in that little boat we're pulling behind us, and then you vamoose and go to Harwich – or hell if you like. I'll be damned if I care. And you can take it from me, now, brother, you've got to put me ashore whether you like it or not. And if you don't like it, I'm going to turn right here and make you. See? All this darned shinanyking makes me tired. I'm through with it and it's time you tumbled to who's boss here – you one-armed, mutt-faced, sawn-off little son of a b— you! You steer this boat for Ramsgate, *now* pronto, and land me like I said, or by Gor, I'll scrape that fool face off the front of your silly head and smear the rest of you all over the boat. So – jump to it! Let's see some action, quick!'

If Smith had not been born and bred in the midst of a habitually peaceful and law-abiding community, he might perhaps have understood that Lichtensteiger meant to do what he said. But Smith had never encountered a really *bad* and utterly unscrupulous human being in all his life before. In spite of the feeble imitations of the breed which he had seen inside the cinemas, Smith did not believe in such things as human wolves. It is even doubtful if Smith had ever envisaged himself as being involved in a fight by the Marquis of Queensberry's rules. It is a fact that Smith would never have dreamed of kicking a man when he was down or hitting anyone below the belt, and he made the mistake of believing that Lichtensteiger must, after all, be more or less like himself. Smith believed that Lichtensteiger's threats, though alarming, were not to be taken seriously. He therefore said, 'Here! I say! You can't say things like that, you know. This is my boat and I won't –'

But Smith did not get any further. Lichtensteiger interrupted him. He drove his heel with all his might into Smith's stomach, and Smith doubled up with a grunt and dropped on the cockpit floor. Lichtensteiger then kicked him in the back and the mouth, spat in his face and stamped on him. When Smith came to he heard Lichtensteiger saying, 'You'll be wise, my buck, to get on to the fact that I took pains, that time, not to hurt you. Next time, though, I reckon to beat you up good. So – cut out the grunting and all that sob-stuff and let's hear if you're going to do what I say. Let's hear from you. Or do you want another little dose? Pipe up, you –'

Smith vomited. When he could speak, he said, 'I can't – Ah, God! Don't kick me again. I'll do it. I'll do what you want. But – I can't – get up. Wait – and I'll do it – if I can. I think my back's – broken.'

Smith lay still and gasped, until his breath and his wits returned to him. He explored his hurts with his fingers gingerly, and then he sat up and nursed his battered face in his hands. He was thinking. He was shocked and amazed at Lichtensteiger's strength and brutal ferocity, and he knew that, for the moment, he dare do nothing which might tempt Lichtensteiger to attack him again. Smith was sorely hurt and frightened, but he was not daunted. And deep down in the soul of that under-sized bank clerk there smouldered a resolute and desperate determination to have his revenge. Presently he said, 'Better now. But it hurts me to move. Bring up the chart from the cabin. I'll find out a quiet place to land you and see what course to steer.'

Lichtensteiger laughed. 'That's right, my son,' said he. 'Pity you didn't see a light a bit sooner, and you'd have saved yourself a whole heap of grief.' He brought the chart and Smith studied it carefully for some minutes. Then he put his finger on the coastline between Deal and Ramsgate and said, 'There, that looks the best place. It's a stretch of open beach, with no houses shown anywhere near. It looks quiet and deserted enough on the chart. Look for yourself. Will that spot suit you?'

Lichtensteiger looked and grunted. He was no sailor, and that small-chart of the southern half of the North Sea did not convey very much to him. He said, 'Huh! Guess that'll do. Nothing much doing around that way by the look of it. What's this black line running along here?'

'That's a road. I'll put you on the beach here, and you walk inland till you get to the road and then turn left. It's only two miles to Deal that way.'

'Let her go then,' said Lichtensteiger. 'The sooner you get me ashore the sooner you'll get quit of me, which ought to please you some, I guess. And watch your step! I reckon you know enough now not to try and put anything over on me; but if you feel like playing any tricks – *look out*. If I have to start in on you again, my bucko, I'll tear you up in little bits.'

'I'll play no tricks,' replied Smith. 'How can I? For my own sake, I can't risk you being caught. You're making me do this against my will, but nobody will believe that if they catch me doing it. I promise to do my best to land you where no one will see you. It shouldn't be hard. In four or five hours we'll be close to the land, and you'll see the lights of Ramsgate on one side and Deal on the other. In between there oughtn't to be many lights showing, and we'll run close inshore where it's darkest and anchor. Then I'll row you ashore in the dinghy, and after that it'll be up to you.'

'Get on with it, then,' said Lichtensteiger, and Smith trimmed the *Kate's* sails to the northerly wind and settled down to steer the compass course he had decided on. The yacht slipped through the darkness with scarcely a sound. Smith steered and said nothing, while Lichtensteiger looked at the scattered lights of the shipping which dotted the blackness around him and was silent too.

At the end of an hour Lichtensteiger yawned and stretched himself. 'Beats me,' he said, 'how in hell you can tell where you're going to.' And Smith said, 'It's easy enough, when you know how.'

At the end of the second hour Lichtensteiger said, 'Gee, this is slow. Deader'n mud. How long now before we get there?' And Smith replied, 'About three hours. Why don't you sleep? I'll wake you in time.'

Lichtensteiger said, 'Nothing doing. Don't you kid yourself. I'm keeping both eyes wide open, constant and regular. I've got 'em on you. Don't forget it either!'

Another hour went by before Lichtensteiger spoke again. He said, 'What's that light in front there? The bright one that keeps on going in and out.'

'Lighthouse,' said Smith. 'That's the South Foreland light. I'm steering for it. The lights of Deal will show up to the right of it presently, and then we'll pick out a dark patch of coast somewhere to the right of that again and I'll steer in for it.'

By 2 a.m. the land was close ahead, a low black line looming against the lesser blackness of the sky. 'Looks quiet enough here,' said Lichtensteiger. 'Just about right for our little job, I reckon. How about it?'

'Right,' said Smith, sounding overside with the lead-line. 'Four fathoms. We'll anchor here.' He ran the *Kate* into the wind, lowered the jib and let go his anchor with a rattle and a splash.

'Cut out that flaming racket,' hissed Lichtensteiger. 'Trying to give the show away are you, or what? You watch your step, damn you.'

'You watch yours,' said Smith, drawing the dinghy alongside. 'Get in carefully or you'll upset.'

'You get in first,' replied Lichtensteiger. 'Take hold of my two bags and then I'll get in after. And you want to take pains we don't upset. If we do, there'll be a nasty accident – to your neck! I guess I can wring it for you as quick under water as I can here. You watch out now and go slow. You haven't done with me yet, don't you kid yourself.'

'No, not yet,' said Smith. 'I'll put you on shore all right. I'll promise you that. It's all I can do under the circumstances; but considering everything, I think it ought to be enough. I hope so, anyhow. Get in now and we'll go.'

Smith rowed the dinghy towards the shore. Presently the boat grounded on the sand and Lichtensteiger jumped out. He looked around him for a while and listened intently; but, except for the sound of the little waves breaking and the distant lights of the town, there was nothing to be heard or seen. Then, 'All right,' said Lichtensteiger. And Smith said nothing. He pushed off from the beach and rowed away silently into the darkness.

Lichtensteiger laughed. He turned and walked inland with a suitcase in each hand. He felt the sand under his feet give way to shingle, the shingle to turf, and the turf to a hard road surface. Lichtensteiger laughed again. It amused him to think that the business of getting himself unnoticed into England should prove, after all, to be so ridiculously easy. He turned to the left and walked rapidly for half a mile before he came to a fork in the road and a signpost. It was too dark for him to see the sign; but he stacked his suitcases against the post and climbing on them struck a match. He read: 'Calais – $1\frac{1}{2}$.'

John Masefield

THE DERELICT

(from *The Bird of Dawning*)

John Masefield is usually remembered by his nostalgic sea poems like Sea Fever *and* Cargoes, *and as Poet Laureate, but he began life as a cadet on board H.M.S.* Conway *and went to sea at the age of 15 as an apprentice in a square-rigged ship in which he rounded Cape Horn. The following extract from his novel* The Bird of Dawning, *which describes the race home of the tea clippers, deals with the sighting of a derelict at sea.*

A boatload of seamen, who have survived a collision when their own ship was run down by a steamer which failed to stop, have been 8 days in a lifeboat. 'Cruiser' Trewsbury, the mate, is in command and they sight a vessel abandoned and low down in the water, a mystery ship.

As they drew near her, she looked perhaps more to be pitied than feared. The little disorders against which the sailor is always contending now triumphed unchecked and stamped her as deserted. They came quartering up to her, sometimes seeing her stern, sometimes her port broadside. Her boat's falls dragged in the sea on both sides. Sometimes in one of her rolls she hove them well out, as though she had hooked a fish, and swung them high and crashed them into her rail. Her staysails swung, jangling their sheets. She was groaning, cracking and jangling from blocks and ports and framework: her bells jangled sometimes; and buckets or paint pots which had rolled loose on her deck sometimes made a rattling roll from side to side, like the flourish of a little devil's drum delighting in the ruin. Now and again as the steady wind caught some fold of sail as she sheered, it would blow out with a roar, and flog and collapse, or lift high, trumpeting.

'She'll condemn some wealth in sails, sir,' Mr Fairford said. 'If she goes on like this much longer.'

'She will,' Cruiser said. 'Look, all of you, along her waterlines: the paint doesn't seem to have blistered.'

'No, sir,' they agreed, 'the paint hasn't blistered. She hasn't been on fire below, sir.'

'Not badly on fire, anyway; but she's got some water in her.'

'If you'll excuse me saying it, sir,' Kemble said, 'I only say it to warn you. They've got deadly disease on board her, that's my theory, and opened the cocks to sink her before they cleared out.'

'That's very likely,' Cruiser said. 'And it is just possible that they've left some dying men on board. It may be yellow fever: it may be small-pox. Now I shall go aboard alone, or with you, Rodmarton, as you know her, and when I'm aboard you'll drop astern on a line till I know what's the matter with her. You understand, Mister; let the two of us aboard, then shove off and keep clear, for I don't like the look of her.'

'Nor I, sir,' Fairford agreed. 'I'll keep clear of her all right, if you'll pitch me a line off a pin.'

'George! I've been wrong about her all the time. She's got a lovely stern,' Cruiser said as they drew up to it, under oars, having now dropped the sail. The ellipse of it rose up high above them, and showed to all in a gilt grummet her name and port:

Bird of Dawning.
London.
The Light comes after me.

Above and below the gilt grummet was her device, of a white cock with scarlet hackles, gripping a perch with gilt spurs.

'The Light comes after me,' Edgeworth spelled. 'Well, we're coming after you, you she-cow, and don't you forget it.'

'Half a moment, before we come alongside,' Cruiser said. 'We must hail before we board. Sing out, all hands.'

All hands lifted up their voices in a hail:

'*Cock*, ahoy. *Bird of Dawning*, ahoy.'

They had not expected an answer to their hail: but an answer came. From the hen-coop abaft the mainmast, a cock faintly crowed at them.

'My word, a cock,' Cruiser said.

'She can't be deserted, sir,' Rodmarton said. 'They'd never have left the poultry . . . They must be all dead of the plague.'

'Who took the boats, then?' Cruiser asked. 'They left in a hurry, thinking she was going down, and she hasn't gone.' He knitted his brows, puzzled at the case. Standing up, he hailed again. '*Bird of Dawning*, ahoy.' Again the cock crowed back at him, as though the ship herself were answering. Most of the men said that they were damned.

'The sooner we examine into her the better,' Cruiser said. 'She'll scare us all white, until we know.' He was scared himself at the thought of the scenes of horror that might be in the houses there, only a few fathoms away. With the terror, there was hope of finding more stores, before the ship went down.

'Edge her in to the falls, Coates,' he said. 'Stand by to catch the forward life-line, Rodmarton, while I catch the one aft. Look out, port oars, that you don't smash any oars against her. Tend her with a ricker, Edgeworth; you too, Kemble.'

They pulled up alongside gingerly, Coates steering, Rodmarton forward, Cruiser in the stern-sheets ready to leap, the two old men ready to fend. The ship loomed up immense, as she rolled away from them, heaving out her grassy copper, and showing bare, bright patches where the fall-blocks had stricken her. She paused in her roll for an instant, then with a rapidly increasing rattling angle she rolled down towards them, till her yardarms looked like spears descending. 'In your port oars,' Cruiser said. 'Half a stroke, starboard, lively now. Watch your tip, Rodmarton.'

Nimbly as a cat, in spite of his fatigue, he leaped at the life-line that swung from the after-davit, caught it, went up it, swung to the rail and leaped down on to the deck. Rodmarton followed him rather less nimbly. Cruiser took a coil of running gear from the pin and leaned over the fife-rail. 'Stand from under,' he called. 'Catch this line. Catch a turn with it round the forward thwart and drop astern on it till I tell you.'

He paid out the line to them, and watched them drop astern, till they lay off the quarter, with all hands clustered forward in her staring. Rodmarton stood by the starboard main fife-rail, looking thoroughly scared. The words of Kemble and the others had gone well home to him: he was thinking that his brother Joe might lie dead in his bunk in one of the deckhouses within a few yards of him.

Cruiser went to the well and hove up the rod: there were three feet three inches of water in her.

'See that, Rodmarton?' he called. 'She's got just over three feet in her. Try it, you: and check it.'

Rodmarton tried it and made it the same.

'Yes, sir, three feet three, sir.'

'And why should they desert her with only that?'

'I don't know, sir.'

'It must have been much less than that. The ship was deserted yesterday, and she must have been leaking gaily ever since.'

'It may have been like what Kemble said, sir: a fish got into it.'

'A fish,' Cruiser said. 'An obliging fish, I should say.'

'Yes, sir.'

Cruiser stepped to the hen-coop and flung back its slide. A cock chuckled, hopped down to the deck and flapped and crowed: five hens followed him. Cruiser reached to the bin on the coop-top and flung them some grain, and filled their pan at the scuttle-butt.

'Won't you drink, sir?' Rodmarton said.

'You drink,' Cruiser said. 'I'll speak to the boat's crew.' Going to the rail, he hailed the boat. 'Give all hands a biscuit each and a pannakin of water, Mister,' he cried. Going back to the scuttle butt, he took a small drink himself. 'This butt is full,' he said. 'It must have been filled in the dog-watch yesterday or the day before I should think the day before, since the hens were shut up for the night. We'll go forward, first, Rodmarton, to see about your brother Joe.'

'Joe was a good brother to me, sir,' Rodmarton said, snivelling. 'And if I'd not been so proud, I could have been with him now.'

'I don't believe for a moment that this is a pest-ship,' Cruiser said. 'She's had men enough to get both boats over and haul up the courses and get the mainyards aback. You wouldn't have thought would you, that being able to stand up straight and walk forward would be such a pleasure? It is like having a new life.'

'It is indeed, sir.'

They were now near the after-end of the long, forward deck-house which stretched from the foremast to the main hatch. A green door swung open and crashed and clattered at the roll, in the after end of this deck-house. 'That's the round-house door, sir,' Rodmarton said, 'where my brother Joe used to berth. I went to tea there with him only two days before we sailed, and he give me those little London pantiles, all square, not like we got. And I don't think I dare look in, please sir, for fear of seeing them all dead.'

Cruiser's habits of order were strong upon him. 'Lay aft, Rodmarton,' he said, 'and get a pull on that main royal clue-line before the sail splits.' He went to the round-house door, hooked it back open, and looked in.

It had been the round-house or cabin for the ship's idlers, the two chief boatswains, the two sailmakers, the cook and the carpenter. The two junior boatswains no doubt berthed in the fo'c'sle. The house was a neat cabin, with no trace of pestilence about it. The six bunks were deserted, with their curtains of green Min cloth swaying to the roll: the blankets neatly stored, ready for the night. The six chests were still lashed to the ringbolts, some to serve as seats at the tiny table, the others under the bunks. In the two spare bunks their canvas bags were piled. In the locker were their allowances, a tin of cold sea-pie with a spoon in it, a corked bottle half full of lime-juice, and a bread-barge full of broken biscuit. Cruiser pocketed some of the bread, and looked about for some clue that would tell him what had happened. No clue was there.

The pipes were in the pipe-racks. Tacked to the matchboard on the bulkheads in the bunks were odds and ends which showed something of the tastes of the men who had slept there. The cook had two texts printed in colours, 'God is Love' and 'God bless our Home', the one with a decoration of partridges, the other with a Shetland pony. They had probably been sent to him by his children: they seemed unbearably pathetic there. In a shelf at the foot of the carpenter's bunk was a model of the *Bird of Dawning*, rigged with spars of beef-bone, and very nearly finished, save for the running rigging of the mizen mast. In what Cruiser took to be brother Joe's bunk there were a couple of chest-shackles, not yet finished, with the pointing still in progress on them.

Cruiser went out to Rodmarton, gave him a hand at bunting up the main-royal, and handed him some biscuit.

'There's nobody dead there,' he said. 'You'd better eat this bread slowly. I'm going to the fo'c'sles. If I were you, I'd go into the round-house and take over your brother Joe's gear.'

'Thank you, sir; I will, sir.' Rodmarton, like most Englishmen, was a man of very deep affections not usually shown. Cruiser left him in the round-house, and went into the starboard fo'c'sle, which was in the same superstructure just forward from it.

It was a big, roomy place; dry, clean and well lighted, with bunks for fifteen seamen, whose chests and bags were still there. From what he could see, this starboard watch had been below, turned in, when the alarm of all hands had been given. There was no trace of sickness or death there. From what he could see, the alarm had been in the day-time or the dog-watch, because the men had been lying on their blankets, not beneath them. The prints of their bodies lay stamped there; he could tell their sizes, and something of their characters.

At the forward end of the fo'c'sle was a hanging place for oil-skins, which swung there on pegs, rather like a row of desiccated pirates upon a gibbet. The chests had not been emptied, even of their tobacco. The men had apparently sprung up, snatched a few things and had then left the ship. Their whackpots were in the lockers still, and hook-pots half full of lime-juice still hung on the edges of the bunks. As in all homeward-bound ships, the bunks contained things that the men were making, such as models of the *Bird of Dawning*, with the little blocks made of guji seed, sharks' back-bones carefully dried and about to become walking-sticks, narwhals' horns on which the scrimshaw-worker was cutting crude designs of rope, sennits, ladies, hearts, arrows and clipper-ships; albatrosses' feet being made into tobacco-pouches; chest-shackles for going ashore; sail-makers' rubbers in beef-bone, representing shroud and stopper knots; and ships with their masts prone which were soon to be thrust down the necks of bottles half full of putty, coloured to represent the sea, and then by an adroit twitch of a thread, rigged, with the masts erect, to rouse wonder in all beholders how the ships ever got there. All these little treasures had been left behind, unfinished, at the feet of bunks: some of them were good of their kind; and all had been made by blunt fingers, with the aid of a knife and a few pins, at the sacrifice of sleep in many watches below.

Cruiser crossed the deck to the port fo'c'sle on the other side of the bulkhead. It resembled its fellow, except that a meal had not been cleared away from the table when the crew left the fo'c'sle. The wreck of the meal had now been rolled off the table and flung hither and yon under bunks and behind chests. What meal it was, Cruiser found it hard to say: probably breakfast or supper, for the skilly-can which may have contained a hot drink of some sort, was rolling with the whack-pots. Cruiser picked it up and scooped from it something of the molasses which had once sweetened its brew.

Forward of the fo'c'sle in the same superstructure was the ship's galley, shut up, either before or after the day's work, at the time of the desertion of the ship: the range was in good order, and the fire laid for kindling. Immediately forward of this was the donkey-house, containing the engine which had once been in charge of Rodmarton. Here Cruiser was startled indeed.

Both doors of the engine-room were open. The deck was strewn with coal-bags, spanners, and lumps of coal. Plainly, the vanished crew had been set to work to get the engine to work the pumps. He knew a little about engines; from what he could see this one was in good order: he did not doubt for a moment that it was in excellent order, like all the things under Captain Miserden's command. It was all greased and oiled, and its bright parts kept polished. Its canvas cover lay folded beside it. The fires had been lit, but steam had not been raised, and the drive to the pumps had never been rigged. Rodmarton joined him here. Rodmarton was white and scared at the thought of his brother gone into a mystery: the deserted ship terrified him: he came to Cruiser for company.

'Look here, Rodmarton,' Cruiser said, 'this engine's in order, yet they haven't got steam and cleared her. Why not? Why on earth not?'

'It beats me, sir,' Rodmarton said. 'But I'll tell you what I'm afraid of, sir. I'm afraid one of them giant squid has come up and picked all hands off and ate them.'

'What, and the boats too?'

'Yes, sir, pulled the boats down.'

'You can tell that to the marines, not to the deck department. Man, can't you see that she's sprung a leak somehow, some sudden, appalling leak, that leaped on them suddenly, and scared them all stiff and drove them out of her when they had the chance to be taken off? But why haven't they rigged the drive to the pump and got the engine on to it? They've the power here to free her. Why haven't they tried it?'

'Sir,' Rodmarton said, 'they have the hand pumps rigged by the main bitts there, and I took a heave round on them, and could get nothing. It's my belief, sir, that the tea's got into the pump-box and jammed the suck. The pump's jammed, sir, that's why they never rigged the drive.'

'Jammed,' Cruiser said. 'I never thought of that. The tea leaves have jammed the intake of the pumps?'

'Yes, sir.'

'Of course, if the pumps are jammed,' he said slowly, 'it would explain a good deal.' But he thought to himself, 'How would the intake jam here? The ship has been swept and garnished, and all her timbers almost polished before any tea went into her: and her tea is all in tiers of boxes chinsed tight with grass-mat; how would loose tea leaves get down to the well?'

He found no answer to that question, so thrust it aside till he had settled something more pressing. He took a pannikin from the fo'c'sle, passed under the fo'c'sle head, and there pushed back the scuttle that led below.

He looked down into a darkness that was all close, hot and heavy, yet fragrant with the smell of the tea leaf. It was very dark below, he could see nothing but the gleam of a coaming below, and hear nothing but the crying of a ship's fabric that can never be wholly silent.

'I'm going down here,' he said to Rodmarton, 'I want to find this leak.'

Rodmarton plainly showed that he believed that the giant squid was down below; and something of his fear touched Cruiser as he swung over the coaming, and clambered down the nine iron rungs into the 'tween-decks. He went down slowly, feeling his way below him with his feet. He knew that somewhere in the dark was something evil which had driven nearly forty men in a hurry out of the ship. What that was, he had now to find and face. He did not believe in giant squid, but the light that he had left, shining at the scuttle-entrance, seemed dearer to him than any light that he had seen.

Soon his feet touched the coaming of the forepeak hatch; he swung round on to the laid 'tween-decks and looked about him. By the light from the scuttle above he saw close to him some casks lashed to the coaming bolts. Putting an arm into them, he found that they were half filled with sand for the scrubbing of decks, and with small pieces of holystone, wads of canvas, and suji-muji brushes, all designed for the smartening of the ship for London River. As his eyes became used to the gloom, he saw the slope of the cables on each side, and the frame of strong scantlings which held in the coal for the cook and engine. Further aft he could see the barrier of the shifting-boards, which fenced the tea in the waist. All the close heavy air was fragrant with the tea. The noise of the ship labouring and plowtering, the clang of her freeing-ports, and the gurgling ominous running suck of the sea along her, making her whine, and whicker, were all more intense down below there. The gear was still tugging and jangling. Every now and then all the dark 'tween-decks seemed to shudder with patterings and goings: he knew that the noises were strains passing in the beams, but they sounded like feet. As he stood listening, and somewhat daunted, something heavy and swift ran across his feet. He leaped and kicked out, but the thing was already gone: it was only a big ship's rat, perhaps driven from the lower hold by the leak. His heart beat the quicker for it for some moments.

Remembering an old method of the sea, he groped to the ship's port side, pressed the pannikin against it and laid his ear to the pannikin. The sea-stethoscope brought to his ear a noise of gurgling and lapping, which he knew to be the noise of the water already in the ship. It was not the rushing noise of a dangerous leak. He took his pannikin from place to place, going to the breast-hooks, then to the starboard side, then moving aft to the cargo, then crossing again to the port side, and listening like a doctor for some irregular murmur, some dangerous sign or sound. There was no such sound in the forward part of the ship. 'There's nothing dangerous at the moment, forward,' he told himself. 'Yet the water in her gives her a horrid feel at the end of each roll.'

He felt at each roll that the ship had her death upon her, and might at any moment go suddenly down, and shut that little bright scuttle above him with the green weight of the sea.

He climbed back on deck to the great relief of Rodmarton. 'Rodmarton,' he said, 'get up on to the top of the deckhouse here with me. Clamber up to that ventilator and listen.'

He himself clambered to the other forward ventilator, and listened at its frowsy mouth to what it had to say. It told just the same story that the pannikin had told, that there was a dead weight of water in the lower hold, but no shattering inrush.

'And yet,' he said to himself, after he had tried both ventilators, 'there must have been a shattering inrush. What has stopped it, and for how long is it stopped?' He shook his head at Rodmarton and said: 'We'll move along aft and try there.' In his head the thought ran, 'She has probably started some butt amidships, and in some odd way the cargo has caulked and chinsed it. If we could find the place we might get a mat over it and save her.'

As he walked aft, he asked Rodmarton if he had ever known the *Cock* to leak. 'No, sir,' Rodmarton said, 'not when I was in her: she's as tight as a nut. She's still a new ship and she goes into graving dock every time. We never had to pump her. The last time I saw Joe I asked him if she'd opened at all, and he said the same.'

They came to the booby hatch under the standard compass between the boat-skids. Cruiser pushed back the scuttle and let a waft of hot air blow by him. 'If it isn't forward, it must be somewhere here,' he said. He clambered slowly down, and stood in the 'tween-decks to accustom his eyes to the gloom.

As he stood there, holding to the iron ladder, and looking aft, he saw two green eyes looking at him from the bulkhead. They did not blink, they watched him intently, and for an instant they made him think of the squid. 'Who's there?' he called. 'Come out of it.'

There was a rustling in the studding-sail locker, and a faint mew: the thing came to his feet and rubbed his ankles: it was a little black cat. 'Poor pussy,' he said. 'And couldn't they find you when they left her?' He stooped, stroked the little head, caught the purring creature to him and carried her up on deck. 'Here's a pet for you,' he said. 'Give her a drink of water, and see that she doesn't eat the hens.'

He walked to the port side and applied his pannikin as before. There was no sound of any inpour on that side. When he tried the starboard side, it seemed to him that there was a new noise at his ear. He tried forward, with no result, then, trying aft, was convinced that somewhere on that side water was struggling and lapping into the ship. He tried as far aft as the bulkhead, which went right across the 'tween-decks to screen off the sail-locker and lazarette. The noise seemed to come from rather far aft, now as a tinkle, now a splash, according to the roll of the ship: undoubtedly, a leak was there, of sorts.

He could not keep from wondering whether it were not at the stern-post, or some difficult place, where a mat could not be put. He climbed up to the deck and hailed Rodmarton. 'She seems to be weeping somewhere aft on the starboard side. Come aft with me, will you?'

The break of the *Bird of Dawning*'s poop was recessed, in a curve, amidships. Within this curve a green door led to an alleyway, with the saloon at the end. As usual with those ships, the cabins of the first and second mates lay on each side of the alleyway; then came the steward's pantry and cabin, then the companion leading up to the charthouse, then the saloon itself stretching right across the ship. Cruiser, who had been on board the ship at Pagoda Anchorage, remembered his way: Rodmarton had been aft as a seaman coming for tobacco and slops.

Stopping at the pantry, Cruiser groped in the half-darkness for candle and matches on the shelf, and finding them struck light, and then saw, in a bucket of water (for coolness) a bundle of tallow dips, which he took.

Just beyond him was the ship's big saloon, lit by a skylight and full of the sun. Only a few weeks before Cruiser had entered it as a suppliant, seeking for work; now here he was again: what was he now, and what was the ship now?

There was the table where Captain Miserden had sat to receive him, a big, white-faced, black-bearded man, with strange eyes. The saloon was finer than most ships' saloons. It had been designed for passengers making the Australian passage: its panels were of polished bird's-eye maplewood; there was much brass about the skylight: still bright, Cruiser noticed, as though it had been polished only the day before.

An open locker against the after-bulkhead caught his eye: it was the likeliest place for the ship's chronometers; he stepped to look within it, and saw that it had contained the chronometers (there were notes of the rates still in the nest) but that the instruments were gone.

He hove up the hatchway which led to the lazarette, and after 'tween-decks. A warm compound smell wafted up at him, from the variety of things stored there. Tea from the cargo was the dominant smell, but other suggestions of a grocer's shop were there. When he had clambered down and surveyed the place with his candles, he was freed from his fear that the crew had been starved away. It was a 'homeward-bound' lazarette, but what stores remained seemed enough for the passage still before her. He stuck the lights where they would not fall and then stood to listen.

As he had dreaded, the sound of water running into the ship could be heard there without the help of any pannikin. Water was coming in, somewhere close to him, in some abundance or so it seemed, for the echoes in that hollow place made the noise greater.

'No doubt about this,' he said to himself. 'She's got it somewhere aft here, on the starboard side. Now perhaps I can find it.'

He laid his ear to the pannikin on the ship's side: the noise at once sharpened and seemed to draw near: it was close to him, under his feet and rather further aft. By moving aft, he reached a place at which it seemed to be directly below him in the ship's side, rather far aft. A pipe leading up the ship's side there gave him a clue. He ran up into the saloon, and opened a door on the starboard side aft. As he had hoped, it led to the captain's lavatory and bathroom. He tried plugs and taps, but got no water from them; and at once a hope sprang up in him that he had found the cause of the trouble. Instantly, however, he had to beat down the thought. 'It cannot be only that,' he told himself. 'It must be more than that. This ship must have had a flood pouring into her, and something or other has stopped the flood.'

'Have you found anything, sir?' Rodmarton asked.

'I'm just going down for another look-see,' he said. 'Come on down, I've got to get a man-hole-lid open, and get down into the after-hold.'

Down in the lazarette, close to where he had stood, was a man-hole-lid, which had certainly been lifted not long before. Cruiser hove it out of its place and peered down on to what looked like a little waterfall. Water was spouting in a jet through the ship's side into the hold there. As he held the candle he saw the jet arched almost like a pipe of bright metal shooting in and curving and splashing down.

'See that, Rodmarton,' he said, 'that's a part of it, anyhow. It's the intake of the captain's lavatory, gone at the joint. Light some more candles from the bunch, I'm going down to have a look at it.'

Very carefully, he swung himself down, got foothold, and crawled with a light to the place. He had not expected what he found. The intake pipe had been cut through close to the ship's side; it had then been wilfully prised and wrenched aside, and splayed open to let water into the ship. There was no doubt about it. Someone had worked to let water into the ship.

'Do you find the skin gone, sir?' Rodmarton asked.

'No. It's the pipe. Nip forward to the carpenter's shop and see if he's got any big spigots: there are sure to be some. And get a slush-can and a maul, and any old clout you can come across.'

While he waited for these things, he marvelled still more at his discovery. 'Who did this, and why, and when?' he asked. 'It cannot be the only leak. And yet, no other seems to be running. And there must have been another, to scare the crew out of the ship. The jammed pump of course came as an extra scare.'

He remembered very clearly his own time with a captain who had wished to put his ship ashore. What if Captain Miserden had wished to be rid of the *Bird of Dawning*? What if the man, whoever he might be, who had cut through the pipe, had also jammed or choked the suction of the pumps?

Rodmarton appeared with gear from the carpenter's shop. 'I've got some spigots, sir,' he said. 'And a maul and slush and stuff.'

'Well, nip on down here, with some lights, and we'll tom this hole tight.'

Rodmarton swung down and stared at the cut pipe.

'Why, sir: it's been cut through on purpose.'

'No doubt of that, but we can stop this easily enough, with a spigot, till we can get down to it and make a neat job of it.'

'But can this be the only leak, sir?'

'Why, no,' Cruiser said. 'I don't see how it can be. But it may be the only active leak. I believe, now, that this ship knocked a hole in herself somewhere, somehow on a bit of wreck, or wrenched a butt apart, or sheared off a rivet or something. Then she began to leak like fun. But water exerts a great pressure, and it often happens that when some weight of water is in a ship the very weight of the water will keep more from coming in. Now I believe that this ship has checked her leak in the same way. But I also believe that someone wanted her cast away, and cut through this pipe, and in some way got down to the well and choked the intake of the pumps. Then all hands were scared, and when the chance came to desert ship they deserted her. However, we'll soon know more about this. We'll chinse up this pipe and get those poor chaps out of the boat.'

It was one minute's work to slush the hard-wood spigot, wrap it in a clout of worn canvas, slush the end, thrust it into the pipe and beat it home. The spigot dripped for an instant after it was in, then the drippings ceased.

'We'll get some putty or cement along presently,' Cruiser said, 'and make a good job of it; this will hold for the time. Now we'll get the boat on board.'

He clambered back into the lazarette, hoisted up the gear with the candles and helped Rodmarton to replace the man-hole-lid.

'By the way, Rodmarton,' he said, 'when you were in this ship what hoses had you?'

'The usual wash-deck hoses forward, sir; and two long fire-hoses, with copper nozzles, in racks just forward of the mizen mast. The ship carried passengers her first voyage or two and the hoses were in case of fire in the quarters.'

'I saw those hoses,' Cruiser said, 'when I came aboard this ship in the Min River. They're not in the racks now. The racks are empty.'

'I didn't notice, sir.'

'I did,' Cruiser said, thinking to himself that the man who had removed the hoses had helped to the desertion of the ship. 'Now on deck here, Rodmarton, by this little companion ladder, and get the ship's crew aboard.'

As Rodmarton went up the captain's companion, Cruiser went along the alleyway, locked the door which led to the deck and pocketed the key. 'Just as well,' he thought, 'to have no second road open to the rum, with men like Stratton and Efans about.' He then went up the ladder to the poop, and found the boat's crew hauling their boat forward to the falls that dangled from the starboard davits.

'Up on board with you,' he said. 'We can salve this hooker, I do believe. Coates and Chedglow, you both stay in the boat till she's on the skids. MacNab, you, too; you'll only crock your bones again if you go trying to climb.'

They brought the boat to the falls, and hooked her on. Man by man they swarmed up the life-lines, with ejaculations of wonder and delight to be out of the boat, able to stand erect, and to walk and to feel the deck of a ship below them. The two and a half days had taken the strength out of them. They had to take the boat's falls to the deck-capstan, and to hoist her one fall at a time. They got her up, swung her in, secured her, and helped MacNab out of her.

'Hold on a minute, all hands,' Cruiser said, as the crowd stood below him, ready to scatter forward to raid the fo'c'sles.

He went to the boat's locker and removed the brandy.

'You've all had a hard time in the boat,' he said. 'You must splice the main brace. Keep aft here, till I give the word.' He served out to each man there a strong grog, which they drank with thankfulness. After the grog he gave each man a handful of raisins. They sat about the main bitts eating for a few minutes; they were all smiling foolishly, looking up at the spars, touching deck and bitts to make sure that they were real, and anon rising to their feet, to walk a few steps for the pleasure of being able to do it.

Cruiser and Mr Fairford ate their raisins at the break of the poop.

'What do you think, Mister?' he asked. 'Will the crowd sail this hooker to London?'

'They're mostly English, sir,' old Fairford said, 'and my experience is, that you can get the English to do anything, if you put it to them the right way. The trouble with the English is they try all the wrong ways first.'

'I'm not much of a hand at speaking,' Cruiser said.

'They're not much judges of oratory, sir. "Do this, damn your eyes," is the oratory they're used to.'

'I know,' Cruiser said. 'But we've been in an open boat together for over two days.' He walked on to the little platform which led to the standard compass: Mr Fairford followed him.

'D'ye hear there?' Cruiser said, as the men started up at his approach. 'We've been in a tight place together. Thank God we're out of it. We've got out of our boat into one of the crack ships of the fleet. Don't think you're out of danger in her. You're not. She's got more than three feet of water in her hold, and her pumps are jammed. I don't know what leaks she may still have. I've only stopped one small one. You've had a hard time in the boat and I'm going to see that you are well fed and rested. If you go eating and drinking in great quantities you'll suffer. Eat a very little every hour for the rest of the day, then you won't suffer. This ship has been left in a hurry. She may have a bad leak in her. She may flood suddenly again and go down like a stone. The first thing we'll do, is to provision this boat against our having to take to her again. We'll see this time that she has abundant water and thoroughly mended topsides. The gear of this ship's crew is in the fo'c'sles there: you're not to loot it and fight for it. It's going to be whacked out to you:

then each will have a share. Now this ship may sink. We may have to take to the boat again. On the other hand, we may be able to salve her. I believe that we can salve her. I believe that we can sail her home and dock her in London Docks, and perhaps even come home first and win the prize. Why not try for that? You know what sailorizing is, two pounds ten a month and hard going. If you salve this ship and bring her home each man's share may be a couple of hundred pounds. If you'll try for that, I'll promise you hard work, but such good treatment that you'll remember this ship for ever. What do you say? Shan't we sail her home?'

The men looked about sheepishly.

'Come boys,' old Fairford said. 'You're not going to hang back when Captain Trewsbury asks you. You've all seen him in the boat, a young officer up against it, and how he has thought for you. Why, I don't think any old sailor of you all would have thought more for you and brought you through better. I say, you may thank God for him. Shan't we sail this ship home with him and get our names up? Don't leave the race to the *Min and Win,* and the *Natuna* and tripe of that sort.'

'We'll sail her home, sir,' Edgeworth said.

'We'll sail her home with you, sir,' Rodmarton said.

'I wass say, sir,' Efans said, 'we wass not far from Fayal. I say we put into Fayal and claim to be sent home. We wass all shipwrecked men, look you. It wass our rights to be sent home, not to work our ways. Let a new crews ship, look you, in Fayal, yess, and we co home in the mail-steamers, with a nurse at our pedsides.'

'Fayal your Welsh grandmother,' Kemble said, 'shut your head about your rights. Are you going to do us all out of two hundred pounds?'

'I say the same as Efans,' Stratton said. 'I'm not going to be bullied out of my rights, because old walrus-whiskers believes he'll get salvage-money. We have a right to be taken to the nearest port and shipped for home.'

'Come away from that,' Tarlton said. 'You and your right to be shipped for home! You may have a right to be shipped for home. Do you suppose you'll find a Consul who'll ship you home? Do you suppose the mail-ships haven't fixed it with the Consuls so that

they shall not carry shipwrecked men? Lord, I've been shipwrecked. I thought, Lord save us, that I'd be sent home in a mail
steamer, with a stewardess to ask if the sheets were aired. Did I
get? Did I, hell? No, the Consul said to me, "There's a fine ship in
the bay short of hands. You can sign in her and get the advance:
that's my last word to you, my man." So I signed on board the "fine
ship": one of these down-easters put in with her topmasts gone.
Hard? She worked her iron into me and out of me. And that's the
kind of mail-steamer you'll get sent home in: a New Bedford
whaler, put in with scurvy, who'll be at sea for the next three years
as like as not.'

'And that's God's truth,' Kemble said. 'We'll sail her home, Captain Trewsbury. If Stratton and Efans are set on going to Fayal
they can walk there and count the milestones.' He looked round for
support, and plainly had it from nearly all there. Jacobson might
have spoken up for Fayal, but had had most of the devil knocked
out of him by the time in the boat. Bauer would have liked a spree
in Fayal, but the thought of a two-hundred-pound spree in London
was too much for him: the others were for Cruiser. Young Coate
spoke out his mind, as was his way. 'And I say we're damned lucky,
and the sooner we get her on her course, as the Captain asks, I say
the damned well better.'

'Thank you,' Cruiser said. 'We'll try for the London River. But
bear in mind, that this ship may go down on us. Stratton, Efans, and
Jacobson, you will put this ship's scuttle-butt into the boat, and fill
it with fresh water. Then you'll fill all the buckets in the boat with
fresh water. This time we'll see that you do it. Mr Fairford, will
you take Kemble forward, and whack out all the gear, clothes and
blankets and stuff, so that each man has a fair kit? But before you
go, Mister, I must rearrange the watches a bit. Perrot, who is in my
watch, will be cook, and MacNab, who can't do much except look-
out and steward's jobs at present, will be steward, and look-out and
lamp-man. Nailsworth, I want you to be in my watch as boatswain.
Kemble, I want you to be boatswain in Mr Fairford's watch. You
will both bunk in the round-house. Chedglow, you will go to Mr
Fairford's watch. Nailsworth, and you, Tarlton, you can get at the
boat in a short while, and give her a thorough overhaul; but the

rst thing is to fill the mainyards and get this ship on to her course.'

He was, perhaps, more thoroughly fagged than anybody there, or he had had less rest, and all the life in him had been given to put fe into the crowd. He felt dead-beaten, yet saw endless things to e done. The fact that he was out of the boat, even if it were to be nly for part of a day, was such bliss that it was hard to keep from ears. He felt that the first thing to do was to get the chronometers ut of the boat to safety. 'And I must go through the captain's aings,' he thought, 'and I must get the pumps rigged. And I must ke the sun, and give these fellows a course.'

When he had stowed the chronometers safely, he came on deck, here Mr Fairford was serving out the gear of the vanished crew, eginning with the fine weather things. Mr Fairford, helped by .emble and Edgeworth, was building up fourteen little heaps of lothes. 'Dungaree trousers for this fellow. A pair of dungaree ousers here. Now another pair here. That makes decency for ll hands; now the shirts and jumpers.'

Cruiser called to the men who were hanging about, to clap on to me of the gear and snug it up: while they did this, singing out at ae ropes, he went to the pump at the main bitts. It was a strong inch pump, rigged with a traveller to the donkey-engine, and ith hand brakes for six hands when steam was not being used. odmarton had said that it was jammed in the intake, which emed to Cruiser to be likely. He took the winch-brake and hove pon it, and called to two hands to come to heave upon it. 'Hand-mely, now,' he said. 'Don't break anything.'

They did not break anything, something was so jamming the ction that the winch-brakes would not go round.

'Der tea was jam up der suck,' Bauer said. Cruiser did not aswer, because to him it felt as though something had jammed or oken in the mechanism close to the winch-brakes. He knew that ae ship had had foul play, and that someone had wanted her to be ink. Someone had cut through that pipe. Someone had removed ae fire-hoses from their handy racks on deck. Why should not mebody have wrecked the pump so as to finish his dirty job?

'Rodmarton,' he said, 'you're the best mechanic we've got. Go rward to the carpenter's shop and get what wrenches and span-

ners you can find. And Perrot, get forward, too, and get the galle
fire lit. Chedglow, lay aft into the steward's pantry; you, too
MacNab and Coates, and get out some bully-beef tins, or soup
and-bully: make us a strong soup, Doctor, as soon as you can.'

While Rodmarton brought the spanners, Cruiser brought som
lanterns from the steward's pantry and called Rodmarton dow
into the 'tween-decks. The tea rose in a cone to the main hatch, bu
a space had been built clear round the main mast with strong shift
ing boards. Cruiser came to the shaft of the pump and held hi
lantern to it. 'Look here,' he said. 'And look here, sir,' Rodmarto
said, stooping to the deck, 'here's all a kit of tools.'

Just below the deck, at a height convenient for a man to ge
at the nuts and bolts, there was a strong iron clamping-join
which had been opened and still was open. Its nuts and bolts lay o
the deck, methodically screwed together and so stowed in a kit-ba
that they could not roll away. Having cast loose the joint, someone
evidently a sailor, and a man of considerable strength had put a
chain stopper on the plungers and bowsed the stopper well home t
the main mast by means of a handy-billy. Anyone trying to forc
the pump-brakes round from the deck above would be almost cer
tain to smash the plungers across.

'Well, of all the wicked sights,' Rodmarton said. 'It looks a
though someone might have done it a purpose.'

'That was done on purpose,' Cruiser said. 'Surely you can se
that. Now let's get to it.'

He cast loose the hitch on the handy-billy fall, unhooked th
tackle, and slowly and carefully removed the chain, which migh
have been a length of old topgallant sheet. The plungers did no
seem to have been bent. The putter-on of the stopper, whoever h
was, had used so much chain that he had, if anything, overdone i
and made a cushion of it.

'Whatever would he go for to do a thing like that for?' Rod
marton asked.

'He was up to no good,' Cruiser said, as he began to re-fix th
clamping-joint.

'Whoever could it have been?' Rodmarton asked.

'Strange things happen at sea,' Cruiser said. As Rodmarton too
the spanner to the nuts, Cruiser examined the tool-kit-bag that ha

been lying on the deck. He saw that they were new tools, in a new kit-bag: they looked to him like a set indented for by the captain for the ship's use and only just out of store. As it occurred to him that the point would be important in an enquiry, he called Rodmarton's attention to them before he removed them.

When they were again on deck, he sounded the well. The leak still stood at three feet three inches. He had been on board for rather more than seventy minutes, during which the leak had not increased.

'Turn to here, half a dozen of you,' Cruiser said. 'Man this pump a moment. Heave round as handsomely as if you were walking on eggs. Handsomely does it.'

They manned the brakes and very gently began to turn them round. After half a dozen turns the water spouted on to the deck and away into the scuppers. Cruiser took a place at the brakes, and felt for himself that the pump was working easily. 'There it is,' he said, 'the pump is all clear. You can shift a ton of water in a minute and a half with her. You could free this ship in a couple of hours. But I'm not going to break your backs with pumping. Rodmarton, you go forward with Clutterbuck and see if you can get steam and rig the drive along.'

He went to Fairford, and told him the news. 'Someone had jammed the pump,' he said. 'But had not wrecked it, luckily; perhaps he was afraid of making a noise. I'm getting steam, or hope to get it, and then we'll free her by the donkey. What I'm afraid of is, that there's some other leak that is being kept under by the pressure of the water, and that when we start freeing her, she'll fill again.'

'As to that, sir, we might find the place and get a mat over it, or a sail into it, if it should be anything big. I would not worry, Captain Trewsbury: if we have to go back into the boat, we'll still be a lot better off than we were this morning. I suppose you haven't found anything to show why they left her, sir?'

'Nothing at all. It's a mystery to me.'

'If I might make a suggestion, sir, I would not lose time getting her to a course. No doubt this ship and the *Blackgauntlet* were leading the fleet, but others will be near, sir, if you'll forgive my saying so.'

'Yes, I shall get her to her course, as soon as I've got a fix.' He
went aft into Captain Miserden's chart-room, just abaft the mizen
mast; the door had been hooked open, and some of the drawers in
the lockers were wide open and untidy. The captain's sextant and
barometer had gone: the tell-tale compass had gone from the ceiling. Cruiser noted these things with the mental comment that both
barometer and compass had been unscrewed, as though the desertion of the ship had been expected and prepared for at leisure. The
log-book, meteorological log, abstract, and the ship's clearance
papers had gone: also all the charts. Thrusting back the slide of the
window, he reached for the log-slate hooked to the outer bulkhead.
On the slate, someone had written with a bold sea hand:

> 'D.R.2. Winds variable light N.E.
> Sq with R.'

There was no date to the entry, which might have referred to a
voyage made with Noah.

All the jottings and rough-books, all the tables and logarithms
that had been used in that room until the day before in finding the
ship's position, had been removed. Cruiser took those that he had
used in the boat, worked up a hasty fix, that would serve till he
could check it by observation, then having shaped a course, he
prepared to go on deck. As he was about to leave the chart-room,
he noticed a little drawer underneath the mahogany stand in which
the water-carafe stood; he pulled it open, thinking it might contain
some jottings of the ship's position. It did not: it contained a pistol,
with five chambers loaded. He put it into his pocket and walked
out on deck. 'Man the wheel here,' he said. 'Stand by all hands.'

At his orders, the great mainyards swung and filled, the ship
which had been kicking and bucking for so long, steadied for a few
instants, then leaned in her roll, then leaned further, rolled back a
little, and then slid forward, so that a wave splashed high at her
bow and rolled over abaft her waist and crumbled away into pale
green bubbles astern. The ship was on her course and under way
again.

There was a good deal to be done on deck, getting pulls on the
braces and freshening the nips on nearly all the gear: it was full

half an hour before anyone had any leisure; but when the yards were trim, a little party of malcontents came aft together and hung about the booby-hatch waiting for Cruiser to notice them. He had seen them, indeed he had expected them, but for a little while he took no notice of them. They were Efans, in command, Stratton, second in command, Jacobson of the party because he was half-witted, and Bauer of the party because it offered some little variety to the life. They were coming aft 'to see the captain' in the time-honoured way. The rest of the crew were giving them no sympathy and in no way supporting them, yet it was plain that all hands knew what was toward. They were not hanging back in the jobs they were doing, indeed all seemed to be suspiciously eager at them, yet all, without exception, had an eye on the group and on the Captain.

'Here are these four come-day-go-days wants to see you, sir,' Fairford explained.

'I'll deal with them later, Mister,' Cruiser said, going aft to look at the compass. He stood there an instant, looking now at the card, now at the mizen topgallant sail, full of wind and sharp-edged with it. 'How is she, Edgeworth?' he asked the helmsman.

'Steering as easy as an old shoe, sir.'

'The water in her is holding her down.'

'Yes, sir, she's not herself.'

'This is better than that ship's boat.'

'Yes, sir,' Edgeworth said. 'You may just bet it is , sir.' He watched the trim of the sails, and glancing aft at the stream of the wake judged that she was going about seven knots, and could be made to do more. There was exhilaration in feeling her striding away thus: the bliss of it after the boat was untellable. Yet he dared not give way to exultation, just behind the joy was still that spectre: 'This ship has been abandoned in a hurry. She has her death about her and may even now go down like a stone.'

He strolled quietly to the rail at the break of the poop and looked down at the party of growlers. 'What's the matter?' he asked.

'This ship, sir, look you,' Efans said. 'It was not right, sir, to take poor men to their teaths. This ship has peen apandoned, look you,

full of water, yess. We will not work her, sir, no, unless you go for
Fayal. We will not go to watery teath in her, it wass not right.'

'No, sir,' Stratton said. 'We're not going to work her, unless you
take her to Fayal and have her into dry dock.' He nudged Bauer
and Jacobson. Jacobson said nothing. Bauer said: 'It was a tam
shame to risk men's lives, so.'

'If this ship leaks,' Cruiser said, 'so that she is a danger, I shall
sail her to her nearest port. If not, she'll keep the course I set. And
if you refuse to obey my commands I'll shoot the whites out of your
eyes.' He took the pistol from his pocket, so that they could see it.

'Let me hear no more from any of you about not working her.
Get to the jobs I set you, putting water into the boat. Get to it.'
They got to it: Cruiser had the pleasure of hearing Efans say:
'Cot's sake, man Stratton, I nefer knew that he had a pig pistol,
nefer.'

Stratton muttered something under his breath, probably about
some people being funny dogs, and that was the end of the breeze;
it had been what old Fairford called, 'a bit of kite-flying to see
which way the wind set.' Cruiser watched the rebels till they had
watered the boat, he then sent the three of them to the royal yards
to loose the sails. By the time the royals were set and trimmed it
was time to take the sun. He got a good observation, worked out his
position exactly, pricked it off upon the chart, had the log hove and
saw that she was making eight knots. The cook had dinner, of sorts,
for all hands at about noon, when Cruiser's watch on deck began.

'Mr Fairford,' he said, as he took the deck, 'you can choose any
cabin you like down below. I shall keep the chart-room here for
when I'm not on deck, but as I have still some hope of a passage, I
may not be much below.'

'Perhaps I shan't be much either, sir,' old Fairford said. 'When
one comes to be my age, one doesn't need as much sleep as one did,
but I'll be glad of a watch below now, sir, I'll confess, after that
boat.'

After he had turned-in, Rodmarton reported the rigging of the
drive, and the getting of steam. Cruiser came down to the main
deck to watch the setting going of the pumps. The leak had not
increased since the morning, it was still a steady three feet three.

'Had you much of a bother with the engine?' Cruiser asked.

'No, sir, none,' Rodmarton said. 'I know this engine like an old friend: and they've got all the spare parts put away in oil in the bosun's locker. I knew where to put my hand on everything. Captain Miserden always was very particular about the engine; he said it saved him an anchor once. She started up just like a bird.'

'Still; go handsomely,' Cruiser said.

The steam was applied, the drive throbbed along to the barrels, and in a moment the pump was flinging two jets of water on to the deck. The water came up brown with tea, for the lowest tiers of cargo were ruined. They watched it carefully, Cruiser anxiously, for he expected to hear a ripping crack from somewhere in the pumpbox putting the pump out of action.

'I can't understand,' he said, 'why the man who tried to wreck the pump didn't drop a few spanners down the shaft, instead of securing the plungers.'

'Perhaps he did, sir,' Rodmarton said.' We shall very soon see.'

However, there came no jolting, stripping final crash from inside the pump-box, the pump worked and the water gushed. Cruiser watched the well anxiously now, lest his fear should be justified, that the leak was controlled and held under by the weight of water in the ship. He expected a sudden inrush as the weight was lessened. He watched the leak dropping, to three feet, to two feet nine, then down to two feet, yet still no more came in; the water dropped regularly, so much pumping, so much decrease in the well, so many minutes of pump, so many inches less leak.

'I can't understand it,' he said to himself. 'They could have freed her. If they had made the least little search, they could have found the leak and the stopper on the pump. Who was it that wanted her put away, and contrived all this?'

He was desperately short-handed. With a man at the wheel there were six men to a watch and of those six one or two were weakly youths, and all were much the worse for being in the boat.

'What coal have you, Rodmarton?' he asked.

'I should think about three and a half tons in the fore-peak, sir.'

'Could you keep steam in her with that till we dock?'

'Yes, sir, enough to work the deck-capstans. You could swing the braces with the engine if you'd a mind to it.'

Even so, that afternoon watch was hard work for the man on deck. The wind was fresh and fair, the ship going well before it under most of her plain sail, and going the livelier as the water came out of her. The gear aloft was good, yet with the ship moving as she was, the men were at it all the time, getting a small pull of this and that, or a better set on the other thing. Cruiser would gladly have set a foretopmast studding sail, but thought it wiser to wait till the crew had had some more food and rest. By four bells in the watch the pumps sucked dry, the well was empty: by six bells he had satisfied himself that there was no more water coming into the ship. He sent Nailsworth with Rodmarton down to the cut pipe in the lazarette. There with some cement from the carpenter's shop they made a good job of the repair, so that it was as tight as a nut.

All through the rest of the watch, whenever the work of the ship gave him a moment's pause, he wondered at the change in his fortunes and at the reasons for it. He could see no reason why the ship should have been deserted: no amount of thought made the matter clearer to him.

'I must have some sleep, sometime,' he said to himself: 'then, when I have slept perhaps I may have some light on it, or find something that may explain it.'

He had a word with Nailsworth towards the end of the watch. 'What do you think of it, Nailsworth?' he asked. 'Why was this ship deserted?'

'I cannot think, sir. It seems to me to lie between somebody's madness and somebody's wickedness. It has been very fortunate for us, sir.'

'It has indeed.'

'What would you recommend, Nailsworth, for men who have been through what we have been through?'

'Food and rest, sir. They won't expect much rest in a ship, for the work has to be done; but you could feed them up a bit, if there are the stores for it.'

'Yes, I can do that. There are the stores.'

He gave orders for a good supper for all hands. After his watch he turned-in in the chart-room for a blessed dog-watch of sleep which gave him a new lease of life. When he came on deck at four bells, just before sunset, he was told that a ship was in sight. Mr Fairford was examining her through a telescope which he had found in the cabin of the mate.

'She's hull down, sir. I can't see what she is. A lofty ship; one of the China fleet, I should say. Will you take a look-see, sir?'

Cruiser took the telescope for a look. It was a good old glass, much the worse for wear and difficult to adjust. When he had focused it, he saw the little smudge take a shape which he knew to be that of a ship with a skysail, and with studding sails set. He watched her for a minute or two, till he was satisfied that she was on the same course as the *Bird of Dawning*. He handed the glass back to Mr Fairford.

'She's one of the fleet,' he said. 'She looks to me like the *Streaming Star*.'

'I thought that, at first, sir,' Fairford said, 'Kemble thought she's the *Natuna*.'

'We seem to be holding her.'

'Yes, sir, she's not gaining. If they'd only stayed by her this ship would have been just about leading by twenty-four hours clear.'

'She's in the first flight still,' Cruiser said.

'Yes, sir, but short-handed as we are we can't drive her.'

'Can't we?' Cruiser said. 'We will, though. Forward there, rig out your gear and get the foretopmast stunsail set.'

He drove her all through that night, with a fair wind blowing fresh. When he came on deck for the forenoon watch next morning, the wester was still blowing strong and true, heaping the sea astern them, and wetting the foresail to the yard. The ship was not in sight; it was a dirtier day with a smudged horizon. She might have been close to them and they none the wiser. They were now tearing through it at ten knots an hour, under conditions which showed the *Bird of Dawning* at her best. She liked a lot of wind on her quarter; with that she would run at ease without strain, 'steady as the Scripture,' old Fairford called it, hardly filling a scupper as she ran.

Cruiser left the deck in charge of Fairford for an hour, while he took a survey of the ship.

The well had no water in it, the only leak must therefore have been the cut pipe. Perhaps some thing or paper in the ship might show why she had been abandoned.

Coates had given him an account of the ship's stores. As he had judged for himself in passing through the lazarette, these were ample for the passage home: some seven cwt. of bread, three casks of salt pork, one cwt. of peas, two cwt. of rice, 150lb. of soup-and-bouilli, much Australian tinned mutton, plenty of small stores, much marmalade, 200lb. of raisins, one cwt. of currants, some gallons of lime-juice, a cask of molasses, half a cask of sugar and a cask of flour. In the captain's private stores were jam, pickles, sardines, and a tin of butter, which had gone across the equator twice and may have lost some of its dairy freshness. There were also some tinned plum-puddings and tongues. Altogether, there was ample food to feed the survivors of the *Blackgauntlet* or double rations to London River. The water in the tanks was abundant. The boatswain's stores were also abundant as the stores of a China clipper had to be. She had rope, sails, canvas, small stuff, spare spars and tar enough to take her round the world and back.

Cruiser took the cabin-keys from the labelled keyboard in the chart-room and went down into the cabin, asking himself what manner of man the Captain of the *Bird of Dawning* had been. He had seen him and remembered him from the meeting as a big black-haired man with a white face and a kindly manner. He had heard no ill spoken of him except that he was 'a religious man, fond of his glass.' All the captains in the China fleet were religious men, and fond of a glass on occasion. Men under Cruiser had sailed with Captain Miserden: they had never seen him drunk nor the worse for drink: but Cruiser had to answer the question why the ship had been abandoned: drunkenness in the Captain was one possible explanation. Cruiser felt that he would begin with that.

At a first glance, it looked as though the Captain had been fond of a cocktail. There were two big glass carafes in the saloon, one containing rum, the other gin; by them were bottles of liquid sugar and orange bitters and two glasses containing swizzle sticks. Yet, on examining the steward's stores account-book, which hung from a hook in the pantry, he found that the rum and gin in the ship at

Foochow amounted to only twelve quart bottles of each, or barely enough to allow Captain and mates one modest cocktail a day apiece. Certainly, the Captain could not have been a drinker. Even the medical comforts contained only three dozen bottles of brandy, not more than two of which had been opened. It was among the medical comforts that Cruiser first found some suggestion of what Captain Miserden was.

All the stores were in excellent order, arranged in lockers on each side of the rudder shaft. The locker to port was the usual ship's medicine-chest with bandages, splints, dressings, and diagrams of men, clamped to cabin tables, undergoing simple operations; some thirty jars of drugs, and scales for weighing the same. The starboard locker at a first glance seemed to contain similar things, there were tins of arrowroot and of beef-jelly, a few tins of preserved milk, and a little ginger and camphor. The main bulk of the goods in this locker proved to be patent medicines for the Captain's private consumption. There were so many of these that Cruiser turned them out on to the cabin deck.

The first to come to hand was a box almost full of 'Dr Jenkinson's Cholera Powders, the only known specific for this Fatal Complaint.' Next came a discreet bottle for Female Ailments, not otherwise described, and a large assortment of cheap medicines:

Doctor Hoborow's Mixture for the Blood.

Old Doctor Gubbins's Liver Remedy, with a picture of old Doctor Gubbins being told by an Eminent Scientist that the Remedy was essential to Health.

Rhubarb Pills, for use in the Spring.

Dr Mainspring's Mariner's Joy, for the most obstinate cases.

Bile Pills.

Liver Pills.

Dr Primrose's Kidney Pellets, as prescribed by the famous Dr Primrose to the Unfortunate Queen of the French.

Dr Gubbins's Spring Mixture, for the Blood.

Dr Gubbins's Autumn Mixture, for the Blood.

'These Sovereign specifics correct Nature in those difficult seasons when the Body politic is adjusting itself to changed conditions.'

Nature's Remedy, 'Vegetable Pills prepared from plants known to the Red Indians, who by their daily use attain to the ages of 100: even 120 being not uncommon.'

Senna Tea, 'two tablets dissolved in the cup that cheers ensures a happy household.'

'The Salt of Life, being the active principle of Epsom and Glauber Salts extracted by a new process.'

In addition to these, there were wrappers and empty boxes which marked where others had lain.

'Dr Gubbins's Nutrient Corrective, being a Medical Food derived from Active Vegetable Principles by the World Famous Lemuel Gubbins.' There was a picture of Dr Gubbins, who seemed to be a mixture of Euripides and the Duke of Wellington.

'Use Olopant and smile at Disease.' A Mother of seven wrote to say that she had and did.

There were many, many others, most of which had been opened and tried: plainly Captain Miserden must have dosed himself with some of these remedies every day and night since his ship left England. 'That is something to go upon, perhaps,' he thought. 'He had a bee in his bonnet about patent medicines.' He turned his mind back to his one memory of Captain Miserden, that strange-looking, white-faced bright-eyed man who had spoken to him there in that cabin. 'He looked a bit odd,' Cruiser thought. 'But then ships' captains often do look odd: it's a very lonely life.'

There was nothing else in the lockers that showed anything of the Captain's mind. There were some jars of ginger, and of lichees, some China ham and a few cases of nutmegs, which were no doubt his own private venture: there were also about two piculs of tea, carefully stowed at the ship's side, either a private venture or brought as gifts to friends. There was nothing in all this to show why the ship had been deserted. Why, in the name of wonder, had she been deserted?

The slop-chest was the next thing examined. It was in one of the little cabins off the alleyway. It had been neatly kept. All the stores were in pigeon-holes, marked with tickets that showed the contents and the quantity remaining. Though the ship was homeward-bound, the slop-chest contained a fair number of articles, pipes, tobacco, matches, foul-weather clothing, sou'-westers, knives, shoes, etc., not yet taken up. Cruiser helped himself to several things of which he stood in need. There was a neatly-kept account-book of the slops. Cruiser, looking through it, saw that Rodmarton's brother had drawn a pound of tobacco from them only three days before.

'There'll be nothing down here,' Cruiser thought to himself. 'I'd better search the chart-room.'

He went up again to the little hard, bare, chart-room which still seemed haunted by Captain Miserden. He had looked through the upper drawers in the lockers there, when hoping to find instruments, charts or the ship's log. These had all been removed; but there were other lockers in the cabin, under the settee, and these he had not yet looked at. He pulled open one. It contained a few blue linen handkerchiefs, some writing pads and pencils, a box of dividers, a pair of protractors, a little French guide to Navigation, and a cardboard box containing spare sextant mirrors done up in tissue paper. He shut this drawer and opened another, wondering where the Captain had kept his clothes. 'I suppose,' he thought, 'I suppose his steward has them in some locker below.'

The second drawer contained a row of books, placed backs upward along the drawer so as to chock each other. These books had seen a good deal of service, they were much used, and had been more than once in salt water. Cruiser took out the first volume which came to hand: it had not been thrust well home into the row and seemed indeed to be offering itself to his hand. It was a mean sort of book in a bad binding and ill print. He opened it at the title page and read:

> Habakkuk Unveiled.
> Mudde.

On the flyleaf was the Captain's signature, in a bold, flowing, well-formed sea-hand – R. Miserden, Capt. 1857 – with a note below, in fainter ink:

'I bought this Book for my Eternal Salvation at the house of the Prophet, 27, Seacole Lane, Millwall, on my 35th Birthday –

R.M.'

On the title page, the purpose of the book was declared.

Habakkuk Unveiled
being an Interpretation of the Prophecies
Concerning the Destruction of the World
Now shortly to happen
The whole being a Revelation of the Prophet's
Mission
granted in Vision to the Prophet's Follower,
Ebenezer Mudde
of the First church of Habakkuk. The year of
Wrath, 1853.

He glanced at the book, which contained a fiery doctrine about the coming of the end of the world. Miserden had read it very carefully, with ejaculations pencilled in the margin, such as: 'Lord grant it.' 'O that I may see it.' 'Hark to truth,' etc. Under one fiery passage at a chapter ending he had written: 'This light is too blinding.'

*

(Masefield's explanation of a ship abandoned as a consequence of the master's religious mania was not as uncommon as might be supposed. There are several such reported occurrences, one of the most intriguing being the voyage of the barque *Usk* from Newport towards Valparaiso in 1860 which changed course off the Falkland Islands, the Captain appearing on deck and ordering the vessel home because of a vision of the Almighty in which he saw the ship destroyed by fire. He explained that he could not proceed around Cape Horn with such a threat hanging over him and the vessel put back for Newport with her cargo hatches unopened. The Captain was instantly dismissed but on the next voyage with a new master, the *Usk* rounded the Horn, exploded into flames and was quickly destroyed off Valparaiso Bay.)

Nicholas Monsarrat

FLYING DUTCHMAN COUNTRY

(from *The Cruel Sea*)

FOR *Compass Rose*, there were special times which stuck in the memory, like insects of some unusually disgusting shape or colour, transfixed for ever in a dirty web which no cleansing element could reach.

There was the time of the Dead Helmsman (all these occasions had distinctive labels, given them either when they happened, or on later recollection. It simplified the pleasure of reminiscence). This particular incident had a touch of operatic fantasy about it which prompted Morell to say, at the end: 'I think we must have strayed into the Flying Dutchman country': it was a cold blooded dismissal, but that was the way that all their thoughts and feelings were moving now.

The ship's lifeboat was first seen by Baker, during the forenoon watch: it was sailing boldly through the convoy, giving way to no man, and pursued by a formidable chorus of sirens as, one after another, the ships had to alter course to avoid collision. The Captain, summoned to the bridge, stared at it through his glasses: he could see that it must have been adrift for many days – the hull blistered, and the sail, tattered and discoloured, had been strained out of shape and spilled half the wind. But in the stern the single figure of a helmsman, hunched over the tiller, held his course confidently: according to the strict rule of the road he had, as a sailing-ship, the right of way, though it took a brave man to put the matter to the test without, at least, paying some attention to the result.

It seemed that he was steering for *Compass Rose*, which was a sensible thing to do, even if it did give several ships' captains heart failure in the process: the escorts were better equipped for dealing with survivors, and he probably realized it. Ericson stopped his ship, and waited for the small boat to approach: it held its course steadily, and then, at the last moment, veered with a gust of wind and passed close under *Compass Rose*'s stern. A seaman standing on the depth-charge rails threw a heaving-line, and they all shouted: the man, so far from making any effort to reach them, did not even look up, and the boat sailed past and began to draw away.

'He must be deaf,' said Baker, in a puzzled voice. 'But he can't be blind as well . . .'

'He's the deafest man you'll ever meet,' said Ericson, suddenly grim. He put *Compass Rose* to 'slow ahead' again and brought her round on the same course as the boat was taking. Slowly they overhauled it, stealing the wind so that presently it came to a stop, someone in the waist of the ship threw a grappling-hook across, and the boat was drawn alongside.

The man still sat there patiently, seeming unaware of them.

The boat rocked gently as Leading-Seaman Phillips jumped down into it. He smiled at the helmsman: 'Now then, chum!' he called out encouragingly – and then, puzzled by some curious air of vacancy in the face opposite, he bent closer, and put out his hand. When he straightened up again, he was grey with shock and disgust.

He looked up at Lockhart, waiting above him in the waist of the ship.

'Sir,' he began. Then he flung himself across and vomited over the side of the boat.

It was as Ericson had guessed. The man must have been dead for many days: the bare feet splayed on the floor-boards were paper thin, the hand gripping the tiller was not much more than a claw. The eyes that seemed to stare so boldly ahead were empty sockets, some sea-bird's plunder: the face was burnt black by a hundred suns, pinched and shrivelled by a hundred bitter nights.

The boat had no compass, and no chart; the water-barrel was empty, and yawning at the seams. It was impossible to guess how long he had been sailing on that senseless voyage – alone, hopeful in death as in life, but steering directly away from the land, which was already a thousand miles astern.

There was the time of the Bombed Ship, which was the finest exercise in patience they ever had.

It started, in mid-ocean, with a corrupt wireless message, of which the only readable parts were the prefix 'S.O.S.' and a position, in latitude and longitude, about four hundred miles to the north of their convoy. The rest was a jumble of code-groups which, even when 'reconstructed', did not yield much beyond the words 'bomb', 'fire', and 'abandon'. It must have been difficult for *Viperous* to decide whether it was worth detaching an escort for this forlorn effort of detection: there was no reason to suppose that the position given was accurate, and they could ill spare a ship for a long search; and this quite apart from the fact that the message might be false – the result of a light-hearted wireless operator amusing himself, or an attempted decoy by a U-boat, both of which had happened before. But evidently *Viperous* decided that it was worth a chance: her next signal was addressed to *Compass Rose*, and read: 'Search in accordance with S.O.S. timed 1300 today.' A little later she re-opened R/T communication to add: 'Goodbye.'

The first part of the assignment was easy: it boiled down to turning ninety degrees to port, increasing to fifteen knots, and holding that course and speed for twenty-six hours on end. It was the sort of run they all enjoyed, like a dog let off a leash normally in the grasp of the slowest old lady in the world: now there was no restraint on them, no convoy to worry about, no Senior Officer to wake from his siesta and ask them what on earth they were doing. *Compass Rose* raced on, with a rising wind and sea on her quarter sometimes making her sheer widely, till the quartermaster could haul her back on her course again: she was alone, like a ship in a picture, crossing old grey waves towards an untenanted horizon.

She ran all through the night, and all next morning: not a stick, not a sail, not a smudge of smoke did she see: it was a continuous reminder of how vast this ocean was, how formidable a hiding-place. There were hundreds of ships at sea in the Atlantic all the time, and yet *Compass Rose* seemed to have it to herself, with nothing to show that she was not, suddenly, the last ship left afloat in the world.

But when they had run the distance and reached the likely search-area, the phrase 'hiding-place' returned again, this time to mock them. It was mid-afternoon of a brisk lowering February day,

with darkness due to fall within three hours: they were looking fo
a ship which might have been bombed, might have been sunk
might have been playing the fool, might be in a different longitud
altogether, and half-way round the world from this one. On a shee
of squared tracing paper Ericson plotted out a 'box-search' –
course for *Compass Rose* consisting of a series of squares, graduall
extending down wind in the direction the ship should have drifte
Its sides were each seven miles long: every two hours, the are
shifted another seven miles to the north-eastward. Then he laid
off on the chart, so as to keep a check on their final position, an
they settled down to quarter the ocean according to this pattern.

It was very cold. Darkness came down and with it the first dri
of snow: as hour succeeded hour, with nothing sighted and no hir
of a contact on the radar-screen, they began to lose the immediat
sense of quest and to be preoccupied only with the weather. Th
wind was keen, the snow was penetratingly cold, the water racin
past was wild and noisy: these were the realities, and the earl
feeling of urgency in their search was progressively blunted, pro
gressively forgotten. Hours before, it seemed, there *had* been som
thing about a carefully worked out, meticulous investigation
this area; but that was a very long time ago, and the bombed shi
(if she existed) and her crew (if they still lived) were probabl
somewhere quite different, and in the meantime it was excru
ciatingly cold and unpleasant ... At midnight the snow was
whirling blizzard: at 4 a.m., when Lockhart came on watch, it wa
to a bitter, pitch-black darkness that stung his face to the marro
when he had scarcely mounted the bridge.

'Any sign of them?' he shouted to Morell.

'Nothing ... If they're adrift in this, God help them.'

It was 'nothing' all that watch, and 'nothing' when dayligh
came, and 'nothing' all the morning: at midday the wind fell ligh
and the snow diminishing to an occasional drift, wafting gently pas
them as if hoping to be included in a Christmas card. Individuall
without sharing their doubts, they began to wonder if the thing ha
not gone on long enough: the search had taken two days alread
and during the last twenty-four hours they had 'swept' nearly si
hundred square miles of water. The contract could not call for ver

much more . . . 'I've just remembered it's St Valentine's Day,' said Ferraby suddenly to Baker, during the idle hours of the afternoon watch. 'Put it down in the log,' growled Ericson, overhearing. 'There won't be any other entries . . .' It was unusual for him to admit openly to any sort of doubt or hesitation: they felt free now to question the situation themselves, even to give up and turn back and forget about it.

The solid echo which was presently reported on the radar hardly broke through to their attention at first.

But it was the ship all right, the ship they had been sent to find. They came upon her suddenly: she was masked until the last moment by the gently whirling snow, and then suddenly she emerged and lay before them – a small untidy freighter with Swedish funnel-markings. She was derelict, drifting down wind like some wretched tramp sagging his way through a crowd: she listed heavily, her bridge and fore-part were blistered and fire-blackened, and her fore-bridge itself, which seemed to have taken a direct hit from a bomb or a shell, looked like a twisted metal cage from which something violent and strong had ripped a way to freedom. One lifeboat was missing, the other hung down from the falls, half-overturned and empty. There was nothing else in the picture.

Compass Rose circled slowly, alert for any development, but there was no sound, no movement save the snow falling lightly on the deserted upper deck. They sounded their siren, they fired a blank shot: nothing stirred. Presently they stopped, and lowered a boat: Morell was in charge, and with him were Rose, the young signalman, Leading-Seaman Tonbridge, and a stoker named Evans. As they pulled away from *Compass Rose*, Ericson leant over the side of the bridge, megaphone in hand.

'We'll have to keep moving,' he called out. 'This ship is too much of an attraction . . . Don't worry if you lose sight of us.'

Morell waved, but did not answer. He was no longer thinking about *Compass Rose*: he was thinking, with a prickling of his scalp, of what he was going to find when he boarded the derelict.

I am not good at this, he thought, as they pulled across the short stretch of water that separated the two ships: no good at bombs, no good at blood, no good at the brutal elements of disaster . . . When

Leading-Seaman Tonbridge jumped on to the sloping deck with the painter, and made the boat fast, it was all Morell could do to follow him over the side: '*You* go,' his subconscious voice was saying to Tonbridge: 'I'll wait here, while you take a look.' It was not that he was afraid, within the normal meaning of the word: simply that he doubted his ability to deal with the disgusting un-known.

In silence he climbed up and stood on the deck: a tall grave young man in a yellow duffle-coat and seaboots, looking through falling snow towards the outline of the shattered bridge. He said to Stoker Evans: 'Have a look below – see how deep she's flooded, and to Tonbridge: 'Stay by the boat,' and to Signalman Rose 'Come with me.' Then they began to walk forward: their feet rang loudly on the iron deck, their tracks in the snow were fresh, like children's in a garden before breakfast: round them was complete silence, complete empty stillness, such as no ship that was not fun damentally cursed would ever show.

It was not as bad as Morell had expected – in the sense that he did not faint, or vomit, or disgrace himself: the actual details were horrifying. The bridge had taken the full force of a direct hit by a bomb: there had been a small fire started, and a larger one farther forward, between the well-deck and the fo'c'sle. It was difficult to determine exactly how many people had been on the bridge when it was hit: none of the bodies was complete, and the scattered frag ments seemed at a first glance to add up to a whole vanished regiment of men. There must have been about six of them: now they were in dissolution, and their remnants hung like some ap palling tapestry round the bulkheads, gleaming here and there with the dull gleam of half-dried paint. The whole gory enclosure seemed to have been decorated with blood and tissue: ' "When father papered the parlour",' hummed Morell to himself, 'he never thought of this . . .' The helmsman's hand was still clutching the wheel – but it was only a hand, it grew out of the air: tatters of uniforms, of entrails, tufts of hair, met the eye at every turn: on one flat surface the imprint of a skull in profile, impregnated into the paintwork, stood out like a revolting street-corner caricature, sten cilled in human skin and fragments of bone. 'You died with your nouth open,' said Morell, looking at this last with eyes which eemed to have lost thir capacity to communicat sensation to the brain. 'I hope you were saying something polite.'

He walked to the open side of the bridge, high above the water, and looked out. The snow still fell gently and lazily, dusting the surface of the sea for a moment before it melted. There was nothing round them except anonymous greyness: the afternoon light was failing: *Compass Rose* came into view momentarily, and then vanished. He turned back to Rose who stood waiting with his signal lamp, and they stared at each other across the space of the bridge: each of their faces had the same serious concentration, the same wish to accept this charnel-house and be unmoved by it. It was part of their war, the sort of thing they were trained for, the sort of thing they now took in their stride – sometimes without effort, sometimes with . . . I suppose Rose has looked at all this, and looked away again, thought Morell: I suppose he is waiting for me to say something, or to take him down the ladder and away from the bridge. That would be my own choice too . . . He cleared his throat.

'We'll see what Evans has to say, and then send a signal.'

The ship could not be got going again, but she was fit to be towed: though the engine-room and one hold were deeply flooded, the water was no longer coming in and she might remain afloat indefinitely. That was the outline of the signal which Rose presently sent across to the *Compass Rose*: reading it, Ericson had to make up his mind whether to start the towing straight away, or to cast around for the missing boat and its survivors. After two nights adrift in this bitter weather, there was little chance of their being alive; but if the bombed ship would remain afloat, it would not matter spending another day or so on the search. Perhaps Morell had better stay where he was, though: he could keep an eye on things, and there must be a lot of tidying up to do.

'Remain on board,' he signalled to Morell finally. 'I am going to search for the lifeboat, and return tomorrow morning.' Something made him add: 'Are you quite happy about being left?'

Happy, thought Morell: now *there* was a word . . . It was now nearly nightfall: they were to be left alone in this floating coffin for over twelve hours of darkness, with the snow to stare at, the sea to listen to, and a bridge full of corpses for company. ' "Happiness is relative",' he began dictating to Rose, and then he changed his mind. The moment did not really deserve humour. 'Reply: "Quite all right",' he said shortly. Then he called to Tonbridge and Evans, and took them back with him to the bridge. That was where a start must be made.

Morell was never to forget that night. They used the remains of daylight for cleaning up: the increasing gloom was a blessing, making just tolerable this disgusting operation. They worked in silence, hard-breathing, not looking closely at what they were doing: the things they had to dispose of disappeared steadily over the side, and were hidden by the merciful sea. Only once was the silence broken, by Leading-Seaman Tonbridge. 'Pity we haven't got a hose, sir,' he said, straightening up from a corner of the bridge which had kept him busy for some minutes. Morell did not answer him: no one did. The place where they stood, though blurred now by shadow, was eloquent enough.

They made a meal off the emergency rations in the boat, and boiled some tea on the spirit-stove they found in the galley; then they settled down for the night, in the cramped chart-room behind the bridge. There were mattresses and blankets, and a lamp to give them some warmth: it was good enough for one night on board, if they did not start thinking.

Morell started thinking: his thoughts destroyed the hope of sleep, and drove him outside on to the upper deck – there was no comfort in the sleeping men close to him, only anger at the relief they had found: he felt that if he stayed he would have to invent some pretext for waking them up. He made his footfalls soft as he went down the ladder, he made his breathing imperceptible as he crossed the well-deck: the hand that pushed aside the canvas curtain screening the fo'c'sle was the hand of a conspirator. He took a step forward, and felt in front of him a hollow emptiness: he struck a match, and found that he was in a large mess-hall, full of shadows, full of its own deserted silence. The match flared: he saw a long table, with plates set out on it – plates with half-eaten helpings of stew, crumbled squares of bread, knives and forks set down hurriedly at the moment of crisis. None of those meals would ever be finished now: all the men who had set down the knives and forks were almost certainly dead. I am thinking in clichés, he thought, as the match spluttered and went out. But clichés were as effective as thoughts freshly minted, when the reality which they clothed pressed in so closely and backed by such weight of crude fact.

Pursued by ghosts, he walked aft along the snow-covered upper deck. The wind whined on a strange note in the rigging: the water gurgled close under his feet: the ship was restless, needing to fight the sea all the time. There was no comfort to be found under the open sky: the deck held too many shadows, the unfamiliar shape of it had too many surprises. And suppose there were *other* surprises: suppose the ship were not deserted, suppose a mad seaman with an axe rushed him from the next blind corner: suppose he found fresh footprints in the snow, where none of them had trodden.

At the base of the mast a shadow moved. Morell gripped the pockets of his duffle-coat, his nerves screaming. The shadow moved again, sliding away from him.

He roared out: 'Stop!'

The cat mewed, and fled.

Morning came, and with it *Compass Rose*. She had nothing to report – no boats, no survivors – and Morell, in a sense, had nothing to report either. A heaving-line was passed from *Compass Rose*, and then a light grass rope, and then the heavy towing-hawser: there was no windlass to haul this on board the bombed ship, and Morell's party had to man-handle it in foot by foot, straining against a dead weight of wire which at times seemed as if it would never reach them. But finally they made it fast, and gave the signal, and the tow started.

They made less than three knots, even in good weather: it took them ten days of crawling to finish the journey. Each morning, as soon as it was light, Morell waved a greeting to Lockhart: each evening, as 'Darken Ship' was piped, Lockhart waved goodbye to Morell. Day after day, night after night, the two ships crept over the water, both useless save for this single purpose, both doomed by the umbilical tie to be any U-boat's sitting shot. When, at the mouth of the Mersey, they parted at last and Morell came aboard, it was like waking from a nightmare which one had despaired of surviving.

'Sorry to leave?' asked Lockhart ironically, as Morell came up to the bridge.

'No,' answered Morell, fingering his ten-days' growth of beard, 'no, I'm not.' He looked at the ship astern of them, now in the charge of two harbour tugs. 'I may say that the idea of the convict missing his chains is purely a novelist's conception of life.'

There was the time which was rather difficult to label: they mostly knew it as the time of the Captain's Meeting.

This time was on a Gibraltar convoy, a convoy in the same bad tradition of most of the Gibraltar runs: there had been a steady wastage of ships all the way southwards, and although they were now within two days of the end of the trip the U-boat pack was still with them. Ericson seemed to be showing particular interest in a ship in the front line of the convoy: often he would train his glasses on her for minutes at a time, and she was the one he always looked for first as soon as daylight came up. She survived until the last day; and then, when dawn broke after a night of disaster, she was no longer in her station, and her place in the van of the convoy had been taken by the next ship astern.

At first light the customary signal came from *Viperous*:

'Following ships were sunk last night: *Fort James, Eriskay, Bulstrode Manor, Glen MacCurtain*. Amend convoy lists accordingly.'

There was something in Ericson's manner as he read this signal which discouraged comment. He remained on the bridge for a full hour, staring silently at the convoy, before saying suddenly to Wells:

'Take a signal . . . "To Escorts in company, from *Compass Rose*. Please report any survivors you may have from *Glen MacCurtain*".'

The answering signals came in very slowly: they did not make cheerful reading. *Viperous* and two other escorts sent 'NIL' reports. The corvette in the rear position signalled: 'Two seamen, one Chinese fireman.' The rescue-ship detailed to look after survivors sent: 'First Officer, two seamen, one fireman, five lascars.'

They waited, but that seemed to be all. *Glen MacCurtain* must have gone down quickly. Ferraby, who had the watch, said tentatively:

'Not many picked up, sir?'

'No,' said Ericson. 'Not many.' He looked towards the horizon astern of them, and then walked to his chair and sat down heavily.

Presently a merchant ship in the rear of the convoy started flashing to them. Wells took the signal, muttering impatiently to himself: evidently the operating was not up to acceptable Naval standards.

'Message from that Polish packet, sir,' he said to Ericson. 'It's a bit rocky . . . "We did see your signal by mistake",' he read out, his voice slightly disparaging. ' "We have one man from that ship." '

'Ask them who it was,' said Ericson. His voice was quiet, but there was such acute tension in it that everyone on the bridge stared at him.

Wells began to flash the question, signalling very slowly, with frequent pauses and repetitions. There was a long wait; then the Polish ship began to answer. Wells read it out as it came across:

' "The man is fourth officer",' he began. Then he started to spell, letter by letter: ' "E-R-I-C-S-O-N." ' Wells looked up from the signal-lamp. 'Ericson . . . Same name as yours, sir.'

'Yes,' said Ericson. 'Thank you, Wells.'

There was a time, a personal time for Lockhart, which he knew as the time of the Burnt Man.

Ordinarily, he did not concern himself a great deal with looking after survivors: Crowther, the sick-berth attendant, had proved himself sensible and competent, and unless there were more cases than one man could cope with, Lockhart left him to get on with his work alone. But now and again, as the bad year progressed, there was an overflow of injured or exhausted men who needed immediate attention; and it was on one of these occasions, when the night had yielded nearly forty survivors from two ships, that Lockhart found himself back again at his old job of ship's doctor.

The small, two-berth sick-bay was already filled: the work to be done was, as in the old days, waiting for him in the fo'c'sle. As he stepped into the crowded, badly-lit space, he no longer felt the primitive revulsion of two years ago, when all this was new and harassing; but there was nothing changed in the dismal picture, nothing was any the less crude or moving or repellent. There were the same rows of survivors – wet through, dirt-streaked, shivering: the same reek of oil and sea-water: the same relief on one face, the same remembered terror on another. There were the same people drinking tea or retching their stomachs up or telling their story to anyone who would listen. Crowther had marshalled the men needing attention in one corner, and here again the picture was the same: wounded men, exhausted men, men in pain afraid to die, men in a worse agony hoping not to live.

Crowther was bending over one of these last, a seaman whose filthy overalls had been cut away to reveal a splintered kneecap: as soon as he looked the rest of the casualties over, Lockhart knew at once which one of them had the first priority.

He picked his way across the fo'c'sle and stood over the man, who was being gently held by two of his ship-mates. It seemed incredible that he was still conscious, still able to advertise his agony: by rights he should have been dead – not moaning, not trying to pluck something from his breast . . . He had sustained deep and cruel first-degree burns, from his throat to his waist: the whole raw surface had been flayed and roasted, as if he had been caught too long on a spit that had stopped turning: he now gave out, appropriately, a kitchen smell indescribably horrible. What the first touch of salt water on his body must have felt like, passed imagination.

'He got copped by a flash-back from the boiler,' said one of the men holding him. 'Burning oil. Can you fix him?'

Fix him, thought Lockhart: I wish I could fix him in his coffin right now . . . He forced himself to bend down and draw close to this sickening object: above the scored and shrivelled flesh the man's face, bereft of eyelashes, eyebrows, and the front portion of his scalp, looked expressionless and foolish. But there was no lack of expression in the eyes, which were liquid with pain and surprise.

If the man could have bent his head and looked at his own chest, thought Lockhart, he would give up worrying and ask for a revolver straight away . . . He turned and called across to Crowther:

'What have you got for burns?'

Crowther rummaged in his first-aid satchel. 'This, sir,' he said, and passed something across. A dozen willing hands relayed it to Lockhart, as if it were the elixir of life itself. It was in fact a small tube of ointment, about the size of a toothpaste tube. On the label was the picture of a smiling child and the inscription: 'For the Relief of Burns. Use Sparingly.'

Use sparingly, thought Lockhart: if I used it as if it were platinum dust, I'd still need about two tons of it. He held the small tube in his hand and looked down again at the survivor. One of the men holding him said: 'Here's the doctor. He'll fix you up right away,' and the fringeless eyes came slowly round and settled on Lockhart's face as if he were the ministering Christ himself.

Lockhart took a swab of cotton-wool, put some of the ointment on it, swallowed a deep revulsion, and started to stroke, very gently, the area of the burnt chest. Just before he began he said: 'It's a soothing ointment.'

I suppose it's natural that he should scream, thought Lockhart presently, shutting his ears: all the old-fashioned pictures showed a man screaming as soon as the barber-surgeon started to operate, while his friends plied the patient with rum or knocked him out with a mallet . . . The trouble was that the man was still so horrifyingly alive: he pulled and wrenched at the two men holding him, while Lockhart, stroking and swabbing with a mother's tenderness, removed layer after layer of his flesh. For the *other* trouble was that however gently he was touched, the raw tissue went on and on coming away with the cotton-wool.

Lockhart was aware that the ring of men who were watching had fallen silent: he felt rather than saw their faces contract with pity and disgust as he swabbed the ointment deeper and deeper, and the flesh still flaked off like blistered paint-work. I wonder how long this can go on, he thought, as he saw, without surprise, that at one point he had laid bare a rib which gleamed with an astonishing cleanness and astringency. I don't think this is any good, he thought again, as the man fainted at last, and the two sailors holding him turned their eyes towards Lockhart in question and disbelief. The ointment was almost finished: the raw chest now gaped at him like the foundation of some rotten building. 'Die!' he thought, almost aloud, as he sponged once more, near the throat, and a new layer of sinew came into view, laid bare like a lecturer's diagram. 'Please give up, and die. I can't go on doing this, and I can't stop while you're still alive.'

He heard a dozen men behind him draw in their breath sharply as a fresh area of skin suddenly crumbled under his most gentle hand and adhered to the cotton-wool. Crowther, attracted by the focus of interest and now kneeling by his side, said: 'Any good, sir?' and he shook his head. I'm doing wonders, he thought: they'll give me a job in a canning-factory ... Some blood flowed over the rib he had laid bare, and he swabbed it off almost apologetically. Sorry, he thought: that was probably my fault – and then again: Die! Please die! I'm making a fool of myself, and certainly of you. You'll never be any use now. And we'll give you a lovely funeral, well out of sight ...

Suddenly and momentarily, the man opened his eyes, and looked up at Lockhart with a deeper, more fundamental surprise, as if he had intercepted the thought and was now aware that a traitor and not a friend was touching him. He twisted his body, and a rippling spasm ran across the scorched flesh. 'Steady, Jock!' said one of his friends, and: Die! thought Lockhart yet again, squeezing the last smear of ointment from the tube and touching with it a shoulder muscle which immediately gave way and parted from its ligament. Die. Do us all a favour. Die!

Aloud, he repeated, with the utmost foolishness: 'It's a soothing ointment.' But: Die now! his lips formed the words. Don't be obstinate. No one wants you. You wouldn't want yourself if you could take a look. Please die!

Presently, obediently, but far too late, the man died.

There was the time of the Skeletons.

It happened when *Compass Rose* was in a hurry, late one summer afternoon when she had been delayed for nearly half a day by a search for an aircraft which was reported down in the sea, a long way south of the convoy. She had not found the aircraft, nor any trace of it: *Viperous* had wirelessed: 'Rejoin forthwith,' and she was now hurrying to catch up before nightfall. The sea was glassy smooth, the sky a pale and perfect blue: the hands lounging on the upper deck were mostly stripped to the waist, enjoying the last hour of hot sunshine. It was a day for doing nothing elegantly, for going nowhere at half speed: it seemed a pity that they had to force the pace, and even more of a pity when the radar operator got a 'suspicious contact' several miles off their course, and they had to turn aside to investigate.

'It's a very small echo,' said the operator apologetically. 'Sort of muzzy, too.'

'Better take a look,' said Ericson to Morell, who had called him to the bridge. 'You never know . . .' He grinned. 'What does small and muzzy suggest to you?'

To Morell it suggested an undersized man tacking up Regent Street after a thick night, but he glossed over the thought, and said instead:

'It might be wreckage, sir. Or a submarine, just awash.'

'Or porpoises,' said Ericson, who seemed in a better humour than he usually was after being woken up. 'Or seaweed with very big sand-fleas hopping about on top . . . It's a damned nuisance, anyway: I didn't want to waste time.'

In the event, it wasted very little of their time, for *Compass Rose* ran the distance swiftly, and what they found did not delay them. It was Wells – the best pair of eyes in the ship – who first sighted the specks on the surface, specks which gradually grew until, a mile or so away, they had become heads and shoulders – a cluster of men floating in the water.

'Survivors, by God!' exclaimed Ericson. 'I wonder how long they've been there.'

They were soon to know. *Compass Rose* ran on, the hands crowding to the rail to look at the men ahead of them. Momentarily Ericson recalled that other occasion when they had sped towards men in the water, only to destroy them out of hand. Not this time, he thought as he reduced speed: now he could make amends.

He need not have bothered to slow down: he might well have ploughed through the same as last time. He had thought it odd that the men did not wave or shout to *Compass Rose*, as they usually did: he had thought it odd that they did not swim even a little way towards the ship, to close the gap between death and life. Now he saw, through his glasses, that there was no gap to be closed: for the men, riding high out of the water, held upright by their life-jackets, were featureless, bony images – skeletons now for many a long day and night.

There was something infinitely obscene in the collection of lolling corpses, with bleached faces and white hairless heads, clustered together like men waiting for a bus which had gone by twenty years before. There were nine of them in that close corporation: they rode the water not more than four or five yards from each other: here and there a couple had come together as if embracing. *Compass Rose* circled, starting a wash which set the dead men bobbing and bowing to each other, like performers in some infernal dance. Nine of them, thought Morell in horror: what is the correct noun of association? A school of skeletons? A corps?

Then he saw – they all saw – that the men were roped together. A frayed and slimy strand of rope linked each one of them, tied round the waist and trailing languidly in the water: when the ripples of the ship's wash drove two of them apart, the rope between them tightened with a jerk and a splash. The other men swayed and bowed, as if approving this evidence of comradeship . . . But this is crazy, thought Ericson: this is the sort of thing you hope not to dream about. *Compass Rose* still circled, as he looked down at the company of dead men. They must have been there for months. There was not an ounce of flesh under the yellow skins, not a single reminder of warmth or manhood. They had perished, and they had gone on perishing, beyond the grave, beyond the moment when the last man alive found rest.

He was hesitating about picking them up, but he knew that he would not. *Compass Rose* was in a hurry. There was nothing to be gained by fishing them out, sewing them up, and putting them back again. And anyway . . .

'But why roped together?' asked Morell, puzzled as the ship

completed her last circle, and drew away, and left the men behind. It doesn't make sense.'

Ericson had been thinking. 'It might,' he said, in a voice infinitely subdued. 'If they were in a lifeboat, and the boat was being swamped, they might tie themselves together so as not to lose touch during the night. It would give them a better chance of being picked up.'

'And they weren't,' said Morell after a pause.

'And they weren't. I wonder how long – ' But he did not finish that sentence, except in his thoughts.

He was wondering how long it had taken the nine men to die: and what it was like for the others when the first man died: and what it was like when half of them had gone: and what it was like for the last man left alive, roped to his tail of eight dead shipmates, still hopeful, but surely feeling himself doomed by their company.

Perhaps, thought Ericson, he went mad in the end, and started to swim away, and towed them all after him, shouting, until he lost his strength as well as his wits, and gave up, and turned back to join the majority.

Quite a story.

There was the time that was the worst time of all, the time that seemed to synthesize the whole corpse-ridden ocean; the time of the Burning Tanker.

Aboard *Compass Rose*, as in every escort that crossed the Atlantic, there had developed an unstinting admiration of the men who sailed in oil-tankers. They lived, for an entire voyage of three or four weeks, as a man living on top of a keg of gunpowder: the stuff they carried – the lifeblood of the whole war – was the most treacherous cargo of all; a single torpedo, a single small bomb, even a stray shot from a machine-gun, could transform their ship into a torch. Many times this had happened, in *Compass Rose*'s convoys: many times they had had to watch these men die, or pick up the tiny remnants of a tanker's crew – men who seemed to display not the slightest hesitation at the prospect of signing on again, for the same job, as soon as they reached harbour. It was these expendable seamen who were the real 'petrol-coupons' – the things one could

wangle from the garage on the corner: and whenever sailors sa
or read of petrol being wasted or stolen, they saw the cost in lives a
well, peeping from behind the head-line or the music-hall jok
feeding their anger and disgust.

Appropriately, it was an oil-tanker which gave the men i
Compass Rose, as spectators, the most hideous hour of the whol
war.

She was an oil-tanker they had grown rather fond of: she was th
only tanker in a homeward-bound convoy of fifty ships which ha
run into trouble, and they had been cherishing her, as they some
times cherished ships they recognized from former convoys, o
ships with queer funnels, or ships that told lies about their capacit
to keep up with the rest of the fleet. On this occasion, she had wo
their affection by being obviously the number one target of th
attacking U-boats: on three successive nights they had sunk th
ship ahead of her, the ship astern, and the corresponding ship in th
next column; and as the shelter of land approached it became o
supreme importance to see her through to the end of the voyag
But her luck did not hold: on their last day of the open sea, with th
Scottish hills only just over the horizon, the attackers found thei
mark, and she was mortally struck.

She was torpedoed in broad daylight on a lovely sunny after
noon: there had been the usual scare, the usual waiting, the usua
noise of an under-water explosion, and then, from this ship the
had been trying to guard, a colossal pillar of smoke and flame cam
billowing out, and in a minute the long shapely hull was on fir
almost from end to end.

The ships on either side of her, and the ships astern, fanne
outwards, like men stepping past a hole in the road: *Compass Ros*
cut in towards her, intent on bringing help. But no help had ye
been devised that could be any use to a ship so stricken. Alread
the oil that had been thrown skywards by the explosion had bathe
the ship in flame: and now, as more and more oil came gushing ou
of the hull and spread over the water all round her, she became th
centre-piece of a huge conflagration. There was still one gap in th
solid wall of fire, near her bows, and above this, on the fo'c'sle, he
crew began to collect – small figures, running and stumbling i

rious haste towards the only chance they had for their lives. They uld be seen waving, shouting, hesitating before they jumped; and *mpass Rose* crept in a little closer, as much as she dared, and lled back to them to take the chance. It was dangerously, unbearly hot; even at this distance: and the shouting, and the men ving their arms, backed by the flaming roaring ship with her rtain of smoke and burning oil closing round her, completed an thentic picture of hell.

There were about twenty men on the fo'c'sle: if they were going jump, they would have to jump soon . . . And then, in ones and os, hesitating, changing their minds, they did begin to jump: ccessive splashes showed suddenly white against the dark grey of e hull, and soon all twenty of them were down, and on their way ross. From the bridge of *Compass Rose*, and from the men ronging on her rail, came encouraging shouts as the gap of water tween them narrowed.

Then they noticed that the oil, spreading over the surface of the ter and catching fire as it spread, was moving faster than any of e men could swim. They noticed it before the swimmers, but soon e swimmers noticed it too. They began to scream as they swam, d to look back over their shoulders, and thrash and claw their y through the water as if suddenly insane.

But one by one they were caught. The older ones went first, and en the men who couldn't swim fast because of their life-jackets, d then the strong swimmers, without life-jackets, last of all. But rhaps it was better not to be a strong swimmer on that day, beuse none of them was strong enough: one by one they were overken, and licked by flame and fried, and left behind.

Compass Rose could not lessen the gap, even for the last few o nearly made it. Black and filthy clouds of smoke were now ursing across the sky overhead, darkening the sun: the men on e upper deck were pouring with sweat. With their own load of el-oil and their ammunition, they could go no closer, even for ese frying men whose faces were inhumanly ugly with fear and o screamed at them for help; soon, indeed, they had to give und to the stifling heat, and back away, and desert the few that re left, defeated by the mortal risk to themselves.

Waiting a little way off, they were entirely helpless: they stood on the bridge, and did nothing, and said nothing. One of the look outs, a young seaman of not more than seventeen, was crying as he looked towards the fire: he made no sound, but the tears were streaming down his face. It was not easy to say what sort of tears they were – of rage, of pity, of bitterness of watching the men dying so cruelly, and not being able to do a thing about it.

Compass Rose stayed till they were all gone, and the area of sea with the ship and the men inside it was burning steadily and remorselessly, and then she sailed on. Looking back, as they did quite often, they could see the pillar of smoke from nearly fifty miles away: at nightfall, there was still a glow and sometimes a flicker on the far horizon. But the men of course were not there any more; only the monstrous funeral pyre remained.

Oliver Onions

PHANTAS

As Abel Keeling lay on the galleon's deck, held from rolling down it only by his own weight and the sun-blackened hand that lay outstretched upon the planks, his gaze wandered, but ever returned to the bell that hung, jammed with the dangerous heel-over of the vessel, in the small ornamental belfry immediately abaft the main-mast. The bell was of cast bronze, with half-obliterated bosses upon it that had been the heads of cherubs; but wind and salt spray had given it a thick incrustation of bright, beautiful, lichenous green. It was this colour that Abel Keeling's eyes liked.

For wherever else on the galleon his eyes rested they found only whiteness – the whiteness of extreme eld. There were slightly var-ying degrees in her whiteness: here she was of a white that glistened like salt-granules, there of a greyish chalky white, and again her whiteness had the yellowish cast of decay; but everywhere it was the mild, disquieting whiteness of materials out of which the life had departed. Her cordage was bleached as old straw is bleached, and half her ropes kept their shape little more firmly than the ash of a string keeps its shape after the fire has passed; her pallid timbers were white and clean as bones found in sand; and even the wild frankincense with which (for lack of tar, at her last touching of land) she had been pitched had dried to a pale hard gum that sparkled like quartz in her open seams. The sun was yet so pale a buckler of silver through the still white mists that not a cord or timber cast a shadow; and only Abel Keeling's face and hands were black, carked and cinder black from exposure to his pitiless rays.

The galleon was the *Mary of the Tower*, and she had a frightful list to starboard. So canted was she that her mainyard dipped one of its steel sickles into the glassy water, and, had her foremast remained, or more than the broken stump of her bonaventure

mizzen, she must have turned over completely. Many days ago they
had stripped the mainyard of its course, and had passed the sail
under the *Mary*'s bottom, in the hope that it would stop the leak.
This it had partly done as long as the galleon had continued to
glide one way; then, without coming about, she had begun to glide
the other, the ropes had parted, and she had dragged the sail after
her, leaving a broad tarnish on the silver sea.

For it was broadside that the galleon glided, almost imperceptibly, ever sucking down. She glided as if a loadstone drew her,
and, at first, Abel Keeling had thought it was a loadstone, pulling
at her iron, drawing her through the pearly mists that lay like face-
cloths to the water and hid at a short distance the tarnish left by
the sail. But later he had known that it was no loadstone drawing
at her iron. The motion was due – must be due – to the absolute
deadness of the calm in that silent, sinister, three-miles-broad
waterway. With the eye of his mind he saw that loadstone now as
he lay against a gun-track, all but toppling down the deck. Soon
that would happen again which had happened for five days past.
He would hear again the chattering of monkeys and the screaming
of parrots, the mat of green and yellow weeds would creep in
towards the *Mary* over the quicksilver sea, once more the sheer
wall of rock would rise, and the men would run . . .

But no; the men would not run this time to drop the fenders.
There were no men left to do so, unless Bligh was still alive.
Perhaps Bligh was still alive. He had walked halfway down the
quarter-deck steps a little before the sudden nightfall of the day
before, had then fallen and lain for a minute (dead, Abel Keeling
had supposed, watching him from his place by the gun-track), and
had then got up again and tottered forward to the forecastle, his
tall figure swaying, and his long arms waving. Abel Keeling had
not seen him since. Most likely he had died in the forecastle during
the night. If he had not been dead he would have come aft again
for water . . .

At the remembrance of the water Abel Keeling lifted his head.
The strands of lean muscle about his emaciated mouth worked,
and he made a little pressure of his sun-blackened hand on the
deck, as if to verify its steepness and his own balance. The main-

mast was some seven or eight yards away ... He put one stiff leg under him and began, seated as he was, to make shuffling movements down the slope.

To the mainmast, near the belfry, was affixed his contrivance for catching water. It consisted of a collar of rope set lower at one side than at the other (but that had been before the mast had steeved so many degrees away from the zenith), and tallowed beneath. The mists lingered later in that gully of a strait than they did on the open ocean, and the collar of rope served as a collector for the dews that condensed on the masts. The drops fell into a small earthen pipkin placed on the deck beneath it.

Abel Keeling reached the pipkin and looked into it. It was nearly a third full of fresh water. Good. If Bligh, the mate, was dead, so much the more water for Abel Keeling, master of the *Mary of the Tower.* He dipped two fingers into the pipkin and put them into his mouth. This he did several times. He did not dare to raise the pipkin to his black and broken lips for dread of a remembered agony, he could not have told how many days ago, when a devil had whispered to him, and he had gulped down the contents of the pipkin in the morning, and for the rest of the day had gone waterless ... Again he moistened his fingers and sucked them; then he lay sprawling against the mast, idly watching the drops of water as they fell.

It was odd how the drops formed. Slowly they collected at the edge of the tallowed collar, trembled in their fullness for an instant, and fell, another beginning the process instantly. It amused Abel Keeling to watch them. Why (he wondered) were all the drops the same size? What cause and compulsion did they obey that they never varied, and what frail tenuity held the little globules intact? It must be due to some Cause ... He remembered that the aromatic gum of the wild frankincense with which they had parcelled the seams had hung on the buckets in great sluggish gouts, obedient to a different compulsion; oil was different again, and so were juices and balsams. Only quicksilver (perhaps the heavy and motionless sea put him in mind of quicksilver) seemed obedient to no law ... Why was it so?

Bligh, of course, would have had his explanation; it was the

Hand of God. That sufficed for Bligh, who had gone forward th
evening before, and whom Abel Keeling now seemed vaguely and
as at a distance to remember as the deep-voiced fanatic who had
sung his hymns as, man by man, he had committed the bodies of
the ship's company to the deep. Bligh was that sort of man; ac
cepted things without question; was content to take things as they
were and be ready with the fenders when the wall of rock rose ou
of the opalescent mists. Bligh too, like the waterdrops, had his
Law, that was his and nobody else's . . .

There floated down from some rotten top up aloft, a flake o
scurf, that settled in the pipkin. Abel Keeling watched it dully as i
settled towards the pipkin's rim. When presently he again dipped
his fingers into the vessel the water ran into a little vortex, drawing
the flake with it. The water settled again; and again the minute
flake, determined towards the rim and adhered there, as if the rim
had power to draw it . . .

It was exactly so that the galleon was gliding towards the wall o
rock, the yellow and green weeds, and the monkeys and parrots
Put out into mid-water again (while there had been men to put her
out) she had glided to the other wall. One force drew the chip i
the pipkin and the ship over the tranced sea. It was the Hand o
God, said Bligh . . .

Abel Keeling, his mind now noting minute things and now
clouded with torpor, did not at first hear a voice that was
quakingly lifted up over by the forecastle – a voice that drew
nearer to an accompaniment of swirling water.

> 'O Thou, that Jonas in the fish
> Three days didst keep from pain,
> Which was a figure of Thy death
> And rising up again – '

It was Bligh singing one of his hymns:

> 'O Thou, that Noah keptst from flood
> And Abram, day by day,
> As he along through Egypt passed,
> Didst guide him in the way – '

The voice ceased, leaving the pious period uncompleted. Bligh was alive, at any rate . . . Abel Keeling resumed his fitful musing.

Yes, that was the Law of Bligh's life, to call things the Hand of God; but Abel Keeling's Law was different. The Hand of God, that drew chips and galleons, must work by some method; and Abel Keeling's eyes were dully on the pipkin again as if he sought the method there . . .

Then conscious thought left him for a space, and when he resumed it was without obvious connection.

Oars, of course, were the thing. With oars, men could laugh at calms. Oars, that only pinaces and galliasses now used, had had their advantages.

But oars (which was to say a method, for you could say if you liked that the Hand of God grasped the oar-loom, as the Breath of God filled the sail) – oars were antiquated, belonged to the past, and meant a throwing-over of all that was good and new and a return to fine lines, a battle-formation abreast to give effect to the shock of the ram, and a day or two at sea and then to port again for provisions. Oars . . . no. Abel Keeling was one of the new men, the men who swore by the line-ahead, the broadside fire of sakers and demi-cannon, and weeks and months without a landfall. Perhaps one day the wits of such men as he would devise a craft, not oar-driven (because oars could not penetrate into the remote seas of the world) – not sail-driven (because men who trusted to sails found themselves in an airless, three-mile strait, suspended motionless between cloud and water, ever gliding to a wall of rock) – but a ship . . . a ship . . .

> 'To Noah and his sons with him
> God spake, and thus said He:
> A cov'nant set I up with you
> And your posterity – '

It was Bligh again, wandering somewhere in the waist. Abel Keeling's mind was once more a blank. Then slowly, slowly, as the water drops collected on the collar of rope, his thought took shape again.

A galliasse? No, not a galliasse. The galliasse made shift to be two things, and was neither. This ship, that the hand of man should one day make for the Hand of God to manage, should be a ship that should take and conserve the force of the wind, take it and store it as she stored her victuals; and rest when she wished, going ahead when she wished; turning the forces both of calm and storm against themselves. For, of course, the force must be wind – stored wind – a bag of the winds, as the children's tale had it – wind probably directed upon the water astern, driving it away and urging forward the ship, acting by reaction. She would have a wind-chamber, into which wind would be pumped with pumps. Bligh would call that equally the Hand of God, this driving-force of the ship of the future that Abel Keeling dimly foreshadowed as he lay between the mainmast and the belfry, turning his eyes now and then from ashy white timbers to the vivid green bronze-rust of the bell above him . . .

Bligh's face, liver-coloured with the sun and ravaged from inwards by the faith that consumed him, appeared at the head of the quarter-deck steps. His voice beat uncontrolledly out.

> 'And in the earth here is no place
>   Of refuge to be found,
> Nor in the deep and water-course
>   That passeth under ground – '

2

Bligh's eyes were lidded, as if in contemplation of his inner ecstasy. His head was thrown back, and his brows worked up and down tormentedly. His wide mouth remained open as his hymn was suddenly interrupted on the longdrawn note. From somewhere in the shimmering mists the note was taken up, and there drummed and rang and reverberated through the strait a windy, hoarse, and dismal bellow, alarming and sustained. A tremor ran through Bligh. Moving like a sightless man, he stumbled forward from the head of the quarter-deck steps, and Abel Keeling was aware of his gaunt figure behind him, taller for the steepness of the deck. As that vast empty sound died away, Bligh laughed in his mania.

'Lord, hath the grave's wide mouth a tongue to praise Thee? Lo, again – '

Again the cavernous sound possessed the air, louder and nearer. Through it came another sound, a slow throb, throb – throb, throb – Again the sounds ceased.

'Even the Leviathan lifted up his voice in praise!' Bligh sobbed.

Abel Keeling did not raise his head. There had returned to him the memory of that day when, before the morning mists had lifted from the strait, he had emptied the pipkin of the water that was the allowance until night should fall again. During that agony of thirst he had seen shapes and heard sounds with other than his mortal eyes and ears, and even in the moments that had alternated with his lightness, when he had known these to be hallucinations, they had come again. He had heard the bells on a Sunday in his own Kentish home, the calling of children at play, the unconcerned singing of men at their daily labour, and the laughter and gossip of the women as they had spread the linen on the hedge or distributed bread upon the platters. These voices had rung in his brain, interrupted now and then by the groans of Bligh and of two other men who had been alive then.

Some of the voices he had heard had been silent on earth this many a long year, but Abel Keeling, thirst-tortured, had heard them, even as he was now hearing that vacant moaning with the intermittent throbbing that filled the strait with alarm ...

'Praise Him, praise Him, praise Him!' Bligh was calling deliriously.

Then a bell seemed to sound in Abel Keeling's ears, and as if something in the mechanism of his brain had slipped, another picture rose in his fancy – the scene when the *Mary of the Tower* had put out, to a bravery of swinging bells and shrill fifes and valiant trumpets. She had not been a leper-white galleon then. The scrollwork on her prow had twinkled with gilding; her belfry and stern-galleries and elaborate lanterns had flashed in the sun with gold; and her fighting-tops and the warpavasse about her waist had been gay with painted coats and scutcheons. To her sails had been stitched gaudy ramping lions of scarlet say, and from her mainyard, now dipping in the water, had hung the broad two-tailed pennant with the Virgin and Child embroidered upon it ...

Then suddenly a voice about him seemed to be saying, '*And a*

half-seven – and a half-seven – ' and in a twink the picture in Abel
Keeling's brain changed again. He was at home again, instructing
his son, young Abel, in the casting of the lead from the skiff they
had pulled out of the harbour.

'*And a half-seven!*' the boy seemed to be calling.

Abel Keeling's blackened lips muttered: 'Excellently well cast,
Abel, excellently well cast!'

'*And a half-seven – and a half-seven – seven – seven –* '

'Ah,' Abel Keeling murmured, 'that last was not a clear cast –
give me the line – thus it should go . . . ay, so . . . Soon you shall sail
the seas with me in the *Mary of the Tower*. You are already perfect
in the stars and the motions of the planets; tomorrow I will instruct
you in the use of the backstaff . . .'

For a minute or two he continued to mutter; then he dozed.
When again he came to semi-consciousness it was once more to the
sound of bells, at first faint, then louder, and finally becoming a
noisy clamour immediately above his head. It was Bligh. Bligh, in
a fresh attack of delirium, had seized the bell-lanyard and was
ringing the bell insanely. The cord broke in his fingers, but he thrust
at the bell with his hand, and again called aloud:

'Upon an harp and an instrument of ten strings . . . let Heaven
and Earth praise Thy Name! . . .'

He continued to call aloud, and to beat on the bronze-rusted
bell.

'*Ship ahoy! What ship's that?*'

One would have said that a veritable hail had come out of the
mists; but Abel Keeling knew those hails that came out of the mists.
They came from ships which were not there. 'Ay, ay, keep a good
look-out, and have a care to your lode-manager,' he muttered
again to his son . . .

But, as sometimes a sleeper sits up in his dream, or rises from his
couch and walks, so all of a sudden Abel Keeling found himself on
his hands and knees on the deck, looking back over his shoulder. In
some deep-seated region of his consciousness he was dimly aware
that the cant of the deck had become more perilous, but his brain
received the intelligence and forgot it again. He was looking out
into the bright and baffling mists. The buckler of the sun was of a

more ardent silver; the sea below it was lost in brilliant evaporation; and between them, suspended in the haze, no more substantial than the vague darknesses that float before dazzled eyes, a pyramidal phantom-shape hung. Abel Keeling passed his hand over his eyes, but when he removed it the shape was still there, gliding slowly towards the *Mary*'s quarter. Its form changed as he watched it. The spirit-grey shape that had been a pyramid seemed to dissolve into four upright members, slightly graduated in tallness, that nearest the *Mary*'s stern the tallest and that to the left the lowest. It might have been the shadow of the gigantic set of reed-pipes on which that vacant mournful note had been sounded.

And as he looked, with fooled eyes, again his ears became fooled:

'*Ahoy there! What ship's that? Are you a ship? . . . Here, give me that trumpet –* ' Then a metallic barking. '*Ahoy there! What the devil are you? Didn't you ring a bell? Ring it again, or blow a blast or something, and go dead slow!*'

All this came, as it were, indistinctly, and through a sort of high singing in Abel Keeling's own ears. Then he fancied a short bewildered laugh, followed by a colloquy from somewhere between sea and sky.

'*Here, Ward, just pinch me, will you? Tell me what you see there. I want to know if I'm awake.*'

'*See where?*'

'*There on the starboard bow. (Stop that ventilating fan; I can't hear myself think.) See anything? Don't tell me it's that damned Dutchman – don't pitch me that old Vanderdecken tale – give me an easy one first, something about a sea-serpent . . . You did hear that bell, didn't you?*'

'*Shut up a minute – listen –* '

Again Bligh's voice was lifted up.

> 'This is the cov'nant that I make:
> From henceforth nevermore
> Will I again the world destroy
> With water, as before.'

Bligh's voice died away again in Abel Keeling's ears.

'Oh – my – fat – Aunt – Julia!' the voice that seemed to come from between sea and sky sounded again. Then it spoke more loudly. 'I say,' it began with careful politeness, 'if you are a ship, do you mind telling me where the masquerade is to be? Our wireless is out of order, and we hadn't heard of it . . . Oh, you do see it, Ward, don't you? . . . Please, please tell us what the hell you are!'

Again Abel Keeling had moved as a sleep-walker moves. He had raised himself up by the belfry timbers, and Bligh had sunk in a heap on the deck. Abel Keeling's movement overturned the pipkin, which raced the little trickle of its contents down the deck and lodged where the still and brimming sea made, as it were, a chain with the carved balustrade of the quarter-deck – one link a still gleaming edge, then a dark baluster, and then another gleaming link. For one moment only Abel Keeling found himself noticing that that which had driven Bligh aft had been the rising of the water in the waist as the galleon settled by the head – the waist was now entirely submerged; then once more he was absorbed in his dream, its voices, and its shape in the mist, which had again taken the form of a pyramid before his eyeballs.

'Of course,' a voice seemed to be complaining anew, and still through that confused dinning in Abel Keeling's ears, 'we can't turn a four-inch on it . . . And, of course, Ward, I don't believe in 'em. D'you hear Ward? I don't believe in 'em, I say . . . Shall we call down to old A.B.? This might interest His Scientific Skippership . . .'

'Oh, lower a boat and pull out to it – into it – over it – through it – '

'Look at our chaps crowded on the barbette yonder. They've seen it. Better not give an order you know won't be obeyed . . .'

Abel Keeling, cramped against the antique belfry, had begun to find his dream interesting. For, though he did not know her build, that mirage was the shape of a ship. No doubt it was projected from his brooding on ships of half an hour before: and that was odd . . . But, perhaps, after all, it was not very odd. He knew that she did not really exist; only the appearance of her existed; but things had to exist like that before they really existed. Before the *Mary of the Tower* had existed she had been a shape in some man's imagination; before that, some dreamer had dreamed the form of a ship with oars, and before that, far away in the dawn and infancy of the world, some seer had seen in a vision the raft before man had ventured to push out over the water on his two planks. And since this shape that rode before Abel Keeling's eyes was a shape in his, Abel Keeling's, dream, he, Abel Keeling, was the master of it. His own brooding brain had contrived her, and she was launched upon the illimitable ocean of his own mind . . .

> 'And I will not unmindful be
> Of this, My cov'nant, passed
> 'Twixt Me and you and every flesh
> Whiles that the world should last.'

sang Bligh, rapt . . .

But as a dreamer, even in his dream, will scratch upon the wall by his couch some key or word to put him in mind of his vision on the morrow when it has left him, so Abel Keeling found himself seeking some sign to be a proof to those to whom no vision is vouchsafed. Even Bligh sought that – could not be silent in his bliss, but lay on the deck there, uttering great passionate Amens and praising his Maker as he said, upon an harp and an instrument of ten strings. So with Abel Keeling. It would be the Amen of his life to have praised God, not upon a harp, but upon a ship that should carry her own power, that should store wind or its equivalent as she stored her victuals, that should be something wrested from the chaos of uninvention and ordered and disciplined and subordinated to Abel Keeling's will . . . And there she was, that ship-shaped thing of spirit-grey, with the four pipes that resembled a phantom organ now broadside and of equal length. And the ghost-crew of that ship were speaking again . . .

The interrupted silver chain by the quarter-deck balustrade had now become continuous, and the balusters made a herring-bone over their own motionless reflections. The spilt water from the pipkin had dried, and the pipkin was not to be seen. Abel Keeling stood beside the mast, erect as God made man to go.

With his leathery hand he smote upon the bell. He waited for the space of a minute, and then cried:

'Ahoy! . . . Ship ahoy! . . . What ship's that?'

3

We are not conscious in a dream that we are playing a game the beginning and end of which are in ourselves. In this dream of Abel Keeling's a voice replied:

'*Hallo, it's found its tongue . . . Ahoy there! What are you?*'

Loudly and in a clear voice Abel Keeling called: 'Are you a ship?'

With a nervous giggle the answer came:

'*We are a ship, aren't we, Ward? I hardly feel sure . . . Yes, of course, we're a ship. No question about us. The question is what the dickens you are.*'

Not all the words these voices used were intelligible to Abel Keeling, and he knew not what it was in the tone of these last words that reminded him of the honour due to the *Mary of the Tower*. Blister-white and at the end of her life as she was, Abel Keeling was still jealous of her dignity; the voice had a youngish ring; and it was not fitting that young chins should be wagged about his galleon. He spoke curtly.

'You that spoke – are you the master of that ship?'

'*Officer of the watch,*' the words floated back; '*the captain's below.*'

'Then send for him. It is with masters that masters hold speech,' Abel Keeling replied.

He could see the two shapes, flat and without relief, standing on a high narrow structure with rails. One of them gave a low whistle, and seemed to be fanning his face; but the other rumbled something into a sort of funnel. Presently the two shapes became three. There was a murmuring, as of a consultation, and then suddenly a new voice spoke. At its thrill and tone a sudden tremor ran through Abel Keeling's frame. He wondered what response it was that that voice found in the forgotten recesses of his memory.

'*Ahoy!*' seemed to call this new yet faintly remembered voice. '*What's all this about? Listen. We're His Majesty's destroyer Sea-pink, out of Devonport last October, and nothing particular the matter with us. Now who are you?*'

'The *Mary of the Tower*, out of the Port of Rye on the day of Saint Anne, and only two men – '

A gasp interrupted him.

'*Out of WHERE?*' the voice that so strangely moved Abel Keeling said unsteadily, while Bligh broke into groans of renewed rapture.

'Out of the Port of Rye, in the County of Sussex . . . nay, give ear, else I cannot make you hear me while this man's spirit and flesh wrestle so together! . . . Ahoy! Are you gone!' For the voices had become a low murmur, and the ship-shape had faded before Abel Keeling's eyes. Again and again he called. He wished to be informed of the disposition and economy of the wind-chamber . . .

'The wind-chamber!' he called, in an agony lest the knowledge almost within his grasp should be lost. 'I would know about the wind-chamber . . .'

Like an echo there came back the words, uncomprehendingly uttered, '*The wind-chamber? . . .*'

'. . . that driveth the vessel – perchance 'tis not wind – a steel bow that is bent also conserveth force – the force you store, to move at will through calm and storm . . .'

'*Can you make out what it's driving at?*'

'*Oh, we shall all wake up in a minute . . .*'

'*Quite, I have it; the engines; it wants to know about our engines. It'll be wanting to see our papers presently. Rye Port! . . . Well, no harm in humouring it; let's see what it can make of this. Ahoy there!*' came the voice to Abel Keeling, a little strongly, as if a shifting wind carried it, and speaking faster and faster as it went on. '*Not wind, but steam; d'you hear? Steam, steam. Steam in eight Yarrow water-tube boilers. S-t-e-a-m, steam. Got it? And we've twin-screw triple expansion engines, indicated horse-power four thousand, and we can do 430 revolutions per minute; savvy? Is there anything your phantomhood would like to know about our armament? . . .*'

Abel Keeling was muttering fretfully to himself. It annoyed him that words in his own vision should have no meaning for him. How did words come to him in a dream that he had no knowledge of when wide awake? The Seapink – that was the name of this ship;

but a pink was long and narrow – low-cargoed and square-bui
aft ...

'*And as for our armament,*' the voice with the tones that
profoundly troubled Abel Keeling's memory continued, '*we've tu
revolving Whitehead torpedo-tubes, three six-pounders on th
upper deck, and that's a twelve-pounder forward there by t
conning-tower. I forgot to mention that we're nickel steel, with
coal capacity of sixty tons in most damnably placed bunkers, a
that thirty and a quarter knots is about our top. Care to con
aboard?*'

But the voice was speaking still more rapidly and feverishly, as
to fill a silence with no matter what, and the shape that was utte
ing it was straining forward anxiously over the rail.

'*Ugh! But I'm glad this happened in the daylight,*' another voi
was muttering.

'*I wish I was sure it was happening at all ... Poor old spook!*'

'*I suppose it would keep its feet if her deck was quite vertic
Think she'll go down, or just melt?*'

'*Kind of go down ... without wash ...*'

'*Listen – here's the other one now –*'

For Bligh was singing again:

> 'For, Lord, Thou know'st our nature such
>   If we great things obtain,
> And in the getting of the same
>   Do feel no grief or pain,
>
> 'We little do esteem thereof;
>   But, hardly brought to pass,
> A thousand times we do esteem
>   More than the other was.'

'*But oh, look – look – look at the other! ... Oh, I say, wasn't he
grand boy! Look!*'

For, transfiguring Abel Keeling's form as a prophet's form
transfigured in the instant of his rapture, flooding his brain with th
white eureka-light of perfect knowledge, that for which he and h
dream had been at a standstill had come. He knew her, this ship

e future, as if God's finger had bitten her lines into his brain. He
ew her as those already sinking into the grave know things, mir-
ulously, completely, accepting Life's impossibilities with a
dded 'Of course.' From the ardent mouths of her eight furnaces
the last drip from her lubricators, from her bed-plates to the
eeches of her quick-firers, he knew her – read her gauges,
umbed her bearings, gave the ranges from her range-finders, and
ed the life he lived who was in command of her. And he would
t forget on the morrow, as he had forgotten on many morrows,
r at last he had seen the water about his feet, and knew that there
uld be no morrow for him in this world . . .

And even in that moment, with but a sand or two to run in his
ass, indomitable, insatiable, dreaming dream on dream, he could
t die until he knew more. He had two questions to ask, and a
aster-question; but a moment remained. Sharply his voice rang
t.

'Ho, there! . . . This ancient ship, the *Mary of the Tower*,
nnot steam thirty and a quarter knots, but yet she can sail the
aters. What more does your ship? Can she soar above them, as
e fowls of the air soar?'

'*Lord, he thinks we're an aeroplane! . . . No, she can't . . .*'

'And can you dive, even as the fishes of the deep?'

'*No . . . Those are submarines . . . we aren't a submarine . . .*'

But Abel Keeling waited for no more. He gave an exulting
uckle.

'Oho, oho – thirty knots, and but on the face of the waters – no
ore than that? Oho! . . . Now *my* ship, the ship I see as a mother
es full-grown the child she has but conceived – *my* ship, I say –
o! *my* ship shall . . . Below there – trip that gun!'

The cry came suddenly and alertly, as a muffled sound came
om below and an ominous tremor shook the galleon.

'*By jove, her guns are breaking loose below – that's her finish –*'

'Trip that gun, and double-breech the others!' Abel Keeling's
ice rang out, as if there had been any to obey him. He had
aced himself within the belfry frame; and then in the middle of
e next order his voice suddenly failed him. His ship-shape, that
r the moment he had forgotten, rode once more before his eyes.

This was the end, and his master-question, apprehension for the answer to which was now torturing his face and well-nigh bursting his heart, was still unasked.

'Ho – he that spoke with me – the master,' he cried in a voice that ran high, 'is he there?'

'Yes, yes!' came the other voice across the water, sick with suspense. 'Oh, be quick!'

There was a moment in which hoarse cries from many voices, heavy thud and rumble of wood, and a crash of timbers and a gurgle and a splash were indescribably mingled; the gun under which Abel Keeling had lain had snapped her rotten breeching and plunged down the deck, carrying Bligh's unconscious form with it. The deck came up vertical and for one instant longer Abel Keeling clung to the belfry.

'I cannot see your face,' he screamed, 'but meseems your voice a voice I know. *What is your name?*'

In a torn sob the answer came across the water:

'*Keeling – Abel Keeling . . . Oh, my God!*'

And Abel Keeling's cry of triumph, that mounted to a victorious 'Huzza!' was lost in the downward plunge of the *Mary of the Tower*, that left the strait empty save for the sun's fiery blaze and the last smoke-like evaporation of the mists.

Alun Richards

THE SEARCH

(from *Ennal's Point*)

The R.N.L.I. lifeboat Samuel Grail *has been launched to search for a missing fishing vessel, the* Gay Lady, *whose skipper, Billy John Grail, is the son and grandson of previously drowned lifeboat coxwains from the little village of Ennal's Point in the Bristol Channel. Severe storm force winds and a force ten gale are raging and the Lifeboat Secretary, Geoffrey Hannah, a middle-aged schoolmaster who narrates the account, has been taken along as the coxwain, Jack Tustin, is short-handed. Aboard are Stick Watts, a seventy-year-old veteran of forty years lifeboat service, Ned Spelling, a young draughtsman, Animal Morgans, a forklift truck driver, engineer mechanic George Peace, and Benny Dance, a labourer. All are volunteers and the mission is handicapped by lack of definite information as to the whereabouts of the* Gay Lady. *There is also present in every man's mind the knowledge that previous lifeboats from the village have been overwhelmed with total loss of life in precisely the same storm conditions in the same area of search, the Bristol Channel having the second highest rise and fall of tide in the world.*

Our journey to the Taskar Spur had taken us an hour, the run in to the coast along the rocky shelves on either side accounted for another hour and by the time we withdrew to search the approaches, and completed the first of our expanding squares, nearly three hours had gone in all, and now we were still searching continuously under the wide arcs of light cast by the slowly falling parachute flares, and I am sure that everyone in the cockpit had come to realize that there was very little hope of sighting anything off the Taskar. The weather had kept up, the wind continuing to blow from the south-west and joined with the tide which still

173

flooded so that we were continuously feeling the full blast of th
elements, needing the drogue when the sea came lumpily behin
us, and tripping it when we faced it, so that although we foun
nothing, and sighted nothing, the taxing of our energies was a con
stant process, tiredness setting in like premature old age an
making even the act of sitting an effort.

Jack took a spell off the wheel, leaving it to Stick and nov
Animal had replaced Benny Dance in the after part of the littl
cockpit, George Peace assisting him. George had busied himself i
the tiny engine room below the cockpit but he was as familiar witl
all the routine deck jobs as any man aboard, and while Jack rested
his head in his hands in front of me, I maintained my own vigi
beside Stick at the wheel. Stick, a fussier helmsman than Jack
corrected himself more often, increasing our speed slightly, seem
ing to be a more demanding taskmaster, and not allowing th
R.N.L.B. *Samuel Grail* any latitude. He had rested himself and nov
as we began a longer sweep of the sea some five miles off the Spu
it was Jack's hope that some sighting of the *Gay Lady* might b
made if she were being carried back down the channel by th
making tide. We assumed her powerless and the best we coul
hope for was some half submerged wreck being washed in with on
or two half drowned souls aboard. At worst, there would be som
recognizable debris, a lifeboat, a mast or broken spar, perhaps sev
eral bodies roped together in the water. But even these sombr
sights would be some consolation, we felt, and at least would caus
a signal to be made enabling those who still searched along th
shore to relax.

But we saw nothing, hour after hour, and now it had grow
darker and colder and we were all silent once more, each man lef
with his thoughts, and as I stood, holding on to the rim of th
cockpit and peering out at the sloping waves, I was conscious o
Stick Watts beside me, his eyes squinting as he steadied himself, hi
wrists thinner and seeming more frail than Jack's as he fussed at th
wheel. He was giving her no rein with the result that she drov
her bow under more often and clouts of spray came driving bac
along the deck. Animal was on deck, aft of the cockpit with th
parachute gun in his hand, searching to port while I scanned th

ea to starboard, and as the spray came champing back at us,
Animal got wetter and wetter and I could hear him muttering, his
urses drowned by the staccato pounding of the gouts of water
which hammered upon his oilskins. Stick did not nurse her like
ack did, and where you would have expected an older man to be
lower and more patient, it was not so. Stick, like some ancient
ailing-ship helmsman believed in getting the most out of a full
lout, and while Animal kept muttering, Stick kept staring ahead
with a fixed expression on his face that said such men were born to
uffer and why should you be a lifeboatman if you were afraid of a
ttle water! Watching him, I remembered a story of my father's of
he Sveynton copper ore barques when some of the crew would get
rostbite and one of the most notorious captains would instruct the
ailmaker to sew their frostbitten fingers together with a line of
hread so that at best, they could still claw at the canvas with their
njured palms and take in some sail when under special threat of
he fist. Listening to these stories, you knew then what short-
anded meant, and Stick's lined face, orange-tinted by the bin-
acle light, had almost ceased to be human as he drove us on and
n, the spray shooting upwards and returning, making the search
ll the more difficult.

It was between ducking from these clouts of spray that Animal
ot a sight of this object in the water and this sighting marked the
ise of Animal, a change in this relatively subdued creature with us
p to this moment.

'There!' shouted Animal. 'Over there! Starboard!'

'Fix it!' said Stick.

'I am bloody fixing it!'

Stick brought one hand down on the throttle controls, easing her
own and bringing the bow around so that Animal could continue
o fix his eyes on whatever he had seen. But even this slight alter-
tion of course presented the driving sea with an enlarged area
gainst which to strike and within seconds our starboard rail went
nder as we heeled and a green sea came lumpily aboard sweeping
own the deck, three or four feet of water rising like a wall and
eeming undiminished by the scuppers through which it was al-
owed to exit and Animal was forced to cling for his life.

The shout had roused Jack who rose to look aft.

'There!' said Animal. Although waist deep in water, he had never taken his eyes from the object.

'Put her arse to it,' shouted Jack.

Stick brought the bow around once more so that again we felt the seas lurch behind us and with one eye cocked for the sea and another on Jack's outstretched arm which now signalled to him, Stick eased us around, then straightened, and then put her astern so that we dropped backwards, the bow parting the sea once more, a necessary surgery since we did not want to be pitch-poled or to roll under, likely circumstances I did not care to think about.

'Oh, Christ!' I heard Jack swear. 'Benny, get a boathook.'

My own vision was impaired as we inched our way astern. We could not do so continuously since the seas never lessened, one wave in four still topping twenty feet and even this simple manoeuvre was fraught with danger. But finally, there came a moment when we formed a brief lee when the object in the water was caught by the boathook and brought aboard.

It was a diesel fuel can, one of those five gallon Army cans in widespread use after the war and normally painted green, but as they heaved it into the cockpit, it was clear that it had recently been painted grey, and admiralty grey, the colour with which Captain Waldo was said to have transformed the appearance of the old *Venturer* so that she became the *Gay Lady*. Now we all looked at the can as a hateful thing.

'Open it,' Jack said.

The locking cap presented no difficulties.

Benny sniffed inside.

'Diesel,' he said. 'Red, about half full.'

We could tell that the paint was recent since the grey coated sides were free of scratch marks and unchipped. Even around the mouth which would normally have been scratched by the filler cap of a vessel's fuel tank as the diesel was poured out, the paint was unblemished. It had hardly been used since it was painted.

'You don't have to be Scotland Yard to know what that's from,' Animal said. 'It's dockyard paint. Fell off a lorry into Waldo's bloody lap.'

We all looked at the fuel container and then Jack went back out to the mouth of the cockpit to signal the coastguard while we continued to stare, and Stick, who had never looked around, kept her head to the seas.

'Ennal's Point Coastguard, this is Ennal's Point Lifeboat. Ennal's Point Coastguard, this is Ennal's Point Lifeboat. Do you read me?'

Perhaps I have not made it clear how cramped we were but you will do well to imagine the interior of a London taxi travelling backwards, the bonnet pushing the cab, the lifeboat wheel in a place corresponding to the bonnet of the engine where Jack Tustin stood, Stick beside him, and forward of them, under cover at a slightly lower level, the seats ran parallel along each side. Here six men could sit facing each other in the covered part of the cockpit. We could also touch hands if we stretched across, and the floor was divided by a centre rib along which each man braced his feet. Thus, although we faced each other, we could look backwards and upwards at Jack whose face continued to be illuminated by the binnacle light and behind him, on either side of the superstructure, we could see the sea when it rose behind us, and at times that was all we could see for it blotted out the sky, literally seeming to curl over us like an immense cupped hand that never quite closed.

I could look across and see George and Ned while I sat between Benny Dance and Animal and now I was conscious of all eyes upon Animal, and I could even feel Animal through his oilskins for his shoulder was jammed up against mine and as his great thighs began to twitch, and his feet brace harder, I could sense that the monster was weakening. We were all soaking wet, of course, and when we veered from our course, very often gouts of water entered the cockpit from the stern, and below the fiddly grating in the deck which acted as a kind of wooden drain, water was continually sloshing before being emitted through the unseen exit ports. The cockpit was like a colander, and the colander never stopped moving, but it never moved in exactly the same way, and although there was no shame and every excuse for all the wretched feelings in the world, the fact that Animal Morgans was feeling the strain, that the great stomach of Animal Morgans, itself a veteran of countless launches and a thousand self-inflicted tortures, being overworked day and night by whatever was stoked into it on every possible occasion – that this foolproof organ was about to crack was news indeed. So we all watched sharp-eyed like soaking penguins squatting alongside him, noting each desperate pretence of the victim with avid clinical interest. First, he bit his lip savagely in an attempt to stop the continual yawning, then, this failing, attempted by a massive straining of leg and limb to separate the centre rib from the deck, but it was no use and he succumbed suddenly and violently without even time to stand and lurch for the open part of the cockpit, and there was a great and violent outpouring and a marked change of colour upon his face, until gasping and ashen and tearful, he became one with the rest of us.

But the excuses continued, as graphic as the crime.

'It's this bastard carbon-uncle. I got the pus right through me. Affecting the entire blood stream, it is.'

But then he was sick again, and I would do us all less than justice if I did not record that we were happy then, and that even Jack and Stick, who had been able to steal fleeting glances at us, now noted this event, and looked ahead at the raging sea with immense cheerfulness. Stick spoke for the first time.

'Drop of quality stuff, that.'

Even off the Taskar we had our moments, but no sooner had our spirits lifted than the weather began to worsen, and once we had moved away to complete our last sweep in the clover leaf pattern, it soon became obvious that our own safety was a matter of concern and now we experienced the first of those freak waves which defy the logic of the sea. It came as we were preparing to trip the drogue once more as we headed for the Taskar in a final sweep when over our stern there came a wall of water, frothing at the ridge and tumbling downwards, fortunately catching us with the drogue set but boarding us, a small mountain of water dropping neatly along the decks and then broadening out and filling the cockpit so that for a second the men sitting were floating, totally submerged, and then the cockpit being designed to shed water in seconds, it seemed to clear, but did not clear for there was another wave, the Siamese twin of the first and so the cockpit filled again and down we went by the stern, down, down, and under, and in that second Animal slid from his seated position and disappeared from beside me, all of us breathing water while above us, on the partially submerged roof of the cockpit, there came a fearful rattling like the crackling of several whips and we fought to regain our breath, Stick having been swept into the cockpit and knocked partially unconscious. Now we realized that real damage had been done. The crackling noise overhead was caused by the porcelain insulators of the radio aerial which had been brought down by the sea. The radio receiver and all our signal equipment was also soaked and the mouthpiece of the radio telephone twisted on its broken flex like a child's toy as it banged metallically against the instrument cases.

When the cockpit cleared eventually, Benny sat Stick beside him. Stick's false teeth had been lost and his old man's hand rubbed his cheeks ruefully.

Animal squinted across. 'You want to claim on them. A bit sharp.' The R.N.L.I. would hear about the lost teeth if Animal had his way. 'Gold, was they?'

Jack remained married to the wheel. We had not wavered by more than a few points from our course. We saw him try the radio telephone, then grimace.

'U.S.' Jack said. 'We'll have to play it by ear from now on.'

For myself, I expected the search to be called off there and then. But having sighted nothing further Jack told us that he proposed to run down to the Lark's Head. The fuel can might have drifted in from that precise direction, but none of us had the slightest hope of finding even a body and as for anything else the night might bring, I am sure most of us were wholly and totally indifferent by now. It was in this state of sullen and resentful weariness that Ned Spelling resumed his watch beside Jack and saw a loom of light far off in the sky, an orange blush upon the underside of a cloud seen in a second and held there as if the door of a furnace had been momentarily opened and shut.

'There!' came the cry again. 'Starboard – two o'clock!'

But no one else saw it.

'Homesick, are you?' Animal said.

It was the worst thing he had said all night, or ever in my hearing, but I was too weary to protest and I had long ago given up.

'Lightship?' Benny Dance said.

'Not the lightship,' said Stick with a look at the compass. 'Can't be. Not if the compass is right.'

Jack now gave the wheel to Benny as we began the long haul to the Lark, and came himself into the shelter to question Ned after we had all scanned the sky for this mysterious loom of light.

'Orange. I saw it. I definitely saw it,' Ned said.

'They wouldn't have flares on a boat of Waldo's,' George Peace said.

'I didn't say it was a flare, it was just orange, a patch of orange – like from a fire.'

'At two o'clock?'

'Yes. And I saw it,' Ned said. 'I definitely saw it.'

His face was earnest, even tearful, and his mouth drooped. Such were the disapproving glances, you could guess that he wished he hadn't seen it, and now that we had no possibility of checking with the coastguard on the radio, Jack had to make up his mind un-aided. The sighting was far out to sea. It would take us an hour and more to continue on our present course to the Lark's Head, longer if we were distracted by this present sighting, if it was a sighting. And Ned was eighteen, next to myself, the most inex-perienced man there.

'Won't be the lightship,' Stick said. 'Not sou'west of here.' With-out his teeth, his sucked-in cheeks aged him even further, his wizened features in striking contrast to Ned's schoolboy sulkiness.

'Right!' Jack said.

'What?' said Animal.

'We'll do the Lark on the way back.'

'On the way back? From where?'

'If he says he saw a light, he saw a light,' Jack said.

Once more, he resumed his position on the wheel with Benny Dance beside him, and now we headed into the weather once more, our six knots a snail's pace as we pushed onwards free of the drogue since the danger now came from the bow, and slowly, the Taskar fell behind us. In a strange way, once more we had forgotten Billy John, and to a man inside the cockpit, I am sure our resentment fell upon Ned Spelling and Jack Tustin and it was as if these doers amongst us were suddenly surrounded by a well informed committee of doubters who saw them as they really were, a foolish boy and a stubborn obstinate man who conspired to offend us further.

'Can't be the lightship,' Stick said again. He had a picture of the Bay and its approaches in his mind and he knew exactly where the lightship should be in relation to our course. He thought in points of the compass, and not in degrees and kept saying, 'not sou'west – never.'

'I wish you'd shut up about the Lightship,' Animal said.

'Well, it can't be. Not south'ard of here.'

'Well, I definitely saw it,' Ned said. 'No doubt.'

'You sure it wasn't your hair in your eyes? Or maybe a hair clip?' said Animal.

'It was orange,' Ned said. 'Like a furnace door opening. Just a glow.'

'They could be burning rags,' Stick said. He had not forgotten the *Gay Lady*.

'After being out all day in this?'

'He'd know he'd have to show a light,' George said.

'Who would?'

'Billy John.'

It was the first time his name had been openly mentioned. Animal did not reply, but I shared his pessimism. I did not believe in the orange light, and after our experience it was impossible that an old boat, less well found than ours, could possibly have survived. I wanted no false optimism, no vain hope, no wild goose chase. We had tried and failed, I thought. Now let us go back home to bed.

We were now heading for the open sea into the greater reaches of the channel mouth and towards the Atlantic Ocean itself, and there came tiredly drifting into my mind a nagging worm of doubt as to the seaworthiness of our re-engined craft.

For the moment, we were free of the dangers astern, but when we came to turn on our eventual run down to the Lark, we would have

an ocean behind us, a whole ocean, and all its tumbling waters.
Once again, I remembered Amy Tustin's phrase, that we were
little men in a little craft who were sometimes expected to do more
than was humanly possible.

Then there came the voice of the new enemy.

'What's wrong with a bit of a song then?' Jack said from the
wheel – like some benign but demented scoutmaster.

'Yes,' said Animal bitterly. 'I got it. "That old bastard orange
light's still burning . . ." '

Now we headed blindly for the open sea, and the first noticeable
difference from the plunging courses we had made off the Taskar
came with a difference in the movement of the lifeboat. She did
not so much move forward as slither in an upward direction as the
oncoming waves grew higher, and when she climbed, she did not
ascend in a straight line but did so at an angle across the belly of
each wave, and there seemed to be a constant problem in keeping
her in the water at all. If the whole body of the lifeboat were not
picked up equally by the water as we rose to the peak of each wave,
there was an imminent danger that she would stand upon her stern
and be thrown back upon herself, pitch-poled into oblivion like a
lazily thrown caber. Hence we tried to climb at an angle, slithering
upwards and it was a climb that seemed to take an age as the seas
grew in height, but this, with our bodies straining with anticipation
and the boathooks flapping in their strops along the guard rails like
a woman's skirt fluttering above a lift shaft, and every rivet pro-
testing individually – all this was the easiest and safest part of this
mad journey. This was only the ascent, it was the descent which
stole your heart, your stomach, pressed in upon your ears and
squeezed back your eyeballs and in turn, lifted up all reason and
sent it flying away as if reason had taken physical shape and left
you, skidding away as fragile as a leaf in a violent wind.

First we reached the crest of the wave, and the crests were
broken now, a wide lip of white water surging and frothing and
from which curtains of spume rose – but there was still air up there,
air and sky, and the sight of other waves building up ominously
immediately in front. When we eased over the crest and our de-

scent began, however, the downward plunge seemed a sheer drop. You felt you had left the sea and had suddenly taken off as the twenty-three tons of lifeboat became all missile and your legs weakened to pap, twitched and trembled as a hurdler's might after attempting some suicidal jump across a crevice – and failing. Suddenly – but never – never ever predictably – we were hurtled downwards like some weighted beetle inside a great bubble of water. And it was then that the air went, disappeared altogether as we were central in a huge plume of spray created by the weight of the lifeboat itself and you could not breathe at all and you gaped and gasped as a fish gasps, experiencing the sea's final irony, but even this torture did not end anything for having begun a descent, you had to complete it.

And the completion was another minor death to reason for when we landed, nose into the trough, all way was abruptly taken off the lifeboat by her weight and now the engines laboured and whined, faltered and coughed, until the propellers could bite and push forward and it was the same insane slithering upwards once more, the coxswain's hands fighting the wheel in order to stand the boat across the new wave so that once more she would keep her body in the water and not be pitch-poled by the new enemy. The waves came every minute or so, and all the while the spray beat at you from for'ard, from aft, and worst of all, from above, for when we were at our lowest point, the spray descended. But it was not so much spray then as gouts of water coming down as fiercely as from some riot policeman's shrewdly aimed water cannon – and then, often, after some particularly vicious descent, or some minor error of judgement on the coxswain's part – the water hit the back of the neck, spurted down the small of your back, and twice in an hour, Jack Tustin's sea boots were filled with water running down the back of his neck from above. It made a noise too, this spray, beating down upon our oilskins, and when we rose, the second man in the cockpit – it was Benny Dance at first – had to steady the compass which turned over and over in the gimbals, revolving like a metal target in a fairground and presenting its blank underside for inspection as often as its face so that steering an accurate course was by guess and by God for the most part. But on and on we went, upwards and downwards, switchbacking, quartering and 'arsing' as Animal put it, often in danger of coming back upon ourselves, and in the little cockpit which was as full of water as a fish tank, we heard Jack say, 'Sharp look-out!' to Benny while we clung on, heads bent, eyes closed, stomachs capitulated completely, and all the time the worst, most terrifying, most awful suffocating thing, was this feeling of wanting to prise open your nostrils because they had ceased to work on the downward plunge.

'Sharp look-out, port and starboard!' the cry came again – as from an idiot under a waterfall.

Now George Peace was also out there in the exposed part of the cockpit, perhaps the freshest of us, but he was not fresh for long for he too had his boots filled from above. The water not only sapped at your reason, it raped you, violating the body from all sides.

'Have a good squint on the crests,' Jack said. 'A light, remember – you'll see a blush first.'

But it was impossible, I thought, and it was more than impossible, it was madness. Then the cry came once more, the same cry, and the same angle of vision.

'Starboard – on the quarter!'

Fortunately, we seemed to hover on this wave and there was no doubt of the sighting. Now the loom of light was much larger and it was clearly the reflection of a fire.

I did not see it then, I only saw the relief on Ned Spelling's face and the flash of Jack's teeth as he grinned and it was not until another age had passed when I, too, went into the cockpit, and as we rose once more, I saw what Jack had already seen, the awesome shape of an old three island tramp steamer poised like ourselves on another crest, her masts silhouetted, her ancient stove pipe funnel whose casing had been removed, nodding jerkily in the gale, a movement as predictable and regular as a nervous tic, and from around her forward hold, there came an ugly orange billowing of smoke as she rolled to her scuppers, then disappeared again, her steerage crippled. We were close enough now to smell the sickly burning of some sulphurous substance which drifted across the sea and followed us in our next plunge.

'Well, I'm buggered!' Jack said. That was all.

Soon we got her name, *Andrea Z*, and her port of registry was Panama.

The sea had played its usual trick, a complete surprise without rhyme or reason, and from now on, our search for Billy John Grail seemed like a game we had begun to play but abandoned long ago in that dimly remembered past when all of us were warm and dry.

I have said that one of the effects of our battering, sea-sickness and fatigue, was that our reason diminished and our thinking power, like our legs, seemed to be effective only in fits and starts. When you are tired, it is important to do the right thing automatically. The body has to react if the mind does not, but all the rules, all the reasons for training had escaped me, and I, like the others, had but to wait as we approached the casualty. We seemed to be inching towards the *Andrea Z*. At a quarter of a mile she presented a shape to the eye no more than an inch long and we only saw her when we were both on respective crests of ascending waves at the same time. There were minutes when she was not there at all, and the waves soon showed that they were not there for our convenience, for two or three minutes passed when we had no sight of her and I began to hope that she had gone altogether for our spume-choked lungs continued to heave in the downward plunges and I knew that even so simple an act as picking up a lifebelt out of the water would be a hazardous exercise in this boiling sea, leave alone attempting to get alongside a stricken vessel on fire. But Jack had taken a rough bearing and kept our course and told me later that he was glad of the slowness of our passage for it gave him time to work out his plan of action. The longer we took the more detailed could his assessment be. 'I knew it wasn't going to be a dawdle!' he said.

It was not long before we began to realize that the sulphurous fumes did not come alone for soon we heard a series of explosions that came at irregular intervals and then continued for all the time that we were in company with the *Andrea Z* and although we did not know it, the chemical fire beside her hold forward was another attack on reason for she carried drums of sodium, one of the few cargoes which ignites on contact with water, and it was not long

before these explosions were visible as well as audible and we coul
see the drums being hurled upwards into the air, revolving slow
as they were ejected by the heat of the blaze so that we could act
ally read the letters of the manufacturer's imprint painted up
their sides. They did not just erupt in the air like popgun corks, the
burst, and when they burst, a shower of orange flame, sparks ar
billowing yellow smoke haloed the ship and now streams of liqu
fire descended and stayed alight upon the water so that the area
sea forward of the *Andrea Z*'s bow was a lake of fire, a lake fed
further streams which came from her welldeck and ran out of t
forward scuppers, more drums following the others and also e
ploding, to provide a continuous display. To say that there was
cauldron of fire forward is somehow inadequate for the area of fi
was much larger than the ship, the sea itself was on fire in
expanding arc before the bow and the smoke from beside the hol
whose hatches had long disintegrated, blew across the sea towar
us in a great spiral whirled this way and that by the followir
wind, the spiral, small at the base and widening into a mushroo
shape as it rose like the smoke from some infernal Aladdin's lamp
   Thus we could see the top of the mushroom when we could n
see the ship and we knew we were closing. Our next sight includ
the little group of men clustered on her bridge. They had not se
us and it was obvious that the *Andrea Z* was further crippled sin
she seemed to have only partial steerage and maintained an o
course, showing her stern quarter to the following sea and descen
ing each trough sideways, rolling as she did so, so that you could s
into that hold and down her funnel for a second, and then wh
she rolled in the contrary direction, her weather side scuppers we
under and you could see the rust on her bottom, her superstructu
well nigh disappearing. She was also yawning as she rolled and h
lifeboats swung in and out on their davits, one already partial
loosened and destroyed but they would be useless in that sea and
was soon clear that all her master could do was to keep on in th
halting course, attempting always to ensure that the wind stay
behind him so that the fire blew out from the hold away from t
ship and did not come back into his face and destroy the bridge
it would have done if she put her head to the weather. In th

ent, the whole ship would have been engulfed, all steerage way
ne and then she would be totally encircled by flame and the men
oard could not even jump into the water.

We drew closer and closer.

'Parachute flare,' Jack said. 'Show 'em we're here.'

Their view of us, as was ours of them, depended on the courtesy
the sea – of us rising to the crests of separate waves simultane-
sly, and at first, they must have believed that our signal was a part
their own inferno, but soon we closed and it was clear that her
dder was partially jammed in a starboard position, giving her
ly partial steering and her master had to tickle and caress her on
r course. There came a moment when a small figure no bigger
an a matchstick actually came to the edge of her bridge and
red at us, but in those winds heading us and following him, gusts
aching seventy or so miles an hour, no one could stand upright in
exposed position and no signals were exchanged until we had
mped into her. All the dwarfed figures aboard were as still as
ectators at a funeral and as Jack slowly made a heading –
aving a look-see!' – it seemed impossible that we should ever get
em off.

The most obvious course would be to run in at them from the
eather side, breaking all the rules to do so, placing ourselves be-
een the ship and the sea and the wind so that the smoke and fire
uld blow away from us, but such a course of action with the
aves rising and falling from twenty to thirty feet now, would very
ely result in our being smashed against the side of the *Andrea Z*
we were not actually picked up by the sea and deposited on
ard, a circumstance which had happened once in lifeboat history
my knowledge, and was not at all unlikely in these conditions.
t we could not approach from the weather side, and the lee, or
eltered side, when the ship could shelter us with its own bulk, was
ver the same for any length of time as her movement was unpre-
ctable. Now there was a portion of the stern that offered shelter,
t it was momentary for when she wallowed, her bow came round
d then she steamed towards us, then fell away, and then she was
the trough, her decks more clearly visible than her profile. When
e righted, she was barely holding course and now that we had

closed to within a hundred yards, we were ourselves in danger
being struck by the drums which continued to be ejected from h
hold, exploding sometimes in the air as a result of the heat, or
the water whose contact was lethal, in both cases flooding the poi
of impact with a small lake of fire.

It was so bad it was laughable, and there was no exercise,
standard drill, no handbook of instructions which could ever pr
dict such an eventuality, and the closer we got, like a drunken a
lurching around a petrol fire, the more we endangered ourselves.

Jacks' voice came at last like some sleep-walker's with mea
ingless instructions.

'What we're going to do is surf in with her.'

It made no sense. Later we would say that we attempted
steam a converging course, but we simply did not know what w
were doing and if Jack had any idea, it was hardly conveye
Each conversation was difficult for the noises of our own progre
were interrupted by the accompanying sound of explosions an
what we saw also seemed to have a mysteriously diminishing effe
on what we were able to hear. Perhaps we did not want to hear –
certainly did not – nor to see – and all the time, the *Andrea Z* w
never still, pitching and rolling, yawing, dipping her bow, and onc
she showed only her propeller which seemed to come out of th
water like some obscene entrail as she plunged downwards and w
were like men looking after her as she disappeared down into a
immense engulfing hole.

'Sneak in,' Jack said. 'Animal and Benny – ready on the bow.'

Stick took a position beside him at the wheel, while Animal an
Benny left the cockpit and lurched forward. We were now behin
the *Andrea Z*'s lee side to stern of her, a wave or two behind h
and approaching at a slight angle and this was a relief for the fi
was in front and blowing away from us, and for a moment it w
visually one of those situations as might be drawn by a marin
artist and depicted on the Lifeboat Institution's Christmas Card
with Animal and Benny crouched in the bow, busying themselv
with the heaving line, Animal kneeling so that when the bow ros
his head and shoulders rose with it, silhouetted against the blac
lump of the *Andrea Z*'s stern. Ahead of them on the portrait, th

flames would shoot off the canvas and the whole on that wild night was such a sight as would make you click your tongue with admiration beside your Christmas tree. The manoeuvre, in short, looked as if it were going to work, and if recorded, you would be sure that the artist had caught the moment of moments, had amply demonstrated that these were men amongst men who would give their all willingly. Artistically, the odd detail of the unnaturally bright flames and that yellow sulphurous smoke would add a livid hue to the traditional elements of fire and water and naturally, you would presume that the rescue would be neatly effected.

But the position was held only for a second for we fell off when there came a large wave as we manoeuvred and it crashed upon us and our converging course and at that moment, Jack overcorrected the wheel and we were immediately in difficulty for the wave broke over us broadside on and hundredweights of water came pouring over on us, hurtling down on Animal and Benny clinging there on the foredeck in that exposed position. Benny lost his footing and his grip, and was washed half the length of the deck, being hurtled along the scuppers so that Jack left the wheel to grab him as he came shooting past the cockpit and we nearly rolled over, Jack and Benny flattened in an embrace, volumes of water cascading down upon us. When we rose, and by the time Stick had taken the wheel, we had now passed the stern of the *Andrea Z* to the weather side and there was Animal flattened upon the bow, looking up and cursing back at us, his eyes apoplectic, his mouth snarling, water sheeting from his flattened hair and oilskins as we went headlong for the area of fire with the drums now exploding above us and the picture now was of men bent on self-destruction. It took us ten minutes to circle once more, and when Benny was brought into the cabin he could not speak at all and lay on the deck winded while George Peace took his place.

'George,' Jack said. 'When you get out there, remember, I don't want any ropes trailing in the water.'

George went forward, scuttling like a crab and we saw Animal snarl back at us once more as we took up station astern of the *Andrea Z* yet again. We were going to attempt to put our bow nose on to that flame-free area on her stern quarter and now I felt like saying in the manner of the boxing impresario's, on my right, the propeller still turning and visible every thirty seconds or so – and on my left, fire. It was as evenly matched a duel as ever was, and the opponents were equally spaced, but in we went, this time miraculously seeming to catch up with the *Andrea Z*'s own wave and skating in on her and now there were grey faces looking down upon us, one man in particular, small and moustachioed in a blue jersey and somehow still wearing a battened down trilby hat and looking like a comedian's feed man as he hung on to the lee rail, his mouth opening and closing unheard, but strangely comic still as if what he was saying was a comedian's prayer, the only solution to this madness.

In we went, still riding on the same wave, our bow aimed on that narrowing lee of her quarter and when we bumped, it was surprisingly free of impact and there was a second's calm in that shelter provided by the hull of the ship. It was as if the wind had at last allowed us a brief respite when we could come to the sensible conclusion that we should pack up with the knowledge that we had tried and failed.

George it was, who threw the heaving line, a light rope intended to take the strain of a larger rope later. It had to be thrown upwards from a moving object to a moving object, in fact, to the comedian's feed man who seemed to have some responsibility and it had to traverse a distance that varied from twelve to twenty feet. But he threw it and failed, coiled it up once more and failed again, and was about to coil it a third time when the sea took us sliding towards the fire forward so now we were forced to go astern, parting the seas with our stern, and once again we were all soaked and Animal and George lay flat until we could come to weather once more, turn and pursue the *Andrea Z* who seemed to have increased her speed. This time with increased revolutions ourselves, we hit the target, hit the ship's side with a resounding crash that must have pancaked the bow fender but we held our nose there as securely as if we had stuck right into her, and I, no more than an abject spectator in all this, remember feeling aggrieved and that it was monstrous that nothing at all was being done aboard the *Andrea Z*. Why did they not have heaving lines ready to throw

hemselves? I did not know that it was all they could do to hold
ven the erratic course they were making, and that before they got
ny help at all, the fire had run the length of the ship, passing down
he scuppers on both sides, that her men were even more exhausted
han we, and that, as every lifeboatman knows, however bad you
nay be feeling yourself, your own despair is fractional compared to
hat of those aboard any casualty. Consequently, I felt a blind re-
ntment at their lack of preparation, their seeming inability to
nake the slightest contribution to our efforts, and when we bumped,
was thrown on top of Benny Dance who had barely recovered
rom his last winding, so that Benny being Benny said, 'Sorry!' and
hat again was a further reminder of my inadequacy.

It was Animal's turn to attempt to get a line aboard and again
hat comic foreign figure above seemed to delight in his role and
lapped his hands as he looked downwards. Animal picked up a
econd line, a nylon warp, an inch or so in diameter which he
oiled like a mat, steadying himself as he stood, one of the *An-
rea Z*'s lifeboats now swinging crazily in its davits immediately
bove him. He seemed to take an age to curl it, our bow still being
ushed into the *Andrea Z*'s side by our engines and when he
eaved it upwards, he caught the stem of the swinging ship's life-
oat above and it fell across the lifeboat's canvas cover, then slith-
red away, hopelessly out of reach and fell back once more. George
vith Animal pulled it back aboard as quickly as possible since rope
railing in the water was a coxswain's nightmare in case the pro-
eller fouled. This time we seemed to have glued ourselves to the
Andrea Z for now Animal laid down the nylon rope and took up
he manilla breasting line, a heavier rope still, and he coiled it with
nassive deliberation. I will not forget that sight all my life, Animal
vith his hair flattened, his oilskins drenched, his huge bulk under
is lifejacket and sea boots framed against the *Andrea Z*'s rust
itted sides and that ship's lifeboat clattering in its davits above
im and looking likely to break loose and drop down on us any
econd. Finally, the rope coiled to his satisfaction, he steadied him-
elf and squared his shoulders, moving slowly and calmly like a
eteran Olympic athlete, one of those unfashionable hairy
reatures of the secondary events, the shot-putter or the discus

thrower, and finally hurled it bodily upwards and it fell limp inboard like a half-opened parcel and was made fast, and Anima grinned at it, grinned at the moustachioed, trilby-hatted man grinned back at us, taking time off like an actor waiting for a burst of spontaneous applause but he was no actor, he was the least exhausted of all of us and this was the strength and asssurance that beat the sea, his presence there, a vindication of all his critics, the right man in the right place at the right time.

'Shot, Animal!' Jack Tustin said.

'*Service to the MV Andrea Z of Panama – Saved 10*' had begun although our search for the *Gay Lady* was to continue and we did not see the lights of Ennal's Point again that night.

Shalimar

EASTING DOWN

THE *Knightley*, a tramp steamer of about 5,000 tons gross, was lying in Victoria Basin, Cape Town. Breakfast in the saloon was nearly over. It had been eaten in comparative silence, for the *Knightley* was not a particularly happy ship; the captain and the chief officer thought very little of each other, the captain's thoughts being distinctly the less charitable. Towards the end of the meal there had been some talk about the ship's work, which encouraged the chief officer to get on to his favourite subject – cleanliness, and the slapping on of paint.

'The bulwarks on the fore-deck require chipping very badly, but we'll get that done during the next week or so,' he said. 'Luckily we're in for a fine weather passage.'

'Indeed, Mr Wilkins,' the captain remarked loftily.

He rose and left the saloon. The other officers drained their coffee cups and also prepared to go.

'What's he getting at now?' the chief officer growled.

His officers never knew what Captain Hartnell was getting at, and he certainly never took the trouble to enlighten them. He conveyed the impression that he was much too superior to reach down to their meagre intellects, and the impression was probably a correct one; for if ever a man suffered from the reverse of what in modern jargon is termed a complex of inferiority, that man was Captain Hartnell. With one exception not a man in the ship could ignore his own inferiority when in the captain's presence – the exception being the young third officer, a Scotsman from the Buchan district of Aberdeenshire, who, placid and laconic, had never discovered any reason why he should be either intimidated or unduly impressed even by a successful shipmaster like his captain who had never suffered the slightest check to his meteoric career and was, without doubt, an outstanding seaman.

Still only thirty-two Captain Hartnell had got command of a
barque when he was twenty-four – a great, modern slab-sided
barque that sailormen declared was too slow to get out of her own
way. He had been chock-full of confidence from the moment he
boarded her. Her code number in the International Book of Signals
was MNBS, and on the first night out, bowling down-channel
before a fresh breeze, he was heard reciting a rhyme of his own
composing:

> 'MNBS,
> My name brings success,
> Go, you flat-bottomed scow, go.'

The 'flat-bottomed scow' went so well that he drove her out to
Australia in twenty days less than his predecessor had taken on the
previous voyage, and since that first successful passage he had
never tired of proving to his owners that he was the smartest man
in their employ. Because of that, and the fact that he was at all
times acutely aware of his own merits, he was far from being a
favourite with his brother shipmasters. Tall and muscular, he carried himself with a swagger, and when he passed over the gangway
that forenoon even the independent stevedores on the quay wall
greeted him with respect. He was hardly three yards away from the
ship, however, when an able seaman named Kelly brushed against
him, then lurched unsteadily up the gangway. Kelly had evidently
been ashore all night and looked the worse for wear. It was strange,
the captain thought, that the miserable chief officer had not reported one of the men absent without leave. Perhaps the chief
officer did not even know. Pah!

Captain Hartnell walked on towards the town. The *Knightley*
would be ready for sea in a couple of days and he had some preliminary clearing to do at the agent's office. The work done, he
strolled along to the Grand Hotel and entered the lounge, where he
found an acquaintance, a much older man who commanded
another tramp steamer lying in the same dock. Both vessels were
bound for Port Pirie, South Australia, in ballast, to load zinc con-
centrates, and over their drinks the two masters discussed their
coming passages.

'I'm a couple of knots faster than you, so I'll probably pick you up somewhere to the nor'a'd of New Amsterdam, even if I sail a week later,' the old man chaffed.

'You won't pick me up at all, and certainly not on that route,' Captain Hartnell retorted. 'I'm going to run the easting down!'

'You're going to do *what*?'

'Run the easting down!'

'You'll regret it,' the other man said seriously.

'Why? I've done it in a barque not a quarter the size of the *Knightley*.'

'Oh, certainly; but the barque hadn't got a racing propeller under her counter,' the other said drily. 'What's the idea?'

'To make a quicker passage. Lots of steamers used to do it – the Aberdeen White Star, Shaw Savill, the New Zealand Shipping Company.'

'Yes, they *used* to, Hartnell; they don't now.' The other man sat back comfortably in his chair. 'Anyhow, a fine weather passage along the edge of the south-east trades as far as the hundredth meridian, then south-eastward towards the Australian coast will do me,' he declared. 'I'll probably get all the bad weather I want off the Leeuwin at this time of the year, and I'm not hankering after any more. By the way, didn't you have wireless that time I met you in New York?'

'Yes, but they took it out of her after the war. Hard times, couldn't afford it, the owners said.'

'H'm! false economy on these long voyages!'

Two days later on a bright, calm morning, the *Knightley* hauled out of the docks, rounded Green Point, and stood down the shore of the Cape Peninsula. When the chief officer relieved the second on the bridge at four o'clock in the afternoon the faint outline of Cape Point was astern, and no land was visible along the port beam.

'Sou'-sou'-east! Here, what the – ?' the puzzled chief demanded.

'We're going off to do some exploring in the ruddy Antarctic,' the second answered bitterly. 'Now you know what he was getting at.'

*

195

Running the easting down! Sweeping along the troubled four thousand mile track that leads from the south of the Cape of Good Hope to the Leeuwin at the south-west corner of Australia, before the furious west winds and the rushing seas that sweep without let or hindrance half-way round the globe. Away down in that track less waste of waters that lie beyond the parallel of 45° south latitude a succession of beautiful clippers outward bound for Australia to load the wool clip used to storm along under every stitch of canvas they could safely carry. It was there that day after day week after week, they did the grand sailing that made their wonderful passages possible; today it is deserted except for the fluttering Cape pigeon and the hovering albatross. It was of that gale-swept tract of the great Southern Ocean that Kipling's immortal engineer said if you failed you had time to mend your shaft, even eat it, ere you were spoken, or 'Make Kerguelen under sail, three trysails burned with smoke.'

The *Knightley* had reached a position too far east even for the latter expedient; for the Crozets and Kerguelen were well to windward, and, in any case, she had not got a single sail on board. But failure was, of course, impossible for Captain Hartnell! MNBS! He was the only happy man on board, as Mr Birnie, the third officer, was the only one who was indifferent. The weather was bitterly cold; squall after squall of hurricane force and laden with sleet shrieked out of the north-west, and icy spray lashed the after-deck even though the vessel was in ballast trim and standing high out of the water. Lurching and pitching wildly, she swept to the eastward, throwing her bows high towards the dark flying scud of the squalls, dipping them till she tossed three-quarters of her rudder out of the sea. She was never still for a single moment, night or day; for the liquid ridges that rushed at her port quarter were of an almost incredible steepness, and the valleys between them were cavernous.

Captain Hartnell was happy because his vessel's progress was even swifter than he imagined it would be when he abandoned the fine weather route farther north and stood down into the wild westerlies. The terrific thrust of the favouring wind and waves more than made up for the power wasted by a propeller, the blades of which beat the air almost as much as they churned the sea. He got considerable pleasure from picturing the astonished face of the captain who was going to overhaul the *Knightley* somewhere about New Amsterdam, when he arrived at Port Pirie and found her already half loaded. Mr Birnie, the third officer, was indifferent because, in spite of his placidity and apparent laziness, he was cast in an iron mould; neither cold, wet, nor discomfort worried him in the least. The other two officers were miserable and disgruntled; they felt that life was being incommensurately aggravated by this entirely unnecessary attempt to save a few days on the passage. The chief officer, a much older man than the captain, felt the cold and discomfort particularly; he could not get warm, even in his bunk, and when keeping his watch on the bridge he was weary of staying on his feet. The deck-hands had reached a state bordering on passive insubordination which might easily have deteriorated into something worse, and the chief officer, possessed of a fellow-feeling, did little to check them.

If the discomfort on deck was acute, it was worse in the engine-room and stokehold. The engineer on watch had no difficulty about keeping warm; the propeller, with little more solid than air and spray to bite on half the time, would have sent the engines racing so wildly that they must have shaken themselves to pieces but for his unremitting attention to the throttle. Sweat ran in rivulets through the grime on his face, and every limb ached before the four long hours of his watch had passed. In the stokehold the boilers rocked in their saddles with every plunge; coal aimed at an open fire-door rattled against the boiler plates and rebounded; in the bunkers, trimmers were bruised by coal rumbling down on top of them. The chief engineer, stout-hearted in normal times but now feeling for his men, was sullen and resentful – and sufferance, as a rule, is not the badge of the tribe of sea-going engineers. By that time every man on board knew that there was an easier way to Port Pirie farther north.

Just after breakfast one day the hands of the watch below, weary after four hours of buffeting, were about to turn into their bunks for a short spell of uneasy sleep. Mr Birnie was on the bridge pacing unsteadily to and fro, occasionally grabbing a rail to steady himself against a lurch, but keeping a keen look-out. That was Mr Birnie's

way, though there was really nothing to look out for; they had no
seen a vessel since they left Cape Point and did not expect to se
one; Australia was still two thousand miles away. The *Knightley*
her hull sloping upward towards the bows like the roof of a house
climbed to the crest of a huge, foaming roller, wriggled an
dropped heavily into the succeeding trough. There followed a vio
lent thud that shook her fore and aft as if she had thumped on
rock. Men and officers, certain that she had struck wreckage, fo
there were no rocks about in an ocean that was hundreds o
fathoms deep, streamed out on deck. Captain Hartnell staggere
up to the bridge.

'Put her slow!' he shouted from the top of the ladder.

Mr Birnie rang the telegraph to slow and waited for a reply from
the engine-room.

'Get the carpenter along to sound the bilges and peaks,' th
captain ordered.

Bewildered men were staring aft striving to get a view of th
wake when the stern dipped, but no extraneous object appeared o
the crests of the rollers running up behind. The more pessimisti
suggested low-lying ice which would be difficult to see but stou
enough to damage the vessel. The captain turned on the thir
officer.

'Were you keeping a good look-out?' he demanded.

Mr Birnie stared him straight in the face and hesitated as i
deliberating whether he was keeping a good look-out or not. H
was always deliberate and, if possible, his speech was monosyllabic
the 'sir' he had to use when answering the captain seemed to com
out reluctantly, as an extra effort, and always after a distinct pause

'Yes . . . sir,' he replied at last.

'And you saw no wreckage – nor anything else?'

'No . . . sir.'

Even by Captain Hartnell's exacting standard Mr Birnie was
first-class officer and one to be trusted, so there must be anothe
reason for the thud. The chief engineer came up to the bridge wit
it. He said the young engineer on watch, who was the only perso
in authority close to the bottom of the ship, considered that th
bump was due to the stern plunging into the trough of the sea more

iolently than usual. The carpenter reported the bilges and peaks
dry.

'Put her on full speed again,' the captain said.

For the next seven hours the *Knightley* kept on her tortured
eastward way, climbing wind-swept ridges, swooping down into
dark, half-sheltered valleys; then, shortly after four o'clock, she
again shook fore and aft. The second engineer, who had just relieved the third at the throttle, was startled and badly shaken by a
continuous racing of the engines; they jarred and rattled and
created a resounding pandemonium in the comparatively restric-
ted space of the engine-room; the maze of glimmering brass and
steel – of pistons, connecting rods, and cross-heads – danced and
whirled in a frenzy. The second engineer throttled right down, then
signalled to the bridge by ringing the engine-room telegraph to
stop. The chief engineer discarded the cup of tea he was sipping
and dashed down the iron ladder into the engine-room. The engineers off duty followed. They had an idea that the heavy thump of
the morning must have fractured the shaft, and made their way
into the tunnel. They worked their way aft as far as the stern-
gland, but found the shaft intact. The wooden floor was slippery
with oil and grease, and they had great difficulty in keeping their
feet; for the ship, robbed of her steerage-way and under the
influence of her high forecastle-head, had brought the wind and sea
dead aft and was pitching very heavily. As it is almost impossible
for a tail-shaft to break inside the stern-tube, they came to the
conclusion that it had broken just outside – and that, in fact, was
what had happened, as Mr Birnie had just discovered. Getting up
from his settee, on which he had been trying to sleep, he had made
his way aft, got over the taffrail, leaned out as far as he could over
the sea, and looked down. The steamer's stern had just dipped
downward and over to port; it flew up again with a dizzy lift that
exposed the greater part of the arched propeller aperture. It was
empty; the propeller had gone.

Darkness was coming down. The two red lights which indicated
the vessel was not under command were hoisted. Well down by the
stern, she continued to lie with the wind and towering seas almost

right aft – pitching heavily but lazily. Captain Hartnell retired
his cabin, shut himself in and pondered, while all over the ship, i
cabins and in sailors' and firemen's forecastles, officers and me
discussed the awful thing that had happened. They discussed
with voices that were almost reduced to whispering, for th
prospect was indeed appalling. The accident which had robbe
the ship of her mobility had in it a specially heart-rending quali
because of her extreme isolation. The shock to the imagination w
cruel. To present discomfort had been added an immediate futur
that was black and an ultimate future that would not bear thinkin
about.

On the bridge the chief officer, tired of keeping a useless look-o
and with no helmsman to supervise, went into the chart-room an
pored over the outspread general chart of the South Indian Ocea
The captain had pencilled a neat cross at the estimated positio
where the propeller was lost, but beyond that there was little on th
chart but parallels of latitude and meridians of longitude. Ye
there *was* something else; much nearer than any land was an ir
regular dotted line marking the extreme northern limit of iceberg
The chief officer shivered. In that watery abomination of desc
lation the ship might drift for months without being sighted, unles
the drift was suddenly checked by what the irregular dotted lin
indicated; and if the wind remained in the north-west, that woul
probably be the result of their drifting. If they got that far! Befor
then they might starve to death! For reasons connected with th
Australian customs laws, the captain, a keen business man, ha
only taken sufficient provisions in Cape Town to allow for un
foreseen delays. Total disablement had certainly not been allowe
for, and the chief officer doubted if there was sufficient food o
board to give full rations for another fortnight. Again he shivered
The silence – broken only by the wind that howled outside and th
splash of the waves – and the total lack of vibration were depressin
in the extreme. Tears came into his eyes. The weird feeling that h
had a dead thing under him almost overwhelmed him; and a blac
resentment against the captain, who, in the first place, had bee
given command of the vessel over his head and who had now go
her into this plight, surged up in his heart. The supper bell wen

and the third officer came on the bridge to relieve him.

Supper was eaten in silence. The captain sat like a sphinx at the head of the table, and as soon as he had finished his meal he retired to his cabin again. The chief officer and the second – a somewhat colourless individual – would have liked to know what thoughts were working in that self-reliant brain, what pangs of remorse were tugging at the usually unresponsive heart-strings. They were left in ignorance as far as the pangs were concerned, but the thoughts were soon disclosed. At eight o'clock the captain summoned all the officers and engineers to the saloon. The boatswain was sent on the bridge to allow the third officer to attend; the donkeyman relieved the fourth engineer in the silent engine-room. Very soon those assembled discovered that they had not been called to a conference, or a council of war, or even a discussion of ways and means of carrying out a plan. They had come to be told what the captain proposed to do, and to receive instructions – and what the captain proposed to do was to fit the spare propeller and tail-shaft! Blank incredulity showed on every face but one, and the chief engineer voiced it.

'But . . . but you can't do that at sea,' he spluttered indignantly.

'*Can't!*' the captain repeated with apparent surprise.

'If you knew the trouble it is to fit a propeller and shaft in a sheltered harbour you wouldn't talk like that. With this sea running it's impossible. To begin with, you would have to tip her down by the head till the stern-tube is out of the water.'

'Quite right,' the captain answered calmly. 'We'll make a start at that tomorrow morning. We'll pump out the after-peak and ballast tanks, and flood No. 1 hold.'

'Flood No. 1 hold!' the chief officer shouted hysterically. 'You'll wreck the ship! You'll lose her! What bulkheads would stand a few hundred tons of water washing against them? If they do, she'll roll over with us!'

'We'll have to chance that – unless you can suggest anything else, Mr Wilkins.'

The chief officer did not reply. There was a silent, puzzled pause and a shuffling of feet. Nobody *could* suggest anything else, and all knew it. The chief engineer broke the silence.

'Look here, Captain Hartnell, I'm as keen as you are to try something; God knows I don't want to end my life down here,' he said soberly. 'But I tell you it's quite impossible, especially with this sea running. If you would wait for a calm, even.'

'Calms are scarce in this latitude and we might wait a month,' the captain replied. 'By that time we should be so weak with starvation that we could do nothing.'

'And you propose to have men working under the counter with a ship jumping like this! It's murder! They'll either drown or have their brains bashed out! I tell you straight, none of *my* men will go over the stern!'

'They had better wait till they're asked,' the captain said drily. 'I'm going over the stern myself.'

'So am I!'

The assembled men looked round in astonishment. The speaker was the young third officer who up till then had remained unobtrusively in the background, apparently studying, with an absent mind, the rivets in the beams overhead.

'Thank you, Mr Birnie,' said the captain.

The third officer's prompt offer had a definite, and remedying, effect. It dropped the seeds of doubt, in some cases of shame, into men's minds; it stirred something in their souls and made an appeal for a more robust attitude towards the crisis that had overtaken them. In a flash it was realized by most of them that resentment, no matter how much it may have been justified, would get them nowhere; that their present attitude was unworthy of British seamen. They shuffled their feet and looked at each other, trying to read each others' minds, as if they were strikers afraid of being suspected of blacklegging. The captain quickly sensed their hesitation.

'Gentlemen, this is the crux of the matter,' he said. 'Are we to remain inactive while the ship drifts helplessly towards the ice-fields, or are we prepared to make an effort to save ourselves?'

The engineers nodded in apparent agreement, but the chief officer remained obdurate.

'I tell you it's madness to try and flood the for'a'd hold,' he moaned.

'That's enough,' Captain Hartnell said curtly. 'At six o'clock tomorrow morning get all your hands on to lifting the ceiling in No. 1 lower hold, and stowing the boards securely in the 'tween-decks. The loose water in the hold *might* damage the bulkhead; if those heavy boards were washing about in it they certainly *would*. Perhaps you didn't think of *that*. Chief, as soon as Mr Wilkins reports to you that the manhole doors have been taken off No. 1 ballast tank top, open the sea-cocks and get the hold flooded. At the same time start the pumps on the afterpeak and tanks.'

'Very good, sir,' said the chief engineer.

A quarter of an hour later Captain Hartnell went on the bridge, and after some difficulty, for there was no light even in the useless binnacle, found the third officer leaning against the rail behind the canvas dodger, against which sleet was pattering.

'Mr Birnie, I won't forget this,' he said, 'but there's something else I want you to do. I've been thinking things out, and have come to the conclusion that we shall require another hand under the counter; we can't manage the job by ourselves. Now, I don't want to *order* any man to do the job because the chief engineer certainly didn't exaggerate when he spoke of the dangers of drowning and bashing. We are in for a hell of a time, and if any man refused to take his share in it, he might well be upheld in a court of law. That would place me, as a shipmaster, in a very awkward position – but I don't want to *plead* with any man. Will you look around, pick out a suitable man, and broach him on the quiet?'

'Yes . . . sir,' said Mr Birnie.

A wild, wintry dawn was ushered in by the chattering of the winch for No. 1 hold. It was being used for sending a derrick aloft. Down in the bottom of the hold the carpenter, and some of the seamen, were lifting the heavy three-inch ceiling boards. Those were slung and hove up level with the 'tween-decks, where they were stowed and securely lashed. The ballast tank top was exposed along its full length, and the carpenter took off the manhole doors. All was ready for flooding the hold. The engineers opened the sea-cocks for the tank, which was already full, and the water overflowed into the hold. The pumping out of the after ballast tanks and after-peak began. The *Knightley* was drifting with half a gale dead aft, and still pitching heavily; the seas running up astern were rising right up to the counter as her stern dipped, and falling to the middle pintle of the rudder as it rose. It was about noon before the alteration of the trim took effect and she came on to an even keel. Her bow dipped lower in the water, and, no longer holding the wind, came up to windward, bringing the wind and sea abeam so that the steamer lay in the trough and wallowed.

The afternoon watch will long be remembered by every soul on board. The steamer rolled as she had never rolled before, and created a panic. She put a severe strain on the arm and body muscles of men hanging on grimly to keep their footing on the decks; the only reason why those of the watch below were not pitched out of their bunks was that they did not attempt to get into them. They were, however, lucky to *be* below, for there they could feel but not see; they missed the swift swoop of masts and funnel that made men dizzy and brought a sinking feeling to the stoutest heart. Even Captain Hartnell, maintaining his position by the bridge rail by intense, painful, muscular effort, became seriously alarmed, for the first time in his career at sea. From the second his vessel's masts and funnel passed the perpendicular she would lean over somewhat lazily, then, as the great and increasing mass of loose water in the hold washed across, she would fall over with a terrific jerk that almost tore the captain's arms out of their sockets. It was the heavy mass of water that constituted the danger – and absolutely nothing could be done about it; except, perhaps, pump the hold dry again and acknowledge defeat. Even that could not promise immediate relief; and in the meantime, from being almost on her beam-ends on one side, the ship would roll over till she was almost on her beam-ends on the other – and when she was lying over on her side, to men's fevered imagination her masts and funnel seemed to be horizontal.

As she crashed over till the sea lapped over the lee bulwark rail she squashed the water so that it created a smother of foam half an acre in extent; but it was during those seconds, that passed like hours, when she lay on her side as if she would never recover, that her breathless captain suffered his most acute spasms of anxiety. I was then that he cursed illogically the damned chief officer who had prophesied disaster, and assuredly if Mr Wilkins had gone on the bridge with a hint of 'I told you so' on his lips, the captain would have committed manslaughter. Always, however, just as hope had almost died, the powerful righting lever created by her low centre of gravity came reluctantly into play, overcame the mass of water that was listing her and brought her upright – only to fall heavily the other way. Towards four o'clock, when human endurance had almost failed, the rolling eased. The stern rising imperceptibly out of the water was beginning to feel the force of the wind. It blew right off and the *Knightley* came head to wind and sea, and hove herself to. Instead of rolling she pitched, but was comparatively safe. To help to keep her hove-to, two tarpaulins were spread in the main rigging, one on each side, to reinforce the elevated stern which was acting like an after-sail. She was tipped sufficiently soon after dark, when the pumps were stopped and the cocks closed.

Next morning the captain ordered the construction of a sea-anchor. Now, the sea-anchor that will hold a five-thousand-ton steamer, in her ordinary trim of being down by the stern, head to the seas in such a gale as was then blowing, has yet to be constructed; but this was different. The vessel was lying head to sea naturally, and the sea-anchor would serve to steady her. It consisted of a triangular framework of stout awning spars and lifeboat oars, on which was stretched an awning. To the apex of the triangle – which would be inverted when it was in the sea – a five-fathom length of mooring chain with a kedge anchor was attached. A three-and-a-half-inch wire hawser, to which the vessel would ride, was shackled to a triple span of two-inch wire attached to the framework. The end of the hawser had been taken on the forecastle-head, passed out through a chock, and led aft outside the ship before being shackled to the span. The derrick of No. 1 hatch was already up; the end of its fall was attached to the framework by a rope strop; the sea-anchor was lifted and swung out over the sea. The strop was cut, the anchor dropped in the water, and promptly sank. Gradually, as the steamer drifted astern, the wire hawser tightened, and presently the sea-anchor appeared on the crest of a wave about fifty yards ahead. It made an efficient drogue.

Down in the tunnel the engineers had set to work to uncouple and remove the bobbin-piece – a length of shaft in the tunnel recess that connected the main and tail shafts. The broken tailshaft was withdrawn and the spare one, which had been secured by chains in the tunnel, was run out through the stern-tube till it was level with the stern-post. It was much colder work than engineers usually have to do, for while they were changing the shafts the sea poured in through the stern-tube every time the stern dipped; but, working heroically, they completed the job by midnight. As far as they were concerned all was ready for shipping the spare propeller which was lying in No. 4 'tween-decks. Had the vessel been loaded it would have been lying under tons of cargo, an indication that it was intended for use only after the vessel had been towed, disabled, into a foreign port.

At daybreak next day the chief officer with his men descended into the 'tween-decks and very carefully cast adrift the chain lashings securing it. It weighed over five tons, and there was great danger that it might take charge, surge forward along the steeply sloping deck, and maim or kill any man who tried to control it. In the meantime one of the derricks for No. 4 hatch had been rigged up. A heavy chain sling was passed through the boss of the propeller, and the lower block of a stout tackle suspended from the derrick head hooked on. A winch revolved, and a sleet squall howled at the propeller and the struggling men as it swayed up through the hatchway, with guys attached to prevent it from flying forward when it cleared the coaming. It was landed on the port side of the slippery iron deck, and three more chain slings attached to it, one also through the boss, the others on opposite blades. It was ready for being transported aft. From the counter another stout tackle, with its fall leading in through the port quarter chock on the poop, was taken along outside the poop rail, passed in over the bulwarks, and made fast to the chain sling that had just been passed through the boss.

Again the winch revolved, the propeller was lifted off the deck by means of the derrick and swung out over the heaving sea. It had to be taken aft fully fifty feet. Very carefully the fall of the derrick tackle was surged away, while the tackle from the counter, led to another winch, slowly dragged the propeller aft. More and more the stern tackle took the weight, till eventually the propeller was hanging down from the stern, level with the rudder. It was then the magnitude of the task they were committed to, and its danger, became fully realized. To get the stern-tube clear of the water the vessel had been tipped till the eight feet mark was awash; but as her stern dipped, the water was rising to the *sixteen* feet mark, and the sea boiled and swirled under her counter. When the stern rose again there was a violent scour through the propeller aperture. The heavy four-bladed propeller, practically out of control, was surging about, now banging against the rudder, now crunching against the plating round the stern-tube. Darkness was almost on them, yet it could not be left to surge about all night. It was hove up close under the counter and made more secure, and, as there was still some daylight left, the captain decided to complete the preliminaries, all ready for the morning. The job took a good deal longer than he expected, and showed him clearly how laborious the main business was going to be.

Under the counter were two eye-bolts, one on each side, to which lifting tackles were hooked when taking off the propeller for inspection in dry-dock, and for replacing it. Those were the tackles that would be used for suspending the propeller in its correct plumb position, and Captain Hartnell thought there was just time to get them adjusted. Hooking the upper blocks to the eye-bolts was easy enough; the third officer was lowered over the stern in a boatswain's chair, and though on occasion the water rose as high as his waist, he accomplished the job without much difficulty. The lower block on the port side was then attached to one of the chain slings that had been passed round opposite blades; but before the starboard one could be hooked on, it, and the threefold purchase rove through it, had to be passed through the propeller aperture from starboard to port. Down went Mr Birnie, in his boatswain's chair, clinging to the lower block; he was lowered till he gained a footing on the lower plate of the aperture, but the stern dipped and he was washed off it. He regained it with difficulty, and men gasped with horror when the scour through the aperture swung him yards clear. A fathom of ratline line was lowered, and he lashed himself to the rudder-post. A terrific struggle followed. Every time he got the block close to the stern-post the scour tore it from his grasp. The captain shouted to him to give it up till the morning, but he asked for the end of a heaving line, which he passed through the aperture from port to starboard and made fast to the block. By its means the group of men leaning over the taffrail were able to check the block from surging back, and to haul it upward after it had been shoved through the aperture. It was slow work, though; for the third officer had to light the six swollen ropes of the tackle round the stern-post against which it was binding. It became so dark that he could hardly be seen from the taffrail, and the captain grew impatient.

'Come up out of that, Mr Birnie,' he shouted. 'Leave everything as it is till the morning.'

Mr Birnie either could not, or would not hear, for he struggled on.

'He's as full of obstinacy as a mule,' the chief officer, who wanted his supper, cried irritably.

'I prefer to call it determination, and I wish you had some of it, Mr Wilkins,' Captain Hartnell snapped.

The boatswain, who had not heard the captain's order, came along with an iron bucket in which there was a lighted fire made of oakum steeped in tar. By its light the work was continued, and the block pulled up to the taffrail and secured. Mr Birnie, sitting in his boatswain's chair – a flat board with a rope span attached to it – was hauled up on deck and stood shaking himself like a spaniel.

About nine o'clock Captain Hartnell went along to the third officer's cabin. Mr Birnie had been relieved of watch-keeping, and the captain found him lying in his bunk, chocked off with cushions, smoking his pipe and reading a book.

'Any luck, Mr Birnie?' the captain asked.

'Yes . . . sir.'

'Who did you get?'

'Kelly . . . sir,' said Mr Birnie.

*

With the first streak of dawn, while the hands assembled the gear aft, the captain stood at the break of the spray-swept forecastle-head. He looked along aft, and his vessel reminded him of a pig rooting for truffles, its nose in the ground and its stern cocked up towards the sky. He looked ahead; stretching out to the invisible sea-anchor the wire hawser became bar-tight as the *Knightley*'s dripping bows lifted, then slackened and splashed into the water as they dipped. The usual dawn squall howled over the grey waste of foaming ridges, but through the sleet he could see the two red lights dangling mournfully in front of the rust-streaked funnel. Even from where he stood he could hear the heavy wash of water, fore and aft, in No. 1 hold – a dismal, menacing sound. With all his self-confidence he had to admit to considerable anxiety, and he prayed that the bulkheads would stand. He was waiting for the carpenter's report, and when it came it was good. The petty officer had sounded the fore-peak and the bilges of No. 2 hold, and found them dry. The bulkheads were not even leaking. Greatly cheered, the captain went aft prepared for a long day of arduous toil.

Among the others waiting on the poop for him he found Kelly, who prided himself on being the hardest case in the ship – a hard case descended from hard cases, indeed a lineal descendant of the Liverpool Irish packet rats who manned the notorious Western Ocean packet ships in the middle of the last century. Unlike his officers, who were going over the stern with him wearing sea-boots, oilskins well lashed at the wrists and below the knees, and with small towels tucked under the collars of their coats, Kelly was barefooted and clad only in singlet and dungaree trousers. Erect and jaunty, as if he were going for a stroll along the beach at Southport on a summer day, he stood among his blue-lipped, shivering mates whose bodies were bent to the blast; for on that high exposed afterdeck there was little shelter except two winches on which wire hawsers were wound, a small hatchway, some ventilators, and the emergency hand-steering wheel with its wheel-box.

'Going for a bath this morning, Kelly?' Captain Hartnell asked pleasantly.

'I am, sir; and I hope the maid hasn't forgotten to turn on the hot-water tap,' Kelly answered with a grin.

From the counter the propeller was lowered by the stern tackle till the port lifting tackle took its weight. The other tackle was then unhooked, and the sling removed by the third officer who had already gone over the stern. The propeller was lowered still farther and the starboard lifting tackle hove on to drag it into the aperture. The captain and Kelly got into their boatswain's chairs and were slacked down, with life-lines round them, to the eight feet mark. After Mr Birnie's experience of the previous evening they secured themselves to the rudder-post at once. The water was icy cold, and they gasped and choked as it closed over them; from their lower level the foaming crests of the waves seemed to tower to an enormous height.

'Ah, well, we're nice and sheltered down here, sir,' said Kelly.

Under the lee of the counter they were certainly sheltered from the wind, the swirling spray, and the driving snow which swept past the vessel's sides in two streams and united again in the wake a few yards behind them. If the sea was not so infernally cold, the captain thought ruefully as he fingered the heavy hammer slung round his neck. With it he had arranged to make signals by taps on the steel-plating to the engineers in the tunnel, but he did not have occasion to use it that day. Three whole hours elapsed before any of the men were able to lay a hand on the propeller which was grinding and crunching against the sternpost. At first they found the conditions almost terrifying, and all they could do was to hang on grimly and wipe the salt water from their eyes as their heads emerged from the sea. The terrific scour through the propeller aperture seemed as if it would choke the very life out of them. The counter above them would lift dizzily one moment, and dip the next to create a smother of foam in which their heads would be revealed, at the next lift, to the anxious watchers hanging out over the quarters on both sides. A less determined man than Captain Hartnell would have given up the job there and then; men with less powers of endurance than Mr Birnie and Kelly possessed could not have stood it.

It was late in the day before they could get on with the job of coaxing the propeller to lie fairly in the middle of the aperture. Shouted orders were cut short on the captain's lips, but by signalling to those who were leaning out over the quarter it was possible to convey instructions to heave, or slack, on the tackles. The adjustment became delicate. As the propeller was gradually worked into position, the heaving and slacking got down to a matter of inches. Thrice they got the hole through the boss of the propeller to coincide with the outer flange of the stern-tube, but were unable to stop the winch at the exact moment. Darkness put a stop to the work, and the men had to be hauled up on to the poop – soaked, deafened, and exhausted – with the boss and the stern-tube still out of alignment.

The following daybreak brought no change in the weather. Again the suffering seamen mustered on the bleak, wind-swept poop, appropriately christened by one of them Mount Misery. The three men were lowered into the water and secured to the rudder-post. By noon the five-ton propeller was hanging at the correct height and rubbing against the stern-post, but six inches over to starboard. Mr Birnie and Kelly got over to that side and endeavoured to lever it into position. Their combined efforts, coinciding with a lucky surge of the starboard tackle, got it into the exact position. The captain yelled frantically to the watchers to hold on everything, and hammered his signal to the waiting engineers. The sea closed over him and his companions. His head was the first to emerge from the foam.

'Is it still in its place, Kelly?' he spluttered.

'Faith, sir, it's mighty contagious!' Kelly yelled.

Again the captain hammered on the plating. For moments big as days, as it seemed – at any rate for twenty minutes which passed like hours – the three men watched, and then the thimble point of the tail-shaft making its way through the round aperture in the boss of the propeller appeared. Never did the most anxious of terriers watch a rat-hole more keenly than those men watched that aperture.

'It's coming, Birnie; by God! it's coming!' Captain Hartnell cried in triumph.

'Yes . . . sir,' said Mr Birnie.

Inch by inch the tail-shaft moved outward till six inches of it projected abaft the propeller boss; then the first thread of the worming on which the nut to secure the propeller would be screwed came into view. It would take the engineers some time to put the bobbin-piece in its place and get it connected to the tail-shaft and main-shaft; so, after the propeller had been bound hard against the stern-post by ropes leading from the quarter pipes, the three men in the water were hauled up for a welcome meal. Less than an hour of daylight remained when the chief engineer reported the job complete, and Captain Hartnell decided to wait till next morning before tackling the job of screwing on the propeller nut. At twilight, with a good horizon, the second officer got stellar observations and discovered that the *Knightley* had drifted 200 miles to the south-east since she broke down.

Dawn found the little group of watchers mustered on the poop for what they hoped would be the last time; and shortly after that the dauntless three were secured to the rudder-post, waiting for the nut to be lowered to them. It weighed three hundred pounds and had to be slung carefully; for if it had slipped out of the sling and dropped into the sea all the work they had accomplished would have been nothing but wasted effort. There was not another nut on board, and the slinging of it had given the captain food for much anxious thought, till an ingenious engineer came to the rescue by fitting two tap-bolts to it. Even a three-hundred-pound nut takes a lot of handling under the conditions in which the men over the stern worked, and it required their united strength to get it over the thimble point of the shaft and pushed home. With the sling still attached to it they managed to get a round turn of the thread of the nut on to the worm of the shaft; then they reckoned it was safe, and the sling was dispensed with. They got three more turns by hand before the key for tightening the nut was lowered to them.

The key weighed three cwt, and had slats on the rim which fitted projections on the nut. At the end of the handle was a round hole into which the lower block of a tackle from under the counter could be hooked. At first the key could be turned by those above hauling on the tackle by hand, a quarter of a turn of the nut at a time; but to the men in the water fell the almost herculean task of shifting the position of the key on the nut, ready for another quarter of a turn. To save it from dropping into the sea it was suspended by a line from the port quarter, with a smaller line attached to the rudder-post to enable the men down there to haul it towards them when it swung outward. The sea was running as high as ever; the steamer's stern rose and fell continuously. Up it flew till it brought the nut clear of the water and gave them a brief spell in which to work; down it plunged, and they held on for their lives in the seething vortex.

At times it took them half an hour to shift the grip of the key on the nut. The hours passed, the short spell of winter daylight was drawing to a close, but the soaked, exhausted, yet indomitable men worked on, determined to get the job finished. For the last few turns of the nut the fall of the tackle had to be taken to one of the steam winches. The strain on the tackle became so great that the nut must have been nearly home, but it had to be got into a position where the hole bored through it for the locking pin coincided with the hole in the tail-shaft through which the pin had to pass.

Darkness again overtook them, and once more light was obtained from flares made by burning oakum and tar in buckets. The nut was now turning an eighth of an inch at a time. With the strain on the tackle the moisture was being squeezed out of the rope fall, which on occasion surged back round the winch and was torn out of the frozen hands of the man who was holding on to it down on the main-deck. Captain Hartnell was sitting astride the propeller boss, probing the hole in the nut with the pin held in fingers numb and blue with cold. To avoid losing the pin it was attached to his wrist by a length of spun-yarn. He was almost in despair, when he felt the pin entering the hole in the shaft. He drove it home with his hammer, and the completely exhausted men were hauled up on to the poop. When they reached it they could not stand on their feet.

Later in the evening the captain told the steward to take Kelly along to the saloon and give him a good stiff dram of rum. He then did a thing he had never done since he first took command of a ship. He invited an officer – Mr Birnie – to his cabin for a whisky-and-soda. The whisky-and-soda was followed by others, and by the time Mr Birnie said good night he was almost discursive.

*

Only Mr Birnie and Kelly went over the stern next morning, and two hours' work sufficed to cover the job of securing the pin and removing the tackles and slings from the propeller. The two men were hauled up to the taffrail for the last time. The captain gave instructions to fill the after-peak and ballast tanks, and at the same time ordered a full head of steam. Gradually the steamer's stern dropped and she came on to a more even keel, but there was still the flooded hold to be pumped out. Without a doubt as her bow rose she would fall off into the trough of the sea, in spite of the pull of the sea-anchor and the tarpaulins in the main rigging, and they might lose her yet through the mass of loose water in the half-empty hold. The memory of that awful rolling was terrifying; she must be kept head on to the seas till the hold was pumped out; the engine-room telegraph on the bridge was rung to 'stand-by'.

It was not answered at once; the engines had to be turned over both ways. Both on deck and in the engine-room there was now considerable anxiety, heart-burning, and searching of mind. Had there been any flaw in the work carried out in the tunnel, or under the counter? Had anything been left undone? Would the first movement of the engines have as a result a crunching jar that would wreck the efforts of the past week and leave them to drift and starve? Only the actual working of the engines could tell. From the bridge Captain Hartnell listened intently. He heard the first wheezings of steam; were the engines vibrating again? They were, and, unknown to him, spray was being tossed up under the counter. The telegraph from the engine-room clanged its reply; the engines were ready.

The sea-anchor was tripped by a line that had been attached to the crown of the kedge, and hoisted on board. The engines were put ahead at half-speed; the *Knightley* was steering again. The captain did not want to drive her too hard into the pounding seas, nor did he wish to steam far back to the westward and lose valuable time. But she had to be kept head to sea at all costs. For most of the time half-speed sufficed; but frequently a touch of full speed was required to give her more steerage-way and straighten her up when she fell off to a dangerous angle and gave a hint that she was about to resume her rolling. The captain's hand was continually on the telegraph handle. At last the flooded hold was pumped out down to the bilges; the manhole doors on top of the ballast tanks were replaced and secured. The chief officer came on the bridge to report, and the captain banged the telegraph handle down to full speed with an air of finality.

'Course . . . sir?' the third officer inquired.

'Keep her north-east, Mr Birnie; you and I and Kelly are due a spell of warm weather,' the captain answered with a partially concealed grin.

The *Knightley* arrived at Port Pirie only a few days overdue. So well had the work been done that she steamed from that port to the United Kingdom, thence to Singapore and back, before the propeller was attended to in the ordinary way at the regular drydocking. The rival steamer from Cape Town had got to Port Pirie before him; but, later, Captain Hartnell had his compensations. From his owners he received a gold watch, suitably inscribed; and he and his fellow-workers under the counter were awarded Lloyd's medal for meritorious service. That decoration is bestowed irrespective of rank and nationality, but it is not lightly awarded. It is recognized by seafarers all over the world as a great honour, and none has earned it more worthily than those men who were lashed to the *Knightley*'s rudder-post. Captain Hartnell had his placed in a frame and displayed in a prominent place in his cabin; Mr Birnie sent his to his mother and thought little more about it; what happened to Kelly's is unknown; for – true vagabond of the sea that he was – he left the steamer at her home port and no one connected with her ever heard of him again.

PART TWO: FACT

Lawrence Beesley

THE SINKING OF THE 'TITANIC'

Lawrence Beesley, a science master at Dulwich College, London, selected the Titanic *for his Atlantic crossing not only because of the novelty of making the voyage in the newest and largest ship afloat, but also because the ship's 46,000 gross tonnage promised a smooth and stable passage. His account, which was said to be the fullest and clearest account of the disaster, was much quoted by Peter Padfield in defence of the master of the* Californian, *the vessel which lay stopped in pack ice and was said to have failed to have gone to the* Titanic's *assistance, despite distress rockets having been reported. Mr Padfield's book,* The Titanic and the Californian, *refutes this commonly believed story, and quotes Horatio Bottomley in* John Bull *as faithfully reflecting the temper of the outside world, 'a world staggering on its beam ends with the magnitude of the drama, and howling for blood'.*

'Someone ought to hang over this *Titanic* business. Sixteen hundred men and women have been murdered on the high seas.'

Independent assessors have cast doubts on the findings of the Board of Trade Enquiry and Mr Padfield's book makes absorbing reading and suggests the presence in the vicinity of a third mystery ship whose identity has never been revealed. It also contains verbatim reports of the United States Senatorial Investigation and the British Board of Trade Enquiry which, like Mr Beesley's account, gives us a fuller understanding of the events of that dreadful night.

Testimony of Mrs J. Stuart White, a passenger:

'. . . Before we cut loose from the ship two of the seamen with us – the men I should say – I do not call them seamen – I think they were dining room stewards – before we cut loose from the ship they took out cigarettes and lighted them – on an occasion like that! That was one thing we saw. All those men escaped on the pretence of being oarsmen. The man who rowed me took his oar and rowed all over the boat, in every direction. I said to him, "Why don't you put your oar in the rowlock?" He said, "Do you put it in that hole?" I said, "Certainly." He said, "I never had an oar in my hand before!" These were the men that we put to sea with at night . . .'

'I wish you would describe as nearly as you can, just what took place after your lifeboat got away from the *Titanic*.'

'We simply rowed away. We had the order, on leaving the ship, to do that. The officer who put us in the boat – I do not know who he was – gave strict orders to the seamen – or the men – to make for the light opposite and land the passengers and get back just as soon as possible. That was the light that everybody saw in the distance.'

'Did you see it?'

'Yes, I saw it distinctly . . . It was a boat of some kind.'

'How far away was it?'

'Oh it was ten miles away but we could see it distinctly. There was no doubt but that it was a boat. But we rowed and rowed and rowed, and then we all suggested that it was simply impossible for us to get back to it.

'We did what we were ordered to do. We went towards the light. That seemed to be the verdict of everybody in the boat. We had strict orders from the officer . . . to row as fast as possible for that boat, land the passengers and come right back for the others. We all supposed the boat was coming towards us, on account of all the rockets we had sent up.

'As I have said before, the men in our boat were anything but seamen with the exception of one man. The women all rowed, every one of them. Miss Young rowed every minute. The men could not row. Miss Swift from Brooklyn rowed every minute from the steamer to the *Carpathia*. Miss Young rowed every minute also, except when she was throwing up, which she did six or seven times. Countess Rothes stood at the tiller . . . but we could not get there. It was evidently impossible to reach it. It seemed to be going in the same direction in which we were going, and we made no headway towards it at all.'

Robert Patrick Dillon, a trimmer on the *Titanic*, was examined in the Board of Trade Enquiry. He was assisting in the engine room in cleaning the gear. (Not a single engineer aboard was saved.)

'Did you hear the shock when the ship struck?'

'Yes, and a few seconds before I heard the bell ring.'

'What happened?'

'After the ship struck they went slow astern for about two minutes, and then went ahead again.'

'What did the engineers do when the ship struck?'

'They went to their stations.'

'Were the watertight doors closed?'

'Yes, three minutes after the ship struck.'

'Did you get any orders?'

'Yes, we were told to go out of the engine room into the stokehold, and we had to lift up the watertight doors to get there.'

'When you got there what order was given?'

'To keep steam up.'

'Subsequently, was an order given to draw the fires?'

'Yes, but I didn't notice in which stokehold this was done. I went into four stokeholds altogether. I returned through the watertight doors to the engine room. This was done to allow the engineers to get to their duties at the pumps in the bow.'

The President: 'Am I to understand that the doors were closed from the bridge and yet the chief engineer told you to open them so as to allow you to pass beneath?'

'Yes.'

'How could that be done?'

'The chief engineer would telephone up to the bridge in order that this might be done.'

'When you returned to the engine room what happened?'

'We got the order "All hands on deck." '

'How long was that after the ship struck?'

'About an hour and forty minutes.'

'Did you see any water coming in in the boiler rooms?'

'Yes, it was coming up through the floors, but there was very little of it.'

'Where did you go?'

'I went to the well deck on the starboard side, and heard them singing out, "Any more women aboard?" The last boat was leaving the ship, and we chased two women up the ladder on to the boat deck.'

'After that did you see any passengers standing about?'

'Yes, but no women.'

'What did you do then?'

'I went on to the poop.'

'Who was there?'

'Some of the crew and passengers, but no women. I waited there until the ship sank.'

'What did you notice?'

'The ship plunged and righted herself again, and then went down. I went down with the ship and sank about two fathoms, but rose and was picked up by No. 4 boat. I was swimming in the water about twenty minutes.'

'Were there any others in the water?'

'About a thousand in my estimation.'

Lawrence Beesley, whose account follows, was 34 at the time of the disaster.

LOOKING back now on the descent of our boat down the ship's side, it is a matter of surprise, I think, to all the occupants to remember how little they thought of it at the time. It was a great adventure, certainly: it was exciting to feel the boat sink by jerks, foot by foot, as the ropes were paid out from above and shrieked as they passed through the pulley blocks, the new ropes and gear creaking under the strain of a boat laden with people, and the crew calling to the sailors above as the boat tilted slightly, now at one end, now at the other, 'Lower aft!' 'Lower stern!' and 'Lower together!' as she came level again – but I do not think we felt much apprehension about reaching the water safely. It certainly was thrilling to see the black hull of the ship on one side and the sea, seventy feet below, on the other, or to pass down by cabins and saloons brilliantly lighted; but we knew nothing of the apprehension felt in the minds of some of the officers whether the boats and lowering gear would stand the strain of the weight of our sixty people. The ropes, however, were new and strong, and the boat did not buckle in the middle as an older boat might have done. Whether it was right or not to lower boats full of people to the water – and it seems likely it was not – I think there can be nothing but the highest praise given to the officers and crew above for the way in which they lowered the boats one after the other safely to the water; it may seem a simple matter, to read about such a thing, but any sailor knows, apparently, that it is not so. An experienced officer has told me that he has seen a boat lowered in practice from a ship's deck, with a trained crew and no passengers in the boat, with practised sailors paying out the ropes, in daylight, in calm weather, with the ship lying in dock – and has seen the boat tilt over and pitch the crew headlong into the sea. Contrast these conditions with those obtaining that Monday morning at 12.45 a.m., and it is impossible not to feel that, whether the lowering crew were trained or not, whether they had or had not drilled since coming on board, they did their duty in a way that argues the greatest efficiency. I cannot help feeling the deepest gratitude to the two sailors who stood at the ropes above and lowered us to the sea: I do not suppose they were saved.

Perhaps one explanation of our feeling little sense of the unusual in leaving the *Titanic* in this way was that it seemed the climax to a series of extraordinary occurrences: the magnitude of the whole thing dwarfed events that in the ordinary way would seem to be full of imminent peril. It is easy to imagine it – a voyage of four days on a calm sea, without a single untoward incident; the presumption, perhaps already mentally half-realized, that we should be ashore in forty-eight hours and so complete a splendid voyage – and then to feel the engine stop, to be summoned on deck with little time to dress, to tie on a lifebelt, to see rockets shooting aloft in call for help, to be told to get into a lifeboat – after all these things, it did not seem much to feel the boat sinking down to the sea: it was the natural sequence of previous events, and we had learned in the last hour to take things just as they came. At the same time, if any one should wonder what the sensation is like, it is quite easy to measure seventy-five feet from the windows of a tall house or a block of flats, look down to the ground and fancy himself with some sixty other people crowded into a boat so tightly that he could not sit down or move about, then picture the boat sinking down in a continuous series of jerks, as the sailors pay out the ropes through cleats above. There are more pleasant sensations than this! How thankful we were that the sea was calm and the *Titanic* lay so steadily and quietly as we dropped down her side. We were spared the bumping and grinding against the side which so often accompanies the launching of boats. I do not remember that we even had to fend off our boat while we were trying to get free.

As we went down, one of the crew shouted, 'We are just over the condenser exhaust: we don't want to stay in that long or we shall be swamped; feel down on the floor and be ready to pull up the pin which lets the rope free as soon as we are afloat.' I had often looked over the side and noticed this stream of water coming out of the side of the *Titanic* just above the water-line: in fact so large was the volume of water that as we ploughed along and met the waves coming towards us, this stream would cause a splash that sent spray flying. We felt, as well as we could in the crowd of people, on the floor, along the sides, with no idea where the pin could be found – and none of the crew knew where it was, only of its existence somewhere – but we never found it. And all the time we got closer to the sea and the exhaust roared nearer and nearer – until finally we floated with the ropes still holding us from above, the exhaust washing us away and the force of the tide driving us back against the side – the latter not of much account in influencing the direction, however. Thinking over what followed, I imagine we must have touched the water with the condenser stream at our bows, and not in the middle as I thought at one time: at any rate, the resultant of these three forces was that we were carried parallel to the ship, directly under the place where boat 15 would drop from her davits into the sea. Looking up we saw her already coming down rapidly from B deck: she must have filled almost immediately after ours. We shouted up, 'Stop lowering 14'[1] and the crew and passengers in the boat above, hearing us shout and seeing our position immediately below them, shouted the same to the sailors on the boat deck; but apparently they did not hear, for she dropped down foot by foot – twenty feet, fifteen, ten – and a stoker and I in the bows reached up and touched her bottom swinging above our head, trying to push away our boat from under her. It seemed now as if nothing could prevent her dropping on us, but at this moment another stoker sprang with his knife to the ropes that still held us and I heard him shout, 'One! Two!' as he cut them through. The next moment we had swung away from underneath 15, and we were clear of her as she dropped into the water in the

1. In an account which appeared in the newspapers of 19 April I have described this boat as 14, not knowing they were numbered alternately.

space we had just before occupied. I do not know how the bow ropes were freed, but imagine that they were cut in the same way, for we were washed clear of the *Titanic* at once by the force of the stream and floated away as the oars were got out.

I think we all felt that that was quite the most exciting thing we had yet been through, and a great sigh of relief and gratitude went up as we swung away from the boat above our heads; but I heard no one cry aloud during the experience – not a woman's voice was raised in fear or hysteria. I think we all learnt many things that night about the bogey called 'fear', and how the facing of it is much less than the dread of it.

The crew was made up of cooks and stewards, mostly the former, I think; their white jackets showing up in the darkness as they pulled away, two to an oar: I do not think they can have had any practice in rowing, for all night long their oars crossed and clashed; if our safety had depended on speed or accuracy in keeping time it would have gone hard with us. Shouting began from one end of the boat to the other as to what we should do, where we should go, and no one seemed to have any knowledge how to act. At last we asked: 'Who is in charge of this boat?' but there was no reply. We then agreed by general consent that the stoker who stood in the stern with the tiller should act as captain, and from that time he directed the course, shouting to other boats and keeping in touch with them. Not that there was anywhere to go or anything we could do. Our plan of action was simple: to keep all the boats together as far as possible and wait until we were picked up by other liners. The crew had apparently heard of the wireless communications before they left the *Titanic*, but I never heard them say that we were in touch with any boat but the *Olympic*: it was always the *Olympic* that was coming to our rescue. They thought they knew even her distance, and making a calculation, we came to the conclusion that we ought to be picked up by her about two o'clock in the afternoon. But this was not our only hope of rescue: we watched all the time the darkness lasted for steamers' lights, thinking there might be a chance of other steamers coming near enough to see the lights which some of our boats carried. I am sure there was no feeling in the minds of any one that we should not be picked up next day: we knew that wireless messages would go out from ship to ship, and as one of the stokers said: 'The sea will be covered with ships tomorrow afternoon: they will race up from all over the sea to find us.' Some even thought that fast torpedo boats might run up ahead of the *Olympic*. And yet the *Olympic* was, after all, the farthest away of them all; eight other ships lay within three hundred miles of us.

How thankful we should have been to know how near help was, and how many ships had heard our message and were rushing to the *Titanic*'s aid. I think nothing has surprised us more than to learn so many ships were near enough to rescue us in a few hours.

Almost immediately after leaving the *Titanic* we saw what we all said was a ship's lights down on the horizon on the *Titanic*'s port side: two lights, one above the other, and plainly not one of our boats; we even rowed in that direction for some time, but the lights drew away and disappeared below the horizon.

But this is rather anticipating: we did none of these things first. We had no eyes for anything but the ship we had just left. As the oarsmen pulled slowly away we all turned and took a long look at the mighty vessel towering high above our midget boat, and I know it must have been the most extraordinary sight I shall ever be called upon to witness; I realize now how totally inadequate language is to convey to some other person who was not there any real impression of what we saw.

But the task must be attempted: the whole picture is so intensely dramatic that, while it is not possible to place on paper for eyes to see the actual likeness of the ship as she lay there, some sketch of the scene will be possible. First of all, the climatic conditions were extraordinary. The night was one of the most beautiful I have ever seen: the sky without a single cloud to mar the perfect brilliance of the stars, clustered so thickly together that in places there seemed almost more dazzling points of light set in the black sky than background of sky itself; and each star seemed, in the keen atmosphere, free from any haze, to have increased its brilliance tenfold and to twinkle and glitter with a staccato flash that made the sky seem nothing but a setting made for them in which to display their wonder. They seemed so near, and their light so much more intense than ever before, that fancy suggested they saw this beautiful ship in dire distress below and all their energies had awakened to flash messages across the black dome of the sky to each other; telling and warning of the calamity happening in the world beneath. Later, when the *Titanic* had gone down and we lay still on the sea waiting for the day to dawn or a ship to come, I remember looking up at the perfect sky and realizing why Shakespeare wrote the beautiful words he put in the mouth of Lorenzo:

> Jessica, look how the floor of heaven
> Is thick inlaid with patines of bright gold.
> There's not the smallest orb which thou behold'st
> But in his motion like an angel sings,
> Still quiring to the young-eyed cherubims;
> Such harmony is in immortal souls;
> But whilst this muddy vesture of decay
> Doth grossly close it in, we cannot hear it.

But it seemed almost as if we could – that night: the stars seemed really to be alive and to talk. The complete absence of haze produced a phenomenon I had never seen before: where the sky met the sea the line was as clear and definite as the edge of a knife, so that the water and the air never merged gradually into each other and blended to a softened rounded horizon, but each element was so exclusively separate that where a star came low down in the sky near the clear-cut edge of the waterline, it still lost none of its brilliance. As the earth revolved and the water edge came up and covered partially the star, as it were, it simply cut the star in two, the upper half continuing to sparkle as long as it was not entirely hidden, and throwing a long beam of light along the sea to us.

In the evidence before the United States Senate Committee the captain of one of the ships near us that night said the stars were so extraordinarily bright near the horizon that he was deceived into thinking that they were ship's lights: he did not remember seeing such a night before. Those who were afloat will all agree with that statement: *we* were often deceived into thinking they were lights of a ship.

And next the cold air! Here again was something quite new to us: there was not a breath of wind to blow keenly round us as we stood in the boat, and because of its continued persistence to make us feel cold; it was just a keen, bitter, icy, motionless cold that came from nowhere and yet was there all the time; the stillness of it – if one can imagine 'cold' being motionless and still – was what seemed new and strange.

And these – the sky and the air – were overhead; and below was the sea. Here again something uncommon: the surface was like a lake of oil, heaving gently up and down with a quiet motion that rocked our boat dreamily to and fro. We did not need to keep her head to the swell: often I watched her lying broadside on to the tide, and with a boat loaded as we were, this would have been impossible with anything like a swell. The sea slipped away smoothly under the boat, and I think we never heard it lapping on the sides, so oily in appearance was the water. So when one of the stokers said he had been to sea for twenty-six years and never yet seen such a calm night, we accepted it as true without comment. Just as expressive was the remark of another – 'It reminds me of a bloomin' picnic!' It was quite true; it did: a picnic on a lake, or a quiet inland river like the Cam, or a backwater on the Thames.

And so in these conditions of sky and air and sea, we gazed broadside on the *Titanic* from a short distance. She was absolutely still – indeed from the first it seemed as if the blow from the iceberg had taken all the courage out of her and she had just come quietly to rest and was settling down without an effort to save herself, without a murmur of protest against such a foul blow. For the sea could not rock her: the wind was not there to howl noisily round the decks, and make the ropes hum; from the first what must have impressed all as they watched was the sense of stillness about her and the slow, insensible way she sank lower and lower in the sea, like a stricken animal.

The mere bulk alone of the ship viewed from the sea below was an awe-inspiring sight. Imagine a ship nearly a sixth of a mile long, 75 feet high to the top decks, with four enormous funnels above the decks, and masts again high above the funnels; with her hundreds of portholes, all her saloons and other rooms brilliant with light, and all round her, little boats filled with those who until a few hours before had trod her decks and read in her libraries and listened to

he music of her band in happy content; and who were now looking
p in amazement at the enormous mass above them and rowing
way from her because she was sinking.

I had often wanted to see her from some distance away, and only
few hours before, in conversation at lunch with a fellow-passen-
er, had registered a vow to get a proper view of her lines and
imensions when we landed at New York: to stand some distance
way to take in a full view of her beautiful proportions, which the
arrow approach to the dock at Southampton made impossible.
ittle did I think that the opportunity was to be found so quickly
nd so dramatically. The background, too, was a different one
om what I had planned for her: the black outline of her profile
gainst the sky was bordered all round by stars studded in the sky,
nd all her funnels and masts were picked out in the same way: her
ulk was seen where the stars were blotted out. And one other thing
as different from expectation: the thing that ripped away from us
stantly, as we saw it, all sense of the beauty of the night, the
eauty of the ship's lines, and the beauty of her lights – and all
hese taken in themselves were intensely beautiful – that thing was
he awful angle made by the level of the sea with the rows of
orthole lights along her side in dotted lines, row above row. The
ea level and the rows of lights should have been parallel – should
ever have met – and now they met at an angle inside the black
ull of the ship. There was nothing else to indicate she was injured;
othing but this apparent violation of a simple geometrical law –
hat parallel lines should 'never meet even if produced ever so far
oth ways'; but it meant the *Titanic* had sunk by the head until the
west portholes in the bows were under the sea, and the portholes
the stern were lifted above the normal height. We rowed away
rom her in the quietness of the night, hoping and praying with all
ur hearts that she would sink no more and the day would find her
till in the same position as she was then. The crew, however, did
ot think so. It has been said frequently that the officers and crew
elt assured that she would remain afloat even after they knew the
xtent of the damage. Some of them may have done so – and
erhaps, from their scientific knowledge of her construction, with
ore reason at the time than those who said she would sink – but at

any rate the stokers in our boat had no such illusion. One of them, I think he was the same man that cut us free from the pulley rope – told us how he was at work in the stoke-hole, and in anticipation of going off duty in quarter of an hour – thus confirming the time of the collision as 11.45 – had near him a pan of soup keeping hot on some part of the machinery; suddenly the whole side of the compartment came in, and the water rushed him off his feet. Picking himself up, he sprang for the compartment doorway and was just through the aperture when the watertight door came down behind him, 'like a knife,' as he said; 'they work them from the bridge.' He had gone up on deck but was ordered down again once and with others was told to draw the fires from under the boiler, which they did, and were then at liberty to come on deck again. It seems that this particular knot of stokers must have known almost as soon as any one of the extent of injury. He added mournfully, 'I could do with that hot soup now' – and indeed he could: he was clad at the time of the collison, he said, in trousers and singlet, both very thin on account of the intense heat in the stoke-hole; and although he had added a short jacket later, his teeth were chattering with the cold. He found a place to lie down underneath the tiller on the little platform where our captain stood, and there he lay all night with a coat belonging to another stoker thrown over him and I think he must have been almost unconscious. A lady next to him, who was warmly clad with several coats, tried to insist on his having one of hers – a fur-lined one – thrown over him, but he absolutely refused while some of the women were insufficiently clad; and so the coat was given to an Irish girl with pretty auburn hair standing near, leaning against the gunwale – with an 'outside berth' and so more exposed to the cold air. This same lady was able to distribute more of her wraps to the passengers, a rug to one, a fur boa to another; and she has related with amusement that at the moment of climbing up the *Carpathia*'s side, those to whom these articles had been lent offered them all back to her, but as, like the rest of us, she was encumbered with a lifebelt, she had to say she would receive them back at the end of the climb. I had not seen my dressing-gown since I dropped into the boat, but some time in the night a steerage passenger found it on the floor and put it on.

It is not easy at this time to call to mind who were in the boat, because in the night it was not possible to see more than a few feet away, and when dawn came we had eyes only for the rescue ship and the icebergs; but so far as my memory serves the list was as follows: no first-class passengers; three women, one baby, two men from the second cabin; and the other passengers steerage – mostly women; a total of about 35 passengers. The rest, about 25 (and possibly more), were crew and stokers. Near to me all night was a group of three Swedish girls, warmly clad, standing close together to keep warm, and very silent; indeed there was very little talking at any time.

One conversation took place that is, I think, worth repeating: one more proof that the world after all is a small place. The ten months' old baby which was handed down at the last moment was received by a lady next to me – the same who shared her wraps and coats. The mother had found a place in the middle and was too tightly packed to come through to the child, and so it slept contentedly for about an hour in a stranger's arms; it then began to cry and the temporary nurse said: 'Will you feel down and see if the baby's feet are out of the blanket! I don't know much about babies but I think their feet must be kept warm.' Wriggling down as well as I could, I found its toes exposed to the air and wrapped them well up, when it ceased crying at once: it was evidently a successful diagnosis! Having recognized the lady by her voice – as one of my vis-à-vis at the purser's table, I said, 'Surely you are Miss — ?' 'Yes,' she replied, 'and you must be Mr Beesley; how curious we should find ourselves in the same boat!' Remembering that she had joined the boat at Queenstown, I said, 'Do you know Clonmel? A letter from a great friend of mine who is staying there at — [giving the address] came aboard at Queenstown.' 'Yes, it is my home: and I was dining at — just before I came away.' It seemed that she knew my friend, too; and we agreed that of all places in the world to recognize mutual friends, a crowded lifeboat afloat in mid-ocean at — a.m. twelve hundred miles from our destination was one of the most unexpected.

And all the time, as we watched, the *Titanic* sank lower and lower by the head and the angle became wider and wider as the stern porthole lights lifted and the bow lights sank, and it was evident she was not to stay afloat much longer. The captain-stoker now told the oarsmen to row away as hard as they could. Two reasons seemed to make this a wise decision: one that as she sank she would create such a wave of suction that boats, if not sucked under by being too near, would be in danger of being swamped by the wave her sinking would create – and we all knew our boat was in no condition to ride big waves, crowded as it was and manned with untrained oarsmen. The second was that an explosion might result from the water getting to the boilers, and débris might fall within a wide radius. And yet, as it turned out, neither of these things happened.

At about 2.15 a.m. I think we were any distance from a mile to two miles away. It is difficult for a landsman to calculate distance at sea but we had been afloat an hour and a half, the boat was heavily loaded, the oarsmen unskilled, and our course erratic: following now one light and now another, sometimes a star and sometimes a light from a port lifeboat which had turned away from the *Titanic* in the opposite direction and lay almost on our horizon, and so we could not have gone very far away.

About this time, the water had crept up almost to her sidelights and the captain's bridge, and it seemed a question only of minutes before she sank. The oarsmen lay on their oars, and all in the lifeboat were motionless as we watched her in absolute silence – save some who would not look and buried their heads on each others' shoulders. The lights still shone with the same brilliance, but not so many of them: many were now below the surface. I have often wondered since whether they continued to light up the cabins when the portholes were under water; they may have done so.

And then, as we gazed awe-struck, she tilted slowly up, revolving apparently about a centre of gravity just astern of amidships, until she attained a vertically upright position; and there she remained – motionless! As she swung up, her lights, which had shone without flicker all night, went out suddenly, came on again for a single flash, then went out altogether. And as they did so, there came a noise which many people, wrongly I think, have described as an explosion; it has always seemed to me that it was nothing but the engines and machinery coming loose from their bolts and bearings, and falling through the compartments, smashing everything in their way. It was partly a roar, partly a groan, partly a rattle, and partly a smash, and it was not a sudden roar as an explosion would be: it went on successively for some seconds, possibly fifteen to twenty, as the heavy machinery dropped down to the bottom (now the bows) of the ship: I suppose it fell through the end and sank first, before the ship. But it was a noise no one had heard before, and no one wishes to hear again: it was stupefying, stupendous, as it came to us along the water. It was as if all the heavy things one could think of had been thrown downstairs from the top of a house, smashing each other and the stairs and everything in the way.

Several apparently authentic accounts have been given, in which definite stories of explosions have been related – in some cases even with wreckage blown up and the ship broken in two; but I think such accounts will not stand close analysis. In the first place the fires had been withdrawn and the steam allowed to escape some time before she sank, and the possibility of explosion from this cause seems very remote. Then, as just related, the noise was not suddenly and definite, but prolonged – more like the roll and crash of thunder. The noise was probably caused by the engines falling down. As the *Titanic* tilted up they would almost certainly fall loose from their bed and plunge down through the other compartments.

No phenomenon like that pictured in some American and English papers occurred – that of the ship breaking in two, and the two ends being raised above the surface. I saw these drawings in preparation on board the *Carpathia*, and said at the time that they bore no resemblance to what actually happened.

When the noise was over the *Titanic* was still upright like a column: we could see her now only as the stern and some 150 feet of her stood outlined against the star-specked sky, looming black in the darkness, and in this position she continued for some minutes – I think as much as five minutes, but it may have been less. Then, first sinking back a little at the stern, I thought, she slid slowly forwards through the water and dived slantingly down; the sea closed over her and we had seen the last of the beautiful ship on which we had embarked four days before at Southampton.

And in place of the ship on which all our interest had been

concentrated for so long and towards which we looked most of the time because it was still the only object on the sea which was a fixed point to us – in place of the *Titanic*, we had the level sea now stretching in an unbroken expanse to the horizon: heaving gently just as before, with no indication on the surface that the waves had just closed over the most wonderful vessel ever built by man's hand; the stars looked down just the same and the air was just as bitterly cold.

There seemed a great sense of loneliness when we were left on the sea in a small boat without the *Titanic*: not that we were uncomfortable (except for the cold) nor in danger: we did not think we were either, but the *Titanic* was no longer there.

We waited head on for the wave which we thought might come – the wave we have heard so much of from the crew and which they said had been known to travel for miles – and it never came. But although the *Titanic* left us no such legacy of a wave as she went to the bottom, she left us something we would willingly forget forever, something which it is well not to let the imagination dwell on – the cries of many hundreds of our fellow-passengers struggling in the ice-cold water.

I would willingly omit any further mention of this part of the disaster from this book, but for two reasons it is not possible – first, that as a matter of history it should be put on record; and secondly, that these cries were not only an appeal for help in the awful conditions of danger in which the drowning found themselves – an appeal that could never be answered – but an appeal to the whole world to make such conditions of danger and hopelessness impossible ever again; a cry that called to the heavens for the very injustice of its own existence; a cry that clamoured for its own destruction.

We were utterly surprised to hear this cry go up as the waves closed over the *Titanic*: we had heard no sound of any kind from her since we left her side; and, as mentioned before, we did not know how many boats she had or how many rafts. The crew may have known, but they probably did not, and if they did, they never told the passengers; we should not have been surprised to know all were safe on some life-saving device.

So that unprepared as we were for such a thing, the cries of the drowning floating across the quiet sea filled us with stupefaction: we longed to return and rescue at least some of the drowning, but we knew it was impossible. The boat was filled to standing-room, and to return would mean the swamping of us all, and so the captain-stoker told his crew to row away from the cries. We tried to sing to keep all from thinking of them; but there was no heart for singing in the boat at that time.

The cries, which were loud and numerous at first, died away gradually one by one, but the night was clear, frosty and still, the water smooth, and the sounds must have carried on its level surface free from any obstruction for miles, certainly much farther from the ship than we were situated. I think the last of them must have been heard nearly forty minutes after the *Titanic* sank. Lifebelts would keep the survivors afloat for hours; but the cold water was what stopped the cries.

There must have come to all those safe in the lifeboats, scattered round the drowning at various distances, a deep resolve that, if anything could be done by them in the future to prevent the repetition of such sounds, they would do it – at whatever cost of time or other things. And not only to them are those cries an imperative call, but to every man and woman who has known of them. It is not possible that ever again can such conditions exist; but it is a duty imperative on one and all to see that they do not. Think of it! a few more boats, a few more planks of wood nailed together in a particular way at a trifling cost, and all those men and women whom the world can so ill afford to lose would be with us today, there would be no mourning in thousands of homes which now are desolate, and these words need not have been written.

Lieutenant William Bligh R.N.

NARRATIVE OF THE MUTINY
ON THE 'BOUNTY'

Captain Bligh's narrative of his epic 3,618 mile South Sea voyage in the ship's cutter without the loss of a man through sickness begins with his own account of the mutiny. Bligh's legend probably reached the heights of absurdity with the writings of the MGM publicity man who, launching the first Mutiny on the Bounty *film in 1935, wrote that Bligh was 'a sea-going disaster, begotten in a galley and born under a gun! His hair was rope, his teeth were marlin spikes . . .' He was, in fact, the son of an Inspector of Customs and the picture of him as a tyrannical commander is not borne out by the entries in his log book. From the edited narrative which follows he is revealed as being increasingly concerned for the comfort and health of his men. He had awnings rigged so that the crew would not suffer the ill effects of the tropical sun, and when rounding the Horn in fierce gales wrote, 'I cannot expect my men and officers to bear it much longer,' adding later, 'I now ordered my cabin to be appropriated at nights to the use of those poor fellows who had wet berths by which means it . . . rendered happy those who had not dry beds to sleep in.'*

The Bounty's *cutter was a mere 23 feet long which, when heavily loaded, presented a freeboard of only a few inches to the sea with the constant danger of swamping. The seaman, John Norton, who was stoned to death on the island of Tofoa, as here recorded, is commemorated by a cross of bare earth known to this day as Norton's Patch. The patch is in the shape of a cross, the reason being, according to legend, that Norton fell with his arms out-stretched.*

Tuesday the 28th April. Just before sunrising, while I was yet asleep, Mr Christian, with the master-at-arms, gunner's mate, and

Thomas Burkett, seaman, came into my cabin, and seizing me tied my hands with a cord behind my back, threatening me with instant death if I spoke or made the least noise. I, however, called as loud as I could, in hopes of assistance; but they had already secured the officers who were not of their party by placing sentinels at their doors. There were three men at my cabin door, besides the four within: Christian had only a cutlass in his hand, the others had muskets and bayonets. I was hauled out of bed and forced on deck in my shirt, suffering great pain from the tightness with which they had tied my hands. I demanded the reason of such violence, but received no other answer than abuse for not holding my tongue. The master, the gunner, the surgeon, Mr Elphinstone, master's mate, and Nelson were kept confined below, and the fore hatchway was guarded by sentinels. The boatswain and carpenter, and also the clerk, Mr Samuel, were allowed to come upon deck, where they saw me standing abaft the mizen-mast with my hands tied behind my back, under a guard, with Christian at their head. The boatswain was ordered to hoist the launch out, with a threat if he did not do it instantly *to take care of himself*.

When the boat was out, Mr Hayward and Mr Hallet, two of the midshipmen, and Mr Samuel were ordered into it. I demanded what their intention was in giving this order, and endeavoured to persuade the people near me not to persist in such acts of violence; but it was to no effect. 'Hold your tongue, sir, or you are dead this instant,' was constantly repeated to me.

The master by this time had sent to request that he might come on deck, which was permitted; but he was soon ordered back again to his cabin.

I continued my endeavours to turn the tide of affairs, when Christian changed the cutlass which he had in his hand for a bayonet that was brought to him, and, holding me with a strong grip by the cord that tied my hands, he with many oaths threatened to kill me immediately if I would not be quiet; the villains round me had their pieces cocked and bayonets fixed. Particular people were called on to go into the boat, and were hurried over the side; whence I concluded that with these people I was to be set adrift. I therefore made another effort to bring about a change, but with no other effect than to be threatened with having my brains blown out.

The boatswain and seamen who were to go in the boat were allowed to collect twine, canvas, lines, sails, cordage, an eight and twenty gallon cask of water, and Mr Samuel got a hundred and fifty pounds of bread, with a small quantity of rum and wine, also a quadrant and compass; but he was forbidden on pain of death to touch either map, ephemeris, book of astronomical observations, sextant, time-keeper, or any of my surveys or drawings.

The mutineers having forced those of the seamen whom they meant to get rid of into the boat, Christian directed a dram to be served to each of his own crew. I then unhappily saw that nothing could be done to effect the recovery of the ship: there was no one to assist me, and every endeavour on my part was answered with threats of death.

The officers were next called upon deck and forced over the side into the boat, while I was kept apart from every one abaft the mizen-mast; Christian, armed with a bayonet, holding me by the bandage that secured my hands. The guard round me had their pieces cocked, but, on my daring the ungrateful wretches to fire, they uncocked them.

Isaac Martin, one of the guard over me, I saw had an inclination to assist me, and as he fed me with shaddock (my lips being quite parched), we explained our wishes to each other by our looks; but this being observed Martin was removed from me. He then attempted to leave the ship, for which purpose he got into the boat; but with many threats they obliged him to return.

The armourer, Joseph Coleman, and two of the carpenters, M'Intosh and Norman, were also kept contrary to their inclination; and they begged of me, after I was astern in the boat, to remember that they declared they had no hand in the transaction. Michael Byrne, I am told, likewise wanted to leave the ship.

It is of no moment for me to recount my endeavours to bring back the offenders to a sense of their duty. All I could do was by speaking to them in general; but it was to no purpose, for I was kept securely bound, and no one except the guard suffered to come near me.

To Mr Samuel I am indebted for securing my journals and commission, with some material ship papers. Without these I had nothing to certify what I had done, and my honour and character might have been suspected without my possessing a proper document to have defended them. All this he did with great resolution, though guarded and strictly watched. He attempted to save the time-keeper and a box with my surveys, drawings and remarks for fifteen years past, which were numerous, when he was hurried away with, 'Damn your eyes, you are well off to get what you have.'

It appeared to me that Christian was some time in doubt whether he should keep the carpenter or his mates; at length he determined on the latter, and the carpenter was ordered into the boat. He was permitted, but not without some opposition, to take his tool-chest.

Much altercation took place among the mutinous crew during the whole business; some swore: 'I'll be damned if he does not find his way home, if he gets anything with him' (meaning me); and, when the carpenter's chest was carrying away: 'Damn my eyes, he will have a vessel built in a month.' While others laughed at the helpless situation of the boat, being very deep, and so little room for those who were in her. As for Christian, he seemed as if meditating destruction on himself and every one else.

I asked for arms, but they laughed at me, and said I was well acquainted with the people among whom I was going, and therefore did not want them; four cutlasses, however, were thrown into the boat after we were veered astern.

The officers and men being in the boat, they only waited for me, of which the master-at-arms informed Christian, who then said: 'Come, Captain Bligh, your officers and men are now in the boat, and you must go with them; if you attempt to make the least resistance you will instantly be put to death'; and without further ceremony, with a tribe of armed ruffians about me, I was forced over the side, where they untied my hands. Being in the boat, we were veered astern by a rope. A few pieces of pork were thrown to us, and some clothes, also the cutlasses I have already mentioned; and it was then that the armourer and carpenters called out to me to remember that they had no hand in the transaction. After having undergone a great deal of ridicule, and been kept some time to make sport for these unfeeling wretches, we were at length cast adrift in the open ocean.

I had with me in the boat the following persons:

Names	*Stations*
JOHN FRYER	Master
THOMAS LEDWARD	Acting-surgeon
DAVID NELSON	Botanist
WILLIAM PECKOVER	Gunner
WILLIAM COLE	Boatswain
WILLIAM PURCELL	Carpenter
WILLIAM ELPHINSTONE	Master's mate
THOMAS HAYWARD	Midshipmen
JOHN HALLET	
JOHN NORTON	Quartermasters
PETER LINKLETTER	
LAWRENCE LEBOGUE	Sailmaker
JOHN SMITH	Cooks
THOMAS HALL	
GEORGE SIMPSON	Quartermaster's mate
ROBERT TINKLER	A boy
ROBERT LAMB	Butcher
MR SAMUEL	Clerk

There remained on board the *Bounty*:

FLETCHER CHRISTIAN	Master's mate
PETER HEYWOOD	
EDWARD YOUNG	Midshipmen
GEORGE STEWART	
CHARLES CHURCHILL	Master-at-arms
JOHN MILLS	Gunner's mate
JAMES MORRISON	Boatswain's mate
THOMAS BURKETT	Able seaman
MATTHEW QUINTAL	”
JOHN SUMNER	”
JOHN MILLWARD	”

Names	Stations
WILLIAM M'KOY	Able seaman
HENRY HILLBRANT	,,
MICHAEL BYRNE	,,
WILLIAM MUSPRATT	,,
ALEXANDER SMITH	,,
JOHN WILLIAMS	,,
THOMAS ELLISON	,,
ISAAC MARTIN	,,
RICHARD SKINNER	,,
MATTHEW THOMPSON	,,
WILLIAM BROWN	Gardener
JOSEPH COLEMAN	Armourer
CHARLES NORMAN	Carpenter's mate
THOMAS M'INTOSH	Carpenter's crew

In all twenty-five hands, and the most able men of the ship's company.

Having little or no wind, we rowed pretty fast towards Tofoa, which bore NE about ten leagues from us. While the ship was in sight she steered to the WNW, but I considered this only as a feint, for when we were sent away, 'Huzza for Otaheite' was frequently heard among the mutineers.

Christian, the chief of the mutineers, is of a respectable family in the north of England. This was the third voyage he had made with me, and as I found it necessary to keep my ship's company at three watches, I had given him an order to take charge of the third, his abilities being thoroughly equal to the task; and by this means the master and gunner were not at watch and watch.

Heywood is also of a respectable family in the north of England, and a young man of abilities, as well as Christian. These two had been objects of my particular regard and attention, and I had taken great pains to instruct them, having entertained hopes that as professional men they would have become a credit to their country.

Young was well recommended, and had the look of an able stout seaman. He, however, fell short of what his appearance promised.

Stewart was a young man of creditable parents in the Orkneys, at which place, on the return of the *Resolution* from the South Seas in 1780, we received so many civilities, that on that account only I should gladly have taken him with me; but, independent of this recommendation, he was a seaman, and had always borne a good character.

Notwithstanding the roughness with which I was treated, the remembrance of past kindnesses produced some signs of remorse in Christian. When they were forcing me out of the ship I asked him if this treatment was a proper return for the many instances he had received of my friendship? He appeared disturbed at my question, and answered with much emotion:

'That – Captain Bligh – that is the thing. I am in hell – I am in hell.'

As soon as I had time to reflect, I felt an inward satisfaction which prevented any depression of my spirits. Conscious of my integrity and anxious solicitude for the good of the service in which I had been engaged, I found my mind wonderfully supported, and I began to conceive hopes, notwithstanding so heavy a calamity, that I should one day be able to account to my king and country for the misfortune. A few hours before my situation had been peculiarly shattering. I had a ship in the most perfect order and well stored with every necessary both for service and health. By early attention to those particulars I had, as much as lay in my power, provided against any accident in case I could not get through Endeavour Straits, as well as against what might befall me in them; add to this the plants had been successfully preserved in the most flourishing state; so that, upon the whole, the voyage was two-thirds completed, and the remaining part, to all appearance, in a very promising way; every person on board being in perfect health, to establish which was ever amongst the principal objects of my attention.

It will very naturally be asked, What could be the reason for such a revolt? in answer to which I can only conjecture that the mutineers had flattered themselves with the hopes of a more happy life among the Otaheiteans than they could possibly enjoy in England; and this, joined to some female connections, most probably occasioned the whole transaction.

The women at Otaheite are handsome, mild and cheerful in their manners and conversation, possessed of great sensibility, and have sufficient delicacy to make them admired and beloved. The chiefs were so much attached to our people that they rather encouraged their stay among them than otherwise, and even made them promises of large possessions. Under these, and many other attendant circumstances equally desirable, it is now perhaps not so much to be wondered at, though scarcely possible to have been foreseen, that a set of sailors, most of them void of connections, should be led away; especially when, in addition to such powerful inducements, they imagined it in their power to fix themselves in the midst of plenty on one of the finest islands in the world, where they need not labour and where the allurements of dissipation are beyond anything that can be conceived. The utmost, however, that any commander could have supposed to have happened is that some of the people would have been tempted to desert. But if it should be asserted that a commander is to guard against an act of mutiny and piracy in his own ship more than by the common rules of service, it is as much as to say that he must sleep locked up, and when awake be girded with pistols.

Desertions have happened more or less, from most of the ships that have been at the Society Islands, but it has always been in the commander's power to make the chiefs return their people. The knowledge, therefore, that it was unsafe to desert, perhaps first led mine to consider with what ease so small a ship might be surprised, and that so favourable an opportunity would never offer to them again.

The secrecy of this mutiny is beyond all conception. Thirteen of the party who were with me had always lived forward among the seamen, yet neither they, nor the messmates of Christian, Stewart, Heywood, and Young had ever observed any circumstance that made them in the least suspect what was going on. To such a close-planned act of villainy, my mind being entirely free from any suspicion, it is not wonderful that I fell a sacrifice. Perhaps if there had been marines on board, a sentinel at my cabin-door might have prevented it; for I slept with the door always open, that the officer of the watch might have access to me on all occasions, the possibility of such a conspiracy being ever the farthest from my thoughts. Had their mutiny been occasioned by any grievances, either real or imaginary, I must have discovered symptoms of their discontent, which would have put me on my guard; but the case was far otherwise. Christian, in particular, I was on the most friendly terms with. That very day he was engaged to have dined with me, and the preceding night he excused himself from supping with me, on pretence of being unwell; for which I felt concerned, having no suspicions of his integrity and honour.

2

My first determination was to seek a supply of bread-fruit and water at Tofoa, and afterwards to sail for Tongataboo, and there risk a solicitation to Poulaho, the king, to equip our boat and grant us a supply of water and provisions so as to enable us to reach the East Indies.

The quantity of provisions I found in the boat was 150 lb of bread, 16 pieces of pork (each weighing 2 lb.) 6 quarts of rum, 6 bottles of wine, with 28 gallons of water, and 4 empty *barrecoes*.

Fortunately it was calm all the afternoon till about four o'clock, when we were so far to windward that with a moderate easterly breeze which sprung up we were able to sail. It was nevertheless dark when we got to Tofoa, where I expected to land; but the shore proved to be so steep and rocky that we were obliged to give up all thoughts of it and keep the boat under the lee of the island with two oars, for there was no anchorage. Having fixed on this mode of proceeding for the night, I served to every person half a pint of grog, and each took to his rest as well as our unhappy situation would allow.

In the morning, at dawn of day, we rowed along shore in search of a landing-place, and about ten o'clock we discovered a cove with a stony beach at the NW part of the island, where I dropped the grapnel within twenty yards of the rocks. A great surf ran on the shore, but as I was unwilling to diminish our stock of provisions I landed Mr Samuel and some others, who climbed the cliffs and got into the country to search for supplies. The rest of us remained at the cove, not discovering any other way into the country than that by which Mr Samuel had proceeded. It was great consolation to me to find that the spirits of my people did not sink, notwithstanding our miserable and almost hopeless situation. Towards noon Mr Samuel returned with a few quarts of water which he had found in holes, but he had met with no spring or any prospect of a sufficient supply in that particular, and had seen only the signs of inhabitants. As it was uncertain what might be our future necessities, I only issued a morsel of bread and a glass of wine to each person for dinner.

I observed the latitude of this cove to be 19° 41′ S. This is the NW part of Tofoa, the north-westernmost of the Friendly Islands.

The weather was fair, but the wind blew so strong from the ESE that we could not venture to sea. Our detention made it absolutely necessary to endeavour to obtain something towards our support, for I determined if possible to keep our first stock entire. We therefore weighed, and rowed along shore to see if anything could be got, and at last discovered some coconut trees; but they were on the top of high precipices and the surf made it dangerous landing. Both one and the other we, however, got the better of. Some of the people with much difficulty climbed the cliffs and got about twenty coconuts, and others slung them to ropes, by which we hauled them through the surf into the boat. This was all that could be done here, and as I found no place so safe as the one we had left to spend the night at I returned to the cove, and having served a coconut to each person we went to rest again in the boat.

At daylight we attempted to put to sea, but the wind and weather proved so bad that I was glad to return to our former station; where, after issuing a morsel of bread and a spoonful of rum to each person we landed, and I went off with Mr Nelson, Mr Samuel, and some others into the country, having hauled ourselves up the precipice by long vines which were fixed there by the natives for that purpose, this being the only way into the country.

We found a few deserted huts, and a small plantain walk but little taken care of, from which we could only collect three small bunches of plantains. After passing this place we came to a deep gully that led towards a mountain near a volcano, and as I con-

245

ceived that in the rainy season very great torrents of water must
pass through it, we hoped to find sufficient for our use remaining in
some holes of the rocks, but after all our search the whole that we
collected was only nine gallons. We advanced within two miles of
the foot of the highest mountain in the island, on which is the
volcano that is almost constantly burning. The country near it is
covered with lava and has a most dreary appearance. As we had
not been fortunate in our discoveries and saw nothing to alleviate
our distresses except the plantains and water above-mentioned, we
returned to the boat exceedingly fatigued and faint. When I came
to the precipice whence we were to descend into the cove, I was
seized with such a dizziness in my head that I thought it scarce
possible to effect it. However, by the assistance of Nelson and
others they at last got me down, in a weak condition. Every person
being returned by noon, I gave about an ounce of pork and two
plantains to each, with half a glass of wine. I again observed the
latitude of this place 19° 41′ S. The people who remained by the
boat I had directed to look for fish or what they could pick up
about the rocks, but nothing eatable could be found, so that upon
the whole we considered ourselves on as miserable a spot of land as
could well be imagined.

I could not say positively, from the former knowledge I had of
this island, whether it was inhabited or not; but I knew it was
considered inferior to the other islands, and I was not certain but
that the Indians only resorted to it at particular times. I was very
anxious to ascertain this point, for in case there had been only a
few people here, and those could have furnished us with but very
moderate supplies, the remaining in this spot to have made preparations for our voyage would have been preferable to the risk of
going amongst multitudes where perhaps we might lose everything.
A party, therefore, sufficiently strong, I determined should go
another route as soon as the sun became lower; and they cheerfully
undertook it.

About two o'clock in the afternoon the party set out, but after
suffering much fatigue they returned in the evening, without any
kind of success.

At the head of the cove, about a hundred and fifty yards from

he water-side, there was a cave; the distance across the stony
beach was about a hundred yards, and from the country in to the
cove there was no other way than that which I have already de-
cribed. The situation secured us from the danger of being surprised, and I determined to remain on shore for the night with a
part of my people, that the others might have more room to
est in the boat, with the master, whom I directed to lie at a grapnel, and be watchful in case we should be attacked. I ordered one
plantain for each person to be boiled, and having supped on this
scanty allowance, with a quarter of a pint of grog, and fixed the
watches for the night, those whose turn it was laid down to sleep in
he cave, before which we kept up a good fire; yet notwithstanding
we were much troubled with flies and mosquitoes.

Friday the 1st May. At dawn of day the party set out again in a
different route to see what they could find, in the course of which
they suffered greatly for want of water. They, however, met with
two men, a woman, and a child; the men came with them to the
cove and brought two coconut shells of water. I endeavoured to
make friends of these people, and sent them away for bread-fruit,
plantains, and water. Soon after other natives came to us, and by
noon there were thirty about us, from whom we obtained a small
supply; but I could only afford one ounce of pork and a quarter of
a bread-fruit to each man for dinner, with half a pint of water; for
. was fixed in my resolution not to use any of the bread or water in
he boat.

No particular chief was yet among the natives. They were, notwithstanding, tractable, and behaved honestly, exchanging the provisions they brought for a few buttons and beads. The party who
had been out informed me of their having seen several neat plan-
ations, so that it remained no longer a doubt of there being settled
inhabitants on the island; for which reason I determined to get
what I could, and to sail the first moment that the wind and
weather would allow us to put to sea.

I was much puzzled in what manner to account to the natives for
he loss of my ship. I knew they had too much sense to be amused
with a story that the ship was to join me, when she was not in sight
from the hills. I was at first doubtful whether I should tell the real

fact, or say that the ship had overset and sunk, and that we only were saved. The latter appeared to be the most proper and advantageous for us, and I accordingly instructed my people that we might all agree in one story. As I expected, inquiries were made about the ship, and they seemed readily satisfied with our account; but there did not appear the least symptom of joy or sorrow in their faces, although I fancied I discovered some marks of surprise. Some of the natives were coming and going the whole afternoon, and we got enough of bread-fruit, plantains, and coconuts for another day; but of water they only brought us about five pints. A canoe also came in with four men and brought a few coconuts and bread-fruit, which I bought as I had done the rest. Nails were much inquired after, but I would not suffer any to be shown, as they were wanted for the use of the boat.

Towards evening I had the satisfaction to find our stock of provisions somewhat increased, but the natives did not appear to have much to spare. What they brought was in such small quantities that I had no reason to hope we should be able to procure from them sufficient to stock us for our voyage. At sunset all the natives left us in quiet possession of the cove. I thought this a good sign, and made no doubt that they would come again the next day with a better supply of food and water, with which I hoped to sail without further delay; for if in attempting to get to Tongataboo we should be driven to leeward of the islands, there would be a larger quantity of provisions to support us against such a misfortune.

At night I served a quarter of a bread-fruit and a coconut to each person for supper, and a good fire being made, all but the watch went to sleep.

At daybreak the next morning I was pleased to find everyone's spirits a little revived, and that they no longer regarded me with those anxious looks which had constantly been directed towards me since we lost sight of the ship; every countenance appeared to have a degree of cheerfulness, and they all seemed determined to do their best.

As there was no certainty of our being supplied with water by the natives, I sent a party among the gullies in the mountains, with empty shells, to see what could be found. In their absence the natives came about us, as I expected, and in greater numbers; two canoes also came in from round the north side of the island. In one of them was an elderly chief called Macca-ackavow. Soon after some of our foraging party returned, and with them came a good-looking chief called Egijeefow, or perhaps more properly Eefow, Egij or Eghee, signifying a chief. To each of these men I made a present of an old shirt and a knife, and I soon found they either had seen me, or had heard of my being at Annamooka. They knew I had been with Captain Cook, who they inquired after, and also Captain Clerk. They were very inquisitive to know in what manner I had lost my ship. During this conversation a young man named Nageete appeared, whom I remembered to have seen at Annamooka: he expressed much pleasure at our meeting. I inquired after Poulaho and Feenow, who, they said, were at Tongataboo, and Eefow agreed to accompany me thither if I would wait till the weather moderated. The readiness and affability of this man gave me much satisfaction.

This, however, was but of short duration, for the natives began to increase in number, and I observed some symptoms of a design against us. Soon after they attempted to haul the boat on shore, on which I brandished my cutlass in a threatening manner, and spoke to Eefow to desire them to desist; which they did, and everything became quiet again. My people who had been in the mountains now returned with about three gallons of water. I kept buying up the little bread-fruit that was brought to us, and likewise some spears to arm my men with, having only four cutlasses, two of which were in the boat. As we had no means of improving our situation, I told our people I would wait till sunset, by which time perhaps something might happen in our favour; for if we attempted to go at present we must fight our way through, which we could do more advantageously at night, and that in the meantime we would endeavour to get off to the boat what we had bought. The beach was lined with the natives, and we heard nothing but the knocking of stones together, which they had in each hand. I knew very well this was the sign of an attack. At noon I served a coconut and a bread-fruit to each person for dinner, and gave some to the chiefs, with whom I continued to appear intimate and friendly. They frequently importuned me to sit down, but I as constantly refused, for it occurred both to Nelson and myself that they intended to seize hold of me if I gave them such an opportunity. Keeping, therefore, constantly on our guard, we were suffered to eat our uncomfortable meal in some quietness.

After dinner we began by little and little to get our things into the boat, which was a troublesome business on account of the surf. I carefully watched the motions of the natives, who continued to increase in number, and found that instead of their intention being to leave us, fires were made, and places fixed on for their stay during the night. Consultations were also held among them, and everything assured me we should be attacked. I sent orders to the master that when he saw us coming down he should keep the boat close to the shore, that we might the more readily embark.

I had my journal on shore with me, writing the occurrences in the cave, and in sending it down to the boat it was nearly snatched away, but for the timely assistance of the gunner.

The sun was near setting when I gave the word, on which every person who was on shore with me boldly took up his proportion of things and carried them to the boat. The chiefs asked me if I would not stay with them all night. I said, 'No, I never sleep out of my boat; but in the morning we will again trade with you, and I shall remain till the weather is moderate, that we may go, as we have agreed, to see Poulaho at Tongataboo.' Macca-ackavow then got up and said. 'You will not sleep on shore? then *mattie*' (which directly signifies we will kill you), and he left me. The onset was now preparing. Every one, as I have described before, kept knocking stones together, and Eefow quitted me. All but two or three things were in the boat, when I took Nageete by the hand and we walked down the beach, everyone in a silent kind of horror.

While I was seeing the people embark, Nageete wanted me to stay to speak to Eefow, but I found he was encouraging them to the attack, and it was my determination, if they had then began, to have killed him for his treacherous behaviour. I ordered the carpenter not to quit me till the other people were in the boat. Nageete, finding I would not stay, loosed himself from my hold and went off, and we all got into the boat except one man, who, while I was getting on board, quitted it, and ran up the beach to cast the stern fast off, notwithstanding the master and others called to him to return, while they were hauling me out of the water.

I was no sooner in the boat than the attack began by about two hundred men; the unfortunate poor man who had run up the beach was knocked down and the stones flew like a shower of shot. Many Indians got hold of the stern rope and were near hauling the boat on shore; which they would certainly have effected if I had not had a knife in my pocket with which I cut the rope. We then hauled off to the grapnel, every one being more or less hurt. At this time I saw five of the natives about the poor man they had killed, and two of them were beating him about the head with stones in their hands.

We had no time to reflect, for to my surprise they filled their canoes with stones, and twelve men came off after us to renew the attack, which they did so effectually as nearly to disable us all. Our grapnel was foul, but Providence here assisted us; the fluke broke, and we got to our oars and pulled to sea. They, however, could paddle round us, so that we were obliged to sustain the attack without being able to return it, except with such stones as lodged in the boat, and in this I found we were very inferior to them. We could not close, because our boat was lumbered and heavy, of which they well knew how to take advantage. I therefore adopted the expedient of throwing overboard some clothes, which, as I expected, they stopped to pick up, and as it was by this time almost dark, they gave over the attack and returned towards the shore, leaving us to reflect on our unhappy situation.

The poor man killed by the natives was John Norton. This was his second voyage with me as a quartermaster, and his worthy character made me lament his loss very much. He has left an aged parent, I am told, whom he supported.

I once before sustained an attack of a similar nature with a smaller number of Europeans against a multitude of Indians. It was after the death of Captain Cook, on the *morai* at Owhyhee, where I was left by Lieutenant King. Yet, notwithstanding this experience, I had not an idea that the power of a man's arm could throw stones, from two to eight pounds weight, with such force and exactness as these people did. Here unhappily we were without fire-arms, which the Indians knew; and it was a fortunate circumstance that they did not begin to attack us in the cave, for in that case our destruction must have been inevitable, and we should have had nothing left for it but to sell our lives as dearly as we could; in which I found every one cheerfully disposed to concur. This appearance of resolution deterred them, supposing that they could effect their purpose without risk after we were in the boat.

Taking this as a sample of the disposition of the natives, there was but little reason to expect much benefit by persevering in the intention of visiting Poulaho, for I considered their good behaviour formerly to have proceeded from a dread of our fire-arms, and which, therefore, was likely to cease as they knew we were now destitute of them; and, even supposing our lives not in danger, the boat and everything we had would most probably be taken from us, and thereby all hopes precluded of ever being able to return to our native country.

We set our sails and steered along shore by the west side of the island Tofoa, the wind blowing fresh from the eastward. My mind was employed in considering what was best to be done, when I was solicited by all hands to take them towards home; and when I told them that no hopes of relief for us remained (except what might be found in New Holland) till I came to Timor, a distance of full twelve hundred leagues, where there was a Dutch settlement, but in what part of the island I knew not, they all agreed to live on one ounce of bread and a quarter of a pint of water per day. Therefore, after examining our stock of provisions, and recommending to them in the most solemn manner not to depart from their promise, we bore away across a sea where the navigation is but little known in a small boat, twenty-three feet long from stem to stern, deep laden with eighteen men. I was happy, however, to see that every one seemed better satisfied with our situation than myself.

Our stock of provisions consisted of about one hundred and fifty pounds of bread, twenty-eight gallons of water, twenty pounds of pork, three bottles of wine, and five quarts of rum. The difference between this and the quantity we had on leaving the ship was principally owing to our loss in the bustle and confusion of the attack. A few coconuts were in the boat, and some bread-fruit, but the latter was trampled to pieces.

3

It was about eight o'clock at night when we bore away under a reefed lug-foresail, and having divided the people into watches and got the boat in a little order, we returned God thanks for our miraculous preservation, and, fully confident of His gracious support, I found my mind more at ease than it had been for some time past.

At daybreak the gale increased, the sun rose very fiery and red – a sure indication of a severe gale of wind. At eight it blew a violent storm and the sea ran very high, so that between the seas the sail was becalmed, and when on the top of the sea it was too much to have set; but we could not venture to take in the sail, for we were in very imminent danger and distress, the sea curling over the stern of the boat, which obliged us to bale with all our might. A situation more distressing has perhaps seldom been experienced.

Our bread was in bags and in danger of being spoiled by the wet: to be starved to death was inevitable if this could not be prevented. I therefore began to examine what clothes there were in the boat, and what other things could be spared; and having determined that only two suits should be kept for each person, the rest was thrown overboard, with some rope and spare sails, which lightened the boat considerably, and we had more room to bale the water out. Fortunately the carpenter had a good chest in the boat, in which we secured the bread the first favourable moment. His tool-chest also was cleared and the tools stowed in the bottom of the boat, so that this became a second convenience.

I served a teaspoonful of rum to each person (for we were very wet and cold), with a quarter of a bread-fruit, which was scarce eatable for dinner. Our engagement was now strictly to be carried into execution, and I was fully determined to make our provisions last eight weeks, let the daily proportion be ever so small.

Served a few broken pieces of bread-fruit for supper, and performed prayers.

The night turned out fair, and having had tolerable rest, every one seemed considerably better in the morning, and contentedly breakfasted on a few pieces of yams that were found in the boat.

Wednesday the 6th May. Our allowance for the day was a quarter of a pint of coconut milk, and the meat, which did not exceed two ounces to each person: it was received very contentedly, but we suffered great drought. I durst not venture to land, as we had no arms, and were less capable of defending ourselves than we were at Tofoa.

To keep an account of the boat's run was rendered difficult, from being constantly wet with the sea breaking over us; but as we advanced towards the land the sea became smoother, and I was enabled to form a sketch of the islands, which will serve to give a general knowledge to their extent and position. Those we were near appeared fruitful and hilly, some very mountainous, and all of a good height.

To our great joy we hooked a fish, but we were miserably disappointed by its being lost in trying to get it into the boat.

As our lodgings were very miserable and confined for want of room, I endeavoured to remedy the latter defect by putting ourselves at watch and watch; so that one-half always sat up while the other lay down on the boat's bottom, or upon a chest, with nothing to cover us but the heavens. Our limbs were dreadfully cramped, for we could not stretch them out; and the nights were so cold, and we so constantly wet, that after a few hours' sleep we could scarce move.

At dawn of day we again discovered land from WSW to WNW, and another island NNW, the latter a high round lump of but little extent; the southern land that we had passed in the night was still in sight. Being very wet and cold, I served a spoonful of rum and a morsel of bread for breakfast.

The land in the west was distinguished by some extraordinary high rocks, which as we approached them assumed a variety of forms. The country appeared to be agreeably interspersed with high and low land, and in some places covered with wood. Off the NE part lay some small rocky islands, between which and an island four leagues to the NE I directed my course; but a lee current very unexpectedly set us very near to the rocky isles, and we could only get clear of it by rowing, passing close to the reef that surrounded them. At this time we observed two large sailing canoes coming swiftly after us along the shore, and being apprehensive of their intentions we rowed with some anxiety, fully sensible of our weak and defenceless state. At noon it was calm and the weather cloudy; my latitude is therefore doubtful to three or four miles. Being constantly wet it was with the utmost difficulty I could open a book to write, and I am sensible that what I have done can only serve to point out where these lands are to be found again, and give an idea of their extent.

All the afternoon we had light winds at NNE; the weather was very rainy, attended with thunder and lightning. Only one of the canoes gained upon us, which by three o'clock in the afternoon was not more than two miles off, when she gave over chase.

If I may judge from the sail of these vessels, they are of a similar construction with those at the Friendly Islands, which with the nearness of their situation gives reason to believe that they are the same kind of people. Whether these canoes had any hostile intention against us must remain a doubt. Perhaps we might have benefited by an intercourse with them, but in our defenceless situation to have made the experiment would have been risking too much.

I imagine these to be of the islands called Fiji, as their extent, direction and distance from the Friendly Islands answer to the description given of them by those islanders. Heavy rain came on at four o'clock, when every person did their utmost to catch some water, and we increased our stock to thirty-four gallons, besides quenching our thirst for the first time since we had been at sea; but an attendant consequence made us pass the night very miserably, for being extremely wet, and having no dry things to shift or cover us, we experienced cold and shiverings scarce to be conceived. Most fortunately for us the forenoon turned out fair, and we stripped and dried our clothes. The allowance I issued today was an ounce and a half of pork, a teaspoonful of rum, half a pint of coconut milk, and an ounce of bread. The rum, though so small in quantity, was of the greatest service. A fishing-line was generally towing from the stern of the boat, but though we saw great numbers of fish, we could never catch one.

In the afternoon we cleaned out the boat, and it employed us till sunset to get everything dry and in order. Hitherto I had issued the allowance by guess, but I now made a pair of scales with two coconut shells; and having accidentally some pistol balls in the boat, twenty-five of which weighed one pound, or sixteen ounces, I adopted one, as the proportion of weight that each person should receive of bread at the times I served it. I also amused all hands with describing the situation of New Guinea and New Holland, and gave them every information in my power, that in case any accident happened to me, those who survived might have some idea of what they were about, and be able to find their way to Timor, which at present they knew nothing of, more than the name, and some not even that. At night I served a quarter of a pint of water and half an ounce of bread for supper.

Saturday the 9th. In the morning, a quarter of a pint of coconut milk and some of the decayed bread was served for breakfast; and for dinner I divided the meat of four coconuts with the remainder of the rotten bread, which was only eatable by such distressed people.

In the afternoon I fitted a pair of shrouds for each mast, and contrived a canvas weather-cloth round the boat, and raised the quarters about nine inches by nailing on the seats of the stern-sheets, which proved of great benefit to us.

The wind had been moderate all day, in the SE quarter, with fine weather, but about nine o'clock in the evening the clouds began to gather, and we had a prodigious fall of rain, with severe thunder and lightning. By midnight we caught about twenty gallons of water. Being miserably wet and cold, I served to the people a teaspoonful of rum each, to enable them to bear with their distressed situation. The weather continued extremely bad, and the wind increased; we spent a very miserable night without sleep, except such as could be got in the midst of rain. The day brought no relief but its light. The sea broke over us so much that two men were constantly baling, and we had no choice how to steer, being obliged to keep before the waves for fear of the boat filling.

The allowance now regularly served to each person was one-twenty-fifth of a pound of bread, and a quarter of a pint of water, at eight in the morning, at noon, and at sunset. Today I gave about half an ounce of pork for dinner, which, though any moderate person would have considered only as a mouthful, was divided into three or four.

The wind continued strong from SSE to SE, with very squally weather and a high breaking sea, so that we were miserably wet, and suffered great cold in the night.

Monday the 11th May. In the morning at daybreak I served to every person a teaspoonful of rum, our limbs being so cramped that we could scarce move them. Our situation was now extremely dangerous, the sea frequently running over our stern, which kept us baling with all our strength.

In the evening it rained hard, and we again experienced a dreadful night. At length the day came, and showed to me a miserable set of beings, full of wants, without anything to relieve them. Some complained of great pains in their bowels, and every one of having almost lost the use of his limbs. The little sleep we got was no ways refreshing, as we were covered with sea and rain. I served a spoonful of rum at day-dawn, and the usual allowance of bread and water for breakfast, dinner, and supper.

At noon it was almost calm, no sun to be seen, and some of us shivering with cold. Course since yesterday W by N, distance eighty-nine miles; latitude, by account, 14° 33' S; longitude made 13° 9' W. The direction of our course was to pass to the northward of the New Hebrides.

The wet weather continued, and in the afternoon the wind came from the southward, blowing fresh in squalls. As there was no prospect of getting our clothes dried, I recommended to every one to strip, and wring them through the salt water, by which means they received a warmth that while wet with rain they could not have.

This afternoon we saw a kind of fruit on the water which Nelson told me was the Barringtonia of Forster; and as I saw the same again in the morning, and some men-of-war birds, I was led to believe that we were not far from land.

We continued constantly shipping seas, and baling, and were very wet and cold in the night; but I could not afford the allowance of rum at daybreak.

Sunday the 17th May. At dawn of day I found every person complaining, and some of them solicited extra allowances; which positively refused. Our situation was miserable; always wet, and suffering extreme cold in the night, without the least shelter from the weather. Being constantly obliged to bale, to keep the boat from filling, was perhaps not to be reckoned an evil, as it gave us exercise.

The little rum we had was of great service. When our nights were particularly distressing I generally served a teaspoonful or two to each person, and it was always joyful tidings when they heard of my intentions.

At noon a water-spout was very near on board of us. I issued an ounce of pork, in addition to the allowance of bread and water; but before we began to eat, every person stripped, and having wrung their clothes through the sea-water, found much warmth and refreshment. Course since yesterday noon WSW, distance one hundred miles; latitude, by account, 14° 11′ S, and longitude made 21° 3′ W.

The night was dark and dismal, the sea constantly breaking over us, and nothing but the wind and waves to direct our steerage. It was my intention, if possible, to make New Holland, to the southward of Endeavour Straits, being sensible that it was necessary to preserve such a situation as would make a southerly wind a fair one; that we might range along the reefs till an opening should be found into smooth water, and we the sooner be able to pick up some refreshments.

Monday the 18th. In the morning the rain abated, when we stripped and wrung our clothes through the sea-water as usual, which refreshed us greatly. Every person complained of violent pain in their bones; I was only surprised that no one was yet laid up. The customary allowance of one twenty-fifth of a pound of bread and a quarter of a pint of water was served at breakfast, dinner, and supper.

At noon I deduced my situation, by account, for we had no glimpse of the sun, to be in latitude 14° 52′ S; course since yesterday noon, WSW, one hundred and six miles; longitude made from Tofoa 22° 45′ W. Saw many boobies and noddies, a sign of being in the neighbourhood of land. In the night we had very severe lightning, with heavy rain, and were obliged to keep baling without intermission.

Wednesday the 20th. Fresh breezes ENE with constant rain; at times a deluge. Always baling.

At dawn of day some of my people seemed half dead; our appearances were horrible, and I could look no way but I caught the eye of someone in distress. Extreme hunger was now too evident, but no one suffered from thirst, nor had we much inclination to drink, that desire perhaps being satisfied through the skin. The little sleep we got was in the midst of water, and we constantly awoke with severe cramps and pains in our bones. This morning I served about two teaspoonfuls of rum to each person, and the allowance of bread and water as usual. At noon the sun broke out and revived every one.

All the afternoon we were so covered with rain and salt water that we could scarcely see. We suffered extreme cold, and everyone dreaded the approach of night. Sleep, though we longed for it, afforded no comfort: for my own part I almost lived without it. About two o'clock in the morning we were overwhelmed with a deluge of rain. It fell so heavy that we were afraid it would fill the boat, and were obliged to bale with all our might. At dawn of day I served a larger allowance of rum. Towards noon the rain abated and the sun shone, but we were miserably cold and wet, the sea breaking constantly over us; so that notwithstanding the heavy rain, we had not been able to add to our stock of fresh water. Latitude, by observation, 14° 29′ S, and longitude made, by account, from Tofoa, 27° 25′ W; course, since yesterday noon, N 78° W, ninety-nine miles. I now considered myself nearly on a meridian with the east part of New Guinea.

Friday the 22nd May. Strong gales from ESE to SSE, a high sea, and dark dismal night.

Friday the 22nd May. Our situation this day was extremely calamitous. We were obliged to take the course of the sea, running right before it, and watching with the utmost care, as the least error in the helm would in a moment have been our destruction.

At noon it blew very hard, and the foam of the sea kept running over our stern and quarters. I, however, got propped up, and made an observation of the latitude, in 14° 17′ S; course N 85° W, distance one hundred and thirty miles; longitude made 29° 38′ W.

The misery we suffered this night exceeded the preceding. The sea flew over us with great force, and kept us baling with horror and anxiety. At dawn of day I found everyone in a most distressed condition, and I began to fear that another such night would put an end to the lives of several, who seemed no longer able to support their sufferings. I served an allowance of two teaspoonfuls of rum; after drinking which, having wrung our clothes and taken our breakfast of bread and water, we became a little refreshed.

Towards noon the weather became fair, but with very little abatement of the gale, and the sea remained equally high. With some difficulty I observed the latitude to be 13° 44′ S; course since yesterday noon N 74° W, distance one hundred and sixteen miles; longitude made 31° 32′ W from Tofoa.

The wind moderated in the evening and the weather looked much better, which rejoiced all hands, so that they eat their scanty allowances with more satisfaction than for some time past. The night also was fair; but being always wet with the sea, we suffered much from the cold. A fine morning, I had the pleasure to see, produced some cheerful countenances, and the first time for fifteen days past we experienced comfort from the warmth of the sun. We stripped and hung our clothes up to dry, which were by this time become so threadbare that they would not keep out either wet or cold.

At noon I observed in latitude 13° 33′ S; longitude, by account, from Tofoa, 33° 28′ W, course N 84° W, distance one hundred and fourteen miles. With the usual allowance of bread and water for dinner, I served an ounce of pork to each person. This afternoon we had many birds about us which are never seen far from land, such as boobies and noddies.

As the sea began to run fair and we shipped but little water, I took the opportunity to examine into the state of our bread, and found that according to the present mode of issuing there was a sufficient quantity remaining for twenty-nine days' allowance; by which time I hoped we should be able to reach Timor. But as this as very uncertain, and it was possible that after all we might be obliged to go to Java, I determined to proportion the allowance so as to make our stock hold out six weeks. I was apprehensive that this would be ill received, and that it would require my utmost resolution to enforce it; for small as the quantity was which I intended to take away for our future good, yet it might appear to my people like robbing them of life; and some, who were less patient than their companions, I expected would very ill brook it. However, on my representing the necessity of guarding against delays that might be occasioned in our voyage by contrary winds or other causes, and promising to enlarge upon the allowance as we got on, they cheerfully agreed to my proposal. It was accordingly settled that every person should receive one twenty-fifth of a pound of bread for breakfast, and the same quantity for dinner; so that by omitting the proportion for supper, we had forty-three days' allowance.

Monday the 25th May. At noon some noddies came so near to us that one of them was caught by hand. This bird was about the size of a small pigeon. I divided it, with the entrails, into eighteen portions and by a well-known method at sea, of 'Who shall have this?'[1] it was distributed, with the allowance of bread and water for dinner, and eat up bones and all, with salt water for sauce. I observed the latitude 13° 32′ S; longitude made 35° 19′ W; course 89° W, distance one hundred and eight miles.

In the evening several boobies flying very near to us, we had the good fortune to catch one of them. This bird is as large as a duck. Like the noddy, it has received its name from seamen, for suffering itself to be caught on the masts and yards of ships. They are the most presumptive proofs of being in the neighbourhood of land of any sea-fowl we are acquainted with. I directed the bird to be killed for supper, and the blood to be given to three of the people who were the most distressed for want of food. The body, with the

1. One person turns his back on the object that is to be divided; another then points separately to the portions, at each of them asking aloud, 'Who shall have this?' to which the first answers by naming somebody. This impartial method of division gives every man an equal chance of the best share.

entrails, beak, and feet, I divided into eighteen shares, and with a
allowance of bread, which I made a merit of granting, we made
good supper compared with our usual fare.

Tuesday the 26th May. Fresh breezes from the SE, with fir
weather. In the morning we caught another booby, so that Prov
dence appeared to be relieving our wants in an extraordina
manner. Towards noon we passed a great many pieces of tl
branches of trees, some of which appeared to have been no lor
time in the water. I had a good observation for the latitude, an
found our situation to be in 13° 41′ S, longitude, by account, fro
Tofoa, 37° 13′ W; course S 85° W, one hundred and twelve mile
The people were overjoyed at the addition to their dinner, whi
was distributed in the same manner as on the preceding evenin
giving the blood to those who were the most in want of food.

To make the bread a little savoury, most of the people fr
quently dipped it in salt water; but I generally broke mine in
small pieces and eat it in my allowance of water, out of a cocon
shell, with a spoon, economically avoiding to take too large a pie
at a time, so that I was as long at dinner as if it had been a mu
more plentiful meal.

The weather was now serene, which nevertheless was not wit
out its inconveniences, for we began to feel distress of a differe
kind from that which we had lately been accustomed to suffer. T
heat of the sun was so powerful that several of the people we
seized with a languor and faintness which made life indifferent. W
were so fortunate as to catch two boobies in the evening. The
stomachs contained several flying fish and small cuttlefish, all
which I saved to be divided for dinner the next day.

Wednesday the 27th May. A fresh breeze at ESE, with fa
weather. We passed much driftwood this forenoon and saw ma
birds; I therefore did not hesitate to pronounce that we were ne
the reefs of New Holland. From my recollection of Captain Cook
survey of this coast, I considered the direction of it to be NW, ar
I was therefore satisfied that with the wind to the southward of E,
could always clear any dangers.

At noon I observed in latitude 13° 26′ S; course since yesterd
N 82° W, distance one hundred and nine miles; longitude ma

9° 4′ W. After writing my account I divided the two birds, with their entrails and the contents of their maws, into eighteen portions, and as the prize was a very valuable one it was divided as before, by calling out 'Who shall have this?' So that today, with the allowance of a twenty-fifth of a pound of bread at breakfast and another at dinner, with the proportion of water, I was happy to see that every person thought he had feasted.

In the evening we saw a gannet, and the clouds remained so fixed in the west that I had little doubt of our being near the land. The people, after taking their allowance of water for supper, amused themselves with conversing on the probability of what we should find.

Thursday the 28th May. At one in the morning the person at the helm heard the sound of breakers, and I no sooner lifted up my head than I saw them close under our lee, not more than a quarter of a mile distant from us. I immediately hauled on a wind to the NE, and in ten minutes' time we could neither see nor hear them.

I have already mentioned my reason for making New Holland so far to the southward, for I never doubted of numerous openings in the reef through which I could have access to the shore, and knowing the inclination of the coast to be to the NW, and the wind mostly to the southward of E, I could with ease range such a barrier of reefs till I should find a passage, which now became absolutely necessary, without a moment's loss of time. The idea of getting into smooth water, and finding refreshments, kept my people's spirits up. Their joy was very great after we had got clear of the breakers, to which we had approached much nearer than I thought was possible without first discovering them.

In the morning, at daylight, we could see nothing of the land or of the reefs. We bore away again, and at nine o'clock saw the reefs. The sea broke furiously over every part, and we had no sooner got near to them than the wind came at E, so that we could only lie along the line of the breakers; within which we saw the water so smooth that every person already anticipated the heart-felt satisfaction he should receive as soon as we could get within them. I now found we were embayed, for we could not lie clear with the sails, the wind having backed against us, and the sea set in so heavy

towards the reef that our situation was become unsafe. We coul
effect but little with the oars, having scarce strength to pull them
and I began to apprehend that we should be obliged to attemp
pushing over the reef. Even this I did not despair of effecting wit
success, when happily we discovered a break in the reef about on
mile from us, and at the same time an island of a moderate heigh
within it, nearly in the same direction, bearing W½N. I entered th
passage with a strong stream running to the westward, and found i
about a quarter of a mile broad, with every appearance of dee
water. We now returned God thanks for His gracious protectior
and with much content took our miserable allowance of a twenty
fifth of a pound of bread and a quarter of a pint of water fo
dinner.

4

As we advanced within the reefs the coast began to show itself ver
distinctly, in a variety of high and low land, some parts of whic
were covered with wood. In our way towards the shore we fell i
with a point of a reef which is connected with that towards the sea
and here we came to a grapnel and tried to catch fish, but had n
success. The island Direction at this time bore S three or fou
leagues. Two islands lay about four miles to the W by N, an
appeared eligible for a resting-place, if for nothing more; but o
our approach to the nearest island, it proved to be only a heap o
stones, and its size too inconsiderable to shelter the boat. We there
fore proceeded to the next, which was close to it and towards th
main. On the NW side of this I found a bay and a fine sandy poin
to land at. Our distance was about a quarter of a mile from
projecting part of the main, which bore from SW by S, t
NNW¾W. We landed to examine if there were any signs of th
natives being near us. We saw old fire-places, but nothing to mak
me apprehend that this would be an unsafe situation for the nigh
Everyone was anxious to find something to eat, and it was soo
discovered that there were oysters on the rocks, for the tide wa
out; but it was nearly dark, and only a few could be gathered.
determined therefore to wait till the morning, when I should bette

know how to proceed, and I directed that one-half of our company should sleep on shore and the other half in the boat. We would gladly have made a fire, but as we could not accomplish it we took our rest for the night, which happily was calm and undisturbed.

Friday the 29th. The dawn of day brought greater strength and spirits to us than I expected, for notwithstanding everyone was very weak, there appeared strength sufficient remaining to make me conceive the most favourable hopes of our being able to surmount the difficulties we might yet have to encounter.

As there were no appearances to make me imagine that any of the natives were near us, I sent out parties in search of supplies, while others of the people were putting the boat in order, that we might be ready to go to sea in case any unforeseen cause should make it necessary. One of the gudgeons of the rudder had come out in the course of the night, and was lost. This, if it had happened at sea, might have been attended with the most serious consequences, as the management of the boat could not have been so nicely preserved as these very heavy seas required. I had been apprehensive of this accident, and had in some measure prepared for it by having grummets fixed on each quarter of the boat for oars; but our utmost readiness in using them would not probably have saved us. It appears therefore a providential circumstance that it happened in a place of safety, and that it was in our power to remedy the defect, for by great good luck we found a large staple in the boat which answered the purpose.

The parties returned, highly rejoiced at having found plenty of oysters and fresh water. I had also made a fire, by the help of a small magnifying glass; and what was still more fortunate, we found among the few things which had been thrown into the boat and saved, a piece of brimstone and a tinder-box, so that I secured fire for the future.

One of the people had been so provident as to bring away with him from the ship a copper pot. By being in possession of this article we were enabled to make a proper use of the supply we now obtained, for with a mixture of bread and a little pork we made a stew that might have been relished by people of far more delicate appetites, and of which each person received a full pint.

The general complaints of disease among us were a dizziness in the head, great weakness of the joints, and violent tenesmus; most of us having had no evacuation by stool since we left the ship. I had constantly a severe pain at my stomach, but none of our complaints were alarming. On the contrary, every one retained marks of strength that, with a mind possessed of a tolerable share of fortitude, seemed able to bear more fatigue than I imagined we should have to undergo in our voyage to Timor.

As I would not allow the people to expose themselves to the heat of the sun, it being near noon, every one took his allotment of earth where it was shaded by the bushes for a short sleep.

The oysters which were found grew so fast to the rocks that it was with difficulty they could be broken off, and at length we discovered it to be the most expeditious way to open them where they were fixed. They were of a good size and well tasted. To add to this happy circumstance, in the hollow of the land there grew some wire grass, which indicated a moist situation. On forcing a stick about three feet long into the ground we found water, and with little trouble dug a well, which produced as much as our occasions required. It was very good, but I could not determine if it was a spring or not. We were not obliged to make the well deep, for it flowed as fast as we emptied it; which, as the soil was apparently too loose to retain water from the rains, renders it probable to be a spring. On the south side of the island likewise we found a small run of good water.

Besides places where fires had been made, there were other signs of the natives sometimes resorting to this island. I saw two ill-constructed huts or wigwams, which had only one side loosely covered; and a pointed stick was found, about three feet long, with a slit in the end of it to sling stones with; the same as the natives of Van Diemen's Land use.

The track of some animal was very discernible, and Nelson agreed with me it was the kangaroo; but whether these animals swim over from the mainland or are brought here by the natives to breed, it is impossible to determine. The latter is not improbable, as they may be taken with less difficulty in a confined spot like this, than on the continent.

The island is about a league in circuit. It is a high lump of rocks and stones covered with wood, but the trees are small, the soil, which is very indifferent and sandy, being barely sufficient to produce them. The trees that came within our knowledge were the manchineel and a species of purow; also some palm trees, the tops of which we cut down, and the soft interior part or heart of them was so palatable that it made a good addition to our mess. Nelson discovered some fern-roots, which I thought might be good roasted as a substitute for bread, but in this I was mistaken. It, however, was very serviceable in its natural state to allay thirst, and on that account I directed a quantity to be collected to take into the boat. Many pieces of coconut shells and husk were found about the shore, but we could find no coconut trees, neither did I see any on the main.

I had cautioned the people not to touch any kind of berry or fruit that they might find; yet they were no sooner out of my sight than they began to make free with three different kinds that grew all over the island, eating without any reserve. The symptoms of having eaten too much began at last to frighten some of them; but on questioning others, who had taken a more moderate allowance, their minds were a little quieted. The others, however, became equally alarmed in their turn, dreading that such symptoms would come on, and that they were all poisoned, so that they regarded each other with the strongest marks of apprehension, uncertain what would be the issue of their imprudence. Fortunately the fruit proved wholesome and good. One sort grew on a small delicate kind of vine. They were the size of a large gooseberry, and very like in substance, but had only a sweet taste; the skin was a pale red, streaked with yellow the long way of the fruit: it was pleasant and agreeable. Another kind grew on bushes, like that which is called the seaside grape in the West Indies; but the fruit was very different, being more like elderberries, and grew in clusters in the same manner. The third sort was a black berry; this was not in such plenty as the others, and resembled a bullace or large kind of sloe, both in size and taste. When I saw that these fruits were eaten by the birds, I no longer doubted of their being wholesome, and those who had already tried the experiment, not finding any bad effect, made it a certainty that we might eat of them without danger.

Wild pigeons, parrots, and other birds were about the summit of the island, but having no fire-arms relief of that kind was not to be expected, unless we should find some unfrequented spot where the birds were so tame that we might take them with our hands.

The shore of this island is very rocky, except the place at which we landed, and here I picked up many pieces of pumice-stone. On the part of the main nearest to us were several sandy bays, which at low-water became an extensive rocky flat. The country had rather a barren appearance, except in a few places where it was covered with wood. A remarkable range of rocks lay a few miles to the SW, and a high peaked hill seemed to terminate the coast towards the sea, with islands to the southward. A high fair cape showed the direction of the coast to the NW, about seven leagues distant, and two small isles lay three or four leagues to the northward of our present station.

I saw a few bees or wasps and several lizards; and the blackberry bushes were full of ants' nests, webbed like a spider's, but so close and compact as not to admit the rain. A trunk of a tree, about fifty feet long, lay on the beach; from which I conclude that a heavy sea sets in here with a northerly wind.

This day being the anniversary of the restoration of King Charles the Second, and the name not being inapplicable to our present situation (for we were restored to fresh life and strength), I named this Restoration Island, for I thought it probable that Captain Cook might not have taken notice of it. The other names which I have presumed to give the different parts of the coast are meant only to show my route more distinctly.

At noon I observed the latitude of the island to be 12° 39′ S; our course having been N 66° W, distance eighteen miles from yesterday noon. The wind was at ESE, with very fine weather.

In the afternoon I sent parties out again to gather oysters, with which and some of the inner part of the palm-tops, we made another good stew for supper, each person receiving a full pint and a half; but I refused bread to this meal, for I considered that our wants might yet be very great, and was intent on saving our principal support whenever it was in my power. After supper we again divided, and those who were on shore slept by a good fire.

Saturday the 30th May. In the morning I discovered a visible alteration in our company for the better, and I sent them away again to gather oysters. We had now only two pounds of pork left. This article, which I could not keep under lock and key as I did the bread, had been pilfered by some inconsiderate person, but everyone denied having any knowledge of this act. I therefore resolved to put it out of their power for the future, by sharing what remained for our dinner. While the party was out picking up oysters I got the boat in readiness for sea, and filled all our water-vessels, which amounted to nearly sixty gallons.

The party being returned, dinner was soon ready, which was as plentiful a meal as the supper on the preceding evening, and with the pork I gave an allowance of bread. As it was not yet noon, I sent the people once more to gather oysters for a sea store, recommending to them to be as diligent as possible, for that I was determined to sail in the afternoon.

Being ready for sea I directed every person to attend prayers. At four o'clock we were preparing to embark, when about twenty of the natives appeared, running and hallooing to us, on the opposite shore. They were each armed with a spear or lance, and a short weapon which they carried in their left hand; they made signs for us to come to them. On the top of the hills we saw the heads of many more. Whether these were the wives and children, or others who waited for our landing, meaning not to show themselves, lest we might be intimidated, I cannot say; but as I found we were discovered to be on the coast, I thought it prudent to make the best of our way, for fear of being pursued by canoes, though from the accounts of Captain Cook, the chance was that there were very few if any of consequence on any part of the coast. I passed these people as near as I could with safety: they were naked, and apparently black, and their hair or wool bushy and short.

Sunday the 31st May. At daybreak I was exceedingly surprised to find the appearance of the country entirely changed, as if in the course of the night we had been transported to another part of the world; for we had now a low sandy coast in view, with very little verdure, or anything to indicate that it was at all habitable to a human being, except a few patches of small trees or brushwood.

Many small islands were in sight to the NE, about six miles

distant. The E part of the main bore N four miles, and Fair Cape SSE five or six leagues. I took the channel between the nearest island and the mainland, which were about one mile apart, leaving all the islands on the starboard side. Some of these were very pretty spots, covered with wood and well situated for fishing, large shoals of fish were about us, but we could not catch any. In passing this strait we saw another party of Indians, seven in number, running towards us, shouting and making signs for us to land. Some of them waved green branches of the bushes which were near them as a token of friendship, but some of their other motions were less friendly. A little farther off we saw a larger party, who likewise came towards us. I therefore determined not to land, though I much wished to have had some intercourse with these people. Nevertheless I laid the boat close to the rocks and beckoned to them to approach, but none of them would come within two hundred yards of us. They were armed in the same manner as the people we had seen from Restoration Island; they were stark naked, their colour black, with short bushy hair or wool, and in their appearance were similar to them in every respect. An island of a good height bore N$\frac{1}{2}$W, four miles from us, at which I resolved to land, and from thence to take a look at the coast. At this isle we arrived about eight o'clock in the morning. The shore was rocky, but the water was smooth, and we landed without difficulty. I sent two parties out, one to the northward and the other to the southward, to seek for supplies, and others I ordered to stay by the boat. On this occasion fatigue and weakness so far got the better of their sense of duty that some of the people expressed their discontent at having worked harder than their companions, and declared that they would rather be without their dinner than go in search of it. One person, in particular, went so far as to tell me, with a mutinous look, that he was as good a man as myself. It was not possible for me to judge where this might have an end if not stopped in time. Therefore to prevent such disputes in future I determined either to preserve my command or die in the attempt, and seizing a cutlass I ordered him to take hold of another and defend himself; on which he called out that I was going to kill him and immediately made concessions. I did not allow this to interfere further with the harmony of the boat's crew, and everything soon became quiet.

The parties continued collecting what they could find, which were some fine oysters and clams and a few small dog-fish that were caught in the holes of the rocks. We also found some rain-water in the hollow of the rocks on the north part of the island, so that of this essential article we were again so fortunate as to obtain a full supply.

After regulating the mode of proceeding I walked to the highest part of the island to consider our route for the night. To my surprise no more of the mainland could be seen here than from below, the northernmost part in sight, which was full of sand-hills, bearing W by N, about three leagues. Except the isles to the ESE and S that we had passed, I could only discover a small key NW by N. As this was considerably farther from the main than the spot on which we were at present, I judged it would be a more secure resting place for the night; for here we were liable to an attack if the Indians had canoes, as they undoubtedly must have observed our landing. My mind being made up on this point, I returned, after taking a particular look at the island we were on, which I found only to produce a few bushes and some coarse grass, the extent of the whole not being two miles in circuit. On the north side, in a sandy bay, I saw an old canoe, about thirty-three feet long, lying bottom upwards and half buried in the beach. It was made of three pieces, the bottom entire, to which the sides were sewed in the common way. It had a sharp projecting prow rudely carved in resemblance of the head of a fish; the extreme breadth was about three feet, and I imagine it was capable of carrying twenty men. The discovery of so large a canoe confirmed me in the purpose of seeking a more retired place for our night's lodging.

At noon the parties were all returned, but had found much difficulty in gathering the oysters from their close adherence to the rocks, and the clams were scarce. I therefore saw that it would be of little use to remain longer in this place, as we should not be able to collect more than we could eat. I named this Sunday Island: it lies N by W¾W from Restoration Island; the latitude, by a good observation, 11° 58′ S.

We had a fresh breeze at SE by S, with fair weather. At two o'clock in the afternoon we dined, each person having a full pint and a half of stewed oysters and clams, thickened with small beans, which Nelson informed me were a species of dolichos. Having eaten heartily, and completed our water, I waited to determine the time of high-water, which I found to be at three-o'clock, and the rise of the tide about five feet. According to this, it is high-water on the full and change at nineteen minutes past nine in the morning. I observed the flood to come from the southward, though at Restoration Island I thought it came from the northward. I think Captain Cook mentions that he found great irregularity in the set of the flood on this coast.

We steered for the key seen in the NW by N, where we arrived just at dark, but found it so surrounded by a reef of rocks that I could not land without danger of staving the boat, and on that account we came to a grapnel for the night.

Monday the 1st June. At dawn of day we got on shore and tracked the boat into shelter, for the wind blowing fresh without and the ground being rocky it was not safe to trust her at a grapnel, lest she should be blown to sea. I was therefore obliged to let her ground in the course of the ebb. From appearances I expected that if we remained till night we should meet with turtle, as we discovered recent tracks of them. Innumerable birds of the noddy kind made this island their resting-place, so that we had to flatter ourselves with hopes of getting supplies in greater abundance than it had hitherto been in our power. Our situation was at least four leagues distant from the main. We were on the north-westernmost of four small keys, which were surrounded by a reef of rocks connected by sand-banks, except between the two northernmost, and there likewise it was dry at low water; the whole forming a lagoon island into which the tide flowed. At this entrance I kept the boat.

As usual I sent parties away in search of supplies, but to our great disappointment we could only get a few clams and some dolichos. With these, and the oysters we had brought from Sunday Island, I made up a mess for dinner, with the addition of a small quantity of bread.

Towards noon Nelson and some others who had been to the easternmost key returned; but Nelson was in so weak a condition that he was obliged to be supported by two men. His complaint was a violent heat in his bowels, a loss of sight, much drought, and an inability to walk. This I found was occasioned by his being unable to support the heat of the sun, and that when he was fatigued and faint, instead of retiring into the shade to rest, he had continued to attempt more than his strength was equal to. I was glad to find that he had no fever, and it was now that the little wine, which I had so carefully saved, became of real use. I gave it in very small quantities, with some pieces of bread soaked in it, and he soon began to recover. The boatswain and carpenter also were ill, and complained of headache and sickness of the stomach. Others, who had not had any evacuation by stool, became shockingly distressed with the tenesmus, so that there were but few without complaints. An idea prevailed that the sickness of the boatswain and carpenter was occasioned by eating the dolichos. Myself, however, and some others who had taken the same food felt no inconvenience; but the truth was that many of the people had eaten a large quantity of them raw, and Nelson informed me that they were constantly teasing him, whenever a berry was found, to know if it was good to eat; so that it would not have been surprising if many of them had been really poisoned.

Our dinner was not so well relished as at Sunday Island, because we had mixed the dolichos with our stew. The oysters and soup, however, were eaten by everyone, except Nelson, whom I fed with a few small pieces of bread soaked in half a glass of wine, and he continued to mend.

In my walk round the island I found several coconut shells, the remains of an old wigwam, and the backs of two turtle, but no sign of any quadruped. One of the people found three sea-fowl's eggs.

As is common on such spots, the soil is little other than sand, yet it produced small toa-trees, and some others that we were not acquainted with. There were fish in the lagoon, but we could not catch any. Our wants, therefore, were not likely to be supplied here, not even with water for our daily expense; nevertheless, I determined to wait till the morning, that we might try our success in the night for turtle and birds. A quiet night's rest also, I conceived, would be of essential service to those who were unwell.

The wigwam and turtle shell were proofs that the natives at times visited this place, and that they had canoes; the remains of the large canoe that we saw at Sunday Island left no room to doubt; but I did not apprehend that we ran any risk by remaining here a short time. I directed our fire, however, to be made in the thicket, that we might not be discovered by its light.

At noon I observed the latitude of this island to be 11° 47′ S. The mainland extended towards the NW and was full of white sand-hills; another small island lay within us, bearing W by N¼N, three leagues distant. Our situation being very low we could see nothing of the reef towards the sea.

The afternoon was advantageously spent in sleep. There were, however, a few not disposed to it, and those were employed in dressing some clams to take with us for the next day's dinner; others we cut up in slices to dry, which I knew was the most valuable supply we could find here, but they were very scarce.

Towards evening I cautioned everyone against making too large a fire, or suffering it after dark to blaze up. Mr Samuel and Mr Peckover had the superintendence of this business, while I was strolling about the beach to observe if I thought it could be seen from the main. I was just satisfied that it could not, when on a sudden the island appeared all in a blaze that might have been discerned at a much more considerable distance. I ran to learn the cause, and found that it was occasioned by the imprudence and obstinacy of one of the party, who in my absence had insisted on having a fire to himself; in making which the flames caught the neighbouring grass and rapidly spread. This misconduct might have produced very serious consequences, by discovering our situation to the natives, for if they had attacked us we had neither arms nor strength to oppose an enemy. Thus the relief which I expected from a little sleep was totally lost, and I anxiously waited for the flowing of the tide, that we might proceed to sea.

5

At eight o'clock in the evening we once more launched into the open ocean. Miserable as our situation was in every respect, I was secretly surprised to see that it did not appear to affect anyone so strongly as myself. On the contrary, it seemed as if they had embarked on a voyage to Timor in a vessel sufficiently calculated for safety and convenience. So much confidence gave me great pleasure, and I may venture to assert that to this cause our preservation is chiefly to be attributed.

I encouraged everyone with hopes that eight or ten days would bring us to a land of safety; and after praying to God for a continuance of his most gracious protection, I served an allowance of water for supper, and directed our course to the WSW, to counteract the southerly winds in case they should blow strong.

We had been just six days on the coast of New Holland, in the course of which we found oysters, a few clams, some birds, and water. But perhaps a benefit nearly equal to this we received, by having been relieved from the fatigue of being constantly in the boat, and enjoying good rest at night. These advantages certainly preserved our lives; and, small as the supply was, I am very sensible how much it alleviated our distresses. By this time nature must have sunk under the extremes of hunger and fatigue. Some would have ceased to struggle for a life that only promised wretchedness and misery, and others, though possessed of more bodily strength, must soon have followed their unfortunate companions. Even in our present situation we were most deplorable objects, but the hopes of a speedy relief kept up our spirits. For my part, incredible as it may appear, I felt neither extreme hunger nor thirst. My allowance contented me, knowing that I could have no more.

Thursday the 4th June. I served one twenty-fifth of a pound of bread and an allowance of water for breakfast, and the same for dinner, with an addition of six oysters to each person. At noon, latitude observed 10° 48′ S; course since yesterday noon S 81° W, distance one hundred and eleven miles; longitude, by account, from Shoal Cape, 1° 45′ W. A strong trade wind at ESE, with fair weather.

This day we saw a number of water-snakes that were ringed yellow and black, and towards noon we passed a great deal of rock-weed. Though the weather was fair we were constantly shipping water, which kept two men always employed to bale the boat.

Friday the 5th June. At noon I observed in latitude 10° 45′ S; our course since yesterday W¼N, one hundred and eight miles; longitude made 3° 35′ W. Six oysters were, as yesterday, served to each man, in addition to the usual allowance of bread and water.

In the evening a few boobies came about us, one of which I caught with my hand. The blood was divided among three of the men who were weakest, but the bird I ordered to be kept for our dinner the next day. Served a quarter of a pint of water for supper, and to some, who were most in need, half a pint. In the course of the night, being constantly wet with the sea, we suffered much cold and shiverings.

Saturday the 6th June. At daylight I found that some of the clams, which had been hung up to dry for sea-store, were stolen; but everyone solemnly denied having any knowledge of it. This forenoon we saw a gannet, a sand-lark, and some water-snakes, which in general were from two to three feet long.

The usual allowance of bread and water was served for breakfast, and the same for dinner, with the bird, which I distributed in the usual way of 'Who shall have this?' I proposed to make Timor about the latitude of 9° 30′ S, of 10° S. At noon I observed the latitude to be 10° 19′ S; course N 77° W, distance one hundred and seventeen miles; longitude made from the Shoal Cape, the north part of New Holland, 5° 31′ W.

In the afternoon I took an opportunity of examining our store of bread, and found remaining nineteen days' allowance, at the former rate of serving one twenty-fifth of a pound three times a day. Therefore, as I saw every prospect of a quick passage, I again ventured to grant an allowance for supper, agreeable to my promise at the time it was discontinued.

We passed the night miserably wet and cold, and in the morning I heard heavy complaints. The sea was high and breaking over us. I could only afford the allowance of bread and water for breakfast, but for dinner I gave out an ounce of dried clams to each person, which was all that remained.

The sea ran very high all this day and we had frequent showers of rain, so that we were continually wet and suffered much cold in the night. Mr Ledward, the surgeon, and Lawrence Lebogue, an old hardy seaman, appeared to be giving way very fast. I could only assist them by a teaspoonful or two of wine, which I had carefully saved, expecting such a melancholy necessity.

Monday the 8th June. Wind at SE. The weather was more moderate than it had been for some days past. A few gannets were seen. At noon I observed in 8° 45′ S; course WNW¼W, one hundred and six miles; longitude made 8° 23′ W. The sea being smooth I steered W by S.

At four in the afternoon we caught a small dolphin, which was the first relief of the kind that we obtained. I issued about two ounces to each person, including the offals, and saved the remainder for dinner the next day. Towards evening the wind freshened, and it blew strong all night, so that we shipped much water and suffered greatly from wet and cold.

Tuesday the 9th June. At daylight, as usual, I heard much complaining, which my own feelings convinced me was too well founded. I gave the surgeon and Lebogue a little wine, but I could afford them no further relief, except encouraging them with hopes that a very few days longer, at our present fine rate of sailing, would bring us to Timor.

This afternoon I suffered great sickness from the nature of part of the stomach of the fish, which had fallen to my share at dinner. At sunset I served an allowance of bread and water for supper.

Wednesday the 10th June. In the morning, after a very comfortless night, there was a visible alteration for the worse in many of the people, which gave me great apprehensions. An extreme weakness, swelled legs, hollow and ghastly countenances, a more than common inclination to sleep, with an apparent debility of understanding, seemed to me the melancholy presages of an approaching dissolution. The surgeon and Lebogue, in particular, were most miserable objects. I occasionally gave them a few teaspoonfuls of wine out of the little that remained, which greatly assisted them. The hopes of being able to accomplish the voyage was our principal support. The boatswain very innocently told me that he really thought I looked worse than anyone in the boat. The simplicity with which he uttered such an opinion amused me, and I returned him a better compliment.

Our latitude at noon was 9° 16′ S. Longitude from the north part of New Holland, 12° 1′ W. Course since yesterday noon W½S, one hundred and eleven miles. Birds and rock-weed showed that we were not far from land, but I expected such sights here, as there are many islands between the east part of Timor and New Guinea. The night was more moderate than the last.

Thursday the 11th June. Everyone received the customary allowance of bread and water, and an extra allowance of water was given to those who were most in need. At noon I observed in latitude 9° 41′ S; course S 77° W, distance one hundred and nine miles; longitude made 13° 49′ W. I had little doubt of having now passed the meridian of the eastern part of Timor, which is laid down in 128° E. This diffused universal joy and satisfaction.

In the afternoon we saw gannets and many other birds, and at sunset we kept a very anxious look-out. In the evening we caught a booby, which I reserved for our dinner the next day.

Friday the 12th June. At three in the morning, with an excess of joy, we discovered Timor bearing from WSW to WNW, and I hauled on a wind to the NNE till daylight, when the land bore from SW by S to NE by N. Our distance from the shore, two leagues.

It is not possible for me to describe the pleasure which the blessing of the sight of this land diffused among us. It appeared scarce credible to ourselves, that in an open boat, and so poorly provided, we should have been able to reach the coast of Timor in forty-one days after leaving Tofoa, having in that time run, by our log, a distance of 3,618 miles; and that, notwithstanding our extreme distress, no one should have perished in the voyage.

I have already mentioned that I knew not where the Dutch settlement was situated, but I had a faint idea that it was at the SW part of the island. I therefore, after daylight, bore away along shore to the SSW, which I was the more readily induced to do, as the wind would not suffer us to go towards the NE without great loss of time.

The day gave us a most agreeable prospect of the land, which was interspersed with woods and lawns; the interior part mountainous, but the shore low. Towards noon the coast became higher, with some remarkable headlands. We were greatly delighted with the general look of the country, which exhibited many cultivated spots and beautiful situations; but we could only see a few small huts, whence I concluded that no European resided in this part of the island. Much sea ran on the shore, which made landing impracticable. At noon we were abreast of a high headland; the extremes of the land bore SW½W and NNE½E, our distance off shore being three miles; latitude by observation, 9° 59′ S, and my longitude, by dead reckoning from the north part of New Holland, 15° 6′ W.

With the usual allowance of bread and water for dinner, I divided the bird we had caught the night before, and to the surgeon and Lebogue I gave a little wine.

The wind blew fresh at E, and ESE, with very hazy weather. During the afternoon we continued our course along a low shore, covered with innumerable palm-trees, called the fan palm from the leaf spreading like a fan; but here we saw no signs of cultivation, nor had the country so fine an appearance as to the eastward. This, however, was only a small tract, for by sunset it improved again, and I saw several great smokes where the inhabitants were clearing and cultivating their grounds. We had now run twenty-five miles to the WSW since noon, and were W five miles from a low point, which in the afternoon I imagined had been the southernmost land; and here the coast formed a deep bend, with low land in the bight that appeared like islands. The west shore was high, but from this part of the coast to the high cape which we were abreast of at noon the shore is low, and I believe shoal. I particularly remark this situation, because here the very high ridge of mountains that run from the east end of the island terminate, and the appearance of the country changes for the worse.

That we might not run past any settlement in the night, I determined to preserve my station till the morning, and therefore brought to under a close-reefed foresail. We were here in shoal water, our distance from the shore being half a league, the westernmost land in sight bearing WSW½W. Served bread and water for supper, and the boat lying to very well, all but the officer of the watch endeavoured to get a little sleep.

Saturday the 13th June. At two in the morning, we woke, and stood in shore till daylight, when I found we had drifted during the night about three leagues to the WSW, the southernmost land in sight bearing W. On examining the coast, and not seeing any sign of a settlement, we bore away to the westward, having a strong gale, against a weather current, which occasioned much sea. The shore was high and covered with wood, but we did not run far before low land formed the coast, the points of which opening at west, I once more fancied we were on the south part of the island; but at ten o'clock we found the coast again inclining towards the south, part of it bearing WSW½W. At the same time, high land appeared in SW; but the weather was so hazy that it was doubtful whether the two lands were separated, the opening only extending one point of the compass. For this reason I stood towards the outer land, and found it to be the island Roti.

I returned to the shore we had left and brought to a grapnel in a sandy bay, that I might more conveniently calculate my situation. In this place we saw several smokes, where the natives were clearing their grounds. During the little time we remained here the master and carpenter very much importuned me to let them go in search of supplies; to which at length I assented, but not finding any other person willing to be of their party, they did not choose to quit the boat. I stopped here no longer than for the purpose just mentioned, and we continued steering along shore. We had a view of a beautiful looking country, as if formed by art into lawns and parks. The coast is low and covered with woods, in which are innumerable fan palm-trees that look like coconut walks. The interior part is high land, but very different from the more eastern parts of the island, where it is exceedingly mountainous, and to appearance the soil better.

At noon the island Roti bore SW by W seven leagues. I had no observation for the latitude, but by account we were in 10° 12′ S, our course since yesterday noon being S 77° W, fifty-four miles. The usual allowance of bread and water was served for breakfast and dinner, and to the surgeon and Lebogue I continued to give wine.

We had a strong breeze at ESE, with hazy weather, all the afternoon. At two o'clock, having run through a very dangerous breaking sea, the cause of which I attributed to be a strong tide setting to windward, and shoal water, we discovered a spacious bay or sound, with a fair entrance about two or three miles wide. I now conceived hopes that our voyage was nearly at an end, as no place could appear more eligible for shipping or more likely to be chosen for an European settlement. I therefore came to a grapnel near the east side of the entrance in a small sandy bay, where we saw a hut, a dog, and some cattle; and I immediately sent the boatswain and gunner away to the hut to discover the inhabitants.

While we lay here I found the ebb came from the northward, and before our departure the falling of the tide discovered to us a reef of rocks, about two cables' length from the shore; the whole being covered at high-water renders it dangerous. On the opposite shore also appeared very high breakers, but there is nevertheless plenty of room, and certainly a safe channel for a first-rate man-of-war.

The bay or sound within seemed to be of a considerable extent, the northern part being about five leagues distant. Here the land made in moderate risings joined by lower grounds. But the island Roti to the southward is the best mark by which to know this place.

I had just time to make these remarks when I saw the boatswain and gunner returning with some natives; I therefore no longer doubted of our success and that our expectation would be fully gratified. They brought five Indians and informed me that they had found two families, where the women treated them with European politeness. From these people I learned that the governor resided at a place called Coupang, which was some distance to the NE. I made signs for one of them to go in the boat and show us the way to Coupang, intimating that I would pay him for his trouble. The man readily complied and came into the boat.

These people were of a dark tawny colour, had long black hair, and chewed a great deal of betel. Their dress was a square piece of cloth round the hips, in the folds of which was stuck a large knife, a handkerchief wrapped round the head, and another hanging by the four corners from the shoulders, which served as a bag for their betel equipage. They brought us a few pieces of dried turtle and some ears of Indian corn. This last was the most welcome, for the turtle was so hard that it could not be eaten without being first soaked in hot water. They offered to bring us some other refreshments if I would wait, but as the pilot was willing I determined to push on. It was about half an hour past four when we sailed.

By direction of the pilot we kept close to the east shore under all our sail, but as night came on the wind died away and we were obliged to try at the oars, which I was surprised to see we could use with some effect. At ten o'clock, finding we advanced but slowly, I came to a grapnel, and for the first time I issued double allowances of bread and a little wine to each person.

Sunday the 14th June. At one o'clock in the morning, after the most happy and sweet sleep that ever men enjoyed, we weighed and continued to keep the east shore on board, in very smooth water, when at last I found we were again open to the sea, the whole of the land to the westward that we had passed being an island, which the pilot called Pulo Samow. The northern entrance of this channel is about a mile and a half or two miles wide, and I had no ground at ten fathoms.

The report of two cannon that were fired gave new life to everyone, and soon after we discovered two square-rigged vessels and a cutter at anchor to the eastward. We endeavoured to work to windward, but were obliged to take to our oars again, having lost ground on each tack. We kept close to the shore and continued rowing till four o'clock, when I brought to a grapnel and gave another allowance of bread and wine to all hands. As soon as we had rested a little we weighed again and rowed till near daylight, when we came to a grapnel off a small fort and town, which the pilot told me was Coupang.

Among the things which the boatswain had thrown into the boat before we left the ship was a bundle of signal flags that had been used by the boats to show the depth of water in sounding. With these we had in the course of the passage made a small jack, which I now hoisted in the main shrouds as a signal of distress, for I did not think proper to land without leave.

Soon after daybreak a soldier hailed us to land, which I immediately did, among a crowd of Indians, and was agreeably surprised to meet with an English sailor who belonged to one of the vessels in the road. His captain, he told me, was the second person in the town. I therefore desired to be conducted to him, as I was informed the governor was ill and could not then be spoken with.

Captain Spikerman received me with great humanity. I informed him of our distressed situation and requested that care might be taken of those who were with me without delay. On which he gave directions for their immediate reception at his own house, and went himself to the governor, to know at what time I could be permitted to see him; which was fixed to be at eleven o'clock.

I now desired my people to come on shore, which was as much as some of them could do, being scarce able to walk. They, however, were helped to the house, and found tea with bread and butter provided for their breakfast.

The abilities of a painter, perhaps, could seldom have been displayed to more advantage than in the delineation of the two groups of figures which at this time presented themselves to each other. An indifferent spectator would have been at a loss which most to admire, the eyes of famine sparkling at immediate relief, or the horror of their preservers at the sight of so many spectres, whose ghastly countenances, if the cause had been unknown, would rather have excited terror than pity. Our bodies were nothing but skin and bones, our limbs were full of sores, and we were clothed in rags. In this condition, with the tears of joy and gratitude flowing down our cheeks, the people of Timor beheld us with a mixture of horror, surprise, and pity.

The governor, Mr William Adrian Van Este, notwithstanding extreme ill health, became so anxious about us that I saw him before the appointed time. He received me with great affection, and gave me the fullest proofs that he was possessed of every feeling of a humane and good man. Sorry as he was, he said, that such a calamity could ever have happened to us, yet he considered it as the greatest blessing of his life that we had fallen under his protection; and though his infirmity was so great that he could not do the office of a friend himself, he would give such orders as I might be certain would procure us every supply we wanted. A house should be immediately prepared for me, and with respect to my people, he said that I might have room for them either at the hospital or on board of Captain Spikerman's ship, which lay in the road; and he expressed much uneasiness that Coupang could not afford them better accommodations, the house assigned to me being the only one uninhabited and the situation of the few families that lived at this place such that they could not conveniently receive strangers. For the present, till matters could be properly regulated, he gave directions that victuals for my people should be dressed at his own house.

On returning to Captain Spikerman's house I found that every kind relief had been given to my people. The surgeon had dressed their sores, and the cleaning of their persons had not been less attended to, several friendly gifts of apparel having been presented to them.

I desired to be shown to the house that was intended for me, which I found ready, with servants to attend. It consisted of a hall, with a room at each end and a loft overhead; and was surrounded by a piazza, with an outer apartment in one corner, and a communication from the back part of the house to the street. I therefore determined, instead of separating from my people, to lodge them all with me, and I divided the house as follows: One room I took to myself, the other I allotted to the master, surgeon, Mr Nelson, and the gunner; the loft to the other officers; and the outer apartment to the men. The hall was common to the officers, and the men had the back piazza. Of this disposition I informed the governor, and he sent down chairs, tables, and benches, with bedding and other necessaries for the use of every one.

The governor, when I took my leave, had desired me to acquaint him with everything of which I stood in need; but it was only at particular times that he had a few moments of ease or could attend to anything, being in a dying state with an incurable disease. On this account I transacted whatever business I had with Mr Timotheus Wanjon, the second of this place, who was the governor's son-in-law, and who also contributed everything in his power to make our situation comfortable. I had been, therefore, misinformed by the seaman, who told me that Captain Spikerman was the next person in command to the governor.

At noon a dinner was brought to the house, sufficiently good to make persons more accustomed to plenty, eat too much. Yet I believe few in such a situation would have observed more moderation than my people did. My greatest apprehension was that they would eat too much fruit, of which there was great variety in season at this time.

Having seen every one enjoy this meal of plenty, I dined myself with Mr Wanjon, but I felt no extraordinary inclination to eat or drink. Rest and quiet, I considered, as more necessary to the re-establishment of my health, and therefore retired soon to my room, which I found furnished with every convenience. But instead of rest, my mind was disposed to reflect on our late sufferings, and on the failure of the expedition; but, above all, on the thanks due to Almighty God, who had given us power to support and bear such heavy calamities, and had enabled me at last to be the means of saving eighteen lives.

Richard Dana

ON A VOYAGE ROUND CAPE HORN

(from *Two Years Before The Mast*)

*An attack of measles which badly affected his eyesight when at
Harvard University caused Richard Dana to sign aboard the brig
Pilgrim of Boston for a trading voyage to the Pacific seaboard in
1834. Two years later, he returned to Boston in another ship, the
Alert, which he had joined to escape the tyrannical attentions of
the Pilgrim's Master. His eyesight was fully recovered and he had
kept a log book. Publishers were at first chary of his manuscript,
but when it was published in 1840, it was immediately successful
and hailed as 'a voice from the lower deck'.*

*The Pilgrim's passage around Cape Horn was from west to east
and she was heavily laden with a dead weight cargo of hides.*

WE were short-handed for a voyage round Cape Horn in the dead
of winter. Besides S— and myself there were only five in the
fo'c'sle; who, together with four boys in the steerage, sailmaker,
carpenter, etc., composed the whole crew. In addition to this, we
were only three or four days out, when the sailmaker, who was the
oldest and best seaman on board, was taken with the palsy, and was
useless for the rest of the voyage ... By the loss of the sailmaker,
our watch was reduced to five, of whom two were boys, who never
steered but in fine weather, so that the other two and myself had to
stand at the wheel four hours apiece out of every twenty-four; and
the other watch had only four helmsmen. 'Never mind – we're
homeward bound!' was the answer to everything; and we should
not have minded this were it not for the thought that we should be
off Cape Horn in the very dead of winter. It was now the first part
of May; and two months would bring us off the Cape in July,
which is the worst month in the year there, when the sun rises at
9.00 and sets at 3.00, giving 18 hours night, and there is snow and
rain, gales and high seas, in abundance.

The prospect of meeting this in a ship half manned, loaded so deep that every heavy sea must wash her fore and aft, was by no means pleasant. The *Brandywine* frigate, in her passage round had 60 days off the Cape, and lost several boats by the heavy seas. All this was for our comfort; yet pass it we must; and all hands agreed to make the best of it . . .

Sunday, June 19th, were in lat. 34° 15′ S, and long. 116° 38′ W.

There began now to be a decided change in the appearance of things. The days became shorter and shorter; the sun running lower in its course each day, and giving less and less heat, and the nights so cold as to prevent our sleeping on deck; the Magellan Clouds in sight, of a clear, moonless night; the skies looking cold and angry; and, at times, a long heavy, ugly sea, setting in from the southward, told us what we were coming to. Still, however, we had a fine, strong breeze, and kept on our way under as much sail as our ship would bear. Towards the middle of the week, the wind hauled to the southward, which brought us upon a taut bowline, made the ship meet, nearly head-on, the heavy swell which rolled from that direction; and there was something not at all encouraging in the manner in which she met it. Being still so deep and heavy, she wanted the buoyancy which should have carried her over the seas, and she dropped heavily into them, the water washing over the decks; and every now and then, when an unusually large sea met her fairly upon the bows, she struck it with a sound as dead and heavy as that with which a sledge-hammer falls upon the pile, and took the whole of it in upon the fo'c'sle, and, rising, carried it aft in the scuppers, washing the rigging off the pins, and carrying along with it everything which was loose on deck. She had been acting in this way all of our forenoon watch below; as we could tell by the washing of the water over our heads, and the heavy breaking of the seas against her bows, only the thickness of a plank from our heads, as we lay in our berths, which are directly against the bows. At eight bells, the watch was called, and we came on deck, one hand going aft to take the wheel, and another going to the galley to get the grub for dinner. I stood on the fo'c'sle, looking at the seas, which were rolling high, as far as the eye could reach, their tops white with foam and the body of them of a deep indigo blue, reflecting the bright rays of the sun. Our ship rose slowly over a few of the largest of them, until one immense fellow came rolling on, threatening to cover her, and which I was sailor enough to know, by the 'feeling of her' under my feet, she would not rise over. I sprang upon the knight-heads, and, seizing hold of the fore-stay, drew myself up upon it. My feet were just off the stanchion when the stem struck fairly into the middle of the sea, and it washed the ship fore and aft, burying her in the water. As soon as she rose out of it, I looked aft, and everything forward of the mainmast, except the long-boat, which was griped and double-lashed down to the ring-bolts, was swept clear. The galley, the pigsty, the hencoop, and a large sheep-pen, which had been built upon the fore-hatch, were all gone in the twinkling of an eye – leaving the deck as clean as a chin new reaped – and not a stick left to show where anything had stood. In the scuppers lay the galley, bottom up, and a few boards floating about – the wreck of the sheep-pen – and half a dozen miserable sheep floating among them, wet through, and not a little frightened at the sudden change that had come upon them. As soon as the sea had washed by, all hands sprang up out of the fo'c'sle to see what had become of the ship; and in a few moments the cook and Old Bill crawled out from under the galley, where they had been lying in the water, nearly smothered, with the galley over them. Fortunately, it rested against the bulwarks, or it would have broken some of their bones. When the water ran off, we picked the sheep up, and put them in the long-boat, got the galley back in its place, and set things a little to rights; but, had not our ship had uncommonly high bulwarks and rail, everything must have been washed overboard, not excepting Old Bill and the cook. Bill had been standing at the galley-door, with the kid of beef in his hand for the fo'c'sle mess, when away he went, kid beef, and all. He held on to the kid to the last, like a good fellow, but the beef was gone, and when the water ran off, we saw it lying high and dry, like a rock at low tide – nothing could hurt *that*. We took the loss of our beef very easily, consoling ourselves with the recollection that the cabin had more to lose than we; and chuckled not a little at seeing the remains of the chicken-pie and pancakes floating in the scuppers. 'This will never do!' was what some said, and everyone felt. Here we were, not yet within a thousand miles of the latitude of

Cape Horn, and our decks swept by a sea not one half so high as we must expect to find there. Some blamed the captain for loading his ship so deep when he knew what he must expect; while others said that the wind was always south-west, off the Cape, in the winter, and that, running before it, we should not mind the seas so much. When we got down into the fo'c'sle, Old Bill, who was somewhat of a croaker – having met with a great many accidents at sea – said that, if that was the way she was going to act, we might as well make our wills, and balance the books at once, and put on a clean shirt. ' 'Vast there, you bloody old owl! you're always hanging out blue lights. You're frightened by the ducking you got in the scuppers and can't take a joke! What's the use in being always on the lookout for Davy Jones?' 'Stand by!' says another, 'and we'll get an afternoon watch below, by this scrape;' but in this they were disappointed, for at two bells all hands were called and set to work, getting lashings upon everything on deck; and the captain talked of sending down the long top-gallant masts; but as the sea went down towards night, and the wind hauled abeam, we left them standing, and set the studding-sails.

The next day all hands were turned-to upon unbending the old sails, and getting up the new ones; for a ship, unlike people on shore, puts on her best suit in bad weather.

The wind continued westerly, and the weather and sea less rough since the day on which we shipped the heavy sea, and we were making great progress under studding-sails, with our light sails all set, keeping a little to the eastward of south; for the captain, depending upon westerly winds off the Cape, had kept so far to the westward that, though we were within about five hundred miles of the latitude of Cape Horn, we were nearly seventeen hundred miles to the westward of it. Through the rest of the week we continued on with a fair wind, gradually, as we got more to the southward, keeping a more easterly course, and bringing the wind on our larboard quarter, until –

Sunday, June 26th, when, having a fine, clear day, the captain got a lunar observation, as well as his meridian altitude, which made us in lat. 47° 50′ S, long. 113° 49′ W; Cape Horn bearing, according to my calculations, ESE½E, and distant eighteen hundred miles.

RICHARD DANA

Monday, June 27th. During the first part of this day the wind continued fair, and, as we were going before it, it did not feel very cold, so that we kept at work on deck in our common clothes and round jackets. Our watch had an afternoon watch below for the first time since leaving San Diego; and, having inquired of the third mate what the latitude was at noon, and made our usual guesses as to the time she would need to be up with the Horn, we turned-in for a nap. We were sleeping away, 'at the rate of knots', when three knocks on the scuttle and 'All hands, ahoy!' started us from our berths. What could be the matter? It did not appear to be blowing hard, and, looking through the scuttle, we could see that it was a clear day overhead; yet the watch were taking in sail. We thought there must be a sail in sight, and that we were about to heave-to and speak her; and were just congratulating ourselves upon it – for we had seen neither sail nor land since we left port – when we heard the mate's voice on deck (he turned-in 'all-standing', and was always on deck the moment he was called) singing out to the men who were taking in the studding-sails, and asking where his watch were. We did not wait for a second call, but tumbled up the ladder; and there, on the starboard bow, was a bank of mist, covering the sea and sky, and driving directly for us. I had seen the same before in my passage round in the *Pilgrim*, and knew what it meant, and that there was no time to be lost. We had nothing on but thin clothes, yet there was not a moment to spare, and at it we went.

The boys of the other watch were in the tops, taking in the top-gallant studding-sails and the lower and topmast studding-sails were coming down by the run. It was nothing but 'haul down and clew up', until we got all the studding-sails in, and the royals, flying jib, and mizzen top-gallant-sail furled, and the ship kept off a little, to take the squall. The fore and main top-gallant-sails were still on her, for the 'old man' did not mean to be frightened in broad daylight, and was determined to carry sail till the last minute. We all stood waiting for its coming, when the first blast showed us that it was not to be trifled with. Rain, sleet, snow, and wind enough to take our breath from us, and make the toughest turn his back to windward! The ship lay nearly over upon her beam-ends; the spars

290

and rigging snapped and cracked; and her top-gallant-masts bent like whip-sticks. 'Clew up the fore and main top-gallant sails!' shouted the captain, and all hands sprang to the clew-lines. The decks were standing nearly at an angle of forty-five degrees, and the ship going like a mad steed through the water, the whole forward part of her in a smother of foam. The halyards were let go, and the yard clewed down, and the sheets started, and in a few minutes the sails smothered and kept in by clewlines and buntlines. 'Furl 'em, sir?' asked the mate. 'Let go the topsail halyards, fore and aft!' shouted the captain in answer, at the top of his voice. Down came the topsail yards, the reef-tackles were manned and hauled out, and we climbed up to windward, and sprang in to the weather rigging. The violence of the wind, and the hail and sleet, driving nearly horizontally across the ocean, seemed actually to pin us down to the rigging. It was hard work making head against them. One after another we got out upon the yards. And here we had work to do; for our new sails had hardly been bent long enough to get the starch out of them and the new earrings and reef-points, stiffened with the sleet, knotted like pieces of iron wire. Having only our round jackets and straw hats on, we were soon wet through, and it was every moment growing colder. Our hands were soon stiffened, which, added to the stiffness of everything else, kept us a good while on the yard.

No sooner did the mate see that we were on deck than – 'Lay aloft there, four of you, and furl the top-gallant-sails!' This called me again, and two of us went aloft up the fore rigging, and two more up the main, upon the top-gallant-yards. The shrouds were now iced over, the sleet having formed a crust round all the standing rigging, and on the weather side of the masts and yards. When we got upon the yard, my hands were so numb that I could not have cast off the knot of the gasket to have saved my life. We both lay over the yard for a few seconds, beating our hands upon the sail until we started the blood into our fingers' ends, and at the next moment our hands were in a burning heat. My companion on the yard was a lad about sixteen years old, who came out in the ship a weak, puny boy, from one of the Boston schools – 'no larger than a spritsail-sheet knot', nor 'heavier than a paper of lamp-black', and 'not strong enough to haul a shad off a gridiron', but who was now 'as long as a spare topmast, strong enough to knock down an ox, and hearty enough to eat him'. We fisted the sail together, and, after six or eight minutes of hard hauling and pulling and beating down the sail, which was about as stiff as sheet-iron, we managed to get it furled; and snugly furled it must be, for we knew the mate enough to be certain that if it got adrift again we should be called up from our watch below, at any hour of the night, to furl it.

I had been on the lookout for a chance to jump below and clap on a thick jacket and southwester; but when we got on deck we found that eight bells had been struck, and the other watch gone below, so that there were two hours of dog watch for us, and a plenty of work to do. It had now set in for a steady gale from the south-west; but we were not yet far enough to the southward to make a fair wind of it, for we must give Terra del Fuego a wide berth. The decks were covered with snow, and there was a constant driving of sleet. In fact, Cape Horn had set in with good earnest. In the midst of all this, and before it became dark, we had all the studding-sails to make up and stow away, and then to lay aloft and rig in all the booms, fore and aft, and coil away the tacks, sheets, and halyards. This was pretty tough work for four or five hands, in the face of a gale which almost took us off the yards, and with ropes so stiff with ice that it was almost impossible to bend them. I was nearly half an hour out on the end of the fore yard, trying to coil away and stop down the topmast studding-sail tack and lower halyards. It was after dark when we got through, and we were not a little pleased to hear four bells struck, which sent us below for two hours, and gave us each a pot of hot tea with our cold beef and bread, and, what was better yet, a suit of thick, dry clothing, fitted for the weather, in place of our thin clothes, which were wet through and now frozen stiff.

This sudden turn, for which we were so little prepared, was as unacceptable to me as to any of the rest; for I had been troubled for several days with a slight toothache, and this cold weather and wetting and freezing, were not the best things in the world for it. I soon found that it was getting strong hold, and running over all parts of my face; and before the watch was out I went aft to the mate, who had charge of the medicine-chest, to get something for it. But the chest showed like the end of a long voyage, for there was nothing that would answer but a few drops of laudanum, which must be saved for an emergency; so I had only to bear the pain as well as I could.

When we went on deck at eight bells, it had stopped snowing, and there were a few stars out, but the clouds were still black, and it was blowing a steady gale. Just before midnight, I went aloft and sent down the mizzen royal yard, and had the good luck to do it to the satisfaction of the mate, who said it was done 'out of hand and ship-shape'. The next four hours below were little relief to me, for I lay awake in my berth the whole time, from the pain in my face, and heard every bell strike, and, at four o'clock, turned out with the watch, feeling little spirit for the hard duties of the day. Bad weather and hard work at sea can be borne up against very well if one only has spirit and health; but there is nothing brings a man down, at such a time, like bodily pain and want of sleep. There was, however, too much to do to allow time to think; for the gale of yesterday, and the heavy seas we met with a few days before, while we had yet ten degrees more southing to make, had convinced the captain that we had something before us which was not to be trifled with, and orders were given to send down the long top-gallant masts. The top-gallant and royal yards were accordingly struck, the flying jib-boom rigged in, and the top-gallant masts sent down on deck, and all lashed together by the side of the long-boat. The rigging was then sent down and coiled away below, and everything made snug aloft. There was not a sailor in the ship who was not rejoiced to see these sticks come down; for, so long as the yards were aloft, on the least sign of a lull, the top-gallant-sails were loosed, and then we had to furl them again in a snow-squall, and *shin* up and down single ropes caked with ice, and send royal yards down in the teeth of a gale coming right from the south pole. It was an interesting sight, too, to see our noble ship, dismantled of all her top-hamper of long tapering masts and yards, and boom pointed with spearhead, which ornamented her in port; and all that canvas, which a few days before had covered her like a cloud, from the truck to the water's edge, spreading far out beyond her hull on either side, now gone; and she stripped, like a wrestler for the fight. It corresponded, too, with the desolate character of her situation – alone, as she was, battling with storms, wind, and ice, at this extremity of the globe, and in almost constant night.

Friday, July 1st. We were now nearly up to the latitude of Cape Horn, and having over forty degrees of easting to make, we squared away the yards before a strong westerly gale, shook a reef out of the fore topsail, and stood on our way, east-by-south, with the prospect of being up with the Cape in a week or ten days. As for myself, I had had no sleep for forty-eight hours; and the want of rest, together with constant wet and cold, had increased the swelling, so much that my face was nearly as large as two, and I found it impossible to get my mouth open wide enough to eat. In this state the steward applied to the captain for some rice to boil for me, but he only got a – 'No! d – you! Tell him to eat salt junk and hard bread like the rest of them.' This was just what I expected. However, I did not starve, for the mate, who was a man as well as a sailor, and had always been a good friend to me, smuggled a pan of rice into the galley, and told the cook to boil it for me, and not let the 'old man' see it. Had it been fine weather, or in port, I should have gone below and lain by until my face got well; but in such weather as this, and short-handed as we were, it was not for me to desert my post; so I kept on deck, and stood my watch and did my duty as well as I could.

Saturday, July 2nd. This day the sun rose fair, but it ran too low in the heavens to give any heat, or thaw out our sails and rigging; yet the sight of it was pleasant; and we had a steady 'reef-topsail breeze' from the westward. The atmosphere, which had previously been clear and cold, for the last few hours grew damp, and had a disagreeable, wet chilliness in it; and the man who came from the wheel said he heard the captain tell 'the passenger' that the thermometer had fallen several degrees since morning, which he could not account for in any other way than by supposing that there must be ice near us; though such a thing was rarely heard of in this latitude at this season of the year. At twelve o'clock we went below, and had just got through dinner, when the cook put his head down the scuttle and told us to come on deck and see the finest sight that we had ever seen. 'Where away, Cook?' asked the first man who was up. 'On the larboard bow.' And there lay, floating in the ocean, several miles off, an immense, irregular mass, its top and points covered with snow, and its centre of a deep indigo colour. This was an iceberg, and of the largest size, as one of our men said who had been in the Northern Ocean. As far as the eye could reach, the sea in every direction was of a deep blue colour, the waves running high and fresh, and sparkling in the light, and in the midst lay this immense mountain-island, its cavities and valleys thrown into deep shade, and its points and pinnacles glittering in the sun. All hands were soon on deck, looking at it, and admiring in various ways its beauty and grandeur. But no description can give any idea of the strangeness, splendour, and the sublimity of the sight. Its great size – for it must have been from two to three miles in circumference, and several hundred feet in height – its slow motion, as its base rose and sank in the water, and its high points nodded against the clouds; the dashing of the waves upon it, which, breaking high with foam, lined its base, with a white crust; and the thundering sound of the cracking of the mass, and the breaking and tumbling down of huge pieces; together with its nearness and approach, which added a slight element of fear – all combined to give to it the character of true sublimity. The main body of the mass was, as I have said, of an indigo colour, its base crusted with frozen foam; and as it grew thin and transparent towards the edges and top, its colour shaded off from a deep blue to the whiteness of snow. It seemed to be drifting slowly towards the north, so that we kept away and avoided it. It was in sight all the afternoon; and when we got to leeward of it the wind died away, so that we lay-to quite near it for a greater part of the night. Unfortunately, there was no moon, but it was a clear night, and we could plainly mark the long, regular heaving of the stupendous mass, as its edges moved slowly against the stars, now revealing them, and now shutting them in. Several times in our watch loud cracks were heard, which sounded as though they must have run through the whole length of the iceberg, and several pieces fell down with a thundering crash, plunging heavily into the sea. Towards morning a strong breeze sprang up, and we filled away, and left it astern, and at daylight it was out of sight. The next day, which was –

Sunday, July 3rd, the breeze continued strong, the air exceedingly chilly, and the thermometer low. In the course of the day we saw several icebergs of different sizes, but none so near as the one which we saw the day before. Some of them, as well as we could judge, at the distance at which we were, must have been as large as that, if not larger. At noon we were in latitude 55° 12′ S and supposed longitude 89° 5′ W. Towards night the wind hauled to the southward, and headed us off our course a little, and blew a tremendous gale; but this we did not mind, as there was no rain nor snow, and we were already under close sail.

Monday, July 4th. This was 'Independence Day' in Boston. What firing of guns, and ringing of bells, and rejoicings of all sorts, in every part of our country! The ladies (who have not gone down to Nahant, for a breath of cool air and sight of the ocean) walking the streets with parasols over their heads, and the dandies in their white pantaloons and silk stockings! What quantities of ice-cream have been eaten, and what lumps of ice brought into the city from a distance, and sold out by the lump and the pound! The smallest of the islands which we saw today would have made the fortune of poor Jack, if he had had it in Boston; and I dare say he would have had no objection to being there with it. This, to be sure, was no place to keep the Fourth of July. To keep ourselves warm, and the ship out of the ice, was as much as we could do. Yet no one forgot the day; and many were the wishes and conjectures and comparisons, both serious and ludicrous, which were made among all hands. The sun shone bright as long as it was up, only that a scud of black clouds was ever and anon driving across it. At noon we were in latitude 54° 27′ S and longitude 85° 5′ W, having made a good deal of easting, but having lost in our latitude by the heading off of the wind. Between daylight and dark – that is, between nine o'clock and three – we saw thirty-four ice islands of various sizes; some no bigger than the hull of our vessel, and others apparently nearly as large as the one that we first saw; though, as we went on, the islands became smaller and more numerous; and at sundown of this day, a man at the mast-head saw large fields of floating ice, called 'field-ice', at the south-east. This kind of ice is much more dangerous than the large islands, for those can be seen at a distance, and kept away from; but the field-ice, floating in great quantities, and covering the ocean for miles and miles, in pieces of every size – large, flat, and broken cakes, with here and there an island rising twenty and thirty feet, and as large as the ship's hull – this it is very difficult to steer clear of. A constant lookout was necessary; for any of these pieces, coming with the heave of the sea, were large enough to have knocked a hole in the ship, and that would have been the end of us; for no boat (even if we could have got one out) could have lived in such a sea; and no man could have lived in a boat in such weather. To make our condition still worse, the wind came out due east, just after sundown, and it blew a gale dead ahead, with hail and sleet and a thick fog, so that we could not see half the length of the ship. Our chief reliance, the prevailing westerly gales, was thus cut off; and here we were, nearly seven hundred miles to the westward of the Cape, with a gale dead from the eastward, and the weather so thick that we could not see the ice, with which we were surrounded, until it was directly under our bows. At four p.m. (it was then quite dark) all hands were called, and sent aloft, in a violent squall of hail and rain, to take in sail. We had now all got on our 'Cape Horn rig' – thick boots, southwesters coming down over our neck and ears, thick trousers and jackets, and some with oil-cloth suits over all. Mittens, too, we wore on deck, but it would not do to go aloft with them, as it was impossible to work with them. A man might fall; for all the hold he could get upon a rope: so we were obliged to work with bare hands, which, as well as our faces, were often cut with the hailstones, which fell thick and large. Our ship was now all cased with ice – hull, spars, and standing rigging, and the running rigging so stiff that we could hardly bend it so as to belay it, or, still less, take a knot with it; and the sails frozen. One at a time (for it was a long piece of work and required many hands) we furled the courses, mizzen topsail, and fore-topmast staysail, and close-reefed the fore and main topsails, and hove the ship to under the fore, with the main hauled up by the clew-lines and buntlines, and ready to be sheeted home, if we found it necessary to make sail to get to windward of an ice island. A regular lookout was then set, and kept by each watch in turn, until the morning. It was a tedious and anxious night. It blew hard the whole time, and there was an almost constant driving of either rain, hail, or snow. In addition to this, it was 'as thick as muck', and the ice was all about us. The captain was on deck nearly the whole night, and kept the cook in the galley, with a roaring fire, to make coffee for him, which he took every few hours, and once or twice gave a little to his officers; but not a drop of anything was there for the crew. The captain, who sleeps all the daytime, and comes and goes at night as he chooses, can have his brandy-and-water in the cabin, and his hot coffee at the galley; while Jack, who has to stand through everything, and work in wet and cold, can have nothing to wet his lips or warm his stomach.

Eight hours of the night our watch was on deck, and during the whole of that time we kept a bright lookout: one man on each bow, another in the bunt of the fore yard, the third mate on the scuttle, one man on each quarter, and another always standing by the wheel. The chief mate was everywhere, and commanded the ship when the captain was below. When a large piece of ice was seen in our way, or drifting near us, the word was passed along, and the ship's head turned one way and another; and sometimes the yards squared or braced up. There was little else to do than to look out; and we had the sharpest eyes in the ship on the fo'c'sle. The only variety was the monotonous voice of the lookout forward, – 'Another island!' – 'Ice ahead!' – 'Ice on the lee bow!' – 'Hard up the helm!' – 'Keep her off a little!' – 'Stead-y!'.

In the meantime the wet and cold had brought my face into such a state that I could neither eat nor sleep; and though I stood it out all night, yet, when it became light, I was in such a state that all hands told me I must go below, and lie-by for a day or two, or I should be laid up for a long time, and perhaps have the lock-jaw. In the steerage I took off my hat and comforter, and showed my face to the mate, who told me to go below at once, and stay in my berth until the swelling went down, and gave the cook orders to make a poultice for me, and said he would speak to the captain.

I went below and turned in, covering myself over with blankets and jackets, and lay in my berth nearly twenty-four hours, half-asleep and half-awake, stupid from the dull pain. I heard the watch called, and the men going up and down, and sometimes a noise on deck, and a cry of 'ice', but I gave little attention to anything. At the end of twenty-four hours the pain went down, and I had a long sleep, which brought me back to my proper state; yet my face was so swollen and tender that I was obliged to keep my berth for two or three days longer. During the two days I had been below the weather was much the same that it had been – head winds and snow and rain; or, if the wind came fair, too foggy, and the ice too thick, to run. At the end of the third day the ice was very thick; a complete fog-bank covered the ship. It blew a tremendous gale from the eastward, with sleet and snow, and there was every promise of a dangerous and fatiguing night. At dark, the captain called all hands aft, and told them that not a man was to leave the deck that night; that the ship was in the greatest danger, any cake of ice might knock a hole in her, or she might run on an island and go to pieces. No one could tell whether she would be a ship the next morning. The lookouts were then set, and every man was put in his station. When I heard what was the state of things, I began to put on my clothes to stand it out with the rest of them, when the mate came below, and, looking at my face, ordered me back to my berth, saying that if we went down, we should all go down together, but if I went on deck I might lay myself up for life. This was the first word I had heard from aft; for the captain had done nothing, nor inquired how I was, since I went below.

In obedience to the mate's orders, I went back to my berth; but a more miserable night I never wish to spend. I never felt the curse of sickness so keenly in my life. If I could only have been on deck with the rest where something was to be done and seen and heard, where there were fellow-beings for companions in duty and danger; but to be cooped up alone in a black hole, in equal danger, but without the power to do, was the hardest trial. Several times, in the course of the night, I got up, determined to go on deck, but the silence which showed that there was nothing doing, and the knowledge that I might make myself seriously ill, for no purpose, kept me back. It was not easy to sleep, lying, as I did, with my head directly against the bows, which might be dashed in by an island of ice, brought down by the very next sea that struck her. This was the only time I had been ill since I left Boston, and it was the worst time it could have happened. I felt almost willing to bear the plagues of Egypt for the rest of the voyage, if I could but be well and strong for that one night. Yet it was a dreadful night for those on deck. A watch of eighteen hours, with wet and cold and constant anxiety, nearly wore them out; and when they came below at nine o'clock for breakfast, they almost dropped to sleep on their chests, and some of them were so stiff that they could with difficulty sit down. Not a drop of anything had been given them during the whole time (though the captain, as on the night that I was on deck, had his coffee every four hours), except that the mate stole a pot-full of coffee for two men to drink behind the galley, while he kept a lookout for the captain. Every man had his station, and was not allowed to leave it; and nothing happened to break the monotony of the night, except once setting the main topsail, to run clear of a large island to leeward, which they were drifting fast upon. Some of the boys got so sleepy and stupefied that they actually fell asleep at their posts; and the young third mate, Mr H—, whose post was the exposed one of standing on the fore scuttle, was so stiff, when he was relieved, that he could not bend his knees to get down. By a constant lookout, and a quick shifting of the helm, as the islands and pieces came in sight, the ship went clear of everything but a few small pieces, though daylight showed the ocean covered for miles. At daybreak it fell a dead calm, and with the sun the fog cleared a little, and a breeze sprung up from the westward, which soon grew into a gale. We had now a fair wind, daylight, and comparatively clear weather; yet, to the surprise of every one, the ship continued hove-to. 'Why does not he run?' 'What is the captain about?' was asked by every one; and from questions it soon grew into complaints and murmurings. When the daylight was so short, it was too bad to lose it, and a fair wind, too, which every one had been praying for. As hour followed hour, and the captain showed no sign of making sail, the crew became impatient, and there was a good deal of talking and consultation together on the fo'c'sle. They had been beaten out with the exposure and hardship, and impatient to get out of it, and this unaccountable delay was more than they could bear in quietness, in their excited and restless state. Some said the captain was frightened – completely cowed by the dangers and difficulties that surrounded us, and was afraid to make sail; while others said that in his anxiety and suspense he had made a free use of brandy and opium, and was unfit for his duty. The carpenter, who was an intelligent man, and a thorough seaman, and had great influence with the crew, came down into the fo'c'sle, and tried to induce them to go aft and ask the captain why he did not run, or request him, in the name of all hands, to make sail. This appeared to be a very reasonable request, and the crew agreed that if he did not make sail before noon they would go aft. Noon came, and no sail was made. A consultation was held again, and it was proposed to take the ship from the captain and give the command of her to the mate, who had been heard to say that if he could have his way the ship would have been half the distance to the Cape before night – ice, or no ice. And so irritated and impatient had the crew become, that even this proposition, which was open mutiny, was entertained, and the carpenter went to his berth, leaving it tacitly understood that something serious would be done if things remained as they were many hours longer. When the carpenter left, we talked it all over, and I gave my advice strongly against it. Another of the men, too, who had known something of the kind attempted in another ship by a crew who were dissatisfied with their captain, and which was followed with serious consequences, was opposed to it. S—, who soon came down, joined us, and we determined to have nothing to do with it. By these means the crew were soon induced to give it up for the present, though they said they would not lie where they were much longer without knowing the reason.

The affair remained in this state until four o'clock, when an order came forward for all hands to come aft upon the quarter-deck. In about ten minutes they came forward, and the whole affair had been blown. The carpenter, prematurely, and without any authority from the crew, had sounded the mate as to whether he would take command of the ship, and intimated an intention to displace the captain; and the mate, as in duty bound, had told the whole to the captain, who immediately sent for all hands aft. Instead of violent measures, or, at least, an outbreak of quarter-deck bravado, threats, and abuse, which they had every reason to expect, a sense of common danger and common suffering seemed to have tamed his spirit, and begotten in him something like a humane fellow-feeling; for he received the crew in a manner quiet, and even almost kind. He told them what he had heard, and said that he did not believe that they would try to do any such thing as was intimated; that they had always been good men – obedient, and knew their duty, and he had no fault to find with them, and asked them what they had to complain of; said that no one could say that he was slow to carry sail (which was true enough), and that, as soon as he thought it was safe and proper, he should make sail. He added a few words about their duty in their present situation, and sent them forward, saying that he should take no further notice of the matter; but, at the same time, told the carpenter to recollect whose power he was in, and that if he heard another word from him he would have cause to remember him to the day of his death.

This language of the captain had a very good effect upon the crew, and they returned quietly to their duty.

For two days more the wind blew from the southward and eastward, and in the short intervals when it was fair, the ice was too thick to run; yet the weather was not so dreadfully bad, and the crew had watch and watch. I still remained in my berth, fast recovering, yet not well enough to go safely on deck. And I should have been perfectly useless; for, from having eaten nothing for nearly a week, except a little rice which I forced into my mouth the last day or two, I was as weak as an infant. To be sick in a fo'c'sle is miserable indeed. It is the worst part of a dog's life, especially in bad weather. The fo'c'sle, shut up tight to keep out the water and cold air; the watch either on deck or asleep in their berths; no one to speak to; the pale light of the single lamp, swinging to and fro from the beam, so dim that one can scarcely see, much less read, by it; the water dropping from the beams and carlines and running down the sides, and the fo'c'sle so wet and dark and cheerless, and so lumbered up with chests and wet clothes, that sitting up is worse than lying in the berth. These are some of the evils. Fortunately, I needed no help from any one, and no medicine; and if I had needed help I don't know where I should have found it. Sailors are willing enough, but it is true, as is often said – no one ships for nurse on board a vessel. Our merchant ships are always under-manned, and if one man is lost by sickness, they cannot spare another to take care of him. A sailor is always presumed to be well, and if he's sick he's a poor dog. One has to stand his wheel, and another his lookout, and the sooner he gets on deck again the better.

Accordingly, as soon as I could possibly go back to my duty, I put on my thick clothes and boots and southwester, and made my appearance on deck. I had been but a few days below, yet every-thing looked strangely enough. The ship was cased in ice, – decks, sides, masts, yards, and rigging. Two close-reefed topsails were all the sail she had on, and every sail and rope was frozen so stiff in its place that it seemed as though it would be impossible to start any-thing. Reduced, too, to her topmasts, she had altogether a most forlorn and crippled appearance. The sun had come up brightly; the snow was swept off the decks and ashes thrown upon them so that we could walk, for they had been as slippery as glass. It was, of course, too cold to carry on any ship's work, and we had only to walk the deck and keep ourselves warm. The wind was still ahead, and the whole ocean, to the eastward, covered with islands and field-ice. At four bells the order was given to square away the yards, and the man who came from the helm said that the captain had kept her off to NNE.

In our first attempt to double the Cape, when we came up to the latitude of it, we were nearly seventeen hundred miles to the west-ward, but, in running for the Straits of Magellan, we stood so far to the eastward that we made our second attempt at a distance of not more than four or five hundred miles; and we had great hopes, by this means, to run clear of the ice; thinking that the easterly gales, which had prevailed for a long time, would have driven it to the westward. With the wind about two points free, the yards braced in a little, and two close-reefed topsails and a reefed foresail on the ship, we made great way towards the southward; and almost every watch, when we came on deck, the air seemed to grow colder, and the sea to run higher. Still we saw no ice, and had great hopes of going clear of it altogether, when, one afternoon, about three o'clock, while we were taking a *siesta* during our watch below, 'All hands!' was called in a loud and fearful voice. 'Tumble up here, men! – tumble up! – don't stop for your clothes – before we're upon it!' We sprang out of our berths and hurried upon deck. The loud, sharp voice of the captain was heard giving orders, as though for life or death, and we ran aft to the braces not waiting to look ahead, for not a moment was to be lost. The helm was hard up, and the after yards shaking, and the ship in the act of wearing. Slowly, with the stiff ropes and iced rigging, we swung the yards round, everything coming hard and with a creaking and rending sound, like pulling up the plank which has been frozen into the ice. The ship wore round fairly, the yards were steadied, and we stood off on the other tack, leaving behind us, directly under our larboard quarter, a large ice island, peering out of the mist, and reaching high above our tops; while astern, and on either side of the island, large tracts of field-ice were dimly seen, heaving and rolling in the sea. We were now safe, and standing to the northward; but, in a few minutes more, had it not been for the sharp lookout of the watch, we should have been fairly upon the ice, and left our ship's old bones adrift in the Southern Ocean. After standing to the northward a few hours, we wore ship, and, the wind having hauled, we stood to the southward and eastward. All night long a bright lookout was kept from every part of the deck; and whenever ice was seen on the one bow or the other the helm was shifted and the yards braced, and, by quick working of the ship, she was kept clear. The accustomed cry of 'Ice ahead!' – 'Ice on the lee bow!' – 'Another island!' in the same tones, and with the same orders following them, seemed to bring us directly back to our old position of the week before. During our watch on deck, which was from twelve to four, the wind came out ahead, with a pelting storm of hail and sleet, and we lay hove-to, under a close-reefed fore topsail, the whole watch. During the next watch it fell calm with a drenching rain until daybreak, when the wind came out to the westward, and the weather cleared up, and showed us the whole ocean, in the course which we should have steered, had it not been for the head wind and calm, completely blocked up with ice. Here, then, our progress was stopped, and we wore ship, and once more stood to the northward and eastward; not for the Straits of Magellan, but to make another attempt to double the Cape, still farther to the east-ward; for the captain was determined to get round if perseverance could do it, and the third time, he said, never failed.

With a fair wind, we soon ran clear of the field-ice, and by noon had only the stray islands floating far and near upon the ocean. The sun was out bright, the sea of a deep blue, fringed with the white foam of the waves, which ran high before a strong south-wester; our solitary ship tore on through the open water as though glad to be out of her confinement; and the ice islands lay scattered upon the ocean, of various sizes and shapes, reflecting the bright rays of the sun, and drifting slowly northward before the gale. It was a contrast to much that we had lately seen, and a spectacle not only of beauty, but of life; for it required but little fancy to imagine these islands to be animate masses which had broken loose from the 'thrilling regions of thick-ribbed ice, and were working their way, by wind and current, some alone, and some in fleets, to milder climes. No pencil has ever yet given anything like the true effect of an iceberg. In a picture, they are huge, uncouth masses, stuck in the sea, while their chief beauty and grandeur – their slow, stately motion, the whirling of the snow about their summits, and the fearful groaning and cracking of their parts – the picture cánnot give. This is the large iceberg – while the small and distant islands, floating on the smooth sea, in the light of a clear day, look like little floating fairy isles of sapphire.

From a north-east course we gradually hauled to the eastward, and after sailing about two hundred miles, which brought us as near to the western coast of Terra del Fuego as was safe, and having lost sight of the ice altogether – for the third time we put the ship's head to the southward, to try the passage of the Cape. The weather continued clear and cold, with a strong gale from the westward, and we were fast getting up with the latitude of the Cape, with a prospect of soon being round. One fine afternoon, a man who had gone into the fore-top to shift the rolling tackles, sung out at the top of his voice, and with evident glee, 'Sail ho!'

Neither land nor sail had we seen since leaving San Diego; and any one who has traversed the length of a whole ocean alone can imagine what an excitement such an announcement produced on board. 'Sail ho!' shouted the cook, jumping out of his galley; 'Sail ho!' shouted a man, throwing back the slide of the scuttle, to the watch below, who were soon out of their berths and on deck; and 'Sail ho!' shouted the captain down the companion-way to the passenger in the cabin. Beside the pleasure of seeing a ship and human beings in so desolate a place, it was important for us to speak to a vessel, to learn whether there was ice to the eastward, and to ascertain the longitude; for we had no chronometer, and had been drifting about so long that we had nearly lost our reckoning; and opportunities for lunar observations are not frequent or sure in such a place as Cape Horn. For these various reasons the excitement in our little community was running high, and conjectures were made, and everything thought of for which the captain would hail, when the man aloft sung out – 'Another sail, large on the weather bow!' This was a little odd, but so much the better, and did not shake our faith in their being sails. At length the man in the top hailed, and said he believed it was land, after all. 'Land in your eye!' said the mate, who was looking through the telescope; 'they are ice islands, if I can seen a hole through a ladder;' and a few moments showed the mate to be right; and all our expectations fled; and instead of what we most wished to see we had what we most dreaded, and what we hoped we had seen the last of. We soon, however, left these astern, having· passed within about two miles of them, and at sundown the horizon was clear in all directions.

Having a fine wind, we were soon up with and passed the latitude of the Cape, and, having stood far enough to the southward to give it a wide berth, we began to stand to the eastward, with a good prospect of being round and steering to the northward, on the other side, in a very few days. But ill luck seemed to have lighted upon us. Not four hours had we been standing on in this course before it fell dead calm, and in half an hour it clouded up, a few straggling blasts, with spits of snow and sleet, came from the eastward, and in an hour more we lay hove-to under a close-reefed main topsail, drifting bodily off to leeward before the fiercest storm that we had yet felt, blowing dead ahead, from the eastward. It seemed as though the genius of the place had been roused at finding that we had nearly slipped through his fingers, and had come down upon us with tenfold fury. The sailors said that every blast, as it shook the shrouds, and whistled through the rigging, said to the old ship, 'No, you don't!' – 'No, you don't!'

For eight days we lay drifting about in this manner. Sometimes – generally towards noon – it fell calm; once or twice a round copper ball showed itself for a few moments in the place where the sun ought to have been, and a puff or two came from the westward, giving some hope that a fair wind had come at last. During the first two days we made sail for these puffs, shaking the reefs out of the topsails and boarding the tacks of the courses; but finding that it only made work for us when the gale set in again, it was soon given up, and we lay-to under our close-reefs. We had less snow and hail than when we were farther to the westward, but we had an abundance of what is worse to a sailor in cold weather – drenching rain. Snow is blinding, and very bad when coming upon a coast, but, for genuine discomfort, give me rain with freezing weather. A snowstorm is exciting, and it does not wet through the clothes (a fact important to a sailor), but a constant rain there is no escaping from. It wets to the skin, and makes all protection vain. We had long ago run through all our dry clothes, and as sailors have no other way of drying them than by the sun, we had nothing to do but to put on those which were the least wet. At the end of each watch, when we came below, we took off our clothes and wrung them out; two taking hold of a pair of trousers, one at each end – and jackets in the same way. Stockings, mittens, and all, were wrung out also, and then hung up to drain and chafe dry against the bulkheads. Then, feeling of all our clothes, we picked out those which were the least wet, and put them on, so as to be ready for a call, and turned-in, covered ourselves up with blankets, and slept until three knocks on the scuttle and the dismal sound of 'All Starbowlines ahoy! Eight bells, there below! Do you hear the news?' drawled out from the deck, and the sulky answer of 'Aye, aye!' from below, sent us up again.

On deck we were all in darkness, a dead calm, with the rain pouring steadily down, or, more generally, a violent gale dead ahead, with rain pelting horizontally, and occasional variations of hail and sleet; decks afloat with water swashing from side to side, and constantly wet feet, for boots could not be wrung out like drawers, and no composition could stand the constant soaking. In fact, wet and cold feet are inevitable in such weather, and are not the least of those items which go to make up the grand total of the discomforts of a winter passage round the Cape. Few words were spoken between the watches as they shifted; the wheel was relieved, the mate took his place on the quarter-deck, the lookouts in the bows; and each man had his narrow space to walk fore and aft in, or rather to swing himself forward and back in, from one belaying-pin to another, for the decks were too slippery with ice and water to allow of much walking. To make a walk, which is absolutely necessary to pass away the time, one of us hit upon the expedient of sanding the decks; and afterwards, whenever the rain was not so violent as to wash it off, the weather-side of the quarter-deck, and a part of the waist and fo'c'sle were sprinkled with the sand which we had on board for holystoning, and thus we made a good promenade, where we walked fore and aft, two and two, hour after hour, in our long, dull, and comfortless watches.

All washing, sewing, and reading was given up, and we did nothing but eat, sleep, and stand our watch, leading what might be called a Cape Horn life. The fo'c'sle was too uncomfortable to sit up in; and whenever we were below, we were in our berths. To prevent the rain and the sea-water which broke over the bows from washing down, we were obliged to keep the scuttle closed, so that the forecastle was nearly airtight. In this little, wet, leaky hole, we were all quartered, in an atmosphere so bad that our lamp, which swung in the middle from the beams, sometimes actually burned blue with a large circle of foul air about it. Still, I was never in better health than after three weeks of this life. I gained a great deal of flesh, and we all ate like horses. At every watch when we came below, before turning in, the bread barge and beef kid were overhauled. Each man drank his quart of hot tea night and morning, and glad enough we were to get it; for no nectar and ambrosia were sweeter to the lazy immortals than was a pot of hot tea, a hard biscuit, and a slice of cold salt beef to us after a watch on deck. To be sure, we were mere animals, and, had this life lasted a year instead of a month, we should have been little better than the ropes in the ship. Not a razor, nor a brush, nor a drop of water, except the rain and the spray, had come near us all the time; for we were on an allowance of fresh water; and who would strip and wash himself in salt water on deck, in the snow and ice, with the thermometer at zero?

After about eight days of constant easterly gales, the wind hauled occasionally a little to the southward, and blew hard, which, as we were well to the southward, allowed us to brace in a little, and stand on under all the sail we could carry. These turns lasted but a short while, and sooner or later it set in again from the old quarter; yet at each time we made something, and were gradually edging along to the eastward. One night, after one of these shifts of the wind, and when all hands had been up a great part of the time, our watch was left on deck, with the mainsail hanging in the buntlines, ready to be set if necessary. It came on to blow worse and worse, with hail and snow beating like so many furies upon the ship, it being as dark and thick as night could make it. The mainsail was blowing and slatting with a noise like thunder, when the captain came on deck and ordered it to be furled. The mate was about to call all hands, when the captain stopped him, and said that the men would be beaten out if they were called up so often; that, as our watch must stay on deck, it might as well be doing that as anything else. Accordingly, we went upon the yard; and never shall I forget that piece of work. Our watch had been so reduced by sickness, and by some having been left in California, that, with one man at the wheel, we had only the third mate and three beside myself to go aloft; so that at most we could only attempt to furl one yard-arm at a time. We manned the weather yard-arm, and set to work to make a furl of it. Our lower masts being short, and our yards very square, the sail had a head of nearly fifty feet, and a short leech, made still shorter by the deep reef which was in it, which brought the clew away out on the quarters of the yard, and made a bunt nearly as square as the mizzen royal yard. Besides this difficulty, the yard over which we lay was cased with ice, the gaskets and rope of the foot and leech of the sail as stiff and hard as a piece of suction hose, and the sail itself about as pliable as though it had been made of sheets of sheathing copper. It blew a perfect hurricane, with alternate blasts of snow, hail and rain. We had to *fist* the sail with bare hands. No one could trust himself to mittens, for if he slipped he was a gone man. All the boats were hoisted in on deck, and there was nothing to be lowered for him. We had need of every finger God had given us. Several times we got the sail upon the yard, but it blew away again before we could secure it. It required men to lie over the yard to pass each turn of the gaskets, and when they were passed it was almost impossible to knot them so that they would hold. Frequently we were obliged to leave off altogether, and take to beating our hands upon the sail to keep them from freezing. After some time – which seemed for ever – we got the weather side stowed after a fashion, and went over to lee-ward for another trial. This was still worse, for the body of the sail had been blown over to leeward, and, as the yard was a-cock-bill by the lying over of the vessel, we had to light it all up to windward. When the yard-arms were furled, the bunt was all adrift again, which made more work for us. We got all secure at last, but we had been nearly an hour and a half upon the yard, and it seemed an age. It had just struck five bells when we went up, and eight were struck soon after we came down. This may seem slow work; but considering the state of everything, and that we had only five men to a sail with just half as many square yards of canvas in it as the mainsail of the *Independence*, sixty-gun ship, which musters seven hundred men at her quarters, it is not wonderful that we were no quicker about it. We were glad to get on deck, and still more to go below. The oldest sailor in the watch said, as he went down, 'I shall never forget that main yard; it beats all my going a fishing. Fun is fun, but furling one yard-arm of a course at a time, off Cape Horn, is no better than man-killing.'

During the greater part of the next two days, the wind was pretty steady from the southward. We had evidently made great progress, and had good hope of being soon up with the Cape, if we were not there already. We could put but little confidence in our reckoning, as there had been no opportunities for an observation, and we had drifted too much to allow of our dead reckoning being anywhere near the mark. If it would clear off enough to give a chance for an observation, or if we could make land, we should know where we were; and upon these, and the chances of falling in with a sail from the eastward, we depended almost entirely.

Friday, July 22nd. This day we had a steady gale from the southward, and stood on under close sail, with the yards eased a little by the weather braces, the clouds lifting a little, and showing signs of breaking away. In the afternoon, I was below with Mr H—, the third mate, and two others, filling the bread locker in the steerage from the casks, when a bright gleam of sunshine broke out and shone down the companion-way, and through the skylight lighting up everything below, and sending a warm glow through the hearts of all. It was a sight we had not seen for weeks – an omen, a godsend. Even the roughest and hardest face acknowledged its influence. Just at that moment we heard a loud shout from all parts of the deck, and the mate called out down the companion-way to the captain, who was sitting in the cabin. What he said we could not distinguish, but the captain kicked over his chair, and was on deck at one jump. We could not tell what it was; and, anxious as we were to know, the discipline of the ship would not allow of our leaving our places. Yet, as we were not called, we knew there was no danger. We hurried to get through with our job, when, seeing the steward's black face peering out of the pantry, Mr H— hailed him to know what was the matter. 'Lan'o, to be sure, sir! No you hear 'em sing out, "Lan'o"? De cap'em say 'im Cape Horn!'

This gave us a new start, and we were soon through our work and on deck; and there lay the land, fair upon the larboard beam, and slowly edging away upon the quarter. All hands were busy looking at it – the captain and mates from the quarter-deck, the cook from his galley, and the sailors from the fo'c'sle; and even Mr N—, the passenger, who had kept in his shell for nearly a month, and hardly been seen by anybody, and whom we had almost forgotten was on board, came out like a butterfly, and was hopping round as bright as a bird.

The land was the island of Staten Land, just to the eastward of

Cape Horn; and a more desolate-looking spot I never wish to set eyes upon – bare, broken, and girt with rocks and ice, with here and there, between the rocks and broken hillocks, a little stunted vegetation of shrubs. It was a place well suited to stand at the junction of the two oceans, beyond the reach of human cultivation, and encounter the blasts and snows of a perpetual winter. Yet, dismal as it was, it was a pleasant sight to us; not only as being the first land we had seen, but because it told us that we had passed the Cape – were in the Atlantic – and that, with twenty-four hours of this breeze, we might bid defiance to the Southern Ocean. It told us, too, our latitude and longitude, better than any observation; and the captain now knew where we were, as well as if we were off the end of Long Wharf.

In general joy, Mr N— said he should like to go ashore upon the island and examine a spot which probably no human being had ever set foot upon; but the captain intimated that he would see the island, specimens and all, in – another place, before he would get out a boat or delay the ship one moment for him.

We left the land gradually astern; and at sundown had the Atlantic Ocean clear before us.

Lieutenant Commander
Ian Fraser V.C., R.N.R.

H.M. MIDGET SUBMARINE XE3

(from *Frogman V.C.*)

In July 1945 the Japanese cruiser Takao *was anchored in Johore Strait in shallow water. The author took his midget submarine into a depression in the sea bed where explosive charges were laid against the cruiser's bottom. Limpet mines were also placed by one of the ship's crew who had first to get out of the submarine in diving dress and then propel them to the* Takao's *hull where they were attached by magnetism.*

EXCITEMENT was betrayed in my voice. 'There she is,' I cried . . . 'Stand by for a bearing, ship's head now.' . . .

From that moment . . . all fear left me. I felt only that nervous tautness that comes so often in moments of stress. I let each of the others have a quick look at the *Takao* through the periscope, and then we were ready . . .

The only sounds in the boat were the whirr of the main motor, the hiss of escaping oxygen from the cylinder in the engine-room, and an occasional scraping sound of steel on steel in the well greased bearings when the hydroplane wheel was turned. Forty feet, ten feet. 'Up periscope, range.' 'Down periscope.' So it went on until the range had narrowed to 400 yards.

'Up periscope, stand by for a last look round.'

Click! Down went the handles. I fixed my eye to the eye-piece for the hundredth time, slowly swinging to port.

'Ah, there she is, range eight degrees.'

Slowly I swung the periscope round to starboard.

'Flood "Q", down periscope, quick, thirty feet. Bloody hell! There's a boat full of Japs going ashore; she's only about forty or fifty feet away on the starboard bow. God, I hope they didn't see us.'

So close had they been that I could make out their faces quite distinctly, and even had time to notice that one of them was trailing his hand in the water. The boat, painted white, stood out clearly against the camouflaged background of the cruiser. Similar to the cutters used in the Royal Navy for taking liberty men ashore, she was packed with sailors. The helmsman stood aft, his sailor's collar and ribbon gently lifting in the breeze caused by the boat's headway. She was so close that it seemed that her bow waves almost broke over our periscope. I could see the lips of the men moving as they chatted away on their journey ashore. They should have seen us. I do not know why they did not.

'Thirty feet, sir.'

My mind re-focused.

'All right, Magennis, the range is 200 yards, we should touch bottom in a moment.'

To Smith: 'Keep her as slow as you can.'

Followed anxious silence, then a jar and the noise of gravel scraping along the keel as we touched bottom. Reid had to fight hard to keep her on course as we scraped and dragged our way across the bank at depths of only fifteen feet, which meant our upper deck was only ten feet below the surface.

Watching through the night periscope, I could see the surface of the water like a wrinkled window-pane above our heads, until it gradually darkened as we came into the shadow of the great ship. Something scraped down our starboard side, and then, with a re-verberating crash, we hit the *Takao* a glancing blow which stopped us. I thought we had made enough noise to awaken the dead, and I was worried in case someone above might have felt the jar.

'Stop the motor! I wonder where the hell we are?' I said. I could see nothing through the periscope to give me a clear indication of our position in relation to the enemy ship, only her dark shadow on our starboard side. Obviously I was not underneath it, as the depth on the gauge was only thirteen feet.

I began to fear that we might be much too far forward, that the ominous-sounding scraping along our side had been made by an anchor-cable at the target's bows.

'We seem to be too far for'ard,' I reported. 'We'll alter course to

190 degrees and try to run down her side. Port 30, half ahead group down.'

The motor hummed into life again, but we did not budge.

'Group up, half ahead,' I called, and we tried many other movements. The motor hummed even faster, the propeller threshed, but still no sign of movement. We were jammed, and looking back on this afterwards, I am inclined to think that as the *Takao* veered in the tideway, the slacking cable came to rest on us. Then it lifted as she veered away again, or else we were jammed for the same reason under the curve of her hull at this point. It was only after some really powerful motor movements in both directions, and ten minutes of severe strain, that we finally broke loose and dragged our way out across the shingly bottom to the deeper channel.

I had attacked from too fine an angle on the bow, and after running out again, I altered course and steered for a position more on the *Takao*'s beam, which would mean a longer run over the shallow bank, but I decided the risk was worth it, if I were to hit the ship amidships.

At three minutes past three we were ready again, a thousand yards away. Once more we started the run-in for the attack. This time we were successful. We slid easily across the bank with the gauge at one time registering only thirteen feet, and then blackness, as we slid into the hole and under the keel of the *Takao*. It was just as I had practised it so many times before, and I was surprised how easy it was.

The depth gauge began to indicate deeper water, 15 feet, 18 feet, 20 feet, and then a greying of the night-periscope and upper viewing window.

'Stop the motor.'

Then blackness in the night-periscope and upper viewing window.

'Full astern.'

The bottom of the *Takao* showed dimly, and then suddenly it was distinct, encrusted with thick heavy layers of weed as it fell sharply to her keel.

'Stop the motor.'

The hull stopped sliding overhead. We were under her.

We were resting on the bottom with the hull of the *Takao* only a foot above our heads. I wondered if we would be able to go straight through.

'Come and have a look at this,' I called to the crew, and they left their positions to come and see the encrusted bottom of our prize.

'What a dirty bastard,' said one of them; and I couldn't have agreed more. It would have been nice to have gone out and written my name on the years and years of growth on the keel, but time was passing, and the need for haste cut short our conversations. We were anxious to be away. The *Takao* held no interest for us, other than the need to blow her up.

'Raise the antennae,' I called.

Smith operated the lever and the two antennae came up hydraulically from their stowage positions on either side of the bow.

'It doesn't matter about the after one,' I told Smith, 'there's no point in trying to raise it.'

The after antennae, unlike the two for'ard ones, was raised by hand, and sometimes it was an awful struggle, particularly after several days at sea, to get it up, and in any case, it would not have been effective owing to the sharp slope of the ship down on her keel.

Magennis was ready: he must have been stewing in his rubber suit, and I thought, momentarily forgetting the dangers, how pleasant it would be for him to get into the cool water. He strapped on his breathing apparatus. The only instruction I could give him was to place all six limpets in the container as quickly as possible and not to make a noise. I fitted in the Perspex window, patted him on the shoulder, and into the escape compartment he went. Reid closed the door on him; the valves were opened and shut, and the pumps started. Looking through the observation window into the wet-and-dry compartment, I could see Magennis breathing steadily into the bag as the water rose around him, and then I moved over to the night-periscope again, with its larger field of vision and higher magnification. I could see along the keel of the *Takao* for some fifteen yards in either direction, and it was like looking into a dark cave with *XE.3* lying across the centre of the sunlit entrance. I swung around on the periscope so that the keel of the enemy lay against our upper deck, just for'ard of the periscope bracket, and as the bottom rose away, sloping from the keel at a fairly sharp angle, the antennae stuck up from the bow like an ant's feelers. They were not resting on the *Takao's* bottom. Huge lumps and clusters of seaweed hung down like festoons and Christmas decorations, and the faint sunlight danced between them.

Inside the boat we waited patiently. Suddenly, almost as though we hadn't expected it, the pumps stopped and the wheels controlling the valves began to move, as if controlled by a hidden power, as indeed in a sense they were. Reid again moved across from his seat by the wheel to help Magennis to shut them off, and looking through my only means of communication with the diver now that he was outside, I saw the lever which operated the clip on the hatch swing round in an arc of 120 degrees. A few bubbles of free air escaped and gyrated to the surface, wobbling and stretching as they floated through the tangled weed. I saw that there was not enough room between us and the *Takao's* bottom for the hatch to rise fully but, fortunately, it opened enough for Magennis to squeeze through as his hands gripped the sides of the hatch: and he was safely out. He looked all right, safe and confident, and he gave me the 'thumbs up' sign. I noticed a slight leak from the join between his oxygen cylinder and the reducing valve on his breathing set. It wasn't really big enough to cause concern, but I imagine that to Magennis it must have seemed like a full-scale submarine venting its air. He shut the lid and disappeared over the side, and we settled down nervously to await his return.

We counted the limpets as he bumped them out of the containers and moved them one by one along the starboard side, and occasionally I caught a glimpse of him as he worked away under the hull above. Six limpets he took – three towards the for'ard end and three towards the aft end. In all, the total time taken was somewhere round about thirty minutes. To me it seemed like thirty days. I cursed every little sound he made, for every little sound was magnified a thousand times by my nerves. It was a long wait. I couldn't remember if we talked or kept silent through it. I think and hope we were pretty calm superficially.

The inside of the boat was like a boiler, but we had to keep quiet. I dared not start the fan or motor. We had simply to sit and drink tin after tin of orange juice from the Freon container.

The tide was still falling. Although the rise and fall in the Johore Strait is only eight feet, this was more than sufficient to allow the cruiser to sit on us in the shallow hole beneath her hull. High water had been at 1200 zero hour for the attack, and it was now nearly four hours later. I was very anxious to get away. Magennis still seemed to be an age, and just when I could hardly contain myself a moment longer, he appeared on the hatch. He gave the 'thumb up' sign again and in he jumped. I saw the lid shut and the clip go home. He was back, and now at last we could go.

Quickly, we started to release the side cargoes. The fuses on the port charge, four tons of Amytol, had, like the 200-lb limpets, already been set to detonate in six hours' time, so that it was only necessary for us to unscrew the small wheel which started the mechanism, and then to unscrew the larger wheel which released the charge. The first ten turns of this wheel opened a kingston in the charge to allow water to enter the compartment, previously filled by air, and rendered the charge negatively buoyant. The last turn released the charge itself, which should have fallen away and rested on the bottom. In order to relish the full pleasure of placing four tons of high explosive under a Japanese ship, the three of us took it in turns to operate the wheels as Magennis was draining down his compartment. The port charge fell away – we heard it bump down our side, but we hung on for Magennis to re-enter the craft before finally letting the starboard limpet-carrier go. As a result of this delay, it became too heavy and would not release or slide away. Such an emergency had already been thought of by the designers of XE-craft, and an additional wheel had been provided. This operated a pusher to push the side cargo off, and between us we wound the wheel out to its limit, but with no effect. The bottom of the cargo swung out from the ship's side, but the top was still held fast. By now I felt sure that the pins at the top were holding, but I thought to myself that the movement of the craft might shake it loose. We certainly couldn't make headway very far with two tons of dead weight fast to our side.

In the meantime Magennis reported that he had found it very

difficult getting the limpets into position; the work of attaching them successfully had exhausted him. I could well imagine his feelings, as, out on the lonely water with only the sound of his own breathing to accompany him, he struggled and fought, first of all to clear an area of the bottom so that the magnetic hold-fasts could be fitted against the bare plate of the ship's hull. With his diving knife he had to cut away the thick weed waving like the feelers of an octopus above his head, too tough to pull away, and all the time a slow leak from his breathing set. After clearing away the weed he had to tackle the encrustation of barnacles and other shell-fish attached to the bottom. These had to be chipped off as silently as possible. The limpets themselves, clumsily designed (they were big awkward jobs to drag through the water, all angles and projections, and they caught and tangled in the weeds), had to be attached. Unfortunately, owing to the positive buoyancy of the charge itself and the angular bottom of the *Takao*, there was a tendency for the charges to break loose from the magnetic hold-fasts, which, for reasons unknown, had become very feeble, and to run up towards the surface, with Magennis chasing after them to bring them back into position in two groups of three charges. In each group he had secured the limpets some 45–60 feet apart – three away along the cavern to our starboard side, and three along the cavern on either side of the keel, so that they could not dislodge and slide off on to the bottom. He had set the firing mechanism working, but in his exhausted state had become unable to remove three of the counter-mining pins, which ensure that should one limpet blow up the rest will follow immediately, even if the clocks have been wound for the set delay. The counter-mining device, which was lethal after twenty minutes, also ensured that any diver sent down by the Japanese to render the mines safe, or to remove them, would blow himself to eternity should he give the charges the slightest blow.

Looking back on the limpet-placing part of the operation, I see how wonderfully well Magennis did his work. He was the first frogman to work against an enemy from a midget submarine in the manner designed: he was the first and only frogman during the whole X-craft operations ever to leave a boat under an enemy ship and to attach limpet mines: in fact, he was the only frogman to operate from an X-craft in harbour against enemy shipping.

Perhaps I had, in some undetectable way, made him aware of my own nervousness. The limpets should not have been less than 60 feet apart for successful working, but although we should, perhaps, have moved them away a bit further, it was too late now; a final effort had now to be made to get clear of the harbour.

'Group up, half ahead – let's get to hell out of this hole!'

I gave the order with a feeling of relief.

'Main motor, half ahead, sir,' from Smith. 'May I start the fan, sir?'

'Yes, start the fan.'

Magennis began to take off his breathing set and hood.

'What is the course, sir?' asked good, calm, cheerful Reid.

'Two hundred degrees,' I answered. 'Let me know if you have any trouble keeping her on.'

I moved over to the sounding machine and switched it on, and then back to the night-periscope to watch as we moved out under the vast hull which was slowly settling down upon us with the fall of the tide, and through which we hoped our charges would blow a hole big enough to sink her for good.

But although the motor had been running for several seconds, there was no sign of movement.

'Full ahead,' I ordered.

Still no movement!

'Stop, full astern, group up.'

Glancing at Smith, I sincerely hoped I was not becoming hysterical. I felt certain that the *Takao* must have settled down on us, thus preventing any movement whatsoever. We couldn't go astern as the *Takao*'s keel was lower than the rear periscope standard. We must go ahead if we could go anywhere at all.

'Stop, full ahead, group up, lift the red, stop.'

This gave us maximum power, the motors whirred and we could hear the propeller thrusting hard against the water, but it was useless. We seemed to be well and truly stuck, and for a moment I thought of hanging on until half an hour before the charge was due to go off and then abandoning the ship. After all, I consoled myself, it was only 200 yards or so from the shore, and we might be able to hide in the swamps and forests until Singapore fell into British hands again. Our flags and emblems were going to come in useful after all!

We tried pumping the water aft and then for'ard, out and then in, and finally, we even partially blew No. 2 main ballast tank to try to shake loose from what looked like being *XE.3*'s watery grave. I was in despair. Sweat poured into my eyes. But still that black menacing shape stood overhead. Then suddenly, with a final effort, she began to move.

'Ship's head swinging to starboard, can't control her.'

Once again Reid's quiet voice calmed my turmoil. We began to move slowly ahead, the flooded charge dragging like a broken wing on our starboard side. The black roof slid astern, and fresh pure welcome sunlight streamed through the water into my upturned eyes.

We had a bow angle of some five degrees, and slowly the needle of my depth gauge moved in an anti-clockwise direction until it steadied at seventeen feet. The weight on our right swung the ship's head round until we were parallel to the side of the *Takao*, and I reckoned some thirty feet away on her port side.

'Stop the motor, we'll have to try to release the cargo. It'll have to be very carefully done as we're only a few yards away,' I explained.

Magennis was still sweating away in his suit, and I felt he had done enough to make the operation a success. As Reid had little or no experience of underwater swimming in the frogmen gear, and Smith wasn't particularly good at this either, I considered that it was justifiable for me to take the risk of leaving the boat for a few moments, even if I was the commanding officer. Should anything happen, I had enough confidence in Smith to know that he could get her out to rejoin the *Stygian*.

'Come out of the way, Magennis, I'll go out and release it myself. Get me the spare set from the battery compartment.'

'I'll be all right in a minute, sir,' said Magennis, 'just let me get my wind.'

What a wonderful lad he was! He said this with a most hurt expression on his face, quite obviously meaning that since he was the diver it was up to him to do the diving. And so we sat quietly for five minutes, and when he was ready I replaced his hood and Perspex face. 'Thanks,' he said, and into the wet-and-dry compartment he went for the second time.

The wheels spun, the pumps started and the water began to rise. Reid had equipped Magennis with an elephant-size spanner, and as the lid of the hatch opened, I saw this come through the opening immediately behind a mass of air bubbles, followed by Magennis. Once again I wondered what he was thinking about only thirty feet away from a Japanese cruiser in seventeen feet of clear water, his only weapon being a spanner. The bubbles released from opening the hatch were quite enough to cause me a great deal of worry. Had anybody been looking over the side of the *Takao* – perhaps a seaman gazing idly into the water with his thoughts away at home in Yokohama, Nagasaki, or somewhere like that – he must have seen us. The water was as clear as glass, and Magennis in his green diving suit was sending out a steady stream of bubbles from the reducing valve of his set.

Inside the boat it was as quiet as death: none of us spoke. I could hear the ship's chronometer ticking away, the anxious seconds interrupted by an occasional clank as Magennis used his spanner. It took some five minutes to release the cargo; five of the most anxious minutes of my life. Watching through the periscope, I could see the position of both securing pins at which he should have been working, but for some reason or other he was out of sight. I bit my fingers, swore and cursed at him, swore and cursed at the captain and all the staff on board *Bonaventure* who had planned this operation, at the British Admiralty, and finally, at myself for ever having been so stupid as to volunteer for this life, and, having volunteered, for being so stupid as to work hard enough to get myself this particular operation. I wished myself anywhere except lying on the bottom of Singapore harbour.

I don't know what Reid or Smith thought of this little display, but as far as I know they never mentioned my temporary lapse.

I had told Magennis to make no noise, but his hammering and bashing, in what I thought to be really the wrong place, was loud enough to alarm the whole Japanese Navy.

'What the bloody hell is that bloody fool doing?' I asked no one in particular. 'Why the hell doesn't he come on top of the charge. Why didn't I go out myself?' Then I saw Magennis for a moment, and at the same time the cargo came away and we were free. He gave me the 'thumbs up' sign for the third and last time and slid feet first into the wet-and-dry compartment and closed the lid. Wheels turned, pumps started and down came the water.

Right, I thought. Then:

'Starboard twenty steer 090 degrees half ahead group up,' I ordered all in one breath.

'Aye, aye, sir.'

'Twelve hundred revolutions.'

'Aye, aye, sir.'

'O.K.,' I said. 'Home, James, and don't spare the horses.'

I think we all managed a smile at that moment.

Quartermaster John Hooper

THE END OF THE CABLE-SHIP 'LA PLATA'

Quartermaster John Hooper was one of two survivors of the steam vessel La Plata *which foundered in the Bay of Biscay in 1874 with the loss of 68 lives. He had been twice shipwrecked previously and this narrative was much praised by the* Annual Register *at the time – 'as moving as any that has ever been read of adventures at sea'.*

I HAD been twice shipwrecked, and once nearly lost in a fire at sea, before I saw the cable-ship *La Plata* founder in the Bay of Biscay in a winter gale.

I was chief mate of a ship called the *Flying Scud* when she went ashore in a dense fog off California. A big sea swept me overboard and broke my collarbone and otherwise mauled me before I was picked up by some fishermen and sent to hospital in San Francisco.

When the *Flying Scud* struck, there were fifty-seven living souls on board, but when the gale and the lee-shore had done with her, there were only half-a-dozen survivors, including myself and two passengers.

After that, fighting our way round the Horn in the *Morning Cloud*, an American vessel, I was badly damaged by a heavy sea, and three men were swept overboard.

For a quarter of a century I led a life which was packed with peril and adventure, and I was beginning to think that I could not go through any worse experiences than the sufferings I had already known. It is a merciful dispensation of Providence that the future keeps its secrets well hidden from us.

If I could have seen a little ahead I should have hurried away from the Tower Shipping Office in London when I had signed on for the voyage in the steamship *La Plata*; but I had no misgiving or foreboding, because for her day she was a fine, well-found steamboat.

The *La Plata* was an iron screw-steamer of 1218 tons, barque-rigged, and with her machinery well aft. She was specially equipped for cable-laying, and when I joined her on November 22, 1874, which was a Sunday morning, she was ready for sailing from the Telegraph Works at New Charlton, Woolwich, where she was lying.

The steamer had on board 183 nautical miles – that is, about 200 land miles – of deep-sea cable, and had also a great quantity of iron telegraph-poles and telegraph-wire. This was all dead-weight material, and with her 219 tons of coal the *La Plata* had a total weight on board of 1200 tons. As this was mostly stowed in the after part of the vessel, with her bunkers filled with coal, you can understand that she was heavily laden by the stern. I want you to bear that in mind, and also the fact that we were to go across the Bay of Biscay in the winter-time.

Many people in these days dread crossing the Bay at any time, even in the big splendid liners with their great free-board. I wonder what they would have said to starting out in that little steamer, with so much dead weight on board that she was like a log in the water when we started.

On November 26 we left the Thames for Rio Grand do Sul. The steamer had a total crew of ninety-five men, which was a very large number, because it included the telegraph staff, engineers, and hands who were necessary for laying the cable in the deep sea.

It was fine weather when we went down Channel, and it was a glorious morning when we dropped our pilot off the Isle of Wight and stood out to cross the Bay and get out into the Atlantic.

I took a lingering look at the white cliffs of Old England, as did all my comrades who were on deck. I was to see them again, after such suffering as few men have ever lived to describe; but as for them, they had indeed said good-bye.

I was one of the quartermasters of the steamer, so that when I was on duty my post was at the wheel, to steer the ship during my watch. Until Saturday, the 28th, things went well with us, then I knew that we should encounter the full force of a heavy gale. I knew also, that in such a ship, deeply laden as our own was, a heavy gale would be a dangerous one, yet I had no misgivings, even when I saw the great dark clouds gathering in the sky and noticed the huge swirl which was rolling up from the south-west.

There are times when even the boldest sailors feel inclined to turn and seek shelter, and I dare say that more than one bold seaman on board would have been thankful to hear that the *La Plata* was making for some safe spot at which she could anchor until the gale had spent its force. But orders are orders at sea, and our own were to get the steamship out to sea.

The promise of the stormy sky was speedily fulfilled. First the wind came on us like an ordinary gale, then it grew in strength and increased until, by midnight, it was blowing with the force of a hurricane.

The steamer drummed and thrashed into the seas, which had risen to an enormous height and were sweeping her from stem to stern. It is nothing in these days of Atlantic leviathans for a magnificent monster to drive through any ordinary gale, and she can always be held up to any wind that blows and forced to face any sea that runs. But they have such enormously powerful engines – they have their two, three, or four screws, and they have no top hamper; but the little *La Plata* had only a single screw, and low powered engines, and she had to depend on the help of her sails.

When we began driving into the storm we had as much sail set as we could carry, but the sails were blown out of the bolt-ropes, and as the ship was so heavily down by the stern, it was impossible to keep her head to the wind. Her bow was high out of the water, and wind and sea drove against it with such force that the vessel was almost blown round and became unmanageable.

By midnight it was seen that we were in a position of serious danger, if not very great peril, and there was not a man on board who did not know that if she survived the storm at all it would only be through incessant watchfulness on the part of everybody on deck and in the engine-room.

The very life of us depended on the engines being kept working and protecting the engine-room from the enormous masses of water which smashed on board. Time after time the Atlantic waves swept on board, with a deafening and terrifying noise, and a force that promised to smash the ship and overwhelm her.

The almost incredible ill-luck which had followed me ever since went to sea remained with me now. The privations I had been orced to endure had told on even my wonderful constitution, and vhen we began that hard fight with the gale, I was below in my erth, the doctor having ordered me to go there, because I had a ad sore throat, and was suffering from a very severe cold. I was nfitted to go on deck and cope with such bitter weather as was eing experienced. Yet nothing could have been harder for me to ndure than the misery of lying helpless in my bunk, hurled and hrown about by the dreadful labouring of the vessel, and knowing hat any one of the seas which struck us might mean our de-truction.

It is bad enough at such a time of peril to be at one's post on the leck or on the bridge, but it is infinitely worse to be cooped up in he foul air below and battened down. If you are on deck there is at east a chance of salvation, but there is no hope whatever when you re imprisoned as I was in the *La Plata*.

Time after time I heard the ominous thud which told of some ig sea coming on board in the darkness of that terrible night; then, t two o'clock in the morning, there came a crash which told me hat some serious mischief had been done on deck.

I asked for tidings as to what had happened, and learnt that one f the boats had been torn from its fastenings and carried over-oard. That was bad enough, but in such a gale you expect some-hing to be swept away. Boats and stanchions and fittings can be eplaced, and their loss does not greatly matter, but I heard also hat a man had been carried away and had perished.

No more depressing thing can happen at sea than a death on oard ship, especially such a death as this, because it is the end that nay come to any man at any moment. So terrible was the gale by his time that it was almost seeking death to go on deck; yet, in pite of my illness, which had exhausted me and left me almost as veak as a child, I could not bear to remain below any longer. Duty alled me, and I felt bound to obey.

How I clambered out of my berth and got on deck I do not learly remember, but, bit by bit, I fought my way along the deck, truggling through the deep water with which it was now constantly filled, and dodging, as best I could in the darkness, the seas of the Atlantic.

At last I struggled up to the bridge and took my post at the wheel, and from that moment until the ship went down I did not leave my place.

I wish I could find words that would convey to you anything like a strong impression of the dreadful scene on which I looked from the bridge of the struggling steamship; but all I can tell you is that the sky above and all around was perfectly black, and yet there seemed to be enough ghostly, mysterious light to show what an awful, deadly sea was running.

No light, however, was needed to tell us of our danger. We knew that too well from the terrific motion of the ship as she fell away into the trough, or was hurled high by one of the hills of water which swept upon her. It was impossible to do anything more than try to keep her up to it, and yet this could not be accomplished, for the reason I have given.

Steam and steer as we would, the *La Plata* was driven back and hurled about, entirely at the mercy of the wind and sea. She was like some poor, frail human being striving to battle with the wind that has the power to lift him off his feet and throw him away like straw.

For two hours in that night of turmoil – a shriek of wind and a roar of sea in which no human voice could be heard at a distance of more than a few inches – I held to my post and did what I could, more by instinct than by judgement, to help to save the ship. I craved for daylight, although I knew that the dawn would reveal a sea which would appal the stoutest sailor; but it would at least give us the chance of seeing an approaching wave, and doing our best to meet it.

Mercilessly and incessantly the waves crashed on board and swept the deck, carrying away every movable thing, and many things that had been, as we imagined, firmly secured. One boat had already gone; at four o'clock a sea bore down upon us which ripped the lifeboat out of its skids, wrenched bolt-ropes and every fastening from the deck, and swept the entire mass, a heap of shattered wreckage, over the side.

Again, hour after hour, until the dawn broke in the east, the sea continued its work of maiming and destroying. Still things went fairly well. The ship was making a gallant fight and was bearing her punishment nobly. Almost like a living thing she was settling to the contest with wind and water, and it almost looked as if the work of man would triumph over the forces of nature.

Then – about an hour after the cheerless dawn had shown on the horizon – there came to us a report which drove all hope from every heart. We were told that a plate in the engine-room had started, and that the sea was rushing in and threatening to extinguish the engine-room fires, to take away from us the very force on which our safety depended.

Hope abandoned me as soon as I heard the tidings, for I knew that so far as the *La Plata* was concerned, she had received her sentence of death.

From the time I first went on to the bridge until it was reported that the engine-room fires were drowned and that the ship was no longer under control, I had stuck to my post at the wheel, trying as hard as I could to keep her to it. I did not abandon my spokes until the mate came and told me that there was no hope, and that every man must fight for his own life.

A few of the men seemed to be filled with despair, but, for the most part, the crew bore themselves like good Englishmen, and made ready to get the boats free from their lashings and skids, and to clamber into them – the idea being that when the steamship foundered the boats would float and could be rowed away. It was impossible in the sea that was running to attempt to lower them, because they would either have been swamped or smashed to pieces against the steamboat's iron sides.

Captain Dudden, the commander of the *La Plata*, was on the bridge when I finally left it, but all my orders were given to me by the second mate. By the time I got on deck the steamship had been got round, and she was lumbering on before the wind and sea, continually pooped by the terrific following waves.

The water came on board in such enormous masses that the after part of the ship was completely buried, while her fore part was high out of the water. First of all, I made my way to a raft which was on the bridge. The doctor and some of the telegraph men were clustering about the raft, evidently intending to cling to it when it was afloat in the water. It seemed to me that there would be no chance of my own salvation on the raft, so after helping to launch it to windward, I climbed down the bridge and struggled aft towards a lifeboat which the boatswain, whose name was Lamont, and some of the crew had got ready. This was the starboard quarter-boat.

How I got into the boat I do not know, but at last I found myself packed in her, waiting for some stroke of luck to come and get us into the sea, so that we should have a fighting chance.

No sooner had I taken my place in the lifeboat than a tremendous sea swept on board, crashed on to the top of us, burst the lifeboat in two, and by sheer force of water, drove me and the rest of us deep down into the sea.

Now, indeed, I thought that the end had really come. I seemed to go down and down and down into the green depths, until I was almost suffocated in the attempt to hold my breath, and until there seemed to be no chance whatever of rising again to the surface.

I struggled with all the energy within me to get to the top, and at last I found the water getting lighter and lighter, and then I shot up again into the air and took a deep, long breath.

I was still perfectly conscious, and saw that the *La Plata* was just on the point of sinking, and that wreckage was falling all around me.

A number of men were struggling in the water near me, and one of them shouted, 'Look out, quartermaster, for her rigging!'

I saw that I had been sucked over the sinking ship and that the mizzen rigging was crashing upon me. I tried to swim away, but before I could make more than a stroke or two, the mass was upon me and I was netted just as a lion might be by hunters in the forest.

The tangle of rope was over me, and for the second time I was carried down into the depths of the Bay of Biscay. The rigging had caught me over the back, and I sank face downwards. I think this time I went deeper than before, for I could no longer hold my breath, and began to swallow salt water.

The end now seemed sure indeed, yet I made another despairing effort at salvation. I struck out and down – I did anything I could instinctively to clear myself of the toils – and again I had the joy of seeing that my limbs were free and that I was rising rapidly.

I knew that in two or three seconds I should be clear of the water, yet as I rose to the surface my head struck a top-gallant-yard and was cut open by one of the bolts. Stunned and bleeding though I was, I had strength and resourcefulness left to cling to the spar.

It was while I was being sucked down by the sinking ship that I heard and felt a terrible explosion.

The *La Plata* had sunk, and the noise was caused, not, I imagine, by the bursting of her boilers, but owing to the compression of the air.

I was too much occupied with the thought of my own peril to pay any great attention to the foundering of the steamship. I looked about me and saw the boatswain not far away.

The two of us struggled to a broken American air-raft which came floating past us. This raft consisted of a couple of air-tight india-rubber tubes, which were covered and connected with canvas. We knelt in it with our arms over the tubes, immersed in the water, and for the present, at any rate, safe.

I had had time to look around me, and had seen the carpenter, who was clinging to a hencoop, swept off and drowned. In the distance, on the crest of a wave, I saw our only remaining boat, the port quarter-boat, running before wind and sea. She carried fifteen men, who, after many hours of exposure in the Bay, were picked up by a passing ship and afterwards put on board a homeward-bound steamer and landed in England.

It was these survivors who first told the tidings of the disaster and reported that the *La Plata* had gone down with every soul except themselves. Not a word about the boatswain and myself, who were clinging to our frail support and were being hurled about by the angry seas of the Biscay in winter-time, up to our waists in water, with the seas breaking over us any minute, without food or drink, and with very little clothes on to keep off the piercing cold.

There had been no time to make the air-raft thoroughly ready for the water, and the result was that although the air-tubes were sound they were not thoroughly inflated. This was, perhaps, fortunate for us, because we were able to get a better grip than we should have done if the canvas had been thoroughly rigid, and at the same time there was quite buoyancy enough to keep us both afloat.

The boatswain and myself sat on the tube which was most fully inflated, pressing our knees against the other tube, and resting our feet on the canvas connecting the two.

The raft had capsized and the framework had been shattered by the seas, the result being that we had nothing to cling to and were in the water up to the waist, with the breaking seas continually sweeping over our heads.

After the ship had foundered and we were on the raft, I saw a man with a cork lifebelt on. He cried pitifully for help, time after time, but we could do nothing for him, and he drifted away and perished, like the rest of those who had been cast into the waters. Some of them were mercifully spared prolonged suffering, because they were taken down into the vortex, but I fear that many died a lingering death.

Do you clearly understand the terrible position in which we found ourselves? We were not, remember, in an open boat, nor were we even on an ordinary raft. We were simply clinging to the more or less deflated air tubes, deep in the water, in the bitter air of a late November day.

Only one thing kept us from perishing of exposure, and that was the fact that the water in which we were floating was part of that warm current, the Gulf Stream, which flows across the Atlantic and warms certain portions of the English Channel and the Bay of Biscay.

The water itself was not cold, but the air was bitter. I remember that once I raised one of my legs into the air, to give it a rest, but the cold was so bitter that I was glad to put the limb back into the liquid warmth.

The time came when the two of us, who had been talking more or less hopefully, got very silent, and when the hope which had risen within us because of temporary salvation, gave way to dull despair.

The afternoon wore on and the dark night came, followed by what seemed to be a hopeless dawn. Still we clung, sodden, starving, and parched with thirst, to our flabby raft, and all through that day we looked with bloodshot eyes to every point of the compass, hoping and praying for the help which seemed never likely to come. Lamont bore himself wonderfully well, and we did our best to cheer and comfort one another.

Once or twice we saw ships – for we were in the track of the traffic to and from the Near and Far East – across the Bay. More than once it seemed as if our salvation was assured, because ships came so near and we clamoured loudly for help. At one time it seemed certain that we should be rescued, but the ship which could have saved us went away, although I am sure that we must have been within hailing distance.

It was an American three-masted schooner, which seemed to be bearing down directly for us. That was on the Tuesday morning, when the gale had died away and there was fine, clear weather. She got up to within half-a-mile of us, and then a dead calm came, and we had the unspeakable agony of watching her for at least two hours, and then, when the breeze returned, bearing away from us and leaving us to our sufferings and our doom.

A consuming thirst was afflicting us, and yet there was not a drop of water to drink. In my despair I set to work to chew the edge of a medal which I was wearing when the ship went down and which had been presented to me by the Shipwrecked Fishermen and Mariners' Society. This relieved my thirst to some extent, and helped the day on.

The weather varied, and a driving, bitter sleet succeeded the fine spell we had enjoyed. The wind and snow drove pitilessly down upon us, and added to the sufferings, which were now becoming unendurable.

Both of us went almost delirious, and I, at any rate, began to have vivid pictures of sun-bathed fields and green trees, with plenty of clear, pure water to drink and more than enough food to eat. These illusions were shattered from time to time when my senses returned and showed me the cruel reality of the Bay in which we were drifting in the winter.

For four full days and nights the boatswain and myself were in the water; then, on the Wednesday at noon, nearly a hundred hours after we had been cast away, we saw a Dutch schooner, and knew that she had seen us. She was the *Wilhelm Berklesorn*, bound to the Mediterranean.

It was soon clear enough that, having spied us, they were not going to abandon us, but the breeze had freshened again, and the sea was so rough that there was no chance of running the little ship down towards us and rescuing us.

After beating about for a long time the schooner bore down, and Lamont and myself did the only thing it was possible to do to secure ourselves. He had a lifebuoy round his waist, and as the schooner sailed past us, as near as she could get, he slipped away from the raft and managed to seize a rope they threw him and made it fast round his waist. He was too utterly worn out to try and secure it, but the Dutchmen had got him, and they did not mean to let him go until they had dragged him through the water and hauled him, terribly swollen and emaciated, on board.

Then the schooner returned for her second shot, this time at myself. I was perfectly helpless, yet I managed to catch hold of a rope they threw, and which, by a stroke of luck, had fallen around me.

I tried to grasp the rope with my hands, but no strength remained in them. I managed, however, to put the rope round my neck and to grip it with my teeth to prevent myself from being strangled.

The way of the vessel through the water brought me alongside, and reaching over, the Dutchmen caught me by the collar of my shirt and pulled me on board. I collapsed on the deck, but had just breath enough left to utter a few words of thankfulness to God for His mercy in so marvellously preserving me.

The schooner bore away for Gibraltar, and from that port, after being treated in hospital, we sailed for Southampton by the P. and O. mailboat *Cathay*.

It was reported at the time that Lamont died soon after being landed; but I heard afterwards that he did not pass away just then.

As for myself, for a long time I was unable to get about at all, except on crutches; and ever since the disaster I have suffered greatly from the effects of my long stay in the sea.

David Lewis

STRUGGLE WITHOUT HOPE

(from *Ice Bird*)

David Lewis, a New Zealander of Welsh and Irish extraction, sailed alone to Antarctica in 1972 in his yacht Ice Bird, *a voyage which he regarded as the ultimate challenge of the sea. Mountainous seas, constant gales, snowstorms and freezing temperatures accompanied him until the sixth week when, 3,600 miles from Sydney,* Ice Bird *capsized and was dismasted in an area which was the home of 105 foot waves, actually recorded by Russian scientists.* Ice Bird *had been rolled over through a full 360° and an adventure had suddenly become an apparently foredoomed struggle to survive.*

I HASTILY stuffed the nearest floating rag into the gap in the side of the coach roof (later I substituted sealing compound). My Omega wrist watch, kept on Greenwich time for navigation, was providentially still running. In the absence of radio time signals – I correctly assumed that the radios would all be shorted out by salt water – I must rely solely upon it for longitude, estimating its probable error as best I could.

A hurried search for gloves was fruitless. Well, gloves would be no use to me if *Ice Bird* sank. Seizing a bucket (the pump, of course, was useless) I began bailing for life.

The capsize must have occurred soon after first light, or around 2 a.m. Hour after hour I bailed until I was repeating the sequence of operations in a haze of tiredness, mechanically, like an automaton. The glass was beginning to rise, I noted dully, so the cold front must have passed, switching the storm winds to the southwest. This presumption was confirmed when ragged tears began to appear in the driving cloud wrack. Bursts of sunlight momentarily illuminated a scene that, even in my then state, I appreciated was of awesome grandeur. The screaming wind had not let up in the slightest. The tormented sea was a sheet of white water that looked like snow. At least I have seen the sun again before I die, I thought.

By about 8.30 a.m. the yacht was empty down to the floorboards. Then *crash!* I picked myself up from the corner where I had been hurled when this second killer wave had knocked *Ice Bird* flat, this time over to starboard, to find her flooded again to almost exactly the same level as before. The carefully salvaged logbook, charts and sleeping bag were once more awash.

When I wearily recommenced bailing I saw that the life raft was gone from the cockpit. I was without thought; conscious only of pain and weariness; actuated only by some obscure instinct for survival. An age passed until suddenly there was no more water to scoop up. Then I was knocking out the bolts securing the floorboard battens and scooping the remaining thirty or so bucket-fuls out of the bilge.

Noon. *Ice Bird* was dry again. Habit was strong. With numb hands I picked up a ballpoint pen, opened the sodden logbook and laboriously recorded the incident.

'Gale moderating to force 10–9. Heavy seas breaking against us. Everything soaked and destroyed. Must rest a little.' I finished. I had been bailing continuously for something like ten hours.

The thumping of the mast against the hull soon had me on my feet again. Thank goodness the boat was of steel. Crawling out on deck, I set about knocking out split pins to free the shrouds from the rigging screws that anchored them to the deck. The stainless steel wire rigging, like the mast itself, would have to be sacrificed: there was no way in which I could hoist aboard such a weighty tangle of wreckage nor make use of it if salvage had been possible.

So I pried and levered with a screwdriver, pinched and hammered with pliers at those stubborn split pins. The deck's motion was too violent and I was too tired to hit accurately but I carried on until the sunken mast was held by only two wires, never noticing that I had gashed my left hand deeply in two places, as the wounds neither hurt or bled.

By 7.30 that evening I could do no more.

'Hand bleeding and very numb,' I wrote in the logbook, incredibly failing to realize what was wrong or to make the slightest attempt to warm my still uncovered fingers – and I a doctor! The numbing effects upon reasoning power of exhaustion and shock were never more apparent. 'Will have a stiff drink and try to sleep. Sleeping bag soaked,' I added in a barely decipherable scrawl. But the rum bottle was nowhere to be found. Smashed to pieces, I assumed and, after some searching, found another. It was a fortnight before I came upon the original bottle. Driven up through the plywood floor of a locker, it was still intact.

A fitful sleep of utter tiredness followed. In the morning my fingers were too numb to feel the winder on my wrist watch. My first reaction was horror. Should the watch stop I had no way of setting it to the correct time again. Result – the ending at one stroke of any possibility of navigational accuracy and the fading to absolute zero of my already dim chances. I searched feverishly for my glasses. They misted up as soon as I put them on. I squeezed out wet toilet paper and wiped them repeatedly. Now I could *see* the winder turn. This procedure was to be faithfully repeated night and morning from then on and must never, on any account, be omitted.

The wider implications of my fingers' numbness came home to me as I belatedly realized the obvious – that both my hands were frostbitten. From now on I must always keep them covered. The damp woollen gloves or mitts (I had so far salvaged one of each) I would reserve for work on deck, using slightly less damp woollen socks when below. I even learned to write up the log and open cans of corned beef with the socks on my hands.

The remaining shrouds parted of their own accord about the middle of the morning and *Ice Bird* floated free of the wreckage. I laboriously hoisted thirty-five buckets of water out of the companionway and poured them into the self draining cockpit; later in the day eighteen buckets more. I tried to force more sealing compound into the split but had little success. Every single roll of the dismasted yacht put the side decks under and sent a fresh spurt of water into the cabin.

My first pathetic attempt at rigging some sort of a sail was by cutting away the remaining fragments of the canvas dodger and wrapping them round the pulpit forward. It was ineffective. The dry fur coat and fur trousers that had been stowed carefully away in the forepeak in a waterproof plastic bag I found to be soaked, for the bag had chafed through unnoticed during the long weeks at sea. Nevertheless, I changed into them, a procedure which, because of my hands, took over an hour.

The 9 p.m. scribbled entry in the day's log sounds curiously forlorn. 'Blowing up from the west. Both hands fingers frostbitten – attempted to warm them up this p.m. Will now try to run off before the sea.'

And a little later, 'Failed steer. Failed primus. 18 buckets. Estimate watch 4 minutes 33 seconds fast (est. daily gain 6 seconds). Can't be sure if winder turning.'

Depressed by these successive failures, I huddled down in my sleeping bag and pressing my unfeeling hands (which seemed as little part of me as slabs of chilled meat) against my warm body, I dozed the miserable night away.

The first of December. Working in swirling snow, my hands surprisingly well protected by wet woollen gloves, I cleared away the remaining wreckage and set about rigging up a jury mast. The best spar I could find was the surviving spinnaker pole (the other had been broken when the mast had collapsed). It was an aluminium tube ten feet long, far too fragile for the job in hand, as well as being ridiculously short, but I could think of nothing else to use. Shrouds or stays were needed for support and halyards to hoist sails. An old friend, a veteran climbing rope, was sacrificed to make these, supplemented by part of a coil of rope given me by the Stewart Island Fisherman's Cooperative. A deck safety wire was pressed into service as a forestay. I was tired out by the time the task was completed, but at least I was ready to raise the makeshift mast the moment the weather allowed.

I had now time to investigate the motor. Not unexpectedly, it was useless, its electrics brine-soaked. I did succeed, with the expenditure of many waterproof Greenlight matches, in getting one stove burner going erratically and I heated some stew and made coffee over the flaring yellow flame.

338

'This must be Christmas,' I wrote, with my first flash of humour.

The following day, the third since the capsize, was a landmark, for we got under way. The temperature was −2°C and soft ice – frozen sea water – coated the deck. But between the heavy snow showers it was fine and the wind had at last dropped to a normal breeze. This was the opportunity I had been waiting for. I made fast the jury shrouds, one to each side and one to each quarter at the stern and led the forestay wire from the 'mast head' round the bow anchor warp roller and back aft to where I could reach it. Then, planting one end of the spinnaker pole in the mast step, I pushed the light spar upwards and hauled in on the wire forestay until the pole stood vertical, secured laterally and behind by the rope shrouds. The wire was soon made fast and the shrouds tightened down as far as they would go.

The remaining number two storm jib had next to be dragged up from below. I found by trial and error that two knots in the head of the sail reduced its length to that of the short forestay. It only remained to shackle it to the bow, clip the hanks on to the forestay and reeve a pair of sheets. Finally I crawled along to the foot of the mast, braced my back on it against the rolling, and hauled up the jib.

I dared not think how futile was the gesture. The first sights since the accident had shown the stark ice barriers of the Antarctic Peninsula to be around 2,500 miles off, farther than from New York to Seattle or from England to Siberia. It seemed flouting fate as I sheeted in the pathetic rag of sail on the ten-foot mast (the old mast had measured thirty-six feet) and, at the speed of a good one mile an hour, turned the bow towards grim and distant shelter.

Ice Bird had to be steered by hand (from inside the cabin with the tiller lines) whenever the wind was a following one but she could be left to make good her own rather erratic course in beam winds and, with head winds, she could be persuaded to point ever so slightly to windward. My compass could not function inside the steel hull because of the magnetism, so when steering by hand I had to peer up from my seat on the corner of a bunk through the Perspex dome at the strips of sailcloth I had tied to the backstays to indicate the wind direction. Steering was essentially a matter of keeping these at a constant angle.

Since the most common wind directions were approximately from north-west or south-west, the yacht's natural tendency was to sail sideways to the wind and waves (a characteristic that meant ceaseless rapid rolling – a most vile motion); her preferred direction of advance was frequently towards the south-east or north-east rather than due east and we pursued our way, often as not, in a series of zigzags. Sometimes, the wind being more northerly or southerly, *Ice Bird* could be left to her own devices and would follow roughly the desired course for as long as a day or more. At other times, when the wind was more westerly, I would have to steer by hand for twelve or fourteen hours at a stretch, only letting go of the lines to snatch up a biscuit, slice off a hunk of corned beef or answer the call of nature. Time and again, the need for sleep would overwhelm me and all hope of making progress would have to be abandoned for the time being in favour of my body's imperative demand for rest.

The numbness in my swollen hands was beginning to give way to intense and growing agony, showing that some life at least remained in them. Antibiotics offered the one hope of saving my fingers, else infection would make short work of the damaged and devitalized tissue, so I now began taking double doses of Tetracycline capsules and continued this massive therapy for several weeks. To aggravate matters, my left knee became red and swollen. The same antibiotics might be expected to control this infection too. The hope was happily realized, and the pain and swelling subsided in a few days. The Australian Antarctic medical expert and veteran of the Heard Island expeditions, Dr Graeme Budd (he himself had been badly frostbitten), had helped me to plan a joint investigation into the effects of prolonged wet cold that I was expected to encounter during the voyage. This scientific study was accumulating far more information than I had bargained for, I thought ruefully.

Whenever I was not otherwise occupied I turned to escapist novels, so that I could forget for a while the surrounding squalor and misery. But to return to the reality of chilly feet squelching in boots that I had no option but to wear day and night – since my clumsy sausage-like fingers were unequal to the task of unlacing them – to damp sleeping bag and aching hands only served to deepen my depression. The violent rolling in the virtual absence of a steadying sail was physically and mentally exhausting too. Then always at the back of my mind was the reality that I still dare not quite face: one mile an hour – and that in favourable conditions. How far to land? I pushed the thought from me.

Then even this dismally slow progress was halted. After the crippled yacht had been crawling eastward for four days, the foot of the little mast broke off in a gale, and a stormy night and day intervened before I could sort out the cat's cradle of rigging tangled around the deck and raise it again.

'Hands always pain,' I wrote.

Assessed soberly, the situation did, indeed, appear hopeless – in the middle of the stormiest ocean on earth with a makeshift mast that kept crumbling away. I silently cursed the unknown busybody who had added a particular statistic to the *National Geographic World Atlas* that I had aboard: 'World's most distant point from land,' he had written. His totally redundant cross on the map lay due north of *Ice Bird*'s position.

It was impossible for me any longer to ignore the facts. 'A shutter has closed between a week ago when I was part of the living and since. Chance [of survival] negligible but effort in spite of pain and discomfort. These last are very great. Must go on striving to survive, as befits a man. Susie and Vicky without a daddy is worst of all.'

Next day, as blinding snow showers driving up from the south ushered in a new gale, I wrote further. 'Surprising no fear at almost certainly having to die, a lot of disappointment though.'

Would all I could offer the children be memories that would soon fade and the austere comfort of the words I had written in the will made before leaving Sydney? 'In the event of my death attempting to storm new frontiers at sea . . . I want Vicky and Susie to know that I expect them always to face life unafraid, with their heads up, and always remembering to laugh. My grown-up children already know this.'

To my own surprise, I realized that the intolerable thought of the little girls left fatherless did even more to keep me striving than did the urge for self-preservation. Also, surprisingly, the expectation of dying in such utter solitude, about as far from human contact as it was possible to be anywhere on earth, did not occasion me any special despondency; since every one of us must ultimately tread this road alone.

A kind of philosophy seemed to have taken shape about this time. The chances of crossing two and a half thousand miles of Southern Ocean in my leaking, battered boat with its ludicrous mast were too remote for serious contemplation and the far from welcoming blizzard-swept escarpments that were my destination promised no welcoming havens. I must just live for the day, therefore. The awful effort demanded by the daily struggle was worthwhile *in itself*, regardless of its hopelessness; despite its futility this striving would, in some obscure way, not be wasted.

I tried clumsily to express these thoughts in the log. 'Earning membership of humanity – must earn it every day, to be a man.' I proceeded to try for that day's quota by laboriously and painfully emptying out twenty-four buckets of bilge water, clearing the jammed halyard in a snowstorm and hoisting another sail to assist the little jib. This was the storm tri-sail. The head had once again to be knotted so that it could fit the diminutive mast.

If it were not for my hands, how much more I could do, I kept thinking. But even after being outside only long enough to take a sun sight I found myself 'shouting with the pain in my fingers'. The morning of 11 December was relatively calm and I was able to get the stove going, for the first time in five days, to heat up a can of stew and make a lukewarm cup of coffee. I was depressed the greater part of the time, overtired but restless and unable to sleep soundly even when I did have the chance.

By the 12th I had become more obsessed than ever with my terrible hands. Time and again I postponed or put off altogether going on deck to carry out the most urgent and necessary tasks, all for fear of the endless minutes of torture that I knew must inevitably follow. 'Steering by yoke and line from the cabin all after-noon,' I wrote. 'Gashed and frostbitten fingers more painful now. Are they healing? Worry over water [the supply of fresh water aboard was unlikely to prove adequate for reaching land at the present rate of progress], distance, time. Sometimes just get cow-ardly and whimper a bit in my sleeping bag.'

Then at midnight I concluded the tale of the day's tribulations. 'SW gale, force 8, *lower four inches of jury mast crumbled.* Lowered sail and lay a-hull. Hands stand less cold than ever.'

The grim reality behind these laconic phrases had been my claw-ing desperately about the deck, as always on hands and knees, smothering the flapping sails with my body until I could secure them with lashings and then tightening down the shrouds to secure the mast, as I had before – only this time even less of it remained. All this was in darkness out of which streamed volleying snow pellets and stinging half-frozen droplets of spray.

I could not know then that *Ice Bird* was on the eve of another new disaster.

Did I pray? people ask. No. I longed to be able to but, not being religious at other times, I had just enough dignity left not to cry out for help when the going got a bit rough. A higher power, should one exist, might even appreciate this attitude!

I am very often asked about loneliness and I have mentioned the subject previously. Even though my prospects had now changed so radically, I was at least spared this desolate emotion. My little drama was being played out on the vast stage of the Southern Ocean with death lurking in the wings, but my solitude, while full of anguish, was never lonely.

The last day of the eighth week out of Sydney Cove, 13 De-cember (just a fortnight after the capsize) was not a Friday. But it dawned inauspiciously enough – and continued worse. The gale that at midnight had sheered off its four-inch quota of the spin-naker pole mast, had increased until it was blowing at force eleven by 7.30 that morning – only one point in the wind scale below a hurricane. The lashings I had tied so tightly round the sails the night before were totally inadequate in a storm of this intensity.

Frozen snow-filled pockets of heavy sailcloth ballooned out of the ice-sheathed ropes that confined them and proceeded to flog themselves to pieces with the abandon of demented living things. I hastily hunted out more cord and braved the icy deck to wind the cord round the tri-sail and jib, in defiance of the screaming snow-laden wind that strove to wrest the line from my numb hands.

'Dear God,' I thought, 'if only I could set even the smallest headsail to give the yacht steerage way and render her controllable in these terribly high, steep seas.' But I well knew this was a vain ambition – doubly so, because the strongest sail would have disintegrated before ever it could have been sheeted home and, in my case, the frail jury mast could never have stood the added stress. I was left with no option but to try to make the yacht steer down wind under bare poles again. And I had already experienced the futility of attempting that procedure in these Southern Ocean seas (unlike the North Atlantic) and the near-fatal consequences of failure.

Well, no more could usefully be done on deck. Down below I made sure that nothing had been omitted from the gale routine that bitter experience had dictated. I mentally ticked off the items. Hatches fastened, washboards in place. Yes, I had secured the table by spreading across it a piece of strong nylon fishing net, anchored on one side to the port bunk board and, on the other, tied down to the floor battens. This should keep not only the table itself in place, but also the current supply of canned food stored in three boxes underneath it, even if – I hated to admit the possibility even to myself – even if the *Ice Bird* were to be capsized again. One locker only was without a catch and this I attempted less successfully to net down too. A criss-cross of cords (seamanship basically boils down to having quantities of string of all sizes – impossible to have too much) tied down my cardboard files of letters, lists and photostats, many of these papers stuck together and part-pulped from their ducking a fortnight earlier. There were few suitable points to anchor the cord to, so the documents stood to fare little better than before. The heavy bundle of damp, slimy charts – there were so many that I could scarcely lift them – had already been stuffed into the plastic bag with the fewest holes. Now

I pushed the logbook in on top, and after a moment's thought, added a few rolls of toilet paper.

What else? The vital watch, of course. I wrapped it in cotton wool and placed it in a box which I wedged among the plastic bags containing spare batteries and matches in the driest locker. Next the ventilators. I stuffed each one tightly with rags. Fresh air was not at a premium that day – neither was salt water. Finally, laboriously, at the cost of many a bruise and quantities of spilled water, I bailed out twenty bucketfuls from the centre well to leave the bilge dry. This done, I tried once more to steer, but, as in the hurricane that had turned her over, the yacht generally wallowed broadside on and refused to run off before the enormous wind-torn waves, which were becoming more formidable every minute.

By early afternoon the relentless, sustained wind of sixty knots or over had built up huge hollow seas, which differed in two respects from the mighty storm waves I had encountered in other oceans – the rapidity with which they increased in height and their extraordinary steepness.

'They are *jetting* forward,' I noted at 1.30 p.m., with horror. The streaming lines of foam driving across the frothing waste were scarcely distinguishable from the opaque white of the snow blizzard that swept over them. And here and there amid the general turmoil great killer breakers collapsed like tumbling waterfalls in thunderous ruin. Sooner or later one was bound to mark us as its prey. Could we survive?

After watching in helpless misery while the remains of the self-steering gear broke up and was swept away, I made one more attempt to steer. It was hopeless. We lay, helplessly, starboard side to, rolling the decks under. I cowered down on the port bunk, back braced against the cabin bulkhead – as if to seek companionship from the kangaroo and kiwi painted there – about as far into the depths of the cabin as it was possible to get.

It must have been around three o'clock in the afternoon that it came: the dreaded shock that exploded like a bomb: that heart-stopping lift again. Then the little home enclosing me whirled round in a dizzying arc and, for a fraction of a second that seemed an age, I was standing on my head on the roof of the upside-down cabin, before *Ice Bird* crashed over right side up once more.

My preparations had paid off. True, the sleeping bag was soaked through again and my already damaged typewriter, vaulting from its restraining cords, had been smashed into a shapeless tangle of twisted keys and festooned ribbon. Sodden ship's biscuits plastered the sides of the cabin and the deck head (the roof). Sultanas, peanuts, cheese and chocolate had once again been liberally dunked in brine laced with kerosene and, in the case of the first two at least, rendered practically inedible. But the precious charts and the logbook were safe and the netted table had held down most of the cans in the boxes beneath it. Blocking the ventilators had kept the water intake down to a paltry twenty-one bucketfuls. More remarkable still: the little mast, I saw with astonishment, was miraculously still standing.

So far, so good. But we had not escaped unscathed, as I realized when I tried to open the main hatch. It slid back a foot, then jammed. No amount of straining would budge it a millimetre farther. Was I trapped in a steel coffin? My heart began to race unpleasantly until common sense came to my aid. There was always the fore hatch, and the difficulty there was to keep it closed, not to open it. In a calmer frame of mind I pushed and struggled and at length succeeded in squeezing through and locating the trouble. The frame of the pram hood, made of half-inch galvanized steel piping, had been so buckled when the yacht had crashed upside down into the water as to jam the hatch by fouling the Perspex dome. In no way, without the facilities of a machine shop, could I hope to straighten it again. Fortunately, I could just wriggle my way through in my bulky clothes.

The immediate problem, of course, was how to bail. How on earth could I lift a bucket of bilge water past me when I was wedged in the hatchway, not to mention the far more delicate manoeuvre of lifting the toilet bucket out into the cockpit? The answer was found by trial and error. I was able to evolve a set of co-ordinated movements that, when I removed my parka and exhaled deeply, just sufficed to allow me to squeeze the bucket up past my chest and, balancing it precariously above my head, lift it out of the hatch. Bilge water could then be unceremoniously tipped into the cockpit, though the toilet bucket required further contortions before I could gain the bridge deck and empty it safely overside.

The canvas that had covered the twisted pram hood frame had been completely torn away, but this was of little moment. Far more serious, the steel framework had been bent over until it almost touched the steering compass, which was mounted on the main hatch (incidentally, the mounting was damaged). The proximity of the steel tubing must be deflecting the compass needle out of true. This much and the fact that the deviation was easterly was apparent at a glance. But exactly how great was the deviation was a question that could only be answered much later when I had had the opportunity on rare fine days of comparing the compass with sextant readings of the bearing of the sun. It turned out to be a good 20°.

When *Ice Bird* turned over, the barometer had already started rising and, as if satisfied at having so effectively demonstrated its power, the storm now rapidly declined in intensity. The wind eased but, I noted with no enthusiasm, rogue 'killer waves' still continued occasionally to avalanche thunderously. During the night the gale finally blew itself out.

An incongruous note is struck by next day's log. '14 December. My paper is being read before the Royal Society in London today.'

This was an account of ancient Polynesian astronomy, a science that in the islanders' maritime culture was virtually part of navigation. I would much rather be there than here, I thought, wistfully – even at the cost of facing intimidating questions from ranks of eminent astronomers.

No point in wishing. Fortified by ship's biscuits and muesli, I pulled a soggy wool glove up over my right hand and a freezing mitt over my left (their mates had never come to light since the first capsize) and reluctantly issued forth into chilly blustery wind under a low, leaden sky. Dubiously eyeing the split and twisted base of the mast, I hoisted a rag of sail and found my forebodings realized when more shards of the aluminium broke away. Was there anything I could do? Seated on the deck, I stared intently at the mast, willing there to be an answer, oblivious of all else except this life and death problem.

I was not wearing my safety harness, for I often omitted it these days; after all, the precaution seemed rather pointless when the ship itself was doomed. The breaking sea caught me unawares, the shock catapulting me through the air towards the vanished starboard guard wires. Here I brought up agonizingly, if providentially, against the tip of a stanchion. I felt ribs go in a blaze of breath-stopping agony and my right arm went numb as the elbow shared the impact. I can't stand any more pain, I thought, as I writhed in the scuppers, gasping for breath. But there was also relief that I had not gone over the side, where five minutes in the $-1\,°C$ water would have brought oblivion. Such is the mark of our humanity. There is no foreseeable way out of your predicament; you have come to the end of your tether; yet some unsuspected strength within you drives you to keep on fighting.

I dragged myself, moaning and groaning and making a great to-do, along the side deck and down below. As the wind was from the south-south-west there was no need to steer. Bilge water was overflowing the floorboards, though. Cursing mentally – drawing each breath meant stabbing pain enough without aggravating it by speech – I prised up the floor and scooped up twenty-two buckets from the well to tip them into the cockpit. The rest of that pain-fringed day and a restless, chilly night I spent on my bunk, increasingly aware of the vast difference between a merely damp sleeping bag and one still soaked from the recent capsize.

The morrow brought little relief. True this was the day I discovered the missing rum bottle projectile, which had penetrated the floor of the locker; but our poor progress, as revealed by two sun sights, gave little cause for complacency. I hoisted the tri-sail to give us a little more speed and was duly rewarded when the wire span that held the halyard blocks to the mast-head parted and the sails came tumbling down. Three hours in snow showers relieved by intervals of fitful sunshine were taken up in lowering the mast and repairing the damage. I also took the opportunity of fashioning a pair of wire shrouds out of a spare inner forestay, to reinforce the rope stays.

The knife-stabs in my right side that had greeted any sudden body movement during this work on deck became less frequent once I had returned below where I could move with greater caution. But my hands! I rocked back and forth, tears squeezing out from under my eyelids. Would they never mend? Extravasated blood ballooned out each finger end grotesquely so that the finger nails were acutely angled. The bases of the fingers were, in contrast, pale but so swollen that my hands looked like flippers. On the credit side, there was as yet no sign of gangrene. The antibiotics must be taking effect, then, and the healing process beginning, though how complete it would be only time would tell – if time were allowed me. But the pain! The agony resulting from only the briefest moment of chill was worse, much worse than it had been and was lasting longer.

This was the day that my sheepskin trousers, which had shown signs of falling apart, finally disintegrated. Damp and smelly though they were, I was sorry to see the last of them; sorrier still to have to go through the awkwardness and discomfort of getting them off, then pulling over my shivering limbs the mildewed and half-frozen Dacron flying suit I had earlier discarded. How much more of this recurrent misery could I stand? Would it not be easier just to give up the hopeless struggle? And fresh trouble was in store: as I lit the hurricane lamp that evening, I saw with a sinking heart that the glass was dropping again.

I spent a sleepless night as the weather worsened. The number two storm jib, despite the knots that reduced its length to fit the short mast, was setting so badly that periodically it threshed violently. This was my best and strongest sail, a brand-new one, but because I could not immediately think up any way of saving it from the damage it was sustaining, I did not even venture outside to look. Had I done so, ways of dealing with the trouble surely would have become apparent. I would rather not record this, but the sorry fact of the matter is that I had become so demoralized and my dread of pain from fingers and ribs was so great that I did not once go on deck to experiment with the sail's sheeting for three whole days.

Meanwhile the wind rose, fell and rose again, varying between a modest force six breeze and a force eight gale. *Ice Bird* took some heavy buffets and the jib continued to vibrate. Lengths of shock-cord hooked to the tiller lines allowed me to leave them but not for long, so I sat for hours staring miserably out of the transparent dome at the happy-looking ice birds that fluttered around the cockpit. A careless one even flicked the backstay with its wing.

By 18 December a strong gale was building up steep, hollow, tottering seas. This was the third day of my shameful cowering below – I was aware of my own weak-mindedness; I even noted it in the log, but I had not the will power enough to overcome it, taking refuge instead in escapist novels. At 11 a.m. one of the collapsing seas broke aboard, catapulting a volley of pots, aluminium plates and cutlery clear across the cabin.

It was five o'clock that afternoon when the much abused jib split, leaving a portion still drawing. I could have saved it had I only bestirred myself earlier. Now it was too late, so I left up the flapping remnants to give the yacht some steerage way to run before the gale, which had now increased until it was blowing at something like fifty-five to sixty knots with no sign of abatement.

Somewhat belatedly I set about the near hopeless job of trying to stitch up the first storm jib, which had been torn almost in two in the initial capsize. One vital item forgotten in the rush at Sydney had been a sail-mending palm. The best that could be done was to use a book to press the sail needle through the seams of the tough eleven-ounce Terylene, to execute a clumsy repair that I doubted would stand any strong wind. Meanwhile outside my tossing steel shell the south-east gale, fresh chilled from its passage across the polar floes, roared out ever more fiercely over the Southern Ocean, tearing off great gouts of water bodily from the wave crests and driving them horizontally before it.

'Trembling and fearful night,' I wrote, without exaggeration. 'Water washing over floorboards. Shriek wind in spite of blocked ventilators and full battening down washboards.' My thoughts can be imagined.

Blinding snow showers, sweeping across the ocean's face before even stronger squalls, heralded dawn around 2 a.m. The formerly hollow seas now seemed to have been flattened a little by the very fury of the storm – but for how long, I wondered? Then, somewhere around 6 a.m., the stainless steel luff wire of the already split jib tore right through. Now I had to redeem as best I could the cowardice that had kept me so long in the cabin – now that it was much too late to save anything of the sail, unused until three weeks ago, which was now completely split in two, with even its bronze hanks fractured. I brought up the jib I had mended the day before and dragged it along the deck to the forestay, where I hanked it on. But no sail could be hoisted in that storm. Once again we were riding out a severe gale with no means of propulsion so that the ship was out of control and the seas tossed her from side to side at their will.

By now the cabin was well awash and fresh spurts of water were continually being forced under pressure through the split coach roof. It must be got rid of even at the risk of swamping when unbattening the hatchway. Twenty-seven bucketfuls were lifted out, every one paid for in pain: pain in my right ribs with each gasping breath; in my hands as always; from a new bruise whenever a wave smashed me against the side of the cabin. At length it was done, though a worse task awaited me. For a record three days I had held off using the toilet bucket. Now it could not be delayed a moment longer. This was a dreaded chore and a difficult feat of balance at the best of times. In a gale it was a hundred times harder. I dreaded removing my flying suit and, even more, stumbling into my filthy tattered clothes again with one wary eye on the bucket. Emptying the bucket without spilling its contents all over the cabin, myself, the cockpit or the deck was the most delicate operation but, more by luck than otherwise, it was always successfully accomplished.

Afterwards I could not rest; no relaxation being possible while the heavy seas kept crashing on to the resounding metal hull. My morale was very shaky for no respite was in sight even should we survive this particular storm without further damage. Indeed, towards midnight the storm did begin to ease but I was little comforted.

'No progress. Near despair,' I wrote. A half-forgotten fragment of poetry from my schooldays flitted through my mind and was scribbled down in the log.

Though we are ringed with spears,
Though the last hope is gone,
– ? fight on, the – ? gods look on.
Before our sparks of life blow back to Him who gave,
Burn bright, brave hearts, a pathway to the grave.

Though I characterized this as 'corny', it did express a little of what I felt, though at times the implications of this bleak destiny would overwhelm me.

By the following morning, 20 December, except for an occasional last fling, the gale had moved away eastward. We had been nine weeks at sea. Going on deck I found that the rope forestay had parted and that several more inches of the spinnaker mast had crumbled away since the day before. When I hoisted the roughly repaired number one storm jib, the yacht had been forty hours lying a-hull without sail.

Back to bailing, only to find that the cockpit drains had become blocked, probably with pulped paper, so the cockpit needed bailing out too. Depressingly, no amount of poking about in the wet cockpit succeeded in clearing the drains. That job would have to wait for another day. I clambered down into the cabin, to discover that the socks I wore to protect my hands and keep them warm, and which were normally relatively dry, had got wet in the recent gale. All these trials and discomforts were getting me down. The perennial problem was the hopeless inadequacy of my attempts to escape from this fierce, lonely sub-Antarctic ocean.

Why was I bothering to write anything down, I wondered, as I drew the damp logbook out of its plastic bag, opened it on the bunk and scrawled painfully.

'How long will the "mast" and stays last? What sail or gear can stand such gales?' Still less could my makeshift arrangements be expected to cope with them.

All in all, the urge to make a daily record in the log was basically illogical because, now that I was facing the issues squarely, there did not really seem to be a way out. Even should *Ice Bird* continue to ride out these repeated storms without mortal damage, we were for practical purposes getting nowhere and time was slowly but surely running out before the freeze-up would render unattainable even the grim shelter we were seeking. Water, too, would be running short before long, for I had anticipated a quicker passage. The fine rain of high latitudes had been more of a dank mist and impossible to collect. Certainly some handfuls of snow had been scraped off the Perspex dome and cabin top on 3 December and made into several cups of coffee but generally the snow had been too contaminated with spray to be drinkable. The last resort – to seek out floating ice – would probably take all summer in a boat so little mobile as *Ice Bird* then was.

Yet I did have vague hopes that someone, somewhere would read what I was setting down. Even if by then I was dead of thirst and privation, *Ice Bird*, floating half waterlogged or perhaps frozen in, might be found by some whaler or expedition ship. Such thoughts were often in my mind these days, as were speculations about how revolting it would be for someone to come across my decomposing body – unless, of course, time and birds had reduced it to an aseptic skeleton or, more likely, it had been deep frozen like a Siberian mammoth's carcase.

If only it had been possible to erect a stout, dependable mast I could have made it. I mixed a tot of rum (a large one, I see by the log), drank it down resignedly and squirmed into my sleeping bag, for it was night now, the evening of 20 December. This was my darkest hour. But some portion of my mind was far from resigned. All at once the idea, fully formed, burst into consciousness to set me bolt upright, trembling with excitement. The key to survival had come into my hand.

The key to survival was in fact the use of an eleven-foot wooden boom as jury mast which David Lewis managed to erect, despite a badly infected hand. Eight weeks later Ice Bird *made landfall at the U.S. Palmer Antarctic Station where she was repaired and the second leg of the journey was eventually completed.*

Herman Melville

EMIGRANTS

(from *Redburn*)

Although Redburn *was published as fiction, undoubtedly Melville
drew upon his earliest sea experiences as cabin boy upon the packet
ship* St Lawrence *which ran between New York and Liverpool in
1839. This little known account of a cholera epidemic amongst
emigrant passengers in passage to America was followed by a dis-
sertation on the laws governing emigration and gives a vivid picture of conditions which Melville must have seen.*

ALTHOUGH fast-sailing ships, blest with prosperous breezes, have
frequently made the run across the Atlantic in eighteen days; yet, it
is not uncommon for other vessels to be forty, or fifty, and even
sixty, seventy, eighty, and ninety days, in making the same passage.
Though in the latter cases, some signal calamity or incapacity must
occasion so great a detention. It is also true, that generally the
passage out from America is shorter than the return; which is to be
ascribed to the prevalence of westerly winds.

We had been outside of Cape Clear upward of twenty days, still
harassed by head-winds, though with pleasant weather upon the
whole, when we were visited by a succession of rain storms, which
lasted the greater part of a week.

During this interval, the emigrants were obliged to remain
below; but this was nothing strange to some of them; who, not
recovering, while at sea, from their first attack of sea-sickness,
seldom or never made their appearance on deck, during the entire
passage.

During the week, now in question, fire was only once made in
the public galley. This occasioned a good deal of domestic work to
be done in the steerage, which otherwise would have been done in
the open air. When the lulls of the rain-storms would intervene,

354

some unusually cleanly emigrant would climb to the deck, with a bucket of slops, to toss into the sea. No experience seemed sufficient to instruct some of these ignorant people in the simplest, and most elemental principles of ocean-life. Spite of all lectures on the subject, several would continue to shun the leeward side of the vessel, with their slops. One morning, when it was blowing very fresh, a simple fellow pitched over a gallon or two of something to windward. Instantly it flew back in his face; and also, in the face of the chief mate, who happened to be standing by at the time. The offender was collared, and shaken on the spot; and ironically commanded, never, for the future, to throw anything to windward at sea, but fine ashes and scalding hot water.

During the frequent *hard blows* we experienced, the hatchways on the steerage were, at intervals, hermetically closed; sealing down in their noisome den, those scores of human beings. It was something to be marvelled at, that the shocking fate, which, but a short time ago, overtook the poor passengers in a Liverpool steamer in the Channel, during similar stormy weather, and under similar treatment, did not overtake some of the emigrants of the *Highlander*.

Nevertheless, it was, beyond question, this noisome confinement in so close, unventilated, and crowded a den; joined to the deprivation of sufficient food, from which many were suffering; which, helped by their personal uncleanliness, brought on a malignant fever.

The first report was, that two persons were affected. No sooner was it known, than the mate promptly repaired to the medicine-chest in the cabin: and with the remedies deemed suitable, descended into the steerage. But the medicines proved of no avail; the invalids rapidly grew worse; and two more of the emigrants became infected.

Upon this, the captain himself went to see them; and returning, sought out a certain alleged physician among the cabin passengers; begging him to wait upon the sufferers; hinting that, thereby, he might prevent the disease from extending into the cabin itself. But this person denied being a physician; and from fear of contagion – though he did not confess that to be the motive – refused even to enter the steerage.

The cases increased: the utmost alarm spread through the ship: and scenes ensued, over which, for the most part, a veil must be drawn; for such is the fastidiousness of some readers, that, many times, they must lose the most striking incidents in a narrative like mine.

Many of the panic-stricken emigrants would fain now have domiciled on deck; but being so scantily clothed, the wretched weather – wet, cold and tempestuous – drove the best part of them again below. Yet any other human beings, perhaps, would rather have faced the most outrageous storm than continued to breathe the pestilent air of the steerage. But some of these poor people must have been so used to the most abasing calamities, that the atmosphere of a lazar-house almost seemed their natural air.

The first four cases happened to be in adjoining bunks: and the emigrants who slept in the farther part of the steerage, threw up a barricade in front of those bunks; so as to cut off communication. But this was no sooner reported to the captain, than he ordered it to be thrown down; since it could be of no possible benefit; but would only make still worse, what was already direful enough.

It was not till after a good deal of mingled threatening and coaxing, that the mate succeeded in getting the sailors below, to accomplish the captain's order.

The sight that greeted us, upon entering, was wretched indeed. It was like entering a crowded jail. From the rows of rude bunks, hundreds of meagre, begrimed faces were turned upon us; while seated upon the chests, were scores of unshaven men, smoking tea-leaves, and creating a suffocating vapour. But this vapour was better than the native air of the place, which from almost unbelievable causes, was fetid in the extreme. In every corner, the females were huddled together, weeping and lamenting; children were asking bread from their mothers, who had none to give; and old men, seated upon the floor, were leaning back against the heads of the water-casks, with closed eyes and fetching their breath with a gasp.

At one end of the place was seen the barricade, hiding the invalids; while – notwithstanding the crowd – in front of it was a clear area, which the fear of contagion had left open.

'That bulkhead must come down,' cried the mate, in a voice that rose above the din. 'Take hold of it, boys.'

But hardly had we touched the chests composing it, when a crowd of pale-faced, infuriated men rushed up; and with terrific howls, swore they would slay us, if we did not desist.

'Haul it down!' roared the mate.

But the sailors fell back, murmuring something about merchant seamen having no pensions in case of being maimed, and they had not shipped to fight fifty to one. Further efforts were made by the mate, who at last had recourse to entreaty; but it would not do; and we were obliged to depart, without achieving our object.

About four o'clock that morning, the first four died. They were all men; and the scenes which ensued were frantic in the extreme. Certainly, the bottomless profound of the sea, over which we were sailing, concealed nothing more frightful.

Orders were at once passed to bury the dead. But this was unnecessary. By their own countrymen, they were torn from the clasp of their wives, rolled in their own bedding, with ballast-stones, and with hurried rites, were dropped into the ocean.

At this time, ten more men had caught the disease; with a degree of devotion worthy all praise, the mate attended them with his medicines; but the captain did not again go down to them.

It was all-important now that the steerage should be purified; and had it not been for the rains and squalls, which would have made it madness to turn such a number of women and children upon the wet and unsheltered decks, the steerage passengers would have been ordered above, and their den have been given a thorough cleansing. But, for the present, this was out of the question. The sailors peremptorily refused to go among the defilements to remove them; and so besotted were the greater part of the emigrants themselves, that though the necessity of the case was forcibly painted to them, they would not lift a hand to assist in what seemed their own salvation.

The panic in the cabin was now very great; and for fear of contagion to themselves, the cabin passengers would fain have made a prisoner of the captain, to prevent him from going forward beyond the mainmast. Their clamours at last induced him to tell the two mates, that for the present they must sleep and take their meals elsewhere than in their old quarters, which communicated with the cabin.

On land, a pestilence is fearful enough; but there, many can flee from an infected city; whereas, in a ship, you are locked and bolted in the very hospital itself. Nor is there any possibility of escape from it; and in so small and crowded a place, no precaution can effectually guard against contagion.

Horrible as the sights of the steerage now were, the cabin, perhaps, presented a scene equally despairing. Many, who had seldom prayed before, now implored the merciful heavens, night and day, for fair winds and fine weather. Trunks were opened for Bibles; and at last, even prayer-meetings were held over the very table across which the loud jest had been so often heard.

Strange, though almost universal, that the seemingly nearer prospect of that death which any body at any time may die, should produce these spasmodic devotions, when an everlasting Asiatic Cholera is forever thinning our ranks; and die by death we all must at last.

On the second day, seven died, one of whom was the little tailor: on the third, four; on the fourth, six, of whom one was the Greenland sailor, and another, a woman in the cabin, whose death, however, was afterward supposed to have been purely induced by her fears. These last deaths brought the panic to its height; and sailors, officers, cabin passengers, and emigrants – all looked upon each other like lepers. All but the only true leper among us – the mariner Jackson, who seemed elated with the thought, that for *him* – already in the deadly clutches of another disease – no danger was to be apprehended from a fever which only swept off the comparatively healthy. Thus, in the midst of the despair of the healthful, this incurable invalid was not cast down; not, at least, by the same considerations that appalled the rest.

And still, beneath a grey, gloomy sky, the doomed craft beat on; now on this tack, now on that; battling against hostile blasts, and drenched in rain and spray; scarcely making an inch of progress toward her port.

On the sixth morning, the weather merged into a gale, to which we stripped our ship to a storm-stay-sail. In ten hours' time, the waves ran in mountains; and the *Highlander* rose and fell like some vast buoy on the water. Shrieks and lamentations were driven to leeward, and drowned in the roar of the wind among the cordage; while we gave to the gale the blackened bodies of five more of the dead.

But as the dying departed, the places of two of them were filled in the rolls of humanity, by the birth of two infants, whom the plague, panic, and gale had hurried into the world before their time. The first cry of one of these infants, was almost simultaneous with the splash of its father's body in the sea. Thus we come and we go. But, surrounded by death, both mothers and babes survived.

At midnight, the wind went down; leaving a long, rolling sea; and, for the first time in a week, a clear, starry sky.

In the first morning-watch, I sat with Harry on the windlass, watching the billows; which, seen in the night, seemed real hills, upon which fortresses might have been built; and real valleys in which villages, and groves, and gardens, might have nestled. It was like a landscape in Switzerland; for down into those dark, purple glens, often tumbled the white foam of the wave-crests, like avalanches; while the seething and boiling that ensued, seemed the swallowing up of human beings.

By afternoon of the next day this heavy sea subsided; and we bore down on the waves, with all our canvas set; stun'-sails alow and aloft; and our best steersman at the helm; the captain himself at his elbow – bowling along with a fair, cheering breeze over the taffrail.

The decks were cleared, and swabbed bone-dry; and then, all the emigrants who were not invalids, poured themselves out on deck, snuffing the delightful air, spreading their damp bedding in the sun, and regaling themselves with the generous charity of the captain, who of late had seen fit to increase their allowance of food. A detachment of them now joined a band of the crew, who proceeding into the steerage, with buckets and brooms, gave it a thorough cleansing, sending on deck, I know not how many bucketsful of defilements. It was more like cleaning out a stable, than a retreat for men and women. This day we buried three; the next day one, and then the pestilence left us, with seven convalescent; who, placed near the opening of the hatchway, soon rallied under the skilful treatment, and even tender care of the mate.

But even under this favourable turn of affairs, much apprehension was still entertained, lest in crossing the Grand Banks of Newfoundland, the fogs, so generally encountered there, might bring on a return of the fever. But, to the joy of all the hands, our fair wind still held on; and we made a rapid run across these dreaded shoals, and southward steered for New York.

Our days were now fair and mild, and though the wind abated, yet we still ran our course over a pleasant sea. The steerage passengers – at least by far the greater number – wore a still, subdued aspect, though a little cheered by the genial air, and the hopeful thought of soon reaching their port. But those who had lost fathers, husbands, wives, or children, needed no crape, to reveal to others, who they were. Hard and bitter indeed was their lot; for with the poor and desolate, grief is no indulgence of mere sentiment, however sincere, but a gnawing reality, that eats into their vital beings; they had no kind condolers, and bland physicians, and troops of sympathizing friends; and they must toil, though tomorrow be the burial, and their pall-bearers throw down the hammer to lift up the coffin.

How, then, with these emigrants, who, three thousand miles from home, suddenly found themselves deprived of brothers and husbands, with but a few pounds, or perhaps but a few shillings, to buy food in a strange land?

As for the passengers in the cabin, who now so jocund as they? drawing nigh, with their long purses and goodly portmanteaus to the promised land, without fear of fate. One and all were generous and gay, the jelly-eyed old gentleman, before spoken of, gave a shilling to the steward.

The lady who had died, was an elderly person, an American, returning from a visit to an only brother in London. She had no friend or relative on board, hence, as there is little mourning for a stranger dying among strangers, her memory had been buried with her body.

But the thing most worthy of note among these now light-hearted people in feathers, was the gay way in which some of them bantered others, upon the panic into which nearly all had been thrown.

And since, if the extremest fear of a crowd in a panic of peril, proves grounded on causes sufficient, they must then indeed come to perish – therefore it is, that at such times they must make up their minds either to die, or else survive to be taunted by their fellow-men with their fear. For except in extraordinary instances of exposure, there are few living men, who, at bottom, are not very slow to admit that any other living men have ever been very much nearer death than themselves. Accordingly, *craven* is the phrase too often applied to any one who, with however good reason, has been appalled at the prospect of sudden death, and yet lived to escape it. Though, should he have perished in conformity with his fears, not a syllable of *craven* would you hear. This is the language of one, who more than once has beheld the scenes, whence these principles have been deduced. The subject invites much subtle speculation; for in every being's ideas of death, and his behaviour when it suddenly menaces him, lies the best index to his life and his faith. Though the Christian era had not then begun, Socrates died the death of the Christian; and though Hume was not a Christian in theory, yet he, too, died the death of the Christian – humble, composed, without bravado; and though the most sceptical of philosophical sceptics, yet full of that firm, creedless faith, that embraces the spheres. Seneca died dictating to posterity; Petronius lightly discoursing of essences and love-songs; and Addison, calling upon Christendom to behold how calmly a Christian could die; but not even the last of these three, perhaps, died the best death of the Christian.

The cabin passenger who had used to read prayers while the rest kneeled against the transoms and settees, was one of the merry young sparks, who had occasioned such agonies of jealousy to the poor tailor, now no more. In his rakish vest, and dangling watch-chain, this same youth, with all the awfulness of fear, had led the earnest petitions of his companions; supplicating mercy, where before he had never solicited the slightest favour. More than once had he been seen thus engaged by the observant steersman at the helm: who looked through the little glass in the cabin bulkhead.

But this youth was an April man; the storm had departed; and now he shone in the sun, none braver than he.

One of his jovial companions ironically advised him to enter into holy orders upon his arrival in New York.

'Why so?' said the other, 'have I such an orotund voice?'

'No'; profanely returned his friend – 'but you are a coward – just the man to be a parson, and pray.'

However this narrative of the circumstances attending the fever among the emigrants on the *Highlander* may appear; and though these things happened so long ago; yet just such events, nevertheless, are perhaps taking place today. But the only account you obtain of such events, is generally contained in a newspaper paragraph, under the shipping-head. *There* is the obituary of the destitute dead, who die on the sea. They die, like the billows that break on the shore, and no more are heard or seen. But in the events, thus merely initialized in the catalogue of passing occurrences, and but glanced at by the readers of news, who are more taken up with paragraphs of fuller flavour; what a world of life and death, what a world of humanity and its woes, lies shrunk into a three-worded sentence!

You see no plague-ship driving through a stormy sea; you hear no groans of despair; you see no corpses thrown over the bulwarks; you mark not the wringing hands and torn hair of widows and orphans: – all is a blank. And one of these blanks I have but filled up, in recounting the details of the *Highlander*'s calamity.

Besides that natural tendency, which hurries into oblivion the last woes of the poor; other causes combine to suppress the detailed circumstances of disasters like these. Such things, if widely known, operate unfavourably to the ship, and make her a bad name; and to avoid detention at quarantine, a captain will state the case in the most palliating light, and strive to hush it up, as much as he can.

Noel Mostert

THE TANKER MEN

(from *Supership*)

Noel Mostert sailed aboard the S.S. Ardshiel *from Bordeaux to the Persian Gulf and back again in* 1971. *The* Ardshiel, *a quarter of a mile long and wider than a football field, was, by today's standards, only a medium sized supertanker, carrying enough crude oil to supply the total energy needs of a small city for an entire year. The tanker men, he writes, lead an eerie 'Flying Dutchman' existence with no real ports of call and suffer strange psychological pressures. Some of them are described in this edited account of life aboard a modern vessel. The* Ardshiel, 214,085 *tons, flew the house colours of the Peninsular and Oriental Steam Navigation Company, better known simply as the P.& O. Line.*

THERE were moments aboard *Ardshiel* when I felt that I was on one of those very old-fashioned mailboats moving east of Suez a good many decades ago, and never was this more so than at night when, punctually at seven thirty, Basil Thomson led a small procession of his senior officers down from the evening's sundowner's party, or 'pour-out' as they preferred to call it, to the dining saloon, all dressed for dinner in 'Red Sea rig'. An informal dinner dress for warm climates which dispenses with tie and jacket while retaining the decorum of proper change for the evening, the ensemble consists of black dress trousers, silk cummerbund, and white short-sleeved shirt with gold-braided insignia of rank worn on the shoulder tabs. We moved into a dining-room where the Goanese stewards awaited us in stiff white jackets, grouped around their tables of fresh linen, silverware, and individual printed menus in silver holders.

Dinner chimes were broadcast throughout the ship at seven, but these were for the junior officers, who were expected to have

363

finished by the time the captain's party arrived. Cadet Davis, a slow eater apparently, occasionally was still munching when we came in. 'Since you're still there, you'd better bring your plate over here,' Thomson would say sharply, with the tone of a man whose sense of order had been disturbed, and later, when Davis finally had finished, 'You can excuse yourself now!'

The dinner courses came and went silently, arriving upon salvers and served upon hot chinaware. Not much was ever said, except by Captain Thomson, who, as masters are wont to do, exercised the right of monologue.

The food was exceptional, whether breakfast or dinner. A normal breakfast menu might be stewed apples, cornflakes, oatmeal, smoked cod in milk, sausage mince cakes, fried potatoes, cheese or plain omelettes, eggs to order, rolls and toast, tea or coffee. Lunch always featured a curry: birianis, keftas, Madras, dry mince and Deil sauce, vindaloos, Sally Mutton; and it was always served with chutney, popadoms, diced tomato, onion, coconut, and currants. A typical dinner could be mock turtle soup, grilled sole Tartare, roast veal and stuffing, baked and boiled potatoes, cauliflower, peach Melba, and that essentially English course, the savoury, such as bloater paste on toast.

After dinner, the party moved to the coffee-table in the wardroom. 'Who is going to be mum?' someone invariably asked, and whoever was nearest to the coffee began pouring, while others handed around the cups, the milk and the sugar. Thomson usually dominated the conversation, and recounted to the juniors tales of his past experiences, to which they patiently listened. These were stories they'd heard often enough, and would hear many times again before they left the ship. It was not however a lengthy ordeal. After half an hour or so, the master would suddenly announce, 'Well, I suppose I'll go up and do my book of words,' and vanished. As a rule, he was followed by the chief engineer.

The departure of the two most senior officers brought a distinct lightening of atmosphere to the room; but, however much it lightened, the mood of the wardroom always remained somewhat formal and well-mannered. There was seldom any horseplay or ribaldry. One was again aware of the social lassitude of long confinement: that quality of desultory and inactive converse that is not listlessness but rather that emptiness of real mutual interest that settles upon men who have heard each other out too often. And one was aware not so much of the remoteness of the world at large but of most of the ship itself; it was the feeling of being inside a walled-in community upon one end of an otherwise uninhabited island whose opposite shore few ever bothered to visit and some scarcely knew, and which one actually had to wonder about from time to time.

The wardroom in *Ardshiel* was used a great deal more than it was in other tankers, so they all said; on other ships one apparently could seldom expect more than two or three people to be gathered in it at night; yet it struck me that activity in *Ardshiel*'s wardroom died soon enough. They seemed to prefer gathering in each other's cabins, as if in retreat from the huge and impinging emptiness of the ship; and there, in a fog of smoke and a growing litter of beer cans, the hubbub, ribaldry, affectionate jeering, and repartee absent from the wardroom asserted itself.

When people started to drift from the wardroom one evening I decided to follow the path to the other end of our island and went down and started along the catwalk to the bows. The night was overcast and very black, and the farther one went the stranger and lonelier and more frightening the experience became. The front of a ship's superstructure is always dark, all windows heavily curtained, to avoid spoiling night vision from the bridge, so that one walked from a façade that showed no hint of light; but there was at least the sheltering comfort of its towering proximity. After a while one lacked even that; it was distant and only faintly discernible, and still the steel path ran on into the dark as far as one's straining eyes could see. Ships had always had great appeal for me at night, when their peace and detachment seem greatest. I felt quite different on *Ardshiel*'s main deck, and what I felt was close to the fringe of fear, or even terror if one allowed oneself to be impressionable about it, which would not have been too difficult.

An unpleasant loneliness grew from this apprehension of the ship's gloomy distances. One felt the arid metal acreage spreading invisibly all around, and its impact was one of menace: a mechanical desert of indefinable purpose imposed upon the sea's own emptiness, and with forms and shapes that had no reassuring familiarity; it was filled with wind signs, not those of masts and rigging but of abandoned structures upon a plain, and there was no comfort even from the sea. One did not even feel its presence amidships on that path over the somnolent pipes and obscure fittings; the sea lay somewhere a long way below the remote and unseen edge of the deck on either side, and what saltiness reached one's lips had the taste of steel.

The overpowering impression was of desolation and severance from that vague far-off castle one had left; but when I returned there I found it entirely abandoned as well. Those who had been drinking and talking when I left had gone, presumably into the cabins, and, as aboard the *Mary Celeste*, only the fragments of their recent presence lay about: half-emptied glasses of beer, the open magazines, full ashtrays, and cups of cold untouched coffee. One passed from wardroom to dining saloon, to cinema, games room, hospital, emergency room, up the stairways and along the deserted alleyways, encountering no sound or sign of another human. And when, on sudden compulsion, I took the lift down to the engine-room as well, the melancholy surrealism of the experience seemed complete, for the engines are switched to automatic controls at night and over the weekend and left running on their own. The engine-room consequently was as fearful as the deck. It was disturbing to follow those narrow fly-overs, suspended sixty feet over the pounding machinery, and to find one's imagination susceptible once more to aloneness in a mechanical world, especially one of such ceaseless and unaccountable activity.

I returned to the lift and went up to the bridge, the only place where one knew one would find someone without having to knock on a door, and, as it slowly ascended, felt that I could well understand why, as First Officer Alan Ewart-James had informed me, Stanley Kubrick's *2001* had been so unpopular in the theatres of these ships when it was shown.

'You often suddenly get that feeling of ghosts or a presence when you stand alone up here at night,' Third Officer Stephen Tucker remarked when I recounted my various journeys. He had been sitting in the starboard captain's chair gazing into the darkness when I arrived, and he offered it to me. The old man had been gone only ten minutes, he said. He came up every night at ten for his cocoa, which Tucker brewed, checked how things were, gave his orders, and then retired. Once he'd left he never came back unless called, and Tucker then felt he could safely sit in his chairs. On another ship they used to bring the two captain's chairs together and sit and chat the hours away. Tonight he'd been sitting here thinking about that. There were times, he said, when he felt that one could go round the bend on these ships.

Tucker began calculating distances. Did I know it would take a car travelling sixty miles an hour twelve seconds to travel the length of the ship? A sprinter would need five seconds to dash across the main deck! He added, with suddenly diminished spirit, 'I was in good form at dinner and we all had a good giggle at our table. But it's always the same; around half past ten I begin feeling what's the use of it all, this life.'

The principal diversion of the day was sundowner time, when the working day was over for most, enabling the juniors to gather in the wardroom and the seniors to start their pour-out in one or the other of the ship's several executive suites. Pour-out had been suspended on the voyage down through the strains and stresses of the English Channel to Le Verdon and my own first acquaintance of it came on the evening of our departure from the Gironde, when there was an unmistakable relief that the ship was free again and running – no tides or pilots or bloody Frogs and such to depend upon for another thirty days or so; the wider sea ahead, with hopefully fewer strains from surrounding traffic; a greater ease in everybody's manner, a certain cosiness in the sense of the ship gathered in upon itself once more, perhaps even a sort of joy; and yet, underneath it all, a wistfulness, a hint of forlorn, as they retrieved the familiar communion of the hour and sought to get the conversation going.

But it came desultorily, and there were frequent silences as they sat with inward expressions, nursing their glasses; and we all listened gravely to the hum of the bottles as the vibration of the ship jarred them into contact on their tray. 'Oh, ay,' James Jackson would say, leaning forward to pour out another gin, the movement and tone like a sudden resigned assertion of an accepted point of view. There was implicit concurrence in the attentive shift of their eyes as they watched him. Generous dollop of gin. Ice. Sprinkle of bitters. Tonic. Lemon. 'Well, yes,' Basil Thomson agreed, as Jackson leaned back with his full glass. 'There we are, so it goes.'

Those present, aside from Thomson and Jackson and myself, were Harvey Phillips, and Dave Haydon. Ewart-James was on watch and the only other officer eligible, Peter Dutton, had excused himself permanently from pour-out.

We sat in the deep chairs and sofa that were arranged in the master's dayroom around a long coffee-table on which the drinks were set. The evening was still bright but then Thomson's steward, Diaz, came in and drew the curtains along the two windowed bulkheads, encircling us in more soft material and shutting off the outside entirely, and we sat in opulent isolation, with the space beyond the coffee-table having an air of untenanted luxury and unwonted extravagance.

They began talking, as they frequently did, about the past; for most of them, that is for Jackson, Phillips, and Haydon, this meant the recent past of other ships and of those with whom they'd not so long ago sailed, but Thomson preferred the deeper pre-war past, when to his mind P. & O. was still P. & O. 'When old Sir William Currie was chairman he knew by name every one of the thousand or so officers serving on his ships. Every sailing, he came down the day before to make his own inspection, to see that the great P. & O. liner was as it should be. All the officers were assembled in a formal parade in order of rank in the first-class entrance. Sir William was piped aboard by the bo'sun's whistles and met by the captain and staff captain. He greeted every one of the officers lined up by name. When he'd inspected the ship he usually went up to the first officer's cabin for tea and toast. He liked his toast an inch thick, hot, with slabs of butter on it. When I became first officer I thought I'd test his memory to see if he was just memorizing the names of the officers by rank before he came down from London, so I mixed them all up in different order; but Sir William greeted them all by the proper names, and, when he'd done, he said to me, "When I come up to your cabin for tea later, mind you don't get my toast all wrong as well." After he'd gone, the public rooms were locked up again and everyone went over to the Tilbury Hotel to join the wives who were waiting there and who'd been shooed off the ship before the official party came down.'

'They were a fine lot, that generation,' Harvey Phillips said.

'That they were,' Thomson said appreciatively.

'Oh ay,' James Jackson said.

'Well, I dunno,' Dave Haydon said. 'Sometimes the good old days look better from a distance than they did then.'

'Well, we weren't spoiled the way this lot is today,' Thomson said. 'And I think we were a lot better for not being spoiled. When I started, a fourth mate's salary was nine pounds ten a month. A mess kit cost one month's salary and had to be bought. You couldn't get out of it. So, in fact, an officer got only eleven months' salary.'

'The Norwegians used to put British ships to shame the way they treated their seamen, there was a time when their wages were just about double ours,' Dave Haydon said.

'Hold on,' said Thomson.

'I heard they were a pretty grim lot to sail with anyhow,' Harvey Phillips said. 'No humour.'

'Well, you didn't get the stewards dressing up in drag and giving a show the way they do on British ships, I'll grant you,' Haydon said. 'But they had their moments. On that Norwegian ship I sailed in once between Louisiana and Le Havre – well, she was a dry ship, and one night I was telling them about the parties and good times we'd have on the P. & O. tankers. Her old man was a real sour humdinger, a regular Captain Bligh. But he listened to me, and then starts questioning me about the parties and how we ran them. Then he says, "All right, now we have a party. That's an order!" It was an order, all right. Everybody had to be there, cabin boys, stewardesses, the cook, deckhands, all the officers; the lot. He opened up the liquor store, laid it out in the saloon, and yelled, "Okay, you bastards, drink!" It was "Skol," and away you went! Five o'clock the next morning it was still going on. Bodies everywhere, and the old man chasing the chief steward with an axe because he'd chased somebody else. The officer who'd been on watch when it started was still on the bridge.'

'Well, I think that's overdoing it a bit,' Thomson said.

'They never stopped talking about it for months,' Haydon said.

'Well they might,' Harvey Phillips said.

'It reminds me of the trip I made once in an old cargo liner,' James Jackson said. 'She was a two-funnelled job. They built some of them like that after the war. The Greeks got her a long time ago. We took her out of Liverpool to St John's, Newfoundland, and Halifax in December. One of the worst trips of my life. The ship was in a terrible state. The crew nearly walked off. We had to keep the watertight doors closed because the stern gland was leaking. The radiators also leaked. It was warm enough when you went to bed but it all froze up during the night. One of the engineers jumped out of bed in the morning and went flat on his backside. The deck was one sheet of ice from the radiator leakage that had frozen. We were alongside in St John's for Christmas. The second steward was queer and had spent forty quid on a new wardrobe for the trip, new dresses and gowns, golden shoes, even silk underwear. When he was all done up you couldn't tell the difference. He went down to entertain the lads, but there was nothing on hand for us. So we phoned the matron of the hospital to ask for some nurses and she said, "Well, you better send someone up so we can have a look at you!" The third engineer and the second officer went. But there wasn't one under forty of the lot they brought back!'

'Charming!' Haydon said.

'You wouldn't be so fussy these days,' Harvey Phillips said.

'Reminds *me* of that trip in the old *Ellenga*,' cried Thomson, smacking his hands upon the arms of his chair. 'Remember, James?'

'Do I!' Jackson said. 'That was another.'

'Oh yes, but what a time.'

'Rust,' cried Jackson. 'Rust everywhere, you should have seen the hull, she was just a ball of rust. When Dorothy, my wife, came down to join us the taxi driver who'd brought her to the ship asked, "You going in that?"'

'That's because she'd been on the Atlantic run,' Thomson said. 'I don't know how long. She was like a ruddy submarine, with the funnel just sticking out of the water. There had never been a chance to paint her. I joined her in Rijeka and the mate had finally painted her. When we got to Canada it was forty above but when the pilot came aboard he warned us that there was going to be a big drop in temperature. By the time we got to the berth it was thirty below. A seventy-degree drop in an hour and a half! After that, she just crumbled to rust. All that new paint just went. But she was a nice ship. I did eighteen months in her. She was the only tanker except this one in which I have served more than twice; being on her was one of the happiest times I've had.'

The Canaries approached, hidden inside a long featureless Saturday dusk, and they passed after dark as a loom of distant light above the horizon, releasing us toward the great southern Atlantic, and a tropical Sunday. Weekends were an ache, affected by a sudden feeling of void in ship life, which intruded more perceptibly than usual. This was apparent in Stephen Tucker, whom I found sadly watching the fading of that distant glow as though it were a vanishing promise.

'There'll be lots of package tour people there now, swilling down the old vino and having a ball,' he said. 'Probably I'd even find somebody I know from my own street.' He turned moodily to the various phenomena surrounding the duller business of our own progress into the night. In the dusk, in the same quarter as the islands, a large supertanker paced us on a parallel course. There was scarcely a moment on the run down past Iberia, off the Straits of Gibraltar, and along the passage toward the Canaries when one of these ships wasn't in sight: empty ones on the same course as ourselves usually lay to starboard, laden inbound ones to port.

After returning the glasses to their bin, neatly, in the required position, Tucker resumed the task of switching on the ship's riding lights, the various deck floodlights; and then, carefully, set the exact strength of dim stipulated by Thomson for the clock dimmer, which regulated the illumination of all clocks on board; and finally arranged the bridge console's various switches.

Ardshiel was quietly sailing into the onrushing night, falling south-westward with the wind, whose sizeable disturbance ran equably alongside. It had settled in behind us off the Straits of Gibraltar: a powerful Levanter. From the bridge one could smell the crests as they curled and broke. We stood at the bridge rail and quietly talked in a soft windlessness, while the water crashed below, sounding like breakers heard from a height on a still evening.

An approaching tanker, its hull low from its weight of oil, battled toward us against a howling gale, its main deck continually awash from the spray that exploded upward as solid white walls and then collapsed in deluge over the bows and decks. Nobody could have ventured forward there and lived. She was an Esso ship and Tucker, grateful for the diversion, called her on the telephone.

'Esso ship passing, good evening, sir. What is your name? Is that the Esso tanker north-bound, please? Over.'

The telephone rang and Tucker answered. 'Okay, yes, thank you very much. *Esso Skandia*, are you? This is *Ardshiel*, south-bound. You're heading for Le Havre? We've just come from Rotterdam and Le Verdon. Thank you, sir, and I wish you a good trip.'

'I've seen him before,' Tucker said, and we went out to watch the big ship fall away behind. She vanished into the dark, a dwindling sequence of faint white soundless explosions. 'Another Saturday gone,' Tucker said as we watched the ship disappear. 'It's the one day I enjoy when I'm home. I prefer it to Sunday, which gets a bit ragged; I mean, you lie in bed all day reading the papers. But everyone's in a good mood on Saturday, even people who have to work; oh aye. You go out shopping, and then to the pub; Saturdays in pubs, lunchtime; it's great, really great. I like the spirit. You feel you've got all the time in the world ahead of you. I say to the girlfriend. "Shall we have a bite somewhere? Or go off in the car to visit friends?" Then in the evenings we sit reading, make spaghetti, go off to a show, or to the pubs before closing.'

There had been a party in the wardroom before dinner to celebrate the promotion of one of the engineers, Graham Allen, a Geordie of course, from junior to third engineer. It had continued briefly in the wardroom after dinner and, finally, around ten, the survivors had transferred themselves to the newly promoted third engineer's quarters, which were now declared to be in a state of open house for the rest of the night, or until whenever.

Graham Allen's wife, Pat, was the only woman on board. They were a decorative couple, both just over twenty. She was a fresh, clear, and pretty girl and her husband had that dark olive-skinned handsomeness which in Scotland or Ireland one supposes to indicate Armada descent (a myth that has little probability, according to Garrett Mattingly in his *The Defeat of the Spanish Armada*). They had been childhood sweethearts, and an adolescent obsessiveness still clung to their intimacy which, because it was the only one on board, drew longing toward it. Their cabin was next door to mine on the Middle Bridge Deck and it was a favourite rendezvous for the other junior officers, who trekked constantly from the distant corners of the ship to enjoy a taste of feminine company. Tact and manners on both sides were admirable. She was a young woman of great self-possession and she handled with natural discretion and grace a situation that many others her age might understandably have regarded either as an opportunity or an embarrassment. She moved through this company of bored and restless men without any hint of provocation or coquettishness and they for their part regarded her with an admiration that was open and forthcoming and never sly.

The main difference that indicated Sunday on board was the solemn hoisting of Basil Thomson's blue ensign at eight in the morning on the dot. It would remain aloft, fluttering from a halliard abaft the funnel, until struck at sunset. The blue ensign was not flown on weekdays, except in port. The normal flag of the British merchant service is the 'red duster', a red flag with the Union Jack set small into the upper left-hand corner. The blue ensign – blue where the other is red – is the flag of the Royal Navy Reserve and, as a former serving member of the Royal Navy, Thomson was privileged to fly it on his ships instead of the red ensign. It is an honour much esteemed among British masters.

Instead of going up in the clear light of a tropical morning, however, the ritual now coincided with sunrise.

One of Basil Thomson's more confusing habits was that he didn't set the clocks back to accord with the time zone through which we were moving. If we'd changed clocks we would have been doing ten days of it south-bound, half an hour a day. On that Sunday morning we already were more than two hours ahead of the sun; we had been rising in blackest night and breakfasting at dawn and Hattrell, to his chagrin, had been doing his noon position at two in the afternoon, suntime. 'We all like noon at midday but we never get it,' he had been plaintively crying as he did his sums. What it also meant was that the morning swim around the pool, which should have been accomplished in the first strong warmth of the tropical sun, was done instead under the stars; it was a disconcerting exercise, which I soon gave up.

'On the passengers ships they change the clocks for the passengers, who want to know when the sun rises and when it sets,' Thomson remarked at breakfast. 'On these ships it's no skin off anybody's teeth that I don't set the clocks back.' He was in a good mood, and as though to account for it, said: 'I enjoy Sundays, and I'll now go and find my church service.

'I twiddle the knobs on the radio until I get what I want. Then I lean back with my pipe and enjoy the old parson. It may not be the proper way, but I believe that religion should be a thing of joy, light and free. I don't think Jesus would have minded.'

He added, after a brief reflective silence, 'None of us can even tell what God is like, whether he is black, white, blue, or yellow. Whites like to think he is white, the blacks that he is black, but we're all equally ignorant.'

For the navigating officers Sunday was just another working day. They continued through their normal round of watch-keeping. But the engineers, who switched their engines to automatic control at midday Saturday, were free until Monday morning. Sundays they spent at the pool, or raced about the decks before lunch on the bicycles which all supertankers keep on board as one means of defeating the distances of the main deck during working hours. Sunday's curry lunch was somewhat more elaborate than the weekday ones, and at teatime in the afternoon there were special cakes called tabnabs instead of Huntley & Palmer biscuits. None of these diversions was sufficient, however, to appease the restless energies of the engineers and, at the heart of a long humid tranquil tropical afternoon that Sunday, there lay a small pocket of violence in the swimming pool. The junior officers were playing in the water with a polo ball. They played ferociously, long and tirelessly, hurling the ball at each other as though it were a weapon. The pool itself was like a cauldron and the area around it was sodden from their splashing. Graham and Pat Allen sat in deck-chairs, good hu-mouredly watching, oblivious to the stinging showers that drenched them from time to time. Their deck-chairs were raised to give them a better view of the arena and its combat, and they lay with their palms cradling their heads, their arms and elbows spread like small open resting wings and their bodies slack with ease and satisfaction from their own appeased energies.

They all brought into the wardroom that evening the taut skins and glowing alertness set upon them by the day's sun and salt water. They looked very young, healthy, and expectant of some-thing more yet from the day. The barman had been let off to go to the movies, so they had at least a mood of Sunday domestic impro-visation in the wardroom itself, a general sense of lending a hand. Harvey Phillips was barman, playing the role of publican, taking orders, serving them with mock flourish, wiping his counter and setting things straight. Pat Allen was behind the bar with him, washing and drying glasses. Graham Chalmers collected empty beer cans and took out the 'gash'; Graham Allen emptied ashtrays.

As they finished their chores they came over one by one to join the after-dinner group at the coffee-table, where the master himself was lingering over his coffee, watching it all with his benign ex-pression. Harvey Phillips was last, bringing over a tray of drinks. 'I've enjoyed meself,' he said as he served the orders individually. 'Lawrence should go to the pictures more often and leave us to it. It passes the time. It's a change, like on one of the other ships where Sunday nights are always Night Club dinner. It was a good way to finish the weekend.'

'What exactly did that mean?' Basil Thomson asked.

'Well, not too much if you come to think about it. They had the saloon lights off and a candle stuck in the centre of every table and you sat there trying to see your food. But it gave a sort of mood. It was different anyways.'

'If it's just a question of a candle stuck in the centre of the table, I think we can manage that,' Thomson said.

'Actually, there was more to it. They had a cabaret. It depends on the talents you've got aboard. They had some good acts so they could do it. One of the officers was a magician. He dressed up in the clothes of one of the wives on board and then did his magic. It was the star turn.'

'On the *Garonne* they used to do pub lunches on Saturdays,' Graham Allen said. 'A regular buffet was laid out in the wardroom. You could go and help yourself while drinking at the bar, just like in a pub.'

'Was old Peter Simpson chief engineer on her when you were there?' Basil Thomson asked.

'He certainly was,' Graham Allen said. 'He's one of the nicest blokes I've ever met on these ships.'

'Oh yes, a fine man,' Thomson agreed. 'A charming chap, and so is his wife.'

'Yes, what a lovely person,' said Pat Allen. 'A *really* lovely person.'

'So are their children,' said Thomson. 'And they've certainly got enough of them. Six.'

'Oh no, it's five,' Graham Allen corrected.

'No, six,' said Thomson.

'Then they must have had one very recently because Pat and I know them very well and we saw them last time we were home,' Graham Allen said. 'We spent some time with them and she wasn't pregnant then.'

'All I can tell you, young Graham Allen, is that they've got six children,' Thomson said. 'I *know* it's six.'

'In that case, as I say, they must have had another just recently because it was five when we last saw them,' Graham Allen said.

'Well, all I can say to you, Graham Allen, is that I'm glad at least that you admire him; I hope then that you'll take him as an example and not become one of these what I call professional third engineers, and I'm thinking of one in particular who's been on this ship and who said he wasn't interested in further promotion, he was going to stay third engineer and not bother about advancing himself because a chief engineer only got forty pounds a month more than he did, after paying taxes, and he didn't think that so little extra money was worth the responsibility.'

'I plan to study for my second's ticket as soon as I can, so that's not my view,' Graham Allen said. 'But funnily enough, and I don't want to seem disrespectful, but I can understand that point of view, especially since junior officers don't get the perks that a senior officer gets, so they wonder if the life *is* worth so much extra bother to get another promotion.'

'What perks? How am I better off than you?' Thomson demanded. 'I don't even travel first class on the planes. When I go to the office I'm not treated as a captain, not like in the old days. I don't get any better food or drink. Only my quarters are larger, and those I don't need. Now let me remind you of something, young Graham Allen, which is why I mentioned this in the first place; you yourself once told me that if your wife didn't come aboard then you would quit. You said you would leave the ship and the company if you couldn't have her with you. Don't start thinking that that's forgotten, because it's not. It's down in my book of words. It's no use denying it now, it's there.'

'I'm not denying it,' Graham Allen said.

'You couldn't if you wished. I put it down when it was said, so it's there; unarguably there. You said that if your wife couldn't be with you, then you yourself were going!'

Silence settled over his words. The alertness that the sun had fastened upon all of them had crumpled to lassitude. Normally there would have been the sound of Lawrence the barman quietly doing something or other behind the bar, with the bar itself a vacant brightness at the far end. Nobody moved, except occasionally to pick up his glass to drink. Thomson finally rose to go, and the others followed one after another.

'Good night.'

'Good night.'

'Good night.'

Out up the empty stairs, along the empty passages, and out on to the decks for some air; not quite deserted, however. Peter Dutton, the other second engineer, was sitting in a deck-chair near the swimming pool listening to Charlie, one of the Chinese don-keymen, playing his pipes. They were an inseparable pair. Dutton, who had been on the ship for three months already and whose wife had been among those who'd joined *Ardshiel* for the short passage from Rotterdam to Le Verdon, was one of the ship's loners. He kept to himself, never joined pour-out, and seldom lingered in the wardroom. Nobody knew how long Charlie had been on the ship. Some thought he had been aboard since *Ardshiel* came out of the yards. The pipes, slender Pan-like reed ones, were his solace and one often suddenly heard them playing somewhere or other; in this big ship one could never be quite sure where he was playing. They were like an agreeable ghostly presence that constantly shifted its habitation around us, always calling from somewhere different, and they were particularly pleasing to the Geordies and Scotsmen since the lament that lay at the heart of the notes reminded them of their own pipes. 'Charlie's playing his pipes again,' one of them would say, and they would become thoughtful, their heads half turned toward the suspected direction of the sound.

When one heard the pipes thus during one of the long silences of the wardroom they could bring to the room a feeling of great mel-ancholy, but the charm of the music could never make one regret listening. Now, confronting them from the shadows of the deck, visible at last beside the calm green surface of the floodlit pool, one *could* feel a spasm of regret, as though having unwittingly stumbled upon an unsought revelation; but the notes out here were so much freer and clearer and sweeter, and the tableau of the two men, the blond young Geordie and the elderly Chinese, sitting in such quiet and harmonious attachment, was itself so sustaining that one didn't really mind after all.

Peter Scott

FIRE AT SEA

(from *The Eye of the Wind*)

*Peter Scott, although best known as an artist, conservationist, and
founder of The Wild Fowl Trust, had a distinguished war time
career and was awarded the D.S.C. and bar after service in motor
torpedo boats in the English Channel.*

ABOUT twenty minutes after I had been relieved I was informed
in the wardroom that the starboard fore-topmast-backstay had
parted, and I went at once to the bridge to organize the repair.
While I was there a signal was received from *Lincoln* at six-twenty
p.m.:

'HMS *Comorin* seriously on fire in position 54° 39′ N, 21°
13′ W join us if possible. 1600/6.'

We passed this to *Douglas* for permission to go and were detached
at six-forty.

Having told *Lincoln* by radio that we were coming, we made a
further signal: 'Expect to sight you at 2015. Is a U-boat involved?'
to which came: 'Reply No.'

During this time we were able to increase to eighteen knots and
with the following sea the ship's motion was so much easier that the
backstay was quickly repaired and secured. We then began making
preparations for what might turn out to be our sixth load of survivors since war began.

Scrambling nets, lifebuoys, oil drums (to pour oil on to the
troubled waters), heaving lines and heavier bow and stern lines for
boats, line-throwing gun, grass line and manilla – all these were got
ready and the mess decks were prepared for casualties.

At eight minutes past eight in the evening *Glenartney* was
sighted fine on the port bow at extreme visibility range – about

eight miles – and four minutes later *Comorin* was seen right ahead, which was exactly three minutes earlier than expected. There was a lot of white smoke coming from her single funnel.

We asked *Lincoln*, who was lying just to windward of the burning ship, what the situation was and she told us that *Comorin* was being abandoned, that no boats were left, that the *Glenartney* was picking up some rafts and that she, *Lincoln*, was hauling over rafts on a grass line.

When we drew near the scene was awe-inspiring. The great liner lay beam on to the seas drifting very rapidly. A red glow showed in the smoke which belched from her funnel and below that amidships the fire had a strong hold. Clouds of smoke streamed away from her lee side. The crew were assembled aft and we were in communication by lamp and later by semaphore. From the weather quarter the *Lincoln*'s Carley rafts were being loaded up – a dozen men at a time and hauled across to the destroyer lying about two cables away. It was a desperately slow affair and we went in close to see if we could not go alongside.

Various objects were falling from time to time from the *Comorin* into the sea. Each time one looked carefully to see if it was a man but it was not. Some of the things may have been oil drums, in an attempt to make the sea's surface calmer. We looked at the weather side first and passed between *Lincoln* and *Comorin*, only discovering that they were connected by line after we were through. But the line did not part, it had sunk deep enough for us to cross. We turned and tried to lay some oil between the two ships. This meant that we nearly got sandwiched. There were two raft loads going across at the time and the sailors in them waved us to go back. They seemed incredibly tiny and ant-like in their rafts on those angry slopes of grey sea.

The *Lincoln* was rolling wildly and once when her propellers came clear of the water we could see that she had a rope round the starboard one. Her starboard side was black, which we thought at first was burnt paintwork, but discovered afterwards was oil which they had tried to pump out on the weather side and which had blown back all over their side and upper deck.

To go alongside *Comorin* seemed an impossibility. The waves were fifty to sixty feet from trough to crest and the liner's cruiser stern lifted high out of the water at one moment showing rudder and screws and crashed downward in a cloud of spray the next. I thought a destroyer could not possibly survive such an impact.

Round on the leeward side we got our grass line out on to the fo'c'sle and dropped a Carley raft into the water attached to it. The liner drifted to leeward and so did we, but the raft with less wind surface did not drift so fast. So it appeared to float away up wind towards the other ship, and in a very short time was against the liner's lee side. There was a Jacob's ladder over the side and one rating went down and eventually got into the raft. We started to haul in on the grass but we had allowed too much grass to go out, the bight of it had sunk, the great stern had lifted on a wave and come down on the near side of the rope; the bight was round the rudder. When we hauled on the grass it pulled the raft towards the liner and under her. Each time the ship lifted it pounded down on the man in the raft, who began to cry out. At this time we drifted round the stern and could not see him any more. I am not certain if he was drowned, but it can only have been a miracle that saved him.

We were close to the stern now and we fired our Coston line-throwing gun. We fired it well to windward, but a little too high and the wind blew it horizontally clear of the ship like straw. But we were close enough to get a heaving line across – after many had missed – and we connected the Coston line to the departing heaving line as we drew astern and finally pulled an end of the grass rope to it and passed it over to the other ship. Then we put another Carley raft in the water so that they could haul it in to windward but for some time they made no effort to do this and finally their Captain made a signal that he thought the only chance was for *Broke* to go alongside and let the men jump. This was at nine-fifty p.m.

I had various discussions with my Captain as to which side it should be. I must confess that I did not believe we could survive such a venture. By this time it was almost dark and the *Lincoln*'s raft ferry had failed owing to the parting of their grass line. I do not know how many people they had rescued by this ferry, but it cannot have been very many as it was desperately slow. Not that it wasn't enormously worth doing, for at the time it seemed to be the only way at all.

I saw one body floating away and wondered if it was the chap from our raft. Indeed I felt sure it was, though I heard a rumour afterwards that he had managed to climb back on board, and I know that several men were drowned embarking in the *Lincoln*'s ferry service. Obviously a raft secured to the upper deck of a heavily rolling ship cannot be secured close alongside. If it were it would be hauled out of the water by its end whenever the ship rolled away and all those already embarked would be pitched out. The rafts therefore had to remain ten or fifteen yards from the *Comorin*'s side and men had to go down the rope to them. It was here that several men were drowned.

As it gradually got dark the glow from the fire shone redly and eventually became the chief source of light. As soon as we knew we were going alongside I went down to the fo'c'sle, got all the fenders over to the port side, and had all the locker cushions brought up from the mess decks.

I suggested that hammocks should be brought up, but Angus Letty, our Navigating Officer, said that since it was still doubtful if we should get alongside he thought it would be a pity to get them all wet. I wish I had pressed the point but I didn't. Letty had been doing excellent work on the fo'c'sle all the time, but I think his judgement was at fault in this and so was mine in not seeing at once that he was wrong. What are a few wet hammocks by comparison with broken limbs?

So we closed the starboard (leeward) quarter of the *Comorin* and in a few minutes we had scraped alongside.

The absolutely bewildering thing was the relative speed that the ships passed each other in a vertical direction. The men waiting on the after promenade deck were forty feet above our fo'c'sle at one moment and the next they were ten feet below. As they passed our fo'c'sle they had to jump as if jumping from an express lift.

The first chance was easy. About nine jumped and landed mostly on the fo'c'sle, some on B gun deck. They were all safe and uninjured. As they came doubling aft I asked them how they got on and they were cheerful enough.

One petty officer came with this lot – P.O. Fitzgerald – and I immediately detailed him to help with the organization of survivors as they embarked.

There was little, if any, damage to the ship from this first encounter and we backed away to get into position for the next. As we closed in for the second attempt the terrific speed of the rise and fall of the other ship in relation to our own fo'c'sle was again the main difficulty for the jumpers, added to which the ships were rolling in opposite directions, so that at one minute they touched, at the next they were ten yards apart. This very heavy rolling made it almost impossible for us to keep our feet on the fo'c'sle. We had to hold on tightly nearly all the time. I remember I had started the operation wearing a cap as I thought I should be easier to recognize that way, but I so nearly lost it in the gale that I left it in the wireless office for safe keeping.

The second jump was much more difficult than the first. Only about six men came and three of them were injured. From then on I do not remember the chronology of events as one jump followed another with varying pauses for manoeuvring. Our policy was not to remain alongside for any length of time as this would have been very dangerous and might well have damaged us to the point of foundering in these monstrous seas. Instead we quickly withdrew after each brief contact in order to assess the damage and decide upon the seaworthiness of the ship before closing in again for another attempt.

The scene was lit chiefly by the fire, as it was now pitch dark. Occasionally the *Lincoln*'s searchlight swept across us as they searched the sea for the last Carley raft which had somehow broken adrift. At each successive jump a few more men were injured.

We decided to rig floodlights to light the fo'c'sle so that the men could judge the height of the jump. These were held by Leading Telegraphist Davies and Ordinary Seaman Timperon all the time. The pool of light which they formed gave the whole scene an extraordinary artificiality, as if this were some ghastly film scene and I can remember, as I stood impotently waiting for the next jump, feeling suddenly remote as if watching through the wrong end of a telescope.

As soon as the jumping men had begun to injure themselves I sent aft for the doctor who was in bed with a temperature. He came for'ard at once and started to work. At the third jump we drew ahead too far and the whaler at its davits was crushed but several men jumped into it and were saved that way. Another time the Captain changed his mind and decided to get clear by going ahead instead of astern. The ship was struck a heavy blow aft on the port for'ard depth charge thrower.

At this jump there had been a good many injured and as we went ahead into the sea again to circle *Comorin* for another approach the decks began to wash down with great seas. This was awkward for the disposal of the injured and I went up and asked the Captain if in future we could have a little longer to clear away and prepare for the next jump – to which he readily agreed.

My routine was to be down by 'A' gun for the jump. There was a strut to the gun-cover frame which was the best handhold. Here I saw that the padding was properly distributed, the light properly held, the stretcher parties in readiness and hands all ready to receive the survivors.

Then we would crash alongside for a few breathtaking seconds whilst the opportunity did or did not arise for a few to jump. Sometimes there would be two opportunities – first while we still went ahead, and then again as we came astern. The great thing was to get the injured away before the next people jumped on to them. As soon as this had been done I went with the Shipwright to survey the damage and then up to report to the Captain. This was a rather exhausting round trip and before the end I got cramp in my right arm through over-exercise of the muscles.

The damage to the ship was at first superficial, consisting of dents in the fo'c'sle flare and bent guard-rails and splinter shields. But at length one bad blow struck us near the now-crushed whaler on the upper deck level. I ran aft and found a large rent in the ship's side *out* of which water was pouring. I did not think the boiler room could have filled quickly enough for this to be sea water coming out again, and came to the conclusion that it was a fresh-water tank. This was later confirmed by the Shipwright. As I had thought, it was the port 'peace' tank. This was an incredible stroke of good fortune, as a hole of that size in the boiler room would have been very serious indeed in that sea.

Several of *Comorin*'s officers had now arrived and we began to get estimates of the numbers still to come. There seemed always to be an awful lot more. I detailed Lt. Loftus to go down to the mess decks as chief receptionist and went back to my usual round – fo'c'sle for a jump, clear the injured, view the damage, report to the Captain and back to the fo'c'sle.

By now some of the injuries appeared to be pretty bad. There were a good many broken legs and arms and one chap fell across the guard-rail from about twenty-five feet. Letty came aft to me and said, 'That fellow's finished – cut his guts to bits. It appears that A. B. George, a young Gibraltar seaman who was doing excellent work on the fo'c'sle, had put a hand on his back – felt what he took to be broken ribs and withdrawn his hand covered with blood. No such case ever reached the doctor and although there is a possibility that an injured man could have gone over the side owing to the heavy rolling, I am inclined to think that the account was an exaggerated one.

It filled me with gloom, and since at least one-third of the survivors landing on the fo'c'sle had to be carried off it, I became desperately worried by the high percentage of casualties. True, they had improved lately since we had ranged all available hammocks in rows, like sausages. They made very soft padding but a few ankles still slipped between them and got twisted.

On one of my round trips I met an R.N.V.R. Sub-Lieutenant survivor trying to get some photos of the burning ship (I never heard whether they came out). There were a good many officers on board by this time, mostly R.N.R. Of course they did not recognize me, hatless in duffle coat, grey flannel trousers and sea boots, and it took a few moments to persuade them to answer my searching questions.

Still the estimated number remaining did not seem to dwindle. Sometimes there were longish pauses while we manoeuvred into position. Twice we went alongside without getting any men at all. Once the ship came in head on and the stem was stove in, for about eight feet down from the bull ring, and we got no survivors that time either.

Somewhere around eleven-thirty p.m. the fire reached the rockets on the *Comorin*, which went off splendidly, together with various other fireworks such as red Verey's Lights and so on. Later the small arms ammunition began to explode, at first in ones and twos then in sharp rattles and finally in a continuous crackling roar.

The sea was as bad as ever and at each withdrawal we had to go full astern into it. This meant that very heavy waves were sweeping the quarter-deck, often as high as the blast shield of X gun (about eight feet). When these waves broke over the ship she shuddered and set up a vibration which carried on often for twenty or thirty seconds. All this time the hull was clearly under great strain. As we got more used to going alongside some of my particular fears grew less, but the apparent inevitability of casualties was a constant source of worry and there was also the continual speculation upon how much the ship would stand up to.

Once on the first approach there seemed to be a chance for a jump. Two men jumped, but it was too far and they missed. I was at the break of the fo'c'sle at the time, and looked down into the steaming, boiling abyss. With the two ships grinding together as they were there did not seem the slightest chance of rescuing them. More men were jumping now and theirs was the prior claim. The ship came ahead, men jumped on to the flag deck and the pompom deck amidships was demolished: then as we went astern, I ran again to the side to see if there was any sign of the two in the water, but there was none that I could see.

Having got the injured off the fo'c'sle I went aft to examine the damage to the pom-pom deck and see if the upper deck had been pierced. I heard a very faint cry of 'Help', and looking over the side saw that a man was holding on to the scrambling nets which I had ordered to be lowered as soon as we arrived on the scene. We were going astern but he was holding on. I called to some hands by the torpedo tubes and began to haul him up. Eventually he came over the guard-rail unconscious but still holding on by his hands; his feet had never found the net at all. He was very full of water but we got him for'ard at once and he seemed likely to recover.

About this time too they had an injured man of X gun deck who was got down by Neill Robertson stretcher (the kind in which a man can be strapped for lowering). These stretchers were being used all the time. I went for'ard once to find a petty officer. There was a big crowd outside the Sick Bay and I trod on something in the dark shadow there. It was an injured man and I had tripped over his broken leg. I hope and believe it was still numb enough for him not to be hurt, but it was very distressing to me to feel that I had been so careless. I ought to have known that the congestion of stretchers would be there.

When I was reporting damage to the Captain on one occasion we were just coming alongside so I stayed on the bridge to watch from there, as there was hardly time to get down to the fo'c'sle. The Captain was completely calm. He brought the ship alongside in the same masterly manner as he had already done so often. He was calling the telegraph orders to the Navigating Officer who was passing them to the Coxswain in the wheelhouse. As we ground alongside several jumped. One officer was too late, and grabbed the bottom guard-rail and hung outside the flare, his head and arms only visible to us. There was a great shout from the crowd on *Comorin*'s stern. But we had seen it and already two of our men (Cooke and George) had run forward and were trying to haul the officer on board. The ships rolled and swung together. They would hit exactly where the man dangled over the flare; still the two struggling at the guard-rail could not haul the hanging man to safety. Then as if by magic and with a foot to spare the ships began to roll apart again. But still the man could not be hauled on board; still he hung like a living fender. Again the ships rolled together and again stopped a few inches before he was crushed. As they rolled towards each other for the third time, Cooke and George managed to get a proper hold of the man and he was heaved to safety and this time the ships crashed together with a rending of metal. The two seamen had never withdrawn even when the impact seemed certain and they had thus saved the officer's life. It was a magnificently brave thing to see.

Another man was not so lucky. In some way at the time of jumping he was crushed between the two ships, and fell at once into the sea as they separated. On the other hand I saw a steward with a

cigarette in his mouth and a raincoat over one arm step from one
ship to the other, swinging his leg over the guard-rails in a most
unhurried manner, just as if he had been stepping across in harbour. It was one of those rare occasions when the rise and fall of
the two ships coincided. One man arrived on board riding astride
the barrel of 'B' gun and another landed astride the guard-rail.
Both were quite unhurt.

During all this long night Lewis (our Gunner 'T') was with me
on the fo'c'sle. He was a great stand-by, always cheerful and help-
ful. As we saw the damage getting gradually worse we found a
chance to speculate on the leave we should get and even to hope
that the ship would not be 'paid off' because of the terrible paper
work involved and the number of things that each of us had 'on
charge' in our respective departments which we knew would never
be found and for which we should have to account. Letty was full
of activity too on the fo'c'sle head and was doing excellent work
among the survivors as they arrived on board, tending the injured,
heartening the frightened, organizing the stretcher parties.

After the terrible vibrations set up by the huge waves which
broke over the quarter-deck each time that we had to go 'Full
astern both', I became anxious about the state of the after compartments and sent the Gunner and the Shipwright aft to find out
if there was any extensive flooding. They had not long been gone
when one of our officers came up and said there was six feet of
water in the wardroom. I was inclined to take this with a grain of
salt and it was lucky that I did so, for when the Shipwright returned he reported that there were a few inches of water slopping
about on the deck but nothing whatever to worry about in any of
the after compartments. The officer's explanation was that someone had told him this, he didn't know who, and he told this 'someone' to go aft and verify it and then report to me. Nothing of course
had been reported to me.

This same officer only impinged himself once more upon my
consciousness during that night. That was when he came up and
told me in rather a panicky tone that the damage was really getting
very bad on the mess decks and that he did not think that the men
would stand much more of it. His explanation of this remarkable

contribution was that an Engineer Lt-Commander survivor who was down there and evidently (and, I hasten to add, with every justification) slightly shaken, had told him that he had better report the extent of the damage to his First Lieutenant.

Actually, of course, all this damage was above the water line, although, owing to the rolling and pitching a good deal of water was coming inboard through the numerous rents along the port fo'c'sle flare.

Back on the upper deck we saw a man working at the edge of the fire on the weather side of the *Comorin*'s main deck. We couldn't make out what he was doing, but we discovered afterwards that he was burning the confidential books in the blazing signalmen's mess.

Still we were periodically closing the *Comorin*'s bulging stern, with the wicked-looking rudder and propellers bared from time to time as the massive black shape towered above us. Still the men were jumping as the opportunity arose. Each time there was a chorus from the fo'c'sle of 'Jump! – Jump!'

Although we were keen to persuade as many to jump as possible, I thought that it was better to let them judge the time for themselves and told my men not to call out 'jump'.

From one of the survivor officers I discovered there had been two medical officers in *Comorin* – one the ship's doctor, Lt-Commander, R.N.V.R., and another taking passage, a Surgeon Lieutenant, R.N.V.R., but the latter was believed to have gone in one of the boats.

So next time we went into the *Comorin* I shouted that I wanted the doctor at the next jump if possible, as I knew that our own doctor would be hard pressed with so many casualties. No chance arose that time, but a little later as we closed again I could see the Surgeon Lt-Commander poised on the teak rail waiting to jump. Here was the one man that I really wanted safe but he missed his best opportunity and took the last chance, a jump of twenty feet. He landed beyond the padding, at my feet as I stood on the layer's platform of 'A' gun. He fell flat on his back and lay there quite still. But in a few moments he had come round and ten minutes later, very bruised and stiff, he was at work amongst the injured. He too had barely recovered from 'flu and was quite unused to destroyers; I believe also that he felt very seasick. His work that night was beyond praise.

Casualties were not so heavy now, but there were still a good many owing to the fact that jumpers on the downward plunge of the *Comorin* often met the upward surge of *Broke*'s fo'c'sle. This meant that they were hurled against the deck like a cricket ball against a bat.

We were all soaked through with rain and spray and sweat. It was very hot work in a duffle coat. My arms were still inclined to get cramp if I went up ladders by pulling instead of climbing. However I don't think this interfered with my work at all. I still continued with the wearisome anxious round – fo'c'sle for the jump, assess damage, up to report it, and back to the fo'c'sle for the next jump.

These last jumps were very awkward because the remaining ratings were the less adventurous ones whom it was difficult to persuade to jump. Two of them, senior petty officers, were drunk. They had been pushed over and arrived on board in an incapable condition. I thought they were casualties but was relieved, and at the same time furious, to discover that they were only incapably drunk. It seemed too much that my stretcher parties should work on two drunken and extremely heavy petty officers, especially as they were the very two on whom the officers in the other ship would be expecting to be able to rely to set a good example to the rest.

Once I sent up to the Captain and suggested that we might perhaps consider rescuing the last few by raft if the damage got any worse, as with well over 100 survivors on board it would be out of proportion to risk losing the ship and all of them to get the last few if there were a good chance of getting those last few in another way. We agreed that we would try this as soon as the damage gave real cause for alarm but not before.

Quite suddenly the number on *Comorin*'s stern seemed to have dwindled. At last we seemed to be in sight of the end. There were about ten, mostly officers. The Captain and Commander were directing from one deck above, with a torch.

At the next jump they all arrived, unhurt, except the Captain and the Commander, who remained to make sure that the ship was clear.

Five minutes later we came in again. The Commander jumped and landed safely. The Captain paused to make sure that he had gone, then jumped too. He caught in a rope which dangled from the deck above, and which turned him round so that he faced his own ship again. At the same moment the *Broke* dropped away and began to roll outwards. The Captain's feet fell outside the guard-rail and it seemed that he must be deflected overboard. But he sat across the wire guard-rail and balanced for a moment before rolling backwards and turning a back somersault on the padding of hammocks. He was quite unhurt, smoking his cigarette, and he had managed to return his monocle so quickly to his eye that I thought he had jumped wearing it.

He turned out to be Captain Hallett – a destroyer Captain of the First War who had served under my father some thirty-five years earlier.

I took him up to the bridge to see my Captain and at forty minutes past midnight we made the signal to *Lincoln*, 'Ship is now clear of all officers and men.'

Rescue operations were now successfully completed. During the past three hours no less than 685 telegraph orders had been passed from the bridge to the engine-room and executed without a mistake. Captain Hallett told my Captain that there were still some confidential books in the strong room of the *Comorin* and that he would not feel safe in leaving her until she had sunk. He asked us to torpedo her. Having discussed the possibilities of salvage and decided that they were not practical, we prepared to fire a torpedo. It was fired at rather too great a range and did not hit. Nor did the second or the third. Some time elapsed between these attempts and I went below to examine the situation on the mess decks. 'Anyone here down-hearted?' I asked and received a rousing cheer of 'No.' A lot of water was slopping in through the numerous holes and I started a baling party with buckets. The casualties were mostly in hammocks, some on the lockers and some in the starboard hammock netting. The port side of the mess deck was a shambles. However, since everything seemed to be under control, I went aft to the wardroom and found some thirty-five survivor officers ensconced there. The deck was pretty wet and the red shellac colouring had started to come off so that everything soon became stained with red. The flat outside was running with fuel oil and water and baling operations were put in hand.

Then I went back to the bridge and instituted a count of the numbers of survivors which turned out to be correct and never had to be altered. We had exactly 180 on board. Back in the wardroom I found the Engineer Officer baling away with buckets. He told me that the Gunner had been washed overboard, but had been washed back on board again by the next wave. He was very shaken and had turned in. I discovered also that earlier in the evening when struggling with the manilla, P.O. Storrs had been pushed over by the rope, but had managed to hold on and be hauled back to safety. At some time or other A.B. Bates had been washed off the iron deck just by the for'ard funnel and washed back on board again on the quarter deck, a remarkable escape.

As it was now after two a.m. and I had to go on watch at four I tried to get a little sleep in Jeayes's cabin. My own cabin was occupied by a Commissioned Gunner whose arm had been crushed. He had caught hold of the outside of the flag deck. His arm had got between the two ships and been pinched whereupon he had let go and would have fallen into the sea but for the fact that his raincoat was pinched in and held. He hung by it and was hauled in from the flag deck ladder. I afterwards discovered that he had served with my father as an A.B. in the *Majestic* in 1906 when my father had been Cable Officer in her. He occupied my cabin for the rest of the voyage.

I did not sleep much and I missed the torpedoing of the *Comorin*, which was achieved with either the fourth or fifth torpedo. The sixth had a seized-up stop valve and could not be fired. At 0400 I relieved Jeayes on the bridge. The *Comorin* had not sunk; she was appreciably lower in the water and had a marked list to port instead of the slight one to starboard which she had had during the rescue. The Captain had turned in in the charthouse, but came up for a few minutes. I was on watch by myself and we were patrolling up and down to weather of the blazing wreck until dawn.

By about five-thirty the whole of the after promenade deck of
Comorin from which the survivors had jumped was ablaze. It was
satisfactory to know that we had been justified in attempting the
night rescue and that time had been an important factor. At dawn
we left *Lincoln* to stand by *Comorin* till she sank and set off home
with *Glenartney*.

The return journey entailed a lot of hard work. Baling was continuous for the whole two and a half days. *Glenartney* was ordered
to proceed on her journey calling at Freetown to disembark survivors, and we were left alone. The weather worsened and on
Monday night we had to reduce speed during the middle watch
from eight to six knots owing to the heavy head sea set up by the
easterly gale. The water on the mess decks was more than the
balers could cope with and was running out over the watertight
door sills in waterfalls. There were about sixty tons of water on the
upper mess deck – about one foot six inches of water when the ship
was on an even keel, and four feet or more when she rolled, with a
corresponding cataract when she rolled the other way. Life on the
mess decks became very uncomfortable. The forepeak and cable
locker were flooded and the fore store was filling. It was an anxious
night. But when I came on watch at four a.m. on Tuesday the gale
began to moderate suddenly. One of the survivor officers – an
R.N.R. lieutenant – was keeping watch with me. By five the wind
had died away to nothing and an hour later it began to blow from
the west. Almost at once the sea began to go down and we were
able to increase speed. By noon we were steaming at twenty knots
for the Clyde and we arrived there on the morning of Wednesday,
9th April. I spent those two and a half days mainly amongst the
survivors for'ard. Lewis and the others were looking after the
officers as well as possible in the wardroom. The for'ard mess deck
seemed to need most of my efforts, and besides I enjoyed the
company of the rating survivors, so I spent as much time as I could
on the mess deck amongst them. The *Comorin's* commander coop-
erated most kindly by providing three watches of baling parties
with two officers in charge of each watch and by helping with other
work. Three survivor officers shared the night watches with us on
the bridge.

In spite of the apparently heavy casualties during the rescue, so many of these recovered quickly that there were finally only about twenty-five hospital cases out of the whole 180. The worst cases were compound fractures. There were three legs and one arm. The worst of these cases was an old Chief Stoker who was sixty-nine years old. He was in bad pain all the time and to begin with he had been placed on the lockers in the doorway on the starboard side of the mess deck, from which he had had to be moved later on. He was remarkably brave. The doctors were afraid he would die of shock, but on the last morning I had a half-hour's talk with him in which he described in spirited terms how he had once been presented to Queen Victoria. I believe he survived.

I found the youth whom we had pulled up on the net; he was lying stark naked in a hammock. He was still a bit under the weather but I got his clothes brought up from the boiler room and made him sit outside in the afternoon. Next day he was quite well and very bright. He was only eighteen and had been one of Carroll Levis's discoveries. His name was Sturgess and when he left he said, 'Thank you, sir, for saving my life – I'll put in a request as soon as I get to depot to join your ship.'

We arrived at Greenock at about ten-thirty in the morning and were alongside for rather less than one hour before slipping and proceeding to Londonderry. During that hour the hospital cases were taken into the ambulances, the remainder were put into buses, the two P.O.s who had been drunk on the Sunday night and had been under open arrest ever since were taken away under escort from H.M.S. *Hecla*, and our bread and meat that we had ordered by signal were embarked. I went ashore to give parting encouragement to the injured in the ambulance, and met an old school friend, David Colville, Lt. R.N.V.R. That same evening we were back at our base in Londonderry.

To complete the story – we learned that the fire in *Comorin* was an accident. A broken oil pipe at the top of the boiler room had dripped hot oil on a stoker and made him drop a torch which had ignited the oil on the deck. In a flash the boiler room was blazing and had to be closed down at once. This meant that there was no power on the fire main and therefore nothing with which to fight the fire.

Lincoln came into Londonderry two days later and told us of the sinking of *Comorin*. They had fired sixty-three rounds and two torpedoes at her. The torpedoes – not supposed to be fired at all being American pattern – had not hit. They did not reckon at first that their shells did much good. But as the fore hatch cover was near the water, owing to her pronounced list they pounded this and made a hole there large enough to flood the forehold. One of the motor-boats floated off undamaged. Then the ship heeled over and finally the stern came right out of the water and she plunged down. She had sunk by about noon Monday, 7th April. *Lincoln* had saved 121, *Glenartney* about 109. *Lincoln* had most of the army survivors, one of whom had been crushed between boat and destroyer. There was a story that an army officer after embarking in the *Comorin*'s boat had shouted up, 'Of course you'll be sending the boat back for our baggage!'

Captain Joshua Slocum

SAVAGES

(from *Sailing Alone Around the World*)

Joshua Slocum ran away to sea as a ship's cook at the age of 12, and, after an adventurous career as a merchant captain, made the first single-handed voyage around the world. In 1909 he was lost aboard the 35-foot sloop Spray *on another lone voyage.*

I WAS determined to rely on my own small resources to repair the damages of the great gale which drove me southward toward the Horn, after I had passed from the Strait of Magellan out into the Pacific. So when I had got back into the strait, by way of Cockburn Channel, I did not proceed eastward for help at the Sandy Point settlement, but turning again into the north-westward reach of the strait, set to work with my palm and needle at every opportunity, when at anchor and when sailing. It was slow work; but little by little the squaresail on the boom expanded to the dimensions of a serviceable mainsail with a peak to it and a leech besides. If it was not the best-setting sail afloat it was at least very strongly made and would stand a hard blow. A ship, meeting the *Spray* long afterward, reported her as wearing a mainsail of some improved design and patent reefer, but that was not the case.

The *Spray* for a few days after the storm enjoyed fine weather, and made fair time through the strait for the distance of twenty miles, which, in these days of many adversities, I called a long run. The weather, I say, was fine for a few days; but it brought little rest. Care for the safety of my vessel, and even for my own life, was in no wise lessened by the absence of heavy weather. Indeed, the peril was even greater, inasmuch as the savages on comparatively fine days ventured forth on their marauding excursions, and in boisterous weather disappeared from sight, their wretched canoes being frail and undeserving the name of craft at all. This being so,

I now enjoyed gales of wind as never before, and the *Spray* was never long without them during her struggles about Cape Horn. I became in a measure inured to the life, and began to think that one more trip through the strait, if perchance the sloop should be blown off again, would make me the aggressor, and put the Fuegians entirely on the defensive. This feeling was forcibly borne in on me at Snug Bay, where I anchored at grey morning after passing Cape Froward, to find, when broad day appeared, that two canoes which I had eluded by sailing all night were now entering the same bay stealthily under the shadow of the high headland. They were well manned, and the savages were well armed with spears and bows. At a shot from my rifle across the bows, both turned aside into a small creek out of range. In danger now of being flanked by the savages in the bush close aboard, I was obliged to hoist the sails, which I had barely lowered, and make across to the opposite side of the strait, a distance of six miles. But now I was put to my wit's end as to how I should weigh anchor, for through an accident to the windlass right here I could not budge it. However, I set all sail and filled away, first hauling short by hand. The sloop carried her anchor away, as though it was meant to be always towed in this way underfoot, and with it she towed a ton or more of kelp from a reef in the bay, the wind blowing a wholesale breeze.

Meanwhile I worked till blood started from my fingers, and with one eye over my shoulder for savages, I watched at the same time, and sent a bullet whistling whenever I saw a limb or a twig move; for I kept a gun always at hand, and an Indian appearing then within range would have been taken as a declaration of war. As it was, however, my own blood was all that was spilt – and from the trifling accident of sometimes breaking the flesh against a cleat or a pin which came in the way when I was in haste. Sea-cuts in my hands from pulling on hard wet ropes were sometimes painful and often bled freely; but these healed when I finally got away from the strait into fine weather.

After clearing Snug Bay I hauled the sloop to the wind, repaired the windlass, and hove the anchor to the hawse, catted it, and then stretched across to a port of refuge under a high mountain about six miles away, and came to in nine fathoms close under the face of a perpendicular cliff. Here my own voice answered back, and I named the place 'Echo Mountain'. Seeing dead trees farther along where the shore was broken, I made a landing for fuel, taking, besides my axe, a rifle, which on these days I never left far from hand; but I saw no living thing here, except a small spider, which had nested in a dry log that I boated to the sloop. The conduct of this insect interested me now more than anything else around the wild place. In my cabin it met, oddly enough, a spider of its own size and species that had come all the way from Boston – a very civil little chap, too, but mighty spry. Well, the Fuegian threw up its antennae for a fight; but my little Bostonian downed it at once, then broke its legs, and pulled them off, one by one, so dexterously that in less than three minutes from the time the battle began the Fuegian spider didn't know itself from a fly.

I made haste the following morning to be under way after a night of wakefulness on the weird shore. Before weighing anchor, however, I prepared a cup of warm coffee over a smart wood fire in my great Montevideo stove. In the same fire was cremated the Fuegian spider, slain the day before by the little warrior from Boston, which a Scots lady at Cape Town long after named 'Bruce' upon hearing of its prowess at Echo Mountain. The *Spray* now reached away for Coffee Island, which I sighted on my birthday, 20 February 1896.

There she encountered another gale, that brought her in the lee of great Charles Island for shelter. On a bluff point on Charles were signal-fires, and a tribe of savages, mustered here since my first trip through the strait, manned their canoes to put off for the sloop. It was not prudent to come to, the anchorage being within bow-shot of the shore, which was thickly wooded; but I made signs that one canoe might come alongside, while the sloop ranged about under sail in the lee of the land. The others I motioned to keep off, and incidentally laid a smart Martini-Henry rifle in sight, close at hand, on the top of the cabin. In the canoe that came alongside, crying their never-ending begging word 'yammerschooner', were two squaws and one Indian, the hardest specimens of humanity I had ever seen in any of my travels. 'Yammerschooner' was their plaint when they pushed off from the shore, and 'yammerschooner' it was when they got alongside. The squaws beckoned for food, while the Indian, a black-visaged savage, stood sulkily as if he took no interest at all in the matter, but on my turning my back for some biscuits and jerked beef for the squaws, the 'buck' sprang on deck and confronted me, saying in Spanish jargon that we had met before. I thought I recognized the tone of his 'yammerschooner', and his full beard identified him as the Black Pedro whom, it was true, I had met before. 'Where are the rest of the crew?' he asked, as he looked uneasily around, expecting hands, maybe, to come out of the fore-scuttle and deal him his just deserts for many murders. 'About three weeks ago,' said he, 'when you passed up here, I saw three men on board. Where are the other two?' I answered him briefly that the same crew was still on board. 'But,' said he, 'I see you are doing all the work,' and with a leer he added, as he glanced at the mainsail, 'hombre valiente.' I explained that I did all the work in the day, while the rest of the crew slept, so that they would be fresh to watch for Indians at night. I was interested in the subtle cunning of this savage, knowing him, as I did, better perhaps than he was aware. Even had I not been advised before I sailed from Sandy Point, I should have measured him for an archvillain now. Moreover, one of the squaws, with that spark of kindliness which is somehow found in the breast of even the lowest savage, warned me by a sign to be on my guard, or Black Pedro would do me harm. There was no need of the warning, however, for I was on my guard from the first and at that moment held a smart revolver in my hand ready for instant service.

'When you sailed through here before,' he said, 'you fired a shot at me,' adding with some warmth that it was 'muy malo'. I affected not to understand, and said, 'You have lived at Sandy Point, have you not?' He answered frankly, 'Yes,' and appeared delighted to meet one who had come from the dear old place. 'At the mission?' I queried. 'Why, yes,' he replied, stepping forward as if to embrace an old friend. I motioned him back, for I did not share his flattering humour. 'And you know Captain Pedro Samblich?' continued I. 'Yes,' said the villain, who had killed a kinsman of Samblich – 'yes, indeed; he is a great friend of mine.' 'I know it,' said I. Samblich had told me to shoot him on sight. Pointing to my rifle on the cabin, he wanted to know how many times it fired. 'Cuantos?' said he. When I explained to him that that gun kept right on shooting, his jaw fell, and he spoke of getting away. I did not hinder him from going. I gave the squaws biscuits and beef, and one of them gave me several lumps of tallow in exchange, and I think it worth mentioning that she did not offer me the smallest pieces, but with some extra trouble handed me the largest of all the pieces in the canoe. No Christian could have done more. Before pushing off from the sloop the cunning savage asked for matches, and made as if to reach with the end of his spear the box I was about to give him; but I held it toward him on the muzzle of my rifle, the one that 'kept on shooting'. The chap picked the box off the gun gingerly enough, to be sure, but he jumped when I said, 'Quedao [Look out],' at which the squaws laughed and seemed not at all displeased. Perhaps the wretch had clubbed them that morning for not gathering mussels enough for his breakfast. There was a good understanding among us all.

From Charles Island the *Spray* crossed over to Fortescue Bay, where she anchored and spent a comfortable night under the lee of high land, while the wind howled outside. The bay was deserted now. They were Fortescue Indians whom I had seen at the island, and I felt quite sure they could not follow the *Spray* in the present hard blow. Not to neglect a precaution, however, I sprinkled tacks on deck before I turned in.

On the following day the loneliness of the place was broken by the appearance of a great steamship, making for the anchorage with a lofty bearing. She was no Diego craft. I knew the sheer, the model, and the poise. I threw out my flag, and directly saw the Stars and Stripes flung to the breeze from the great ship.

The wind had then abated, and toward night the savages made their appearance from the island, going direct to the steamer to 'yammerschooner'. Then they came to the *Spray* to beg more, or to steal all, declaring that they got nothing from the steamer. Black Pedro here came alongside again. My own brother could not have been more delighted to see me, and he begged me to lend him my rifle to shoot a guanaco for me in the morning. I assured the fellow that if I remained there another day I would lend him the gun, but

I had no mind to remain. I gave him a cooper's draw-knife and some other small implements which would be of service in canoe-making, and bade him be off.

Under the cover of darkness that night I went to the steamer, which I found to be the *Colombia*, Captain Henderson, from New York, bound for San Francisco. I carried all my guns along with me, in case it should be necessary to fight my way back. In the chief mate of the *Colombia*, Mr Hannibal, I found an old friend, and he referred affectionately to days in Manila when we were there together, he in the *Southern Cross* and I in the *Northern Light*, both ships as beautiful as their names.

The *Colombia* had an abundance of fresh stores on board. The captain gave his steward some order, and I remember that the guileless young man asked me if I could manage, besides other things, a few cans of milk and a cheese. When I offered my Monte-video gold for the supplies, the captain roared like a lion and told me to put my money up. It was a glorious outfit of provisions of all kinds that I got.

Returning to the *Spray*, where I found all secure, I prepared for an early start in the morning. It was agreed that the steamer should blow her whistle for me if first on the move. I watched the steamer, off and on, through the night for the pleasure alone of seeing her electric lights, a pleasing sight in contrast to the ordinary Fuegian canoe with a brand of fire in it. The sloop was the first under way, but the *Colombia*, soon following, passed, and saluted as she went by. Had the captain given me his steamer, his company would have been no worse off than they were two or three months later. I read afterwards, in a late California paper, 'The *Colombia* will be a total loss.' On her second trip to Panama she was wrecked on the rocks of the California coast.

The *Spray* was then beating against wind and current, as usual in the strait. At this point the tides from the Atlantic and the Pacific meet, and in the strait, as on the outside coast, their meeting makes a commotion of whirlpools and combers that in a gale of wind is dangerous to canoes and other frail craft.

A few miles farther along was a large steamer ashore, bottom up. Passing this place, the sloop ran into a streak of light wind, and then – a most remarkable condition for strait weather – it fell entirely calm. Signal-fires sprang up at once on all sides, and then more than twenty canoes hove in sight, all heading for the *Spray*. As they came within hail, their savage crews cried, 'Amigo yammerschooner,' 'Anclas aqui,' 'Bueno puerto aqui,' and like scraps of Spanish mixed with their own jargon. I had no thought of anchoring in their 'good port'. I hoisted the sloop's flag and fired a gun, all of which they might construe as a friendly salute or an invitation to come on. They drew up in a semi-circle, but kept outside of eighty yards, which in self-defence would have been the death-line.

In their mosquito fleet was a ship's boat stolen probably from a murdered crew. Six savages paddled this rather awkwardly with the blades of oars which had been broken off. Two of the savages standing erect wore sea-boots, and this sustained the suspicion that they had fallen upon some luckless ship's crew, and also added a hint that they had already visited the *Spray*'s deck, and would now, if they could, try her again. Their sea-boots, I have no doubt, would have protected their feet and rendered carpet-tacks harmless. Paddling clumsily, they passed down the strait at a distance of a hundred yards from the sloop, in an offhand manner and as if bound to Fortescue Bay. This I judged to be a piece of strategy, and so kept a sharp lookout over a small island which soon came in range between them and the sloop, completely hiding them from view, and toward which the *Spray* was now drifting helplessly with the tide, and with every prospect of going on the rocks, for there was no anchorage, at least, none that my cables would reach. And, sure enough, I soon saw a movement in the grass just on top of the island, which is called Bonet Island and is one hundred and thirty-six feet high. I fired several shots over the place, but saw no other sign of the savages. It was they that had moved the grass, for as the sloop swept past the island, the rebound of the tide carrying her clear, there on the other side was the boat, surely enough exposing their cunning and treachery. A stiff breeze coming up suddenly, now scattered the canoes while it extricated the sloop from a dangerous position, albeit the wind, though friendly, was still ahead.

The *Spray*, flogging against current and wind, made Borgia Bay on the following afternoon, and cast anchor there for the second time. I would now, if I could, describe the moonlit scene on the strait at midnight after I had cleared the savages and Bonet Island. A heavy cloud-bank that had swept across the sky then cleared away, and the night became suddenly as light as day, or nearly so. A high mountain was mirrored in the channel ahead, and the *Spray* sailing along with her shadow was as two sloops on the sea.

The sloop being moored, I threw out my skiff, and with axe and gun landed at the head of the cove, and filled a barrel of water from a stream. Then, as before, there was no sign of Indians at the place. Finding it quite deserted, I rambled about near the beach for an hour or more. The fine weather seemed, somehow, to add loneliness to the place, and when I came upon a spot where a grave was marked I went no further. Returning to the head of the cove, I came to a sort of Calvary, it appeared to me, where navigators, carrying their cross, had each set one up as a beacon to others coming after. They had anchored here and gone on, all except the one under the little mound. One of the simple marks, curiously enough, had been left there by the steamship *Colimbia*, sister ship to the *Colombia*, my neighbour of that morning.

I read the names of many other vessels; some of them I copied in my journal, others were illegible. Many of the crosses had decayed and fallen, and many a hand that put them there I had known, many a hand now still. The air of depression was about the place, and I hurried back to the sloop to forget myself again in the voyage.

Early the next morning I stood out from Borgia Bay, and off Cape Quod, where the wind fell light, I moored the sloop by kelp in twenty fathoms of water, and held her there a few hours against a three-knot current. That night I anchored in Langara Cove, a few miles farther along, where on the following day I discovered wreckage and goods washed up from the sea. I worked all day now, salving and boating off a cargo to the sloop. The bulk of the goods was tallow in casks and in lumps from which the casks had broken away, and embedded in the seaweed was a barrel of wine, which I also towed alongside. I hoisted them all in with the throat-yards, which I took to the windlass. The weight of some of the casks was a little over eight hundred pounds.

There were no Indians about Langara; evidently there had not been any since the great gale which had washed the wreckage on shore. Probably it was the same gale that drove the *Spray* off Cape Horn, from March 3 to 8. Hundreds of tons of kelp had been torn from beds in deep water and rolled up into ridges on the beach. A specimen stalk which I found entire, roots, leaves, and all, measured one hundred and thirty-one feet in length. At this place I filled a barrel of water at night, and on the following day sailed with a fair wind at last.

I had not sailed far, however, when I came abreast of more tallow in a small cove, where I anchored, and boated off as before. It rained and snowed hard all that day, and it was no light work carrying tallow in my arms over the boulders on the beach. But I worked on till the *Spray* was loaded with a full cargo. I was happy then in the prospect of doing a good business farther along on the voyage, for the habits of an old trader would come to the surface. I sailed from the cove about noon, greased from top to toe, while my vessel was tallowed from keelson to trunk. My cabin, as well as the hold and deck, was stowed full of tallow, and all were thoroughly smeared.

Stanley Sutherland D.S.M.

BLOCKADE-RUNNER

I AM a bricklayer by trade, now a master builder in my native town of Leith, Scotland. Prior to the outbreak of the Second World War I always had a yearning to go to sea, but couldn't get a ship. Walking down Leith Walk one Sunday night soon after the war started, I ran into a schoolboy pal of mine, Billie Patterson, a bloke who had been to sea a few years, who, having won a rumba competition in Edinburgh with steps brought from South America, earned for himself the name of 'Cuban Pete'. Billie Patterson told me to go down to the S.S. *Cairn Glen* first thing on Monday morning and see the steward for a cabin boy's job, which I did, and got the job. I made a voyage out to St John, New Brunswick, a port which later on in the war was to be my home port for two and a half years. My first voyage lasted two months and two days. When I 'paid-off' I made up my mind to go on deck. The S.S. *Cairn Glen* broke her back on the 'Longships' on her next voyage home from Canada.

My next ship, S.S. *Ruperra*, I joined as ordinary seaman. We sailed from Methil to Dunkirk. While discharging there we got orders to stop discharging and prepare for sea. We lay there for a while, and under bomb fire all the time. Every night we used to sleep in the Seamen's Mission cellars. We heard that the Germans were almost on top of us. Some of the older hands went up to see the Old Man, and find out what was going on. He said he was waiting for tugs to take us out. At this time the local tugs were all lying sunk in the harbour. Finally two tugs came up from Calais to tow us out. We left under heavy bomb fire and the *Ruperra* seemed to be the only floating ship in the harbour. I left the *Ruperra* in Penarth and came home. On her next voyage the *Ruperra* was lost through enemy action.

My third voyage was out to Montreal in the S.S. *Danby*, West Hartlepool. My fourth voyage was not a happy one. I joined the S.S. *Margaux*, Bristol. When we came round to Methil I skinned out, came home on a Friday night, and on Saturday morning I joined the S.S. *Barrwhin*, Glasgow. Sunday morning we were on our way to New York. The convoy we were sailing in had just broken up when we received an S.O.S. When we arrived on the scene the crew had just abandoned their ship, S.S. *Bodnant*, Liverpool. Her bows were stove in, and it fell to our lot to sink her, as she would be a menace to shipping. A mountainous sea was running, and she was a difficult target to hit. I was sightsetter on our four-inch gun. Having a seaman gunner's ticket gave me a six-pence a day extra pay. After firing forty-seven rounds into her we left her going down by the head, and proceeded for New York, where we discharged ballast. First night in New York I walked over the Brooklyn Bridge, got my pocket picked of eighteen dollars, got into a fight with a pro-German in Forty-second Street, got lost, and slept in a doorway for a few hours. When I woke up, frozen stiff, I ran into a kindly taxi-driver, who took me down to my ship. He said that the fare was on the house. On the way back to the ship he drove through Broadway, and pointed out places of interest. A very decent guy.

We went over to Baltimore to load for home. The boys all liked Baltimore with its burlesque shows, etc. The night before we sailed I chummed an O.S. ashore to go and visit an aunt of his. We were broke and walked for a couple of hours till we found her place. While waiting at her door we could smell all kinds of fancy cooking. She came to the door with a piece of chicken in her hand and grease running down her chin. Our hopes were high for a good feed, and possibly a borrow. She told us she was going out, and to call again some time when it was dark. When we got a few blocks down the street I asked my mate if we looked that bad. We joined a convoy in Halifax, and sailed for home. We ran into a storm, and most of the convoy lost their lifeboats. We had to turn back to Halifax and await new ones. Finally we came back to London, and 'paid-off' in Millwall. The S.S. *Barrwhin* was lost through enemy action during 1942.

After being home a few days, being girny and skint, I heard that a ship in the Imperial Dock was 'signing on'. I got off my mark and went down to see about a job as 'sailor'. The *Parracombe* had just come in from Newfoundland, and all was sixes and sevens. The Old Man was very keen to sign me on, and also asked me if I could dig up some A.B.s for him. This was before the 'Manning Pool' started. Being a local he reckoned I would know the lads who hung around the shore corner and outside Rutherford Bar. I dug up two for him, Bob Brown from Leith, and my young stepbrother, James Omand McIntyre. We met in the shipping office next day and signed on. We received a cash advance of five pounds, which didn't last long. After our cargo had been loaded and shifted around a few times by big nobs of the Army and Navy and Air Force we were very glad to batten down for sea. We towed out of the Imperial on the start of our voyage. I thought, this is the life. I was looking after our heavy forrard line, which, as there was a fierce wind blowing, broke with the heavy strain put on it in keeping her away from the quay. On the morning of sailing my mother chummed Jim and I down to the car-stop to cheer us on our way. It was raining cats and dogs. The day previous my mother didn't want us to go in the *Parracombe* as she didn't fancy the name of the ship, and she had a hunch that something might happen to her. Years previously my father had sailed from Leith as carpenter in a ship named *Linmore*. He was washed overboard in the Bay of Fundy. She had seen this ship before sailing and didn't like the look of her. Some Shetland folk have second sight.

Prior to sailing we were well warned by the shore gang that the *Parracombe* was going somewhere dangerous, and that if she went down it would be with a big bang. We put this down to war talk. Steaming out to Methil, I kept my eyes peeled on our bedroom window in the Cuddy Brae, as I knew my mother would be looking out for the ship going out the pierheads. From Methil we steamed round to Oban, where we picked up a Spanish captain, a Luis Diaz, who we learned later was to be our navigator in the Med. We left Oban in a huge convoy. Heaving up anchor we had a load of trouble stowing the cable. The chain-locker was the size of a hanky, Chippy was heaving in too fast for us to stow it, also our paraffin lamp kept going out. Our shouts up the pipes for Chippy to slow down produced no effect. The cable was piling up sky high in the locker, and we jumped out as it was dangerous. The mate came down and caught us laughing our fool heads off. Bob Brown said the ship didn't want to leave. The mate gave us hell for having a carry-on. I'm glad now Bob had a laugh, as his days for laughing are over now. After a few days at sea we were ordered to leave convoy. Three destroyers took us up to the Straits of Gib and left us on our own. We thought we were going into Gib. That evening all hands were mustered midships at the master's order. 'Men,' he says, 'you don't know where we're bound for – well, it's Malta.' He also stated that in the event of aircraft coming over ship we were to carry out our duties in a normal manner and not to panic, as our guns were concealed and ready to go into action if necessary. He ordered the steward to lash the boys up with a stout tot each. That night, freezing cold, we hung stages over her bows and midships and painted the Spanish flag on her bows and name midships. This was a 'barney' in the dark. On my stage, the after bousing line slipped, and Jim and I flew away out past her stem; we were glad to get back on deck again. Next morning we flew the Spanish flag, and steamed on like this for a while, then we switched over to the French flag, which she went down flying. We were all dead keen to get to Malta now as we were told by the Old Man we would have the freedom of Malta when we docked.

May 3, 1941, saw us well up on our way to Cap Bon. That morning when I went to draw the breakfast the old chef lashed up the porridge with curry. He said, 'Honest to God, Jock, I don't know what I'm doing this morning.' He was all sixes and sevens. He told me something was going to happen. He said: 'If it does, I won't come out of it alive.' At noon the same day a huge Italian plane flew low over us fore and aft. She seemed satisfied, and never came back. After this we had a feeling all was not well.

After dinner I nailed back our lavatory door, which had been banging all night, and as I drove in the last six-inch nail I said, 'This bloody door won't bang again.' How very true my words were. I went back into the fo'c'sle for a smoke, and then to have a lie down. When I was preparing to turn in a coloured seaman,

John Sutherland, of Redbraes, Leith, woke up, the colour of death. 'Boys,' he said, 'I've been dreaming about seven white angels.' The previous night he had been dreaming that a priest came to his bunkside and spoke to him. We all scoffed at this. When our ship went down seven out of the fo'c'sle went down with her.

Steaming along, we were going to keep close into the coast pretending we were bound for Sfax, then at night when it was dark we were to double the watch in the stokehold and make a dash across to Malta. In the course of our passage we didn't know that to get to Malta we would have to go over the heaviest minefield in the world. The Old Man knew this on leaving Leith. During the Spanish Civil War he was a blockade-runner many times. While all were arguing there was a terrific explosion. We all made haste for the boat-deck, looking along deck forrard. She looked all right. When I turned back to the fo'c'sle to get my Shepherd Tartan suit, and razor, and gold tooth some lucky lads followed me. While rummaging around there was a series of explosions that tore the bottom out of her and carried away the bridge. This killed all hands on the boat-deck. My brother Jimmie by presence of mind jumped into a potato-locker and closed the lid to escape flying debris. After it cleared he jumped over the wall with right leg broken in three places and two toes off. He didn't know about this till he got ashore. I held on to a stanchion and couldn't let go till my nerves were in order again. The water was pouring down into the fo'c'sle, we got out by shoving a mess-room table against a bulkhead and scrambling out somehow. Aft, the deck looked like a knacker's yard, debris all over the shop. By this time her stern was sky-high in the air, ready for the final plunge. There was nothing else to do but jump over the stern. I jumped feet first, and never thought I would surface again. I swam away from the ship, and slewed round to see her make her final plunge. She went down with a screaming crowd hanging on to her starboard rail aft. Our appeals for them to jump were all in vain. They went down with her. When she disappeared there rose to the surface a terrific amount of wreckage. A couple of rafts well burst up came clear, and played a big part in our rescue. Thirty officers and men went down with the ship, we were seventeen survivors, one Arab died ashore later through exposure. I swam to the nearest raft to see if I could see my brother. I shouted out his name, but no answer. Later, away in the distance, I heard a shout which I didn't recognize. Leaving nothing to chance, I swam away from the raft and came upon Jimmie hanging on to a broken wooden derrick. After much trouble we made a boom defence tank on which was lying the second mate with his right arm hanging off at the shoulder, also a gunner with an ankle injury. The tank couldn't hold four of us. The second mate reckoned it was making water. In the distance I saw a raft with two persons on it. I told the men I would swim across and try to bring it back. I misjudged the distance, and could feel a seizing at my heart. I slipped off my lifejacket as it weighed a ton weight, also my dungarees, and swam a bit easier. On making the raft I discovered it was my pal Andrew Starrs, of Admiral Terrace, Edinburgh, also the second wireless officer. We tried to paddle the raft across to the tank, but the current was too strong.

We spent a cold night with the waves lashing over the raft. I slept in short spells with my head on the second wireless officer's lap. About dusk a plane flew over us, the pilot gave a hail, then sculled off. We thought we were being left to our fate. The reason, we learned later, was that it was too rough to land the seaplane. After being adrift for thirty hours we were picked up by a Vichy French seaplane, and landed at the naval base, Bizerta, where we were stuck in hospital, and severely questioned as to ship, cargo, port of destination. Which we didn't disclose. Later we were shifted to Tunis, and marched through the streets barefooted, and spat on by Italians. We told them 'Bye and bye we'll get you,' which we did when the Eighth Army left Alamein.

We were lodged in a flea- and rat-infested gaol; then sent under heavy guard to the Fort of Kef, where we spent long weary months under heavy Arab guard. The only cheery bit was the sing-songs, which the skipper led, as he had a good voice and was a regular guy, and well liked. There we received 150 francs a month from the American Consul in Tunis, which we spent on fags and eggs. Later we had more company, survivors of the *Empire Pelican* and *Empire Defender*, all Glasgow men, sunk on their own blockade-running. We were crowded out, and shifted to another camp in the village. Again we got more survivors of the big convoy that made for Malta later. One of the men, Hotchka McDaid from Glasgow, was joined by his big brother. The big brother on leaving Glasgow was told by his mother to watch out for Hotchka. Well, it's a small world. We got in touch with the Red Cross, and their parcels kept us alive, as we were living like Arabs on the country's native dish 'cous-cous', stuff like porridge with its brains bashed out. A padre, a Rev. Dunbar from Tunis, used to visit us and bring gifts from Maltese sympathizers in Tunis. We used to also have a wee sermon, and it lifted up our hearts. The padre was a native of Glasgow.

We had a riot in our camp, attacking the guards. Jerry McDyer, Glasgow, and McCafferty, Clydebank, and I were sorted out and sent to Bordj-le-Boeuf, in the desert. It was a long run down there, and we saw a bit of the country. We travelled by train to Gabes, and then on a lorry. At Gabes we bounced a big melon. Travelling through a small village at thirty miles per hour, Jerry flung the melon in among a gang of old Arab gaffers sitting at a corner. Arriving at our destination, we told the commander of the place we were officers, and expected to be treated as such.

Every Tuesday we had a high old time ordering stores from a near-by village. We told the storekeeper the American Consulate would pay all bills. This went on till the storekeeper got a letter saying we were impostors. Then we went back on the hard tack, not to our liking. By good behaviour we got sent back to join our mates in Sfax. They had been shifted down there in cattle-trucks. I was in hospital at this time with a poisoned finger and dysentery, which I forgot about when the lorry called to pick me up. We joined the main party in Sfax, which was near the sea, and healthy.

When the Eighth Army started the big push, and Italy asked two days' grace to bury its dead, we took command of the camp one night. With eighteen rifles and ammunition we got off our mark. A French officer came with us, we picked up a train lying down from the camp, and got steam up and away. An Italian plane flew over us, but it cleared out when a couple of Yank planes appeared. We ran the train to a phosphate mine in Macknassy, and hid in the mine for two days. Later we moved on to Metloui, the first town in North Africa to fly the Free French flag. While we were there we heard that the Americans had arrived at a place called Gafsa the previous night. Ten of us set out on foot to travel forty miles to interview the commander for transport. We stopped a train on the line by waving our shirts and rolled on for Gafsa. The night previous we had slept for a few hours in a railway hut, after we had beaten up a crowd of Arabs who had attacked us for our odds and ends. I smashed in an Arab's face with a dried bull's pizzle, which I was taking home as a memento.

Entering Gafsa, an ancient Foreign Legionary town, we met Colonel Edison Raff. He said he was expecting attack and was going to evacuate the place as he had only a handful of men, and was going to blow up the petrol tanks and airfields before he left. We had a chicken and champagne dinner before we left town that day by train to pick up our waiting mates. From there we travelled to Tebessa, in Algeria, where we met British troops for the first time. We were held up for a day till the line was cleared of the wreckage of a French troop-train which had been sabotaged with a heavy loss of life. The troops in Tebessa thought we were Italians come in to surrender, for we were ragged and torn after being in the desert for thirty days. God, we looked grim. The first bloke we spoke to was a Rab West from Leith, who was a pal of Jimmie's.

From there we travelled to Algiers, where we were marched down to join the troopship *Orontes*. We waited till the troops had left her, then we went aboard. A crowd of Spanish prisoners, political chaps who had joined our crowd at different places, were detained by Naval Intelligence Officers in Algiers. They later joined Pioneer battalions, and wore the British battledress. A fine bunch of blokes, too. We put into Gib on the way home to pick up ammunition. Later we arrived at Greenock, where we received a new suit and ten pounds cash as a present from Billmeir, our owner, to see us home, where we paid off at our local shipping office. Four decorations came to our ship. The master, David L. Hook, Wales, and second deck officer, John Wilson, London, Distinguished Service Cross. Sailor James Omand McIntyre and Sailor Stanley Sutherland, Distinguished Service Medal. We all met again in Buckingham Palace on 9 February 1943, with other blockade-runners, and were presented to the King, to receive our decorations from his hand.

During our captivity it was the sing-songs at night that kept our spirits up, and the parcels from the Red Cross, and the thoughts at the back of our minds to get home and back into the fray. After being home a few months I sailed from Leith in a Fort boat to Canada. I left the Fort boat to join a Canadian ship, and made four voyages in the *Prince Albert Park* from Canada to the States, the West Indies, South America, South Africa, Equatorial Africa, the Gold Coast, back to New York, and back to St John, New Brunswick. I left her and joined the *Rockland Park*, and made three voyages as bos'n round the West Indies.

Paying off on my last voyage, I was swithering whether to make another voyage and then go home. I was sitting in a cafe listening to the radio. I heard a tune coming over the air, *By Yon Bonnie Banks*, that made up my mind. Home. I joined the S.S. *Tortuguiro*, bound for Liverpool, as trimmer. Arriving at Liverpool, I visited my sister. She said, 'You've got very dark-looking.' I said, 'So would you if you had been climbing in and out of coal bunkers for a fortnight.' I spent a day in Liverpool, then caught the train for Edinburgh. It was a great feeling hustling along home in the dark. I fell asleep in the train. When I woke up I asked a pongo where we were. He said, 'Scotland. We have just crossed over the Border.' 'Thank God,' I said. I got home at one o'clock in the morning. I knocked on my door. A frightened voice said, 'Who's there?' 'It's me,' I said. 'Who's me?' from within. 'It's me – how many me's are there in this world?' Mother opened the door, I staggered in, well weighed down with a huge sea-bag and a huge case full of souvenirs and presents. A flush 'homeward-bounder'. We sat up all night talking, and the tea-pot was on and off the gas all night.

In the shipping office, Leith, on 18 March 1946, I took my discharge from the Merchant Service – Reason, Termination of War Service; and came ashore with a host of happy memories spent north and south of the Line, spent with all kinds of guys good and bad who, all flung together, kept the ships sailing and delivered the goods.